MURDER

AT THE

WEEKEND

The re-discovered serials and stories of

FRANCIS DURBRIDGE

Edited by Melvyn Barnes

ISBN 9781912582389

Williams & Whiting (Publishers)

15 Chestnut Grove, Hurstpierpoint,

West Sussex, BN6 9SS

CONTENTS

INTRODUCTION

The lengthy research leading to my book *Francis Durbridge: The Complete Guide* (Williams & Whiting, 2018) produced many fascinating discoveries. These included the fact that Francis Durbridge's first stage play was performed in Birmingham as long ago as 1943, but when in the mid-1960s he resumed his writing for the stage it was in Germany rather than the UK that his theatrical career began. My research also revealed that Durbridge's output over many years, using several pseudonyms as well as his own name, was far more prolific and wide-ranging than was previously known – and it was sheer delight to debunk numerous errors about Durbridge's works that persist on the Internet, while solving various mysteries about them.

It has been acknowledged by Francis Durbridge's sons, Stephen and Nicholas, that many of my discoveries were previously unknown to them. They remain rightly proud of their father's work and international reputation, and I am grateful for their support in bringing to a modern audience the newly collected works in this book.

But firstly, for anyone to whom Durbridge's name is unfamiliar, some background information might be helpful. Francis Henry Durbridge (1912-98) was arguably the most popular writer of mystery thrillers for BBC radio and television from the 1930s to the 1970s, after which he enjoyed a successful career as a stage dramatist with plays such as *Suddenly at Home, Murder with Love* and *House Guest*. His radio serials have been regularly repeated in recent years, the novels based on his radio and television serials are frequently

1

reprinted, and his stage plays remain among the staple fare of amateur and professional companies.

In the 1930s Francis Durbridge was a frequently recurring name on BBC radio, as he was prolific in his production of comedy and dramatic plays, children's stories, musical libretti and short sketches, but it was in 1938 that he found the niche in which he was to carve his name. His radio serial *Send for Paul Temple* became the first of a series that endured until 1968, with Paul Temple and his wife Steve established as icons of detective fiction in such serials as *Paul Temple and the Curzon Case, Paul Temple and the Madison Mystery, Paul Temple and the Vandyke Affair, Paul Temple and the Gilbert Case* and *Paul Temple and the Spencer Affair*. Very small wonder, then, that the Paul Temple mysteries have long survived as books, films, CDs and DVDs, and such was his popularity in his heyday that Temple even became a comic strip hero in newspapers from 1950 to 1971.

But Francis Durbridge was also the master of the thriller serial on BBC television, undoubtedly ruling the roost for nearly thirty years – beginning with *The Broken Horseshoe* in 1952, and continuing with such titles as *Portrait of Alison, My Friend Charles, The Scarf, The World of Tim Frazer, Melissa* and *Bat out of Hell*. His complex plots and cliff-hanger endings attracted enormous viewing figures in the UK and abroad, and he adopted a new approach by introducing one-off protagonists rather than simply transferring Paul Temple to television. It is therefore hardly surprising, when in the 1950s Durbridge was at his peak on the radio and his television serials were commanding huge audiences, that three original Durbridge serials appeared in Sunday newspapers and one in a television magazine. It was a thrill to discover these, and to transcribe them for readers today.

In the 1940s and 1950s Paul Temple was the number one radio detective, so it is similarly no surprise that he appeared in many short stories in newspapers and magazines. Most of them have been subsequently reprinted, but it was a particular pleasure to discover a series of twelve very short Paul Temple stories that appeared in the London *Evening Standard* in early 1947. These have never been reprinted since their original newspaper publication over seventy years ago, and although they might appear a little dated Temple fans will doubtless welcome them and find their atmosphere palpable.

So there we have it – four Francis Durbridge novellas and twelve of his short stories, all of which can be described as the lost (or should it be re-discovered?) stories of this master thriller writer. Three of the novellas originally appeared on Sundays and one on Saturdays, while the twelve Paul Temple stories appeared on Fridays. Hence our title – *Murder at the Weekend.*

Melvyn Barnes

July 2020

THE NYLON MURDERS

Published in the *Sunday Dispatch* in twelve parts, 23 November 1952 – 8 February 1953

This was never published as a book in the UK, but it appeared in Germany as *Kommt Zeit, kommt Mord* (Signum, 1965) and later under the same title (Goldmann, 1968). Under the title *Die Nylonmorde*, it was also included in the Durbridge omnibus *Drei berühmte Kriminalromane in einem Band* (Lingen, 1966). In fact it was very widely published, with rights sold to countries including Italy, Australia and South Africa – which leaves it puzzling that since its original newspaper serialisation it has never re-appeared in the UK in magazine or book form. Its subsequent claim to fame is that numerous websites over the years, and still today, allege that *The Nylon Murders* was the basis of the 1956 British film *Town on Trial* starring John Mills – which is clearly incorrect, as this film shares no common features of plot or characters with Durbridge's serial, he receives no mention on the film credits, and there is nothing whatsoever to link the film to Francis Durbridge.

THE NYLON MURDERS

1

Police Sergeant Cooper turned up the collar of his reefer jacket, as the launch rounded a bend of the river and caught the force of the chill autumn wind. It was growing dusk, and the reflected glow of a green neon sign beyond Tower Bridge transformed the warehouses into gloomy cliffs.

The sergeant glanced across at Tom, his companion, who was steering the launch without any apparent effort. Cooper wondered if he should switch on the lights yet. He decided to wait another five minutes.

After reporting at Wapping Station, they began their leisurely return journey. It was almost dark now, and an occasional riverside lamp was reflected in the water. They were moving under the lee of the north bank to gain as much protection from the wind as possible.

Cooper was mechanically surveying the rows of freighters and warehouses. Suddenly he gripped his companion's arm and pointed towards the piles of a landing stage, over which two crane arms loomed against the sky. He had caught sight of a dark object bobbing gently in the water at the foot of the piles. Tom switched off the engine almost at the same moment as the sergeant switched on the powerful lamp in the bows of the launch. As the launch swung towards the shore, the beam caught the floating object.

"A stiff!" murmured the sergeant almost inaudibly. Within a few seconds they had maneuvered the boat alongside. Even when they were fifteen yards away, his long experience told him that the inert bundle was a dead body.

"A girl … and a good looker at that," said Cooper, as they began to lift the body out of the water.

"Now what would she want to go and do a thing like this for?" asked his companion in a puzzled voice.

"Don't be so sure it's suicide," murmured the sergeant. They had laid the girl in the well of the launch, and he noted that her dark dress was torn and that one of her stockings was missing.

5

The girl's head had slumped forward, partly concealing the fact that there was something tightly knotted around her neck. At first Cooper had mistaken it for a filmy scarf, for it was sodden with water. Now he could see that it had bitten into the flesh.

"This isn't suicide," he exclaimed sharply. "She's been strangled!"

The other man whistled softly and looked down at the delicately moulded features of the dead girl. "So she has," he breathed. "Strangled with a nylon stocking ..."

*****

They took the body to Waterloo Pier, where they found Detective Inspector Charles Merlin of the C.I.D., temporarily attached to H Division. Merlin had previously spent two years in the West End, frequenting the notorious night spots, mixing with crooks and playboys. Merlin had an excellent memory, and never forgot a face.

Merlin pulled back the blanket from the inert figure on the stretcher. The stocking was still tied round the girl's neck, and the water was dripping from her hair and bedraggled clothes. Cooper was telephoning for the police surgeon, and Merlin waited until he had replaced the receiver.

"Where did you find her?" he asked.

The sergeant carefully turned down the collar of his reefer jacket. "Near Hermitage Wharf, off the north bank," he replied, noting the inspector's thoughtful frown. "You wouldn't happen to know her, I suppose?"

"I've certainly seen her before," said Merlin quietly, perching himself on the edge of the desk. "I've an idea she's in show business."

It wasn't until they were carrying the stretcher out to the mortuary that he recalled Andrea Lake. About a year ago he had seen her playing a small part in a West End play called *The Man Within*. He took a rumpled evening paper from his mackintosh pocket and ran his eye down the theatre column. Yes, the play was still on at the Viceroy Theatre.

With a nod to Sergeant Cooper, now busy writing his report, Merlin went out and climbed the stairs up to the road. Twenty minutes later he was making his way along the dusty alley that led to the stage door of the Viceroy Theatre.

Harry Waverley, general manager for The Man Within company, was an ebullient individual whose fresh complexion and rather too heavily waived fair hair belied his forty-five years. He offered the inspector the solitary visitors' chair and pushed a box of cigarettes towards him.

"Haven't seen you for quite a time, Merlin," he smiled. "I'm a bit out of touch with the night spots since I went in for the legitimate. Is this an official visit?"

"In a way," nodded Merlin. "I happen to be interested in Andrea Lake. The stage door keeper tells me she hasn't been on for two nights."

Waverley mouthed an expressive epithet. "Not even as much as a phone call," he said. "She's just walked out on us without a word. We've had a hell of a time breaking in an understudy."

The inspector took stock of the tiny office, and his eyes suddenly came to rest on a photograph of the dead girl. "That's Andrea, inspector," exclaimed Waverley. "And my God, wouldn't I like to get my hands on the little devil!"

"Someone else had the same idea," said Merlin drily. "Miss Lake was murdered – we picked her out of the Thames just over an hour ago."

Waverley's expression changed with an abruptness that was almost comical. "Good God! You don't mean that?"

His air of deep concern aroused the flicker of an ironical smile round the corners of Merlin's mouth. "Didn't it occur to you to make any inquiries when she didn't turn up at the theatre?" he asked.

"Naturally. I telephoned her digs in Chelsea, but they were no wiser than ourselves."

Merlin said: "Tell me all you know about Andrea Lake. Do you know anything about her background?"

Waverley shook his head. "She always kept pretty much to herself and wasn't particularly friendly with anyone in the company. I engaged her at an audition – her agent sent her along. I think she'd been with some repertory company or other just outside Manchester. But she was never a girl to talk about herself much – not like some I could mention!"

Merlin asked for her address, and Waverley took a shabby address book from a pigeonhole in his desk. "She's in digs in some artist's place in Chelsea," he said. "Here's the address."

He pushed the book over to Merlin, who copied the address on the back of an old envelope, then rose to go. "Sorry to rush off like this, but I want to follow up this business while it's hot."

Waverley nodded understandingly. "If there's anything else you want to know, I'll be here till eleven-thirty."

Merlin picked up a taxi outside the theatre and directed the driver to an address in a turning off the Kings Road in Chelsea. Walsingham Street consisted of tall mid-Victorian houses, most of which were artists' studios on the upper floors with living accommodation below.

When the inspector rang the bell, the door was opened by a slim young girl of about eighteen with corn-coloured hair and dark blue eyes. She was wearing an old-fashioned cotton frock and woollen stockings.

Merlin introduced himself and asked if he could speak to the owner of the house. After a momentary hesitation, she showed him into a comfortably furnished study with bookshelves of white pine lining the four walls. A man in a wheelchair, who had been reading a set of publisher's proofs, looked up as Merlin was ushered in.

"Daddy, this is Inspector Merlin from Scotland Yard," said the girl in a soft voice. She hesitated a moment, then at a sign from her father went out, closing the door quietly behind her.

"You must excuse my not getting up, inspector," said the man in the wheelchair. "Usually I hobble about on sticks, but this is one of my bad days."

"That's all right, Mr. -?"

"Everest. Keith Everest."

The inspector nodded. "Yes, of course, sir," he said. "The portrait painter."

In view of his disability, Keith Everest was a popular source of copy for the newspapers, and Merlin had read several accounts of how he had triumphed over his physical handicaps to become a reasonably well-known artist. He remembered too that his picture *The Girl in Gingham* had been a sensation at the Royal Academy a couple of years ago. The picture had been widely photographed and reproduced in many newspapers, and Merlin had no doubt that it was the model for *The Girl in Gingham* who had opened the door to him.

Keith Everest was plainly somewhat gratified that his visitor had recognised him. Merlin noted that he had an easy manner, considerable charm, and seemed in no way perturbed by the visit of an inspector from Scotland Yard. "Nothing seriously wrong, I hope, inspector?" he said.

9

Merlin evaded the question. "Did you have a woman named Andrea Lake living here?" he asked.

"Yes, of course. She's had a room here ever since she came to town."

"When did you last see her?"

"Two days ago," replied Everest promptly. "She said she was going to stay with Clive – that's her boyfriend – for a few days. She visits his family occasionally."

"Have you their address?"

"I'm afraid not. We don't really know this boyfriend, apart from speaking to him on the telephone." He hesitated for a moment. "Why are you asking me all these questions, inspector?"

Merlin said: "Before I answer that, sir – would you mind if I had a word with your daughter?"

Without further ado, Everest leaned across and pressed a bell-push at the side of the fireplace. When the girl came in, Merlin asked her almost the same questions but without eliciting any further information.

"You're sure she never told you about this man Clive?" he persisted.

The girl shook her head. "We discussed most things, but she never would talk about Clive. At times I thought she was ashamed of him, though I can't think why. He sounded quite charming when I spoke to him on the telephone."

"Don't you think you'd better tell us what's happened, inspector?" said Everest quietly.

The inspector nodded. "I'm afraid Miss Lake has met with an accident, Mr. Everest. You knew, of course, that she hasn't been to the theatre for two days?"

The artist nodded. "Yes, they've telephoned several times but we couldn't tell them anything, apart from what we've told you."

"Is Andrea badly hurt?" whispered the girl, an anxious look in the blue eyes.

Merlin turned to Everest. "I suppose you couldn't manage to come with me, sir?" he asked. "It would only be for half an hour."

"Wouldn't I do?" put in Judy. "Daddy hasn't been so well today."

Everest met Merlin's gaze; it was obvious from his expression that he understood the situation. "It's all right, my dear," he said quickly. "Just you run along and get us a taxi." As soon as Judy was out of the room he said to Merlin, "What's happened, inspector – is Andrea dead?"

The inspector nodded. "She's been murdered," he said softly. "I'd like you to identify the body unless, of course, Miss Lake has a relation near at hand."

Everest shook his head. "There again, she kept us very much in the dark. She never discussed her family at all. We sort of took it for granted that she was an orphan. I was very glad to have her here for Judy's sake, and never asked questions. Judy was very much alone when her mother died, and I was struggling to make a name. Of course, Andrea always insisted on paying her way; she was an independent sort of girl."

Waving aside Merlin's offer of assistance, the artist struggled to his feet and picked up the two walking sticks that were leaning against the desk. "This is one of my bad spells," he said gloomily. "Most artists get them. For weeks I've been trying to paint Andrea's picture. There's an expression in the eyes and a curve of the mouth that elude me; I just can't get them on to the canvas."

He leaned against the desk and looked across at the inspector; for a moment his eyes were half closed. "Something seemed to tell me that I never would finish that portrait," he said softly.

*****

When the constable on duty drew back the sheet that covered Andrea Lake's body, the artist's face was inscrutable. He gave the merest nod to Merlin and turned away.

"You are quite certain?" persisted Merlin.

"I could never forget that face," replied Everest quietly, and leaning rather more heavily on his sticks began to move towards the door. On the way back in the taxi, he lit a cigarette and flicked the match through the half-open window. "It's going to be the very devil breaking this to Judy," he said as the taxi turned into the Kings Road.

"Can I be of any help?" began Merlin, but Everest shook his head. "No, no, I'd better just talk to her quietly and wait for the right moment."

"If it isn't inconveniencing you at all, I'd like to take a quick look round Miss Lake's room right away," said Merlin. "There may be some clue there that should be followed up immediately."

Everest nodded. "Yes, of course."

Judy opened the front door the moment the taxi had come to a standstill, and while Merlin turned to pay the driver Everest said to her: "Would you take the inspector up to Andrea's room, then come back to the study?"

12

She seemed to be about to ask a question but changed her mind and merely nodded in reply to her father's request.

Merlin looked round the room that had belonged to Andrea Lake, and found it a fairly typical Chelsea bed-sitter with a comfortable divan behind the door, two small armchairs, a writing desk and a large wardrobe opposite the window. The writing desk was unlocked, and he began to examine its contents at once. Two of the drawers were empty; others contained insurance cards, an old theatrical contract, a make-up chart with several items underlined, and two diaries which did not contain a solitary entry.

Obviously, Andrea Lake was not the sort of person who went around impressing herself upon her private possessions. In fact, Merlin had almost given up hope of discovering any clue to her relations with the outside world, when he saw a letter tucked away at the back of a pigeonhole. It began "Dear Andrea," and bore the address "Prince Edward Hospital, Wolverhampton." Dated a month previously, it was mainly concerned with what the writer described as "a tricky piece of trepanning" … "the first time I've tackled the job..." The letter was signed "Leslie."

Merlin pushed it into his pocket and went on with his search. When Everest came into the room a few minutes later Merlin, acting on an impulse, did not show him the letter.

"I thought you might like to see this, inspector," said the artist, indicating a large canvas he was carrying.

In the artificial light it was difficult to judge the picture, but Merlin could see at once it was of Andrea Lake. Everest had painted her in the modern style. She was sitting in a wing-back chair, wearing a loose blue dressing-gown. Merlin noticed that the artist had done full justice to the girl's

13

attractive figure and shapely legs. He also noticed that she was engaged in darning a nylon stocking.

"That's odd," said Detective Inspector Charles Merlin to himself. "Very odd."

*****

After promising to keep Everest in touch with any new development, Merlin went straight back to the Yard and telephoned the Prince Edward Hospital at Wolverhampton.

It was the duty nurse who answered when he asked to speak to Dr. Leslie. "There's no Dr. Leslie here," she replied. "We have a Dr. Leslie Sanders."

"Can I speak to Dr. Sanders then?"

"I'm afraid not, sir. Dr. Sanders has been away for a couple of days, and won't be back till ten o'clock tomorrow."

Early next morning Merlin was on a train to Wolverhampton and was in the office of the hospital secretary before eleven o'clock. The girl was somewhat taken aback when he introduced himself, but she lifted the house phone and asked to be connected to the doctor. When she replaced the receiver, she said: "If you'll go into the waiting room, Dr. Sanders will be down in a few minutes."

The waiting room was empty, and Merlin went over to the window that looked out on to the hospital courtyard. A couple of night nurses were going out for a morning walk, and a grocer's van was delivering provisions. He was idly watching them, when a door opened and a voice said: "You wish to see me, inspector?"

Merlin swung round and saw an attractive girl in her late twenties standing by the door. "I'm waiting for Dr. Sanders," he said.

The girl nodded. "I am Dr. Sanders."

Merlin hesitated a moment, then took the letter from his inside pocket. "Are you the writer of this letter?" he asked. She took one glance at it and nodded. "I'm sorry to bother you, doctor," said Merlin, "but I'm inquiring into the death of the recipient of this letter – Miss Andrea Lake."

Leslie Sanders gripped the edge of the table, then slowly lowered herself into a chair; the colour had drained from her face.

"I'd no idea you were such a great friend of Miss Lake's," said Merlin, and the girl looked up at him questioningly.

"But I thought you knew," she said. "I'm her sister."

Merlin concealed his surprise, and said quietly: "We can't talk here, doctor. Do you mind if we go along to your office for a few moments?"

The office was just along the corridor and, apart from a row of books that immediately caught Merlin's eye, resembled most doctors' consulting rooms. The books stood on a shelf beneath the window and the titles covered many aspects of criminology, ranging from medical jurisprudence to juvenile delinquency.

"Are you interested in criminology?" asked Merlin.

"It's been a hobby of mine since I first came here," said Leslie. She sat on the arm of a large chair facing the inspector. "Now please tell me all about my sister," she said quietly.

After telling her about the murder, the inspector said: "Now it's my turn to ask the questions, doctor."

Merlin discovered that Leslie was five years older than Andrea, that they each had a small private income, and that the actress had told her sister that she was perfectly happy living in Chelsea with Keith Everest and his daughter.

15

"I believe Mr. Everest was painting Andrea's portrait," said Leslie, and the inspector nodded.

"Yes, I've seen it, doctor," he said quietly.

Sipping his coffee in the dining car on the way back to London, Inspector Merlin reflected that he was very little better off for his trip to the Midlands, apart from the discovery that Andrea Lake had a sister and no other living relative. But the girls apparently knew very little of each other's private lives.

*****

Two days later, after the inquest, where Keith Everest gave evidence of identification and the jury returned a verdict of "Murder by person or persons unknown", the artist came across to Merlin as they were leaving the courtroom.

"If you can spare an hour, inspector, I was asked to invite you back for a cup of tea." He saw Merlin hesitate, then added: "Andrea's sister is staying with us; she seemed quite anxious to see you again."

"You mean she's living down here?" queried Merlin in surprise.

"She has special leave from the hospital," explained Everest as he hailed a taxi. "When she came to see us I told her she could have Andrea's room if she wanted it, and she jumped at the idea."

Merlin, too, found himself intrigued at the idea of meeting Leslie Sanders again. When they got back to the house in Chelsea, Judy and Dr. Sanders were in the living room, sitting in low chairs with a tea table between them.

"So, the police are still no nearer any solution," said Dr. Sanders, after Everest had related briefly what had occurred at the inquest.

"I'm afraid not," Merlin had to admit. "Your sister was rather an elusive person in many ways." Leslie sipped her tea. "Maybe the amateur will have better luck than the professional," she murmured.

"Amateur?" repeated Merlin, a trifle puzzled. "You don't mean you …"

There was a faint smile round the well-shaped mouth that was so reminiscent of her sister's. "The medical superintendent has given me a month's leave and advised me to take things easily. But I didn't make any promises. Criminology has always attracted me, and I've often wondered if I'd ever get an opportunity to apply my theoretical knowledge."

Merlin twisted uncomfortably in his seat. "I don't want to discourage you, doctor," he said, "but criminal detection is a highly specialised business nowadays. Finding a murderer is a job for a particular organisation; the individual can never compete."

Again, the faintly derisive smile flickered around the corners of Leslie Sanders's mouth. Just as she was about to make a retort, the telephone rang, and Everest went to answer it. He returned almost immediately looking somewhat perturbed.

"It's the young man, Clive," he stammered. "He – he doesn't seem to know about Andrea – says he has only just got back from abroad."

"Shall I talk to him?" said Dr. Sanders quickly.

Merlin hesitated a moment, and then nodded. He crossed the room and stood in the doorway, listening to Leslie's side of the conversation. She had a strained look as she replaced the receiver and turned to him.

"He thought I was Andrea," she said. "He's asked me to meet him ... says he'll wait for me in his car at the back of the theatre." Leslie stood facing the inspector, a determined expression on her face. "I've agreed to meet him," she said. "I've got to find out what he knows about Andrea."

"That was pretty smart," approved Merlin. "He obviously hasn't seen the papers."

"What if he hears of Andrea's death before ten o'clock tonight?" asked Keith Everest.

"Then it's my guess he'll keep the appointment out of sheer curiosity," said Leslie.

"On the other hand, if he happened to be indirectly involved in the murder, the news might well frighten him off," said Merlin. "I think you'd better let me go along with you, just in case."

Leslie shook her head. "He may have some valuable information, and I don't want to scare him in any way."

Merlin picked up his hat. "All right, Dr. Sanders, it's on your head," he said.

*****

Leslie arrived at the theatre just as the audience was leaving. There was only one car left in the park. There were no lights in the car park, which was illuminated only by the reflected glow from Shaftesbury Avenue. As Leslie came level with the car, she tapped lightly on the back window.

There was no movement inside. It suddenly occurred to her that this might not be the car at all; yet the instructions on the telephone had been clear enough. She looked round again. The car park was apparently deserted. At last she went up to the car and opened the back door.

The figure of a girl slumped forward, then fell towards her. Even as she stooped to feel the girl's heart, something told Leslie that she was dead. As she lifted her upright, against the side of the car, she saw there was a nylon stocking knotted tightly round her neck.

It was then that Dr. Sanders recognised the girl. It was Judy Everest.

2

Leslie placed her hands under the dead girl's shoulders and lifted her gently back into the car. Then she reached up and switched on the roof light. The light was not very strong, and for a split-second Leslie thought she had made a mistake in thinking that the girl was Keith Everest's daughter. The features were heavily made up; the hairstyle sophisticated. But a further glance revealed that the girl was unquestionably Judy Everest.

Leslie noted that Judy had obviously put up a fight. Her dress was badly torn, her lipstick and makeup smeared across her face. One of her stockings had been torn off completely, and with a sudden feeling of horror Leslie realised that it was Judy's own stocking that the murderer had strangled her with.

For a minute or two Leslie sat on the edge of the seat beside the dead girl, thoughtfully fingering the stocking. She recalled that her sister Andrea had met her death in this way; it was obviously the same killer, a person with a distorted mind and some strange obsession. "An interesting study," reflected Leslie, her professional instincts getting the upper hand for the moment.

She was still considerably puzzled by this strange transformation of Judy Everest. From what Andrea had said about her, and from her own brief acquaintance with the girl, Leslie had imagined that she was a stay-at-home type content to act as her father's housekeeper, without any particular yearning for an artistic career or distant horizons. Why should she have assumed this role of a woman about town which had ended in such a tragic climax?

Death was no new spectacle to Leslie, but this was her first experience of murder, and she was a little surprised to find herself trembling at the thought of the unknown element in the situation. She switched off the roof light, closed the door; and then suddenly, yet for no apparent reason, dropped her head. Later, when she was describing the incident to Inspector Merlin, she couldn't for the life of her say why, at that particular moment, she had suddenly "ducked". But "duck" she did, and the instinct saved her; the bullet missed her by inches, ricocheted off the mudguard, and shattered the windscreen.

Leslie stood with her back to the car, terrified and trembling. She knew that whoever had fired the shot had used a silencer and was probably still watching her from the dark shadows of the deserted car park. At all cost she must get away from the car park and reach the crowded security of Shaftesbury Avenue. Suddenly she made up her mind, took a deep breath, and made a dash for it.

As luck would have it, she reached Shaftesbury Avenue without incident, but there was not a policeman in sight. She was just debating whether she should run down towards Piccadilly Circus, when a familiar figure emerged from the doorway of a tobacconist's opposite and crossed the road to her.

"You look a bit upset, Dr. Sanders," said Detective Inspector Merlin. "Has your boyfriend let you down?"

She swallowed hard and at last found her voice. "There's been another murder," she gasped. "It's horrible!" She gave him the bare facts as they half-ran back to the car park. From the opposite end they saw a dim figure approaching, and when they reached the car there was a police sergeant standing beside it.

"See anything suspicious at your end, sergeant?" asked Merlin. The sergeant shook his head.

"You mean you were both watching this place?" queried Leslie incredulously.

Merlin nodded. "After that telephone call it seemed to be a wise precaution, just in case there was trouble. But the murderer seems to have driven in the car right under our noses. Anyhow, let's have a look at the girl."

He opened the car door. The body was just as Leslie had left it. After a rapid examination, he sent the sergeant to telephone the Yard for the police surgeon, fingerprint experts and a photographer. Leslie could see he was obviously puzzled by the change in Judy's appearance, and when the sergeant had gone he said: "Had you any idea she was dolling herself like this and coming up to town?"

"Not the faintest," replied Leslie, "though I don't know her very well. Her father seemed to think she was the ingenuous type and regarded her as the little mother since his wife died."

Merlin frowned. "Of course, most girls of her age use makeup and go in for nylons," he mused. "We mustn't judge her too harshly just because she has an occasional night out."

"All the same, this is going to be a shock for her father," said Leslie. "I don't think he had the remotest idea that this sort of thing was going on. I don't relish the job of breaking the news to him."

"I'll look after that," said Merlin promptly. "As soon as a police car comes along, I'll send it on there. You can take your time going home."

Leslie looked thoughtful. "Do you think Judy could possibly have known this mysterious Clive?" she said. "It seems significant that he asked me to meet him here but failed to keep the appointment."

Merlin shook his head. "I'm afraid we shan't discover the answer tonight," he replied. "From now on, it'll be mainly routine stuff. You'd much better go home to bed. But give us a chance to break the news to Everest first."

After a little further persuasion, Leslie agreed to do as he suggested. She decided to walk to Charing Cross, have a cup of coffee in the station buffet, then go home by the Underground. As she turned into Charing Cross Road, she had an uncomfortable feeling that she was being followed. There was no tangible evidence — although she stopped several times to look at theatre advertisements and shop windows, she could not see anyone who might possibly be watching her.

She avoided the shortcut down the back of St. Martin-in-the Fields and walked into Trafalgar Square past South Africa House. Crossing the Strand, she saw that crowds were leaving the nearby cinemas, and acting on the spur of the moment she joined them as they poured into the Underground station. There was a long queue at the booking office. She found herself wedged between a hefty middle-aged man, who had obviously been on a pub crawl, and a polite young student who apologised profusely whenever the crowd pushed him against her. Leslie was glad to escape to the platform.

22

But even on the platform she could not entirely throw off the feeling that she was being watched; that somewhere a pair of furtive eyes were focused intently upon her. More people surged along the platform. At last there came that rush of hot air which heralded the approach of a train. The odour of train oil, disinfectant and stale humanity almost overwhelmed her.

Anticipating that there might be some difficulty in boarding the train, the crowd swayed slightly towards the edge of the platform as the train appeared at the far end. When it was about twenty yards away, there was another movement in the crowd; she felt a deliberate pressure from behind that almost flung her right off her balance and on to the rails below. The train was only five yards away, and she was poised right on the edge of the platform.

Suddenly there was a firm grip on her arm, and she was pulled back with an abrupt jerk. "Good Lord! That was a near thing! Hope I didn't hurt you."

Leslie turned to see a slim man in his early thirties standing just behind her. He had rather aquiline features and a friendly smile. The train pulled up with a jerk; he still held on to her arm as they crowded on to it, and he stood beside her in the gangway. "Do you suffer from giddy spells?" he asked when she tried to thank him.

She shook her head. "Someone seemed to push me forward ... of course, it may have been the crowd swaying ..."

"Feel all right now?"

"Yes, thanks. It was lucky you grabbed me."

He chatted for a minute or two, and she began to lose her feeling of apprehension. At Victoria he inquired if she had recovered, and on receiving an assurance that she had, he got out. The train was now little more than half full. She sat rather listlessly scrutinising the row of faces opposite, without evoking a flicker of recognition. The sensation that someone was watching her had returned. One by one, she examined them carefully. Most of them looked tired, and none offered anything to arouse her suspicions. Which of them could possibly be interested in her?

It was almost eleven-thirty when Leslie reached Sloane Square and caught a number eleven bus along the Kings Road. As she turned into Walsingham Street, a police car was just leaving the Everests' house. When she let herself in and closed the front door behind her, she noted that there was a light in the living room, so she knocked gently on the door and put her head inside. Keith Everest was slumped in an armchair, an empty glass on the floor beside him. He hardly seemed conscious of her entering the room.

"The police have been here?" she said softly.

He nodded but seemed afraid to meet her eyes. "I can't believe Judy was like that," he muttered. "She was such a quiet, simple sort of girl. There must be some mistake. She never showed the slightest interest in makeup."

"I assure you she was heavily made up when I found her," said Leslie.

Everest leaned forward in his chair; his features suddenly animated. "You don't think the murderer did that to her after he had killed her?" he suggested eagerly.

"But why should he do a thing like that?"

"The man's obviously crazy. It's probably just the sort of thing he would do."

Leslie pondered upon this for a few seconds. "Maybe you're right," she said at last. There seemed to be no point in disillusioning him, even if she had been able to do so. "Have

24

you any idea whether Judy ever talked to this man Clive on the telephone?" she asked presently.

"I can't remember any occasion …" said Everest, then suddenly stopped short. "Yes, I do! It was several weeks ago. I came back one afternoon when Judy was on the phone, and I could hear her as I came through the hall. When she brought in the tea I asked her who it was she'd been talking to, and she said it was Clive who wanted a word with Andrea." The artist hesitated. "Andrea had a matinée that day, and Judy said she'd told him to ring the theatre. I remember wondering at the time why Judy had taken so long to pass on such a simple message."

Everest emptied his glass and poured himself another drink. Leslie made no attempt to discourage him. It was obvious that he was stunned by the tragedy, and she knew that alcohol would at least dull his imagination. "I always regarded Judy as the essence of simplicity," he mused. "Didn't I paint her as *The Girl in Gingham*? I tell you there wasn't an ounce of guile in her makeup." Everest must have drunk at least a half-bottle of whisky and was fast reaching the maudlin stage. "Ever since her mother died, she's been the pivot of my existence," he said.

Knowing a little about artists, Leslie rather doubted if this were strictly true, but she allowed it to pass without comment. She wanted him to ramble on, hoping that he might let fall some small observation which might prove of use to her during her investigations. But although Keith Everest was ready to talk about himself, his work, and the attack of infantile paralysis that had turned him into a semi-invalid, he told her nothing of any real importance. She encouraged him to talk about Andrea, but again he added no information to what she already knew.

25

"Fine girl, your sister Andrea. Fine girl …" he kept repeating. "That would have been the picture of the year …"

Leslie's thoughts wandered to the portrait in question, Andrea darning a nylon stocking; another stocking thrown over the arm of a chair. "What gave you the idea for that picture?" she asked suddenly. "Andrea was hardly the domesticated type."

He considered the question for a few moments, frowning slightly, before he answered. "It was your sister's idea," he replied at last. "She insisted that a good actress could play any part within reason. She said it would be practice for her … and she looked magnificent … a fine girl, Andrea …" His chin sunk on to his chest and his eyes half closed. Eventually, she persuaded him to go to bed.

When she reached the room that had been Andrea's she closed the door, and as she did so it struck her that she was alone in the house with Keith Everest. She looked for a lock, only to find it had no key. Nor was there a bolt on the door. After a moment's hesitation, she laughed at herself as an alarmist. After all, Keith Everest was a disabled man and half-intoxicated into the bargain. All the same, she would suggest to him in the morning that he should engage a housekeeper who would sleep in.

She sank down on the divan and reviewed the events of the day. Presently she picked up the light coat she had worn that evening and placed it on a hanger, taking her handkerchief out of one of the side pockets. As she did so a slip of paper fluttered on to the floor. It had been torn from a small scribbling pad and folded across the middle. She opened it casually, thinking perhaps it was an old shopping list. Then she saw the strange handwriting. It had been hastily scribbled with a ballpoint pen which flowed rather too freely.

Leslie read: *I only discovered Andrea was murdered after I telephoned you. You have got to find who did it, and I've hit on a clue. Not a word to the police … we must play this our own way. I will be in touch with you tomorrow – Clive.*

Leslie dropped into a chair and restrained a sudden impulse to rush along and tell Keith Everest about the note. It was hardly likely that he would be able to throw any light on it; he was not even in a fit condition to discuss it. How had the note found its way into her pocket? In the Underground? In the lift, perhaps, or on the platform? Obviously, someone had quite deliberately bumped into her and planted the note. After reading the note through several times, she opened a drawer and placed it under the newspaper lining. It seemed as good a hiding place as any. Then she undressed, got into bed and switched off the light.

A distant clock struck one. But her brain was still busy with the mysterious Clive. Why hadn't he spoken to her, instead of following her and waiting an opportunity to slip that note into her pocket? And how could he possibly have discovered a vital clue in such a short time? It could be a bluff of course, to distract her from the real murderer.

Presently she broke into an uneasy dose and dreamed that she was in the studio looking at the portrait of Andrea. The edges of the canvas seemed to dissolve, as if she had been watching a film and the camera had suddenly tracked in for a closer view. All she could see now was Andrea sitting there darning a stocking. And suddenly Andrea's expression seemed to change, until Leslie realised it was the elusive lift of mouth and chin that Keith Everest had been seeking. It was the old Andrea she knew so well … with a quick movement the girl leaned forward in the chair and with both hands outstretched offered Leslie the nylon stocking …

27

She awoke to feel her heart throbbing rapidly, and with that terrifying sense of impending disaster that so invariably follows a nightmare in the small hours. For a few minutes, she lay debating whether to take one of the sleeping tablets she always carried. Then suddenly she sat bolt upright.

There could be no mistaking the sound of soft footsteps moving slowly along the passage and coming nearer and nearer at every moment. Instinctively she sought an obvious explanation. No doubt Keith Everest was feeling the after effects of all that whisky he had drunk, and wanted her to prescribe a sedative.

She stretched out and switched on her bedside lamp, waiting for a knock on the door. The footsteps came to a halt, there was a pause of several seconds, and then she realised that he was not going to knock. She could see the handle slowly begin to turn. The realisation that the door was not locked seemed to paralyse her. Helplessly, she lay and watched the door slowly opening.

Keith Everest stood there, eyes glaring, a strange expression on his mobile features. His mouth was working convulsively, but he made no attempt to speak. When Leslie finally lifted her eyes from his face, she saw that he was wearing a heavy quilted dressing gown over his pajamas. His right hand still clutched the door handle, and as he turned towards her, she saw that he was nervously twisting something round the fingers of his free hand.

It was a nylon stocking.

3

Keith Everest released the door handle and held the nylon stocking stretched out towards her. Leslie raised herself on her right elbow. She felt herself recoil slightly as he took a pace into the room. His eyes seemed to burn with a strange light. As he advanced slowly towards her, she lifted her bare left arm to her throat as if to protect it.

At last he spoke. "I found this in Judy's room," he said in a hoarse, unnatural voice. "I was going through her things … expensive evening frocks, cigarettes, and three different makeup outfits. What does it mean, doctor? I've lived under the same roof with her for nearly twenty years, and I don't know my own daughter."

Leslie had regained her composure by this time, for she realised that there was no sinister objective behind this somewhat unorthodox visit. Everest was obviously very distressed, and all the whisky he had drunk seemed to have agitated rather than soothed him.

With a great effort he groped his way to a chair. "God knows I've seen my share of the seamy side of life," he gasped, "but Judy, of all people! For years I've been living with a complete stranger."

Leslie thrust her feet into her bedroom slippers and pulled on her dressing gown. Everest went on: "It's terrible to think that Judy never confided in me. Since her mother died, I was always under the impression that she told me everything."

"She was a very attractive girl," said Leslie. "Did she ever mention a young man?"

He shook his head. "She didn't seem to have any time for men." He broke off abruptly, and she could see the expression of doubt in his eyes.

"I suppose Judy went out on her own quite a bit," she suggested.

"Yes, she spent quite a lot of time at the reference library. She was very interested in tapestry work, always digging out designs from old books. She said she was going to do a series of articles about it for some women's magazine. She showed the editor some of her work nearly a year ago, and he more or less commissioned the series, but Judy said she wouldn't start it until she had finished the research."

"A year seems to be a long time to do research for a few articles," said Leslie quietly. "How often did she go the library?"

Everest suddenly got up and walked with considerable effort towards the door. "At least three afternoons a week," he answered. "Sometimes in the evening too. I believe the library keeps open till nine."

Leslie wondered if she ought to offer to help him or fetch one of his walking sticks, but he went hobbling along the passage and presently she heard his bedroom door close. She shut her own door, then picked up the nylon stocking that had fallen to the floor. She stood deep in thought, running the fine mesh through her fingers. At last she flung the stocking into a drawer, took off her dressing gown, got into bed and put out the light.

*****

The story of the mysterious murder of Judy Everest was headlined in the morning papers, which recalled Keith Everest's highly successful *The Girl in Gingham* picture at the Royal Academy. Leslie read most of the papers over breakfast, at which the artist did not put in an appearance. After breakfast she picked up a copy of the *Morning Gazette*, which had Judy's picture on the front page, and walked along the Kings Road to the reference library.

She showed Judy's picture to the middle-aged woman in charge of the desk and asked if she recognised her. The woman looked at the picture for a few moments, then nodded. "I have certainly seen her here once or twice, but I wouldn't call her a regular visitor," she said.

"Are you on duty here every day?" queried Leslie.

"Most days. Last time she was here she asked for a book on famous women criminals. I remember thinking what a strange choice it was for such a friendly sort of girl."

Leslie thanked her and, deep in thought, found her way back to the Kings Road. As she approached Walsingham Street, a police car turned the corner and braked to a standstill. "Can you spare a moment, Dr. Sanders?" came the familiar voice of Detective Inspector Merlin. He indicated the vacant seat beside him, and she climbed in.

"I've just been to see Everest," he told her. "He seems to be in rather bad shape."

"That's not surprising," said Leslie. She told him about Keith Everest's discovery in Judy's room, but the inspector did not seem unduly surprised. "It might mean something," he conceded, "but we hear worse things almost every day in the juvenile courts."

Slightly irritated, Leslie decided she would pass on no more information; it had been on the tip of her tongue to tell him about the mysterious note she had received from Clive.

The inspector said: "You'll be interested to know that we've traced the owner of the car in which you found the girl's body. It belongs to Sylvia Graham."

"You mean the actress who plays the lead in *The Man Within*?"

"That's the girl," nodded Merlin. "She drives to the theatre in it every night and leaves it in that particular car park. I've had a long talk with Miss Graham, but it seems she didn't know anything about the murder until she came out rather late and found a policeman on duty by the car. She told me that she'd never set eyes on Judy Everest."

"Maybe it would help if I went and had a talk to her as woman to woman," suggested Lesley.

He eyed her quizzically. "I've warned you about getting your fingers burned," he said. "We've got several very efficient women detectives at the Yard if ever we need the feminine angle on a case."

Leslie clicked open the door of the car. "All the same, I think I'll go on poking my nose where it's not wanted," she said.

As she walked rapidly down Walsingham Street, Leslie felt a trifle ashamed of herself. After all, Merlin had told her about Sylvia Graham's car, she reflected, and it really did seem that he was anxious to help. Nevertheless, her shapely mouth was set in a determined line as she fitted her latchkey into the front door.

She found Keith Everest in his studio, a large portfolio on his knee, moodily tuning over some pencil drawings. He looked up when Leslie entered. "I've had that detective here," he said irritably. "The fellow rattles me. I wish he'd keep away."

"We have to put up with these inconveniences if it means finding the murderer," said Leslie.

Everest nodded. "That's true."

"Has Judy ever mentioned a woman named Sylvia Graham?" asked Leslie.

"I don't think so, though the name's familiar. Isn't she acting in your sister's play?"

"That's right. Did you ever hear Andrea mention her?"

He wrinkled his forehead. "I don't think Andrea liked her very much. Said she was rather a sexy type and got most of her parts on the strength of it."

"That would rile Andrea," said Leslie, recalling her sister's frequently expressed idealistic views about her profession.

"Does Sylvia Graham come into this business at all?"

Leslie shrugged. "That remains to be seen. It just happens that Judy's body was inside her car when I found it last night."

He rubbed his unshaven chin thoughtfully. "Have the police investigated that?"

"They've talked to Sylvia Graham, but nothing came to light. Of course, the body might have been dumped in the car. Still, I suppose there's just a chance that Judy had met Sylvia Graham through Andrea at some time or other."

He shook his head wearily. "It's no use asking me. Outside this house you probably know more about Judy's private life than I do."

"Anyhow, I'll go and see Sylvia Graham."

He sighed and looked at her through half-closed eyes. "Are you resolved to go through with this?"

"Of course. That's why I came."

"You're a determined woman, doctor. But I'm beginning to wonder if we shouldn't leave everything to the police."

"I've no objection at all to your doing that," said Lesley. "After all, you've your work to get on with. But I came down on a month's leave for the express purpose of trying to find out who killed my sister. And the entire strength of Scotland Yard couldn't persuade me to give up the idea."

She left him aimlessly cleaning an old canvas and went down to ask Mrs. Miller, the daily woman, if there had been any telephone messages. There had been only one telephone call, which Keith Everest had answered. "It was from his agent,

33

Miss … He calls him Jimmy boy … I don't know his real name. The agent rang up to say how sorry he was about Miss Judy."

Leslie told her she was expecting a call and asked her to take a message if she was out. She stayed in most of the day, but the mysterious Clive did not telephone. Soon after six she set out for the theatre, arriving there about half an hour before the curtain was due to rise. The stage door keeper seemed a little doubtful about her being able to see Sylvia Graham.

"Tell her I'm Andrea Lake's sister, and it's urgent," said Leslie in a business-like tone. He went off along the corridor and was absent for some minutes. When he returned, he said: "Miss Graham can spare five minutes. Number one dressing room, just round to the right."

Sylvia Graham, with a towel round her curls, barely looked round as Leslie entered the dressing room. She was busily applying the foundation for her make-up and rubbing it evenly with her long delicate fingers. She indicated the visitors' chair. "Any news about Andrea?"

Leslie told Sylvia Graham what little she knew of the developments of the past two days. The actress's back was towards her, but she could see that she was eyeing her shrewdly through the makeup mirror.

"Andrea was a good little actress, but she kept to herself too much," she said in an indifferent tone. "If you want to get on in the theatre, you've got to mix with people." She completed the foundation and picked up a dark brown pencil to start work on her eyebrows. "What was it you wanted from me?" she said at last, in a voice which implied that she was hardened to visitors coming to beg favours from her.

"I just wanted to ask a few questions about what happened last night when Judy Everest was found in your car."

34

Sylvia Graham carefully drew a firm line to the end of her left eyebrow. "The police have already driven me half mad with their silly questions. Besides, how do I know you're genuine? Andrea never even told me she had a sister."

"If you want proof of my identity," began Leslie, opening her handbag, but Sylvia Graham waved the idea aside. "I believe you," she said. "But that doesn't necessarily mean I'm going to tell you all about my private life. The police have already been far too inquisitive in that direction."

She picked up a stick of carmine and began to apply it to her lips. "Where did you say you come from?" she asked presently.

"I didn't. But I'm a doctor attached to a Wolverhampton hospital."

Sylvia Graham completed a rather too elaborate Cupid's bow. "You're strange to all this, aren't you?" she mused. "You know how the Sunday papers describe this bit of London? 'The wickedest square mile in the world.' If you take my tip, honey, you'll catch the next train back to Wolverhampton and let the police sort out this mess."

Before Leslie could offer any protest, there came a sharp rap on the door and a man's voice outside said: "Can I come in?"

He was a man of about thirty-two, tall, energetic and rather carelessly dressed. Leslie recognised the penetrating eyes and aquiline features at once. It was the young man who had saved her from being pushed off the platform the night before. He apologised for his intrusion, and gave Sylvia a paper-backed manuscript. "Here's your piece for the Green Room Rag, dear. Rehearsal tomorrow at ten sharp."

The actress pushed the script on top of a pile of letters, and half turning said: "Dr. Sanders – this is Peter Hamilton, our producer."

He grasped her hand enthusiastically. "Of course, you're Andrea's sister. Do you know, I thought I saw a resemblance last night. She told me quite a lot about you."

Sylvia Graham said somewhat sharply: "I can hardly believe that, Peter. Andrea wasn't the talkative type."

"Andrea was very proud of you in that quiet way of hers," continued Peter Hamilton, ignoring Sylvia's remark. "But she never talked very much about things outside the business. We were all so upset about losing her; it's an absolute tragedy. I haven't had a night's sleep since it happened." He smiled at Leslie. "Why don't you and I have a quiet little chat, doctor?"

Convinced that she would extract no further information from Sylvia Graham, Leslie decided to accept Hamilton's invitation. At least, she reflected, she might get another angle on the murders. They went into a public house opposite the stage door, and for almost an hour Peter Hamilton talked incessantly about Andrea Lake.

"I was terribly fond of your sister," he said, "but quite frankly she never had any time for me." He hesitated. "I had an idea there was somebody else."

"She never mentioned a man named Clive to you?"

He shook his head. "We never discovered if there was a man in her life, and God knows I made all sorts of inquiries. Your sister was a mystery in more ways than one – that's probably what made her so intriguing. I'm confident that she'd have become a really great actress, given the right breaks." He shrugged. "Oh well, what's the use? This profession is just one damned disappointment after another.

36

I suppose you'll be going back to that hospital of yours almost immediately?"

Leslie told him that she proposed to stay in London for three or four weeks in an attempt to solve the mystery of Andrea's murder. He brightened considerably. "If there's anything I can do at any time, don't hesitate to let me know," he urged. "You can always find me at the theatre." He smiled. "After all, things must be pretty strange to you in this part of the world."

Leslie recalled that Sylvia Graham had said much the same thing in rather a different way. On an impulse, she asked him what he thought about Sylvia. "Never stops acting," said Peter laconically. "I wouldn't have said there was any harm in her, but she's always mixed up with some man or other."

"Do you think she murdered Judy Everest?" asked Leslie.

Peter Hamilton shook his head. "The police said she had been killed at about eight o'clock, and Sylvia was in the theatre from six-thirty onwards. Of course, one of her boyfriends might have borrowed the car, but Sylvia says she knew nothing about it and I'm inclined to believe her." He took Leslie by the arm; his manner was quiet and confidential. "Still, if you think our Sylvia's a suspect, I'll keep an eye on her, and if anything arises, I'll give you a ring."

Leslie thanked him, gave him her telephone number and slowly disengaged her arm. She didn't quite know what to make of Peter Hamilton.

*****

There was a mist creeping up from the river and filtering lazily up the old-world streets that led from the Embankment as Leslie came to the Everests' house. She was a little surprised

37

to find the house in complete darkness. It was turning chilly, and Leslie shivered slightly as she opened the front door and fumbled for the light switch. When she pressed it, the hall light did not come on.

Thinking that perhaps someone had turned off the electricity in order to repair a fuse, she called out but there was no reply. She hesitated for a moment, wondering whether to go in search of some candles. Suddenly the telephone rang. She groped her way along the hall to the curtained alcove which housed the instrument and lifted the receiver.

At once she recognised the voice. It was Clive. "Are you alone?" he demanded urgently.

"As far as I know." She hesitated a moment, then said: "Why didn't you keep that appointment last night?"

"I couldn't ... I simply couldn't." He sounded somewhat agitated. "After telephoning you, I found out about Andrea's murder and that upset everything. But I must see you, I simply must. Could we meet tonight?"

Leslie said: "Then you knew it was me you were speaking to last night, before you found out Andrea was dead?"

"Yes ... Andrea often mentioned you. I remembered she said your voice was slightly husky, the same as hers. Where can we meet?"

Leslie spoke softly, but there was a note of authority in her voice. "This is your last chance, Clive," she said. "I'll meet you tonight outside Madame Tussaud's – be there at ten o'clock sharp."

Clive said: "I'll be there. I promise, doctor."

When he had rung off, she replaced the receiver thoughtfully. Had he really recognised her yesterday? Or had some third person told him about her? Was she putting her head into another trap in agreeing to meet him at that time of night?

Her train of thought came to an abrupt halt as she heard a slight movement just behind her. She fumbled for the light switch in the alcove, but no light came. There was another movement close behind her, and a swish of soft silky folds twisted once, twice, three times around her neck. She realised immediately that it was a nylon stocking, and that it was slowly being tightened from behind.

In desperation she snatched at the telephone receiver and swung it madly at arm's length. There was a gasp as it came into contact with human flesh, and the grip on the stocking loosened. She wrenched herself free, rushed down the hall, flung open the front door and ran blindly into the dark street.

Leslie could hear footsteps behind her as she ran along the deserted street towards the Embankment. She turned down a narrow alley that led into a parallel street, and when she came into it she stood against the wall gasping for breath. For a second or two, she thought she had shaken off her pursuer; then she heard quick footsteps along the alley, and almost before she could turn someone had clutched her arm.

"You're in a devil of a hurry," said a familiar voice. By the light of a distant lamp, she recognised the lean features of Peter Hamilton.

4

Peter Hamilton took Leslie by the arm and turned her towards him. Her face was taut, his manner tense and alert. "Is there something wrong?" he asked.

"What are you doing here?" she gasped.

He thrust his hands deep into the pockets of his light coat. "After I left you, an idea occurred to me that I thought might help. So I hopped on the next bus and came to look for you. I was walking along Walsingham Street when your front door suddenly opened, and you came rushing out as if you had ten thousand devils at your heels."

He broke off and eyed her anxiously. "Are you sure you're all right?"

"I will be in a moment. I've had rather a shock." She had regained her breath by now and managed to tell him of the attack that had been made on her in the darkened hall.

"It seems incredible!" he exclaimed. "Maybe you were mistaken for somebody else. After all, if it was pitch dark in the hall ..."

"The person who tried to kill me must have heard me talking on the telephone," she reminded him. "I don't think there could possibly have been any mistake."

"Then we ought to go back at once and see if this mysterious killer is still there. If not, we can at least telephone the police."

She nodded, and they turned to walk back along the alley. "What was it you came to tell me?" she asked.

"When I was passing Sylvia's dressing room this morning, I heard a detective asking her what sort of nylon stockings she wore."

"What did she say?"

"Apparently they're called Five Star and are made by an American firm. It seems they're very fine mesh but extremely strong."

"Did you hear the detective say anything else?"

"No, but I was wondering if you knew what sort of stocking the murderer used ..."

Leslie tried to recall some detail of the stocking that she had seen wound round Judy Everest's neck, but she had been too upset at the time to take in small details. In any case, it would surely be impossible to trace the ownership of a nylon stocking? She had never given the idea a thought.

As they emerged from the alley a slight north-west breeze was blowing down Walsingham Street, and she felt a filmy material brush against her cheek. She put her hand to her throat and stood quite still.

"What is it?" asked Peter Hamilton.

"The stocking ... it's on my shoulder," she replied, almost in a whisper.

He grasped her arm and led her to the nearest street lamp. "So it is! It's caught on your brooch," said Peter Hamilton.

She pulled the stocking off her coat, and they examined it together. Suddenly he turned over the foot of the stocking and gave a low whistle. On a neat little shield were five stars, one in the centre and two on either side. "Five Star, Superfine," he said softly.

She caught her breath. He folded the stocking neatly and pushed it into his coat pocket. "It looks as if you've had a lucky escape. Come on, there's no time to be lost!"

When they came to the house, Leslie noticed there was a light in two of the front windows as well as over the front door, which was now closed. "There must be someone inside," she said. "Somebody has obviously repaired the fuse or whatever it was."

She had left her handbag, containing the latchkey, by the telephone – so they had to ring the bell. For about a minute there was no sound inside, then they heard distant footsteps and finally the front door was opened by Keith Everest. In one hand he held a screwdriver, and in the other a card of fuse

41

wire. "Oh, hallo, doctor," he greeted her in a casual tone. "I've been having a devil of a time – the lights fused, and I had to pop in next door and borrow some fuse wire."

Before she could blurt out her story of the man who had tried to strangle her, Keith Everest, who had been regarding Peter Hamilton with interest, queried rapidly: "This wouldn't be the mysterious Clive, by any chance?"

"No, this is Peter Hamilton. He produced Andrea's play."

The artist invited them into the drawing room, and as they crossed the hall Leslie went along to the alcove. Her handbag had fallen to the floor, and the telephone was still off its stand. She picked it up and replaced it. There was no other evidence of what had happened in the alcove twenty minutes previously. She looked round once again to make quite sure, then retrieved her handbag and slowly walked along the hall to join the two men in the drawing room.

They seemed to be on quite friendly terms. Each had a large whisky, and they were discussing stage décor in a highly technical manner. Though she disliked the taste of whisky, she accepted when Keith Everest held up the decanter. She was just beginning to experience reaction to the recent incident and felt that a stimulant would help her to conceal from Keith Everest that anything unusual had happened.

She hardly knew why she wished to hide this, apart from the fact that if he really knew nothing about it, the sudden news that the murderer had been under his own roof was liable to upset his already badly frayed nerves.

After chatting for a few minutes, Everest excused himself. When the door had closed behind him, Hamilton said: "He seems to me to be in rather a bad way. D'you think you'll be all right staying here alone with him?"

"Mrs. Miller will be back soon."

He shook his head doubtfully. "Everest is a queer bird," he said quietly. He lit a cigarette and went on sipping his drink. Presently he asked: "Who was this Clive that Everest mentioned?"

"He was the fellow Andrea seemed to be very keen about. Didn't she ever mention him to you?"

"Never. I gathered there was somebody, but she never mentioned his name. Do you know anything about him?"

"Not yet," said Leslie, "but I expect to meet him tonight." She told him of the two appointments Clive had made, and of the clue to Andrea's death which he had promised to reveal.

Hamilton appeared to be quite concerned. "Do you think it's safe to meet him tonight?" he asked. "Remember what happened last time."

"But what could possibly happen outside Madame Tussaud's?"

"It all seems very mysterious. If he knows who murdered Andrea, why doesn't he go to the police? It sounds like a trap of some sort." He flicked the ash off his cigarette. "This case seems to become more complicated every day," he said. "I'm wondering if Sylvia Graham is really mixed up in it. She never liked your sister."

"I got the idea that she was trying to warn me about something," said Leslie. "She kept hinting I was out of my depth, and that I should take the next train back to Wolverhampton. Now why should she take that line with a perfect stranger?"

Hamilton finished his drink and put the glass down on the small table "Our Sylvia's a very fine actress," he said, "but she's a difficult girl to understand." He took her hand and clasped it warmly. "I do wish you'd regard me as a friend," he said. "If there's anything I can do for you at any time, please don't hesitate."

When Hamilton had departed, Leslie went upstairs to prepare for her meeting with the mysterious Clive. As she was changing her stockings a thought struck her, and she went over to the drawer into which she had pushed the nylon stocking which Keith Everest had found in his daughter's room. She thought it would be interesting to see if that stocking too was of the Five Star Superfine type. But when Leslie opened the drawer, there was no sign of the stocking.

Thinking that perhaps Everest might know something about it, she went to look for him. At the far end of the passage she saw a light coming from his bedroom, the door of which was partly open. As she came up to it, she could see him standing on the opposite side of the room in front of a large picture. She stood in the doorway for a few seconds, conscious that there was something strange in Keith Everest's manner.

Slowly she looked round the room. It was quite simply furnished, and the only picture was the one before which he was standing. She realised it was the famous *The Girl in Gingham*, and she could not repress an involuntary exclamation. He turned at the sound and saw her, yet hardly seemed conscious of her presence.

"The picture of the year," she heard him mutter to himself. "Two thousand guineas I refused for that picture … Two thousand for the portrait of a slut!"

Then she saw that he was holding a palette knife, and with a sudden movement he slashed at the picture. He did not desist until the canvas was hanging from the frame in ragged ribbons. Then he sank back on his divan bed, his head in his hands, and she could see that he was shaking with silent sobs.

44

"So much for *The Girl in Gingham*," he said at last, in a hoarse unnatural voice.

Leslie went out and got a glass, then poured him a dose of the sedative she had had made up for him earlier in the day. He drank it without argument.

"I hope you aren't going to regret what you've just done," she said quietly. "I have a feeling that it's wrong to judge your daughter's actions until we know a lot more about this business." She shook her head regretfully. "It was a lovely picture ... no matter what Judy may have been."

He looked down at the floor and did not speak for nearly a minute. Then he said: "Yes, it was a lovely picture. I painted it the year after her mother died. It just shows how easily we can be taken in, even by our own daughters."

At last he raised his eyes and surveyed the slashed picture rather ruefully. "I'd be glad if you didn't mention this to anyone, doctor," he said with an effort. "You don't know what torture it was to me every time I looked at that picture."

"I think I can understand," said Leslie. "But you could always have put the picture on a shelf or sold it. And I still feel you're being premature about Judy. We know so little, and I've an idea that there are a lot of things that can be explained."

She debated whether she should tell him of the recent attack on her in the hall, then decided that it could not help matters very much, for she was fairly certain that the person responsible had followed her out of the house and made a getaway.

"That fellow downstairs, is he mixed up in this business?" asked Everest.

"It's difficult to say who is concerned in it," she replied. "He produced Andrea's play, but he says he has never met

45

Judy." She heard a clock outside chime the half-hour, and hastily told him of her appointment with Clive.

"There's something sinister about this man Clive," he said. "Don't forget what happened the last time you went to meet him."

Peter Hamilton had said much the same thing, but she was determined to keep the rendezvous and Mrs. Miller's return from the cinema gave her an excuse to slip away quickly.

*****

It was nearly ten o'clock when Leslie arrived at Baker Street and walked slowly in the direction of Madame Tussaud's. The street was fairly quiet, particularly when the traffic lights held back the stream of buses and cars. There were only one or two pedestrians in front of the Madame Tussaud's building, and although she scanned them closely none gave any sign of recognition.

She looked round for a car coming to a standstill but saw none. Five minutes passed very slowly. A policeman strolled along on his beat, favoured her with an inquiring look, then moved on. A bunch of raucous labourers emerged from a public house farther along and went singing noisily in the direction of Marylebone High Street. Two enormous transport lorries thundered by, heading west.

At ten-fifteen she decided that she would wait no longer, for there was something eerie about this almost deserted stretch of pavement in the shadow of the large buildings. Leslie could see a bus approaching from the direction of Great Portland Street, and she decided to catch it. As she stepped off the kerb, a large American saloon swerved from the rear of the bus and came straight for her. She was two paces into the road before she realised that the car, now some twenty yards away, had no intention of stopping.

She hesitated a second, uncertain whether to dash for the other side of the road or leap back, and at that moment a fruit barrow swung briskly out of a side street and into the main thoroughfare. The owner of the barrow was obviously making for home in an easterly direction and saw at once that the car was heading straight for him. He managed to swing the barrow a couple of feet towards the kerb, then leapt for his life. This distraction diverted the car's course so that it missed Leslie by more than three feet, and she felt the rush of air as it swept past. Its headlights dazzled her, so that she could not see the man at the wheel clearly enough to recognise him.

"Hi, stop him!" shouted the barrow boy, who was half lying on the edge of the pavement. But the car accelerated again and was over the Baker Street traffic lights without any intervention. Leslie rushed up to the barrow boy, who was quite unhurt but in a state of considerable indignation. "Who's going to pay for this ruddy mess?" he demanded truculently of nobody in particular.

"Meantersay you ain't insured?" grinned a stocky little man, who was helping another to restore the barrow to an even keel.

Leslie was still feeling badly shaken, and when she caught sight of a taxi, she hailed it and gave the driver the Chelsea address. Obviously, someone wanted her out of the way. Could it have been Clive at the wheel of that car? Had he waited for a suitable opportunity, and shot out of a side turning a little farther along the Marylebone Road?

*****

47

At the house in Walsingham Street, she found Detective Inspector Merlin waiting for her. He told her that he had come to make a further search through Judy's belongings, and Keith Everest had told him about Leslie's mysterious rendezvous with the elusive Clive.

He had stayed to hear the result. "You look pale," he said. "Something wrong?"

"I had a bit of a shock," she replied, and told him all about the car incident.

"I wish you wouldn't go sticking out your chin like that without at least telling me," he said with a worried look.

"I thought maybe Clive spotted you or one of your men last time he arranged to meet me, and that scared him off. So I didn't want that to happen again."

He regarded her admiringly. "You're pretty plucky, doctor, but very foolish, if you don't mind my saying so. Promise me you won't run into anything like that again without giving me the tip."

Leslie shook her head obstinately. "I might have to take a different line from the official one; in fact, I probably shall. And I don't want the police around cramping my style."

He tried to suppress a grin. "I can't imagine any cop cramping your style," he said.

"It's just that I'd sooner play a lone hand," she explained.

"Mr. Everest was telling me you've found yourself a sort of partner. I was very interested."

"You know Peter Hamilton?" she asked quickly.

"Of course. I was around the West End for quite a while, and I met most of the people in show business at some time or other."

"And what did you make of Peter Hamilton?"

He shrugged. "Much the same as most of the theatre bunch. Never had anything against him, of course. He's made good money for years as a producer." He hesitated for a moment, then inquired: "Why is he poking his nose into this affair?"

"He was very fond of Andrea and told me he'd do anything he could to find out who murdered her."

"And Judy? Was he a friend of hers too?"

Leslie shook her head. "No, he'd never met Judy Everest."

"That's very interesting," said Merlin, putting his hand into his breast pocket. "I found this picture in a frame in Judy's bedroom, hidden behind a photo of her mother."

It was a small cabinet-size picture of the type favoured by stage and film artists for publicity purposes. There was no mistaking the familiar, slightly aquiline features of Peter Hamilton. "Read what it says in the bottom corner."

Lesley did as she was told. Scribbled across the photograph were the words: *To Judy, dearest, with love – Peter.*

5

Various theories raced through Leslie's mind, as she sat there looking at Peter Hamilton's photograph. Why should he wish to conceal the fact that he had met Judy? Why had Judy hidden his photograph? What were they to each other?

She looked up to see that Merlin was regarding her intently, the merest trace of a quizzical smile playing around his tight lips. "You're beginning to get some idea of how difficult it is for one person to investigate a murder case," he said quietly.

"I am sure he told me he had never met Judy," murmured Leslie, almost to herself.

"I daresay you're right," agreed Merlin cheerfully. "As a matter of fact, he told our people the same thing."

She handed the photograph back to him. "Why should he say he had never seen Judy?"

"There's always the possibility that Andrea got him to sign a photo for Judy Everest," he reminded her. "Stage people do a lot of that sort of thing, and quite often they've never seen the person who's getting the picture." He smiled. "Now why don't you leave the mystery to us, and spend the rest of your holiday in that Shropshire cottage you told me about?"

Leslie leaned back in her chair. "Why are you so eager to get rid of me?" she asked.

Merlin said: "Speaking personally, I'm not in the least anxious for you to go. I rather like having you around. But I am anxious about your safety, because it's obvious now that whoever killed your sister is trying to get you out of the way too."

"If he's as anxious as all that, maybe he would follow me into Shropshire, where there are no Scotland Yard experts to keep an eye on me."

"I daresay that could be overcome," he replied.

"If you're as worried about me as all that, why don't you show it by giving me a little more practical assistance with my investigations?" she asked. "I'm not getting what could be described as one hundred per cent co-operation from the Yard."

He grinned at her. "I take off my hat to you for sheer nerve," he said. "Well, supposing the Assistant Commissioner decided to give you the run of the place, what would be your first objective?"

"I'd like that photograph," she replied promptly.

"Why?"

"To confront Peter Hamilton with it next time I see him."

"Somehow I don't think that would be very wise," he said thoughtfully. "For all you know, this man Hamilton might be a pretty dangerous customer."

"Naturally, I shouldn't tackle him about it in the loneliest part of Hampstead Heath," she retorted with some asperity.

"All the same, I think that's the sort of job that's best left to the police." He picked up his hat and moved over to the door. "I have tried to help you," he said somewhat curtly, "but you don't seem to realise that the powers of a detective inspector have their limits."

After he had gone, she paced restlessly up and down the room. Merlin wasn't such a bad sort really, she told herself. Perhaps a shade too conscious of the powers of those set in authority over him, but he was genuinely anxious to solve this case and obviously more than a little concerned about her safety. She felt sorry she had been rude to him.

*****

Next morning there was a letter for her. She slit open the large flat envelope and took out a photostat copy of the inscribed picture of Peter Hamilton. On a sheet of plain notepaper, Merlin had scribbled: "This is a duplicate which should serve the same purpose as the original, but don't stick out your chin too far! And not a word to a soul or I'll be back on the beat."

She slipped the note and picture back into the envelope. Somehow the world seemed much more cheerful. She noticed that Keith Everest, on the other side of the breakfast

51

table, was regarding her curiously but she did not volunteer any explanation.

At the theatre the stage door keeper recognised her, and when she inquired for Hamilton, he went in search of him. He had gone less than five minutes when Leslie noticed Sylvia Graham turning into the stage door keeper's cubbyhole and extracting a small pile of letters from the board on the back wall.

She began turning them over, then suddenly looked up and recognised Leslie. "Oh … good morning," she said, a trifle startled. The greeting was quite formal, and her carefully made-up features became an inexpressive mask.

For a moment, after returning the greeting, Leslie had the impression that Sylvia Graham was about to make some further remark, but she caught sight of Peter Hamilton approaching, nodded to him casually, and went off along the corridor.

Hamilton exchanged a quizzical glance with the stage door keeper who was standing behind him, then crossed to Leslie. "Just ignore the duchess," he grinned. "This is obviously one of her off mornings. Let's go and have some coffee."

He took her to a little Viennese café in Brewer Street, which was almost empty. They settled in a corner, and he leaned across the table. "Now," he said, "what's on your mind, doctor?"

She could not help thinking that this pleasant, disarming manner was hardly typical of a desperate murderer. For a few moments, she slowly stirred her coffee. "I just wanted to make sure that you told me you'd never seen Judy Everest."

"Of course, I told you that. It's perfectly true."

"The police seem to have a different idea," she said deliberately. "Are you sure you never wrote to her, or sent her a signed photograph?"

"Not to my knowledge," he replied. "There was a time, about four years ago, when I was acting fairly regularly, that I gave away quite a number of photos, but certainly I don't remember Judy Everest asking for one." He did not seem in the least perturbed. "As a matter of fact, the police have been on to me already, and they've taken a sample of my handwriting. I can't think why. It all sounds faintly sinister. Do you happen to know what's behind it?"

She hesitated for a second, then told him about the signed photograph. Something restrained her from showing him the photostatic copy in her handbag.

He laughed outright. "I've produced a few thrillers in my time," he chuckled, "but this beats everything!"

When they parted, half an hour later, Leslie was more than a trifle perplexed. Back in Chelsea she was greeted by Mrs. Miller, who told her that Detective Inspector Merlin had telephoned, and left a message asking her to meet him at the Flaneur Restaurant in Gerrard Street at eight o'clock.

On a table in the hall, there was a note addressed to her which had been delivered by hand. She tore it open and read: *Viceroy Theatre. Dear Dr. Sanders, I think there is something you should know about Andrea. Could you come down to my cottage at Clevelode, near Maidenhead, for the weekend? Don't try to get in touch with me at the theatre, or tell anyone about this, but meet me at the entrance to platform four at Paddington to catch the 11.02 on Saturday night. – Sylvia Graham.*

More than a trifle puzzled, she folded the note and pushed it inside her handbag. Sylvia Graham had behaved so coldly towards her at the theatre that she was at a loss to account for this change of attitude. Was it because she had seen Leslie go out with Peter Hamilton, and was anxious to forestall any unpleasantness from that quarter?

*****

Studying the menu at the Flaneur Restaurant, Leslie could not help feeling vaguely flattered that Merlin had invited her out to dinner. "I do hope you get a generous allowance for expenses," she said, regarding him somewhat anxiously across the corner table.

He smiled back at her. "An occasional night out is one of my few extravagances," he said. "I am only too delighted you could come. I want you to regard this evening as a sort of goodwill gesture, and to prove I'm in earnest I thought you might like to know that we've taken a sample of Hamilton's handwriting and it turns out to be quite different from that on the photograph."

"That doesn't surprise me," she said pleasantly, but she did not offer to explain why.

As the meal progressed, Leslie began to realise that Merlin meant what he said. He was interested in her as a person, not merely as the obstinate sister of a murdered girl whose death he had the job of investigating. Indeed, she was quite prepared for it when he suggested that, if she was free on Sunday, she might care for a run into Epping Forest.

"I'm afraid I can't manage this Sunday … and here's the reason," she said, opening her bag and handing him Sylvia Graham's letter. "I feel this is an appointment I ought to keep."

He studied the letter carefully. "If she knows something about Andrea, why didn't she tell us?" he mused. "I spent nearly an hour questioning her. She denied any knowledge of your sister's private life." Merlin put the letter down on the table. "I only hope you won't get mixed up with any more accidents if you accept this invitation," he said. "After all, it might be completely bogus. The note may not even be in her writing." He broke off and caught her eye. "Now what's amusing you?"

"You noticed nothing about the writing?" she asked, trying to sound as casual as possible.

He took a small magnifying glass from his waistcoat pocket and picked up the letter again. "It looks like a typical actress's scrawl to me – over-elaborate capitals, and flourishes at the end of every other word. What's special about it?"

She opened her handbag and took out the photostatic copy of Peter Hamilton's picture. "Compare the handwriting on the note with this on the picture," she suggested.

He placed them side by side and looked at them in turn through his magnifying glass. At last he gave a low whistle. "No doubt about it – they're identical," he said. "That was pretty smart of you."

"But what does it all mean?" she persisted. "Why should Sylvia Graham scrawl on Peter Hamilton's picture and give it to Judy Everest?"

"I shall have to have notice of that question," he replied. "I think perhaps I'd better see you on your way home now. It's getting quite late." She could see that his brain was busy with the possibilities opened up by this new development.

He put her in a taxi and went back to the Yard.

Leslie had told Keith Everest that she was dining with Merlin, and she found him waiting up for her to see if there

55

was any further news about the case. She told him there was nothing new, but that she believed the police were following up several clues. Just as he was going out, Leslie called after him: "I forgot to tell you I'll be away for the weekend."

He stopped at the door. "Going anywhere special?" he inquired.

It was on the tip of her tongue to tell him about Sylvia Graham's cottage, but she changed her mind and said: "Just back to the hospital in Wolverhampton. There are a couple of patients there I'm specially interested in. I'm anxious to check their progress."

He nodded heavily and wished her goodnight. She picked up the evening paper, then decided to go into the kitchen and make herself a hot drink. The table was laid for breakfast, and on top of the refrigerator was a railway guide lying open at the Thames Valley line. As Leslie was bending to open the refrigerator, the word Maidenhead caught her eye. Someone had evidently been looking up trains on this route.

*****

The big clock on number one platform was just coming up to eleven when Leslie caught sight of Sylvia Graham walking briskly through the booking hall. She carried a weekend case and wore a dark green coat.

"There you are!" she said. "I'm so glad you could come, my dear." She sounded as if she really meant it. She led the way to a first class compartment, chatting easily about the journey, explaining that she had left her car at a garage in Maidenhead because the weather had been rather foggy lately and she hated driving into town.

They collected Sylvia's car at an all-night garage and were presently speeding through the night in the direction of Cookham. Sylvia explained that Clevelode was a mere riverside hamlet of not more than half a dozen cottages.

When they arrived, she insisted on cooking bacon and eggs, declaring that she had eaten nothing since teatime. Leslie helped as far as she could but was still considerably mystified that the actress had so far made no attempt to refer to the reason for her visit.

They were drinking their second cup of coffee when Leslie decided that it was time for the showdown. "Why did you ask me down here, Miss Graham – Sylvia?" she demanded, doing her best not to sound like a doctor cross-questioning a patient. "What did you want to tell me?"

Sylvia Graham put down her empty cup and rose. "It's much too late to start on that now," she said quietly. "We'll have a real heart-to-heart talk in the morning. Come on, and I'll show you your room."

It was an attractive little room, with eaves sloping around a dormer window across which gay chintz curtains had been drawn. But it had none of the drawbacks of most cottage bedrooms; there was a small electric fire in one corner, a bedside reading lamp and a washbasin filled with hot and cold water.

Despite these friendly surroundings and a very comfortable bed, Leslie found it difficult to sleep. For half an hour she browsed through an anthology she found on the bedside table, then she switched off the light. She had heard Sylvia's bedroom door close some twenty minutes earlier.

Leslie had just fallen into a half-doze when she heard a movement on the landing outside and realised that someone was going stealthily downstairs. A few moments later, there came what sounded like a subdued knocking on the back door. Presently Leslie heard the door open, and then the hum of distant voices.

She got out of bed and quietly opened her bedroom door. There was no door at the foot of the stairs, and she could hear a man's voice quite plainly. A somewhat heated and very tense conversation was taking place. She caught an occasional phrase, and almost at once realised that the man was Keith Everest. She wondered if he had been in or around the cottage when they arrived, or whether he had only just got there. She recalled the railway guide on the refrigerator, lying open at the Thames Valley timetable.

"You shouldn't have asked her down here," she heard Everest say. "That whole business about Andrea is best forgotten"

"She's entitled to know the truth," retorted Sylvia, "and I'm making it my business to tell her. It's better this way than through the police."

"It's on your own head," replied Everest. "Don't blame me for the consequences. You may be sure that he won't like it."

The argument continued for quite a while, but at last Leslie heard them move into the kitchen and the back door closed. She climbed back into bed, and after a few minutes Sylvia came slowly upstairs. She hesitated for a moment outside Leslie's room, then carefully opened the door and peeped inside. Leslie was turned away from the door, and apparently sound asleep. The door closed softly.

A chain of theories chased each other vividly through Leslie's mind as she lay awake. Finally, she dropped off to sleep, and dreamt that she had to perform a critical operation. She could hear the soft clink of the instruments as the nurse sterilised them. One of them dropped on to the tiled floor with a clatter, and she sat up in bed with a jerk.

A small pebble had struck the dormer window. Someone outside was trying to attract her attention.

6

Leslie opened her weekend case and took out a pencil torch that she had brought with her. Another pebble clinked against the window as she moved towards it. She drew back the curtains a few inches and peered out.

There was a certain amount of light from a sullen moon on the edge of a bank of heavy cloud, but it was only sufficient for her to see that it was a man who stood below the window. She fumbled at the catch, and eventually succeeded in pushing the window wide open. The man slunk into the shadow of the wall. She thrust her arm out, levelled the tiny torch in his direction and pressed the switch. The narrow beam showed her an unkempt young man, shabbily dressed, tie pulled loosely away from his collar, a lock of fair hair falling untidily over his forehead. Despite his anxious expression she could discern that he was a handsome young man, though there was a suspicion of weakness about the regular features.

All this she took in during the split second that elapsed before she heard him exclaim in a hoarse voice: "For God's sake put that light out!"

She snapped off the torch and waited, feeling the pulse in her throat throbbing. "What do you want? Who are you?" she demanded.

"You are Dr. Sanders?" challenged the man below.

"I am."

"Thank God I've found you. I'm Clive!"

"Clive?" she repeated incredulously. "You sounded different on the phone."

"I've been trying to see you for days," said Clive softly. "But something always prevented me. I have to keep on the lookout ..." He spoke jerkily in an agitated fashion. "I'm risking everything in coming here like this. The crowd that tried to get you in that car park and outside Tussaud's are after me as well. They're desperate. They'll stop at nothing."

Despite the fact that Clive knew quite a lot about her movements, Leslie was worried. Why should he contact her in this unorthodox manner? Why attract attention by following her to Maidenhead, when they could have met so easily in London? She said as much to the man down in the shadows.

"You're being watched and so am I. Your phone's tapped, or else there's somebody in the house who gives the game away. This is the first real opportunity I've had to get away from them, and even now I'm taking a big chance."

The moon disappeared behind a cloud. Leslie wondered vaguely if Sylvia Graham had heard anything of this conversation. Fortunately, her room was on the other side of the cottage.

Presently Clive said, in a nervous tone: "If you don't want to have anything to do with me, that's just too bad. I've taken a great risk in trying to get in touch with you, but if you don't want to listen to what I've got to say – well, that's your look-out."

"What do you suggest?" she asked.

"Can you meet me tomorrow night?"

"Why not during the day?"

"It's out of the question," he replied promptly. "I'm taking quite enough chances as it is. Midnight would be the best time. Meet me in the little boathouse at the bottom of the garden here."

Leslie hesitated a moment, then nodded her head. "I can't think why you are surrounding yourself with mystery," she said, "unless you're afraid of being suspected of my sister's murder."

He caught his breath and seemed horrified at the suggestion. "I was in love with Andrea, and she with me," he said earnestly. "You've got to believe that." He sounded tense now, a shade hysterical. "Don't breathe a word about this to anyone," he begged. "Least of all to that policeman friend of yours."

"I promise," said Leslie, a little amused at his description of Detective Inspector Merlin. "Now I must go. I'll see you tomorrow night." She watched him flit silently round the side of the house, then closed the window.

Leslie removed her dressing gown and got into bed. A gentle rattle of the door-latch wakened her some seven hours later. Sylvia Graham came in, carrying a heavily laden breakfast tray. "I hope I didn't wake you too early," she greeted Leslie. "I do hope you regard it as a special treat to have breakfast in bed."

Considerably puzzled by this display of friendliness, Leslie nodded agreeably and said that breakfast in bed was a positive luxury. "Oh, good," approved the actress, setting down the tray on a little table in front of the fire. "Mrs. Goodson, across the way, will come in about eleven to cook lunch," she went on. "So, we won't be interrupted before then, and I thought this would be the best room in which to have our nice cosy chat."

She continued gossiping light heartedly throughout the meal, and it was not until they were drinking their second cup of coffee that Sylvia said: "Looking at me professionally, doctor, would you suspect that I had ever been a drug addict?"

Leslie's cup clattered into the saucer. "Good heavens, no!" she replied.

The actress leaned back in her chair and looked thoughtfully out of the window. "Three years ago, I was in a pretty bad way. I spent several months in a nursing home in Wiltshire. I don't suppose I have to tell you that, during the time I was taking drugs, I met some pretty peculiar people. That's why I am automatically on my guard when any stranger comes to see me.

"You see, there are still a few people at large who knew me in the old days, and they know only too well that a drug addict is always liable to slip … Just one little slip, and she's back where she was and they're in the money. I had a terrible fight to get back in the theatre, so naturally I'm clinging desperately to the ground I've gained."

Leslie nodded. "I quite appreciate that," she said understandingly.

I daresay you've heard that I've quite a reputation where men are concerned," continued Sylvia. "And I don't trouble to deny it. That's a harmless sort of publicity for an actress. I have got quite a number of boyfriends – for one thing, they take my mind off the old temptation. They keep me amused," she added. "I am sometimes contacted by the most unexpected people."

"But if you've conquered the habit, I shouldn't worry too much about other people," advised Leslie. "Try not to be too sensitive about it. Regard it as a closed incident. There was really no need for you to tell me all this, you know. I should never have known."

"I had to tell you," said Sylvia Graham, "because in a way it concerns Andrea."

"Andrea?" repeated Leslie, completely taken aback. "You're not trying to tell me my sister was a drug addict?"

Sylvia took the cigarette out of her mouth. She didn't look at Leslie. "Your sister was an agent for the distribution of drugs," she said softly. "To put it quite brutally, a dope pedlar."

Leslie's first reaction was to laugh outright, but instead she said quietly: "But that's absurd! Why should Andrea get mixed up in that sort of thing?"

Sylvia made a helpless gesture. "It could be for one of a number of reasons," she replied. "Personally, I always suspected she was under the influence of some man or other. I can only tell you that Andrea came into my room after the first dress rehearsal and suggested that I might like a little something to keep up my spirits. I knew what she was referring to, of course. Naturally, I turned the offer down and threatened to expose her."

"What did she say to that?"

"Simply reminded me that she knew enough about my past history to make things very unpleasant for me."

Leslie put down her breakfast tray. "I can't believe all that about Andrea," she said incredulously.

"I gather you haven't seen much of her in recent years."

Leslie nodded. "That's true. I've been studying hard for exams, and she's been working on her own career. We only met occasionally, but I never had the slightest clue that anything like this was happening. She certainly wasn't taking drugs herself, or I'd have spotted it immediately."

"I never said she took drugs herself," said Sylvia. "At least, I had no evidence of it. I don't know what dragged her into

63

this dreadful business, but I'm fairly certain it was directly connected with her murder."

Leslie shook her head in some bewilderment. "I can't think of anything to say. It's all completely new to me. I can't link this news with anything Andrea ever did or said."

Sylvia Graham began to pile the breakfast things on the tray. "Maybe something will suggest itself before tomorrow," she murmured. "Anyhow, I feel better now I've told you." She hesitated for a moment, then added: "All the same, I'd rather you didn't say anything to the police – about the drug business, I mean."

Rather absently Leslie assured her that she would treat the matter as confidential. She was still more than a trifle dazed at hearing of a side of Andrea's life that seemed so utterly repellent. Of course, Sylvia Graham might be lying, but she seemed very genuinely concerned and quite sincere.

Her hostess carried out the breakfast tray, saying that Mrs. Goodson would soon be arriving, and suggesting that Leslie might like to take a little stroll by herself along the river before lunch.

*****

On the way down to the towpath, Leslie peered into the boathouse. Sylvia's car occupied most of the space, for she had had it adapted as a garage. There was an old punt and a pair of oars suspended from one wall. She had half expected to see some signs that Keith Everest or Clive had been there the previous night, but there were none.

Her mind still busy with Sylvia Graham's revelations, Leslie walked rather farther than she had intended and before long found herself within sight of Maidenhead Bridge. She decided to stroll that far and then retrace her steps. As she stood on the bridge for a few minutes, watching the stream of cars flitting past and the play of the watery sunlight on the sullen waters below, she was suddenly conscious of a car pulling up quite near her.

"We certainly meet in some unexpected places," said a voice she knew, and Peter Hamilton's head was thrust out through the window of a Morris Minor. "Can I give you a lift somewhere? I'm on my way to Henley."

"It's quite a coincidence we should both be in this part of the world," she said.

"Are you staying here?"

"I'm with some friend, a little farther up the river." She did not feel inclined to launch into explanations as to how she came to be visiting Sylvia Graham. He seemed rather curious to find out where she was staying, but she contrived to make somewhat vague replies, and presently he looked at his wristwatch and announced that he was already overdue at Henley.

She watched him until he was out of sight, then turned and walked slowly along the towpath, speculating as to whether she ought to tell Detective Inspector Merlin about her discoveries of that morning. Could Merlin have known that Andrea was involved in this dope racket, and was he trying to spare her feelings? It had certainly been a dreadful shock to her.

After lunch she tried to question Sylvia more closely, but the actress now seemed reluctant to discuss the matter any further. She said that after she had rebuffed Andrea; they had had very little to do with each other, and she could throw no light on the girl's associations nor suggest any possible line that Leslie could follow up. Nevertheless, she exerted herself to entertain Leslie and proved an amusing companion.

In the early evening they walked down to the solitary public house in the hamlet, where Sylvia seemed to be on friendly terms with most of the local residents. They stayed there for nearly two hours, but Leslie noticed that Sylvia drank very little, making a couple of shandies last the whole evening. They went back to the cottage, prepared supper, and retired to bed soon after ten.

Leslie switched on her bedside lamp and tried to read, knowing she would never sleep before it was time to get up and keep her midnight rendezvous. She glanced at her wristwatch a dozen times before she decided to make a move. She took her torch from her handbag and slipped it into her overcoat pocket. She did not put on the landing light in case the sound of the switch should wake Sylvia; she used her torch to find her way downstairs and through the kitchen to the back door.

To her surprise it was not locked, yet she distinctly remembered Sylvia locking both the front and back doors. Leslie lifted the latch, and almost immediately heard the sound of a distant scream. A few seconds later the scream was repeated. It came from the direction of the boathouse.

Lesley ran as quickly as she could, but the path was uneven, and she dared not use her torch for fear of attracting attention. It took her several minutes to reach the boathouse. One half of the door had swung open, and inside she could just discern two struggling figures. A man and a woman ...

The man's back was towards her, because he was stooping over the still struggling woman, but Leslie knew instinctively that the woman was Sylvia Graham. She could see that the man was straining to tighten something round Sylvia's throat.

66

As they swayed from side to side, Leslie suddenly rushed at the man with all her strength in an attempt to pull him away. She clutched at him wildly and felt her fingernails gouge into the soft flesh of his cheeks. He gave an exclamation of pain and released his hold on Sylvia. Then, uncertain of the nature of this fresh opposition, he pushed Leslie violently aside and disappeared through the boathouse door.

Leslie took out her torch and quickly examined Sylvia, who was now unconscious. She untied the nylon stocking that had been knotted round her neck, then ran out to the edge of the river and dipped the stocking into the water. Sylvia was still unconscious when she returned, but as soon as Leslie started bathing her face she began to recover.

Leslie was examining the red marks on Sylvia's neck when she heard the sound of approaching footsteps. Had the mysterious stranger realised he was only confronted with a couple of women, one of them almost unconscious? Had he decided that neither of them must survive to give any clue to his identity?

Leslie came to a rapid decision. Leaving Sylvia lying just as she was, she moved to the side of the door. She would wait until the intruder was well inside, then flash her torch on his face to discover his identity once and for all.

The footsteps came nearer. Leslie's thumb found the button of the torch, and she held it slightly away from her just in case he should make a dive for it. They were certainly a man's footsteps, no doubt about that. He fumbled uncertainly at the door, then the door opened. She could see the shadowy outline of a man.

Leslie waited until he was almost level with her, then switched on the torch. The man's startled exclamation was quite eclipsed by Leslie's gasp of surprise and dismay.

The intruder was Detective Inspector Merlin, and both his cheeks were deeply scratched and bleeding profusely.

7

Merlin bent over the semi-conscious form of Sylvia Graham to make certain she was alive, then took a handkerchief from his coat pocket and dabbed at his face. "What's been going on here?" he asked, taking the stocking Leslie held in her hand.

"I was going to ask you the same question," said Leslie.

"Did you see the fellow?"

"Not to recognise him. Did you?"

He shook his head.

She decided that any further questions had better be postponed until they got Sylvia into the cottage. Merlin seemed to appreciate this too, for without further ado he picked up Sylvia and carried her out of the boathouse. Leslie shone the torch, so that he could see his way. Five minutes later, Sylvia was lying on a settee and showing signs of recovering consciousness.

"I never expected to see you in this part of the world," said Leslie curiously.

Merlin dabbed at the wounds on his cheek. "It was my weekend off, and I decided I'd better keep an eye on you," he replied somewhat abruptly. "I'm staying at the local."

"We didn't see you there earlier this evening."

"I thought it best to keep out of your way."

He went on to explain that he had been unable to sleep and had strolled down to the cottage to see if there were any signs of life there. He had heard a distant scream, but it had taken him some time to locate its origin. When he arrived at the boathouse, he was just in time to see the would-be murderer dashing out. He had rushed across a strip of garden and intercepted him.

"The fellow struggled like a madman," continued Merlin. "I knocked him down once, but he recovered, and when he got up, he had either a stone or clinker in his hand. He came for me again and bashed my face with it." He stroked his face, and ruefully felt the lump on the back of his hand. "I was stunned for about a minute, and during that time he made a getaway. I had half a mind to go after him, then I thought that you might be hurt or even … anyhow, thank God you're all right."

Leslie had found the brandy and was pouring some into a small tumbler. "So, you didn't see the man either?" she queried.

"No. The moon was behind the clouds, and it was very dark under that old oak tree where we were struggling. Would you mind if I had a spot of that brandy? And I think you could do with a drop too."

She nodded and poured out the brandy. They tried to make Sylvia drink, but had some difficulty in forcing a few drops between her tightly clenched teeth. However, it obviously had some effect, for a minute or two later she opened her eyes. She put a hand to her throat when she caught sight of Merlin, and her eyes widened in horror.

"It's all right," said Leslie, holding both her hands. "This is Inspector Merlin – you remember him."

Sylvia turned and buried her head in a cushion. "Go away – go away, everybody!" she cried in a muffled voice. "I tell you I can't stand it!"

Leslie exchanged a look with Merlin. "It's the blood on my face," he whispered. "I'll just go and clean up." He went out into the kitchen.

Leslie massaged Sylvia's throat for a few minutes and asked her if she had any other injuries. There was a bad bruise on one foot where her assailant had stamped on it, but no other evidence of the attack.

Presently Merlin returned, looking much more presentable. Sylvia apologised for her outburst and suddenly, without any prompting, she began to tell them about her experience. She said that although she retired early, she developed a headache, and thought a short walk in the fresh air might disperse it. She had taken her favourite route along the towpath, and on her return, she heard a strange noise in the boathouse and went to investigate. She had hesitated in the doorway for a moment, and the next thing she knew was a tight grip on her throat. After that she could not remember anything else coherently.

Merlin did not make an attempt to question her but suggested that Leslie should take her up to bed. Sylvia agreed readily enough and was able to walk upstairs unaided. When she had undressed, Leslie rapidly examined her head and took her pulse. She seemed little the worse for her adventure.

When Leslie came down the stairs into the lounge, Merlin was near the standard lamp examining the soaked stocking which had been used by Sylvia's assailant. He drew the fine mesh gently through his fingers, and slowly looked up as Leslie entered the room. "How is she now?" he inquired.

"I think she'll be all right. It was more shock than anything. If she can get some sleep, she should be fairly normal in the morning."

"It was a lucky thing for her that you arrived on the scene," commented Merlin.

"And lucky for both of us that you came along," she murmured.

"Yes," said Merlin somewhat dryly, "we all seem to have been very fortunate. And now Miss Graham is apparently very anxious to forget the whole thing."

Leslie regarded him curiously. "You think Sylvia wasn't telling the truth?" she asked.

"Not the whole truth. But it seemed hardly fair to pester her with questions in her present state. All the same, I'm quite positive she hasn't told us everything. And if it comes to that, young lady, what were you doing at the boathouse yourself? Don't tell me you suffer from insomnia too."

Leslie hoped he did not notice her hesitation. For a moment she had been going to tell him everything about the proposed rendezvous with Clive. Then a flicker of doubt entered her mind about Merlin. It was certainly a coincidence that he should have been at the boathouse, and that his face should have been so badly scratched. She recalled Clive's parting words: "Don't breathe a word about this to anyone – least of all that policeman friend of yours."

She sipped her brandy for a few moments. "I just happened to hear Sylvia's scream when I went to open my bedroom window. When I got down to the boathouse, I saw the man bending over Sylvia and strangling her with the stocking. I scratched his face pretty badly," she added with just the merest emphasis.

Merlin smiled. "It's a pity you didn't see his face," he said quietly. He picked up his hat. "You can find me at the inn if you want me," he said. He seemed a trifle reluctant to leave, however, and made her promise to bolt every door and fasten the windows.

When she had completed this operation, she went up to Sylvia's room. The actress was half asleep, so Leslie wished her goodnight and quietly closed the door. When she went

71

into her own room, she drew back the curtains and looked out before switching on the light. The clouds had drifted away, and the moon was now clearly visible. She sat there by the window for some minutes, looking at the silent garden below. In the hazy moonlight the garden appeared quite unreal, and Leslie was startled by the sound of a soft footstep.

She withdrew to the side of the window, where she was hidden by the curtain. A man stopped under the window and did not move for several seconds. Very cautiously she peered out and saw that the man below was Detective Inspector Merlin. He was standing, peering down at the path beneath the window. After a few moments he looked round as if to make sure he was not observed, then took a torch from his pocket and began to examine the ground. He was obviously looking at a footprint he had found there. Leslie realised that it would be Clive's footprint, and he had probably left quite a deep impression when he had stood under her window the previous night.

Could Merlin have any clue about that visit, or was he simply prowling around on the off chance? She was tempted to open the window and ask him what he was looking for. In the end, however, she refrained and sat there quietly in the dark until she heard him stealthily move away. Then she drew the curtains and put on the light. Five minutes later, she was lying in bed going over the events of the weekend.

*****

Next morning Sylvia was almost her old self again, but she decided to stay in bed until it was time to leave for town. She was considerably shocked when Leslie suggested that she should telephone the theatre and arrange for her understudy

72

to appear that night. "I daren't take a chance like that," she admitted. "All the old gossip would start about my taking drugs."

"I could give you a certificate," suggested Leslie.

Sylvia shook her head. "That's very sweet of you. But I'll be all right after a few hours' rest."

After she had cleared away the breakfast things, Leslie went out into the garden. It was a pleasant morning, fairly warm for the time of year, and she walked down to the boathouse because Sylvia had asked her to check up whether she had enough petrol to drive back to town.

Leslie had just pushed back the doors, so that she could see the petrol gauge clearly, when she noticed a tiny piece of metal glinting in the sunlight. It was the end of a gold cufflink that had snapped off its chain. She picked it up and turned it over. In the midst of an elaborate design, the letter "M" was plainly discernible.

She examined it more closely. There was only the one letter. Could it belong to Detective Inspector Merlin? It was possible that it had snapped during Merlin's reported struggle outside the boathouse with the mysterious stranger and had only fallen out of his cuff a minute or two later.

When she returned to the cottage, Merlin was waiting for her. "I thought I'd better make sure there have been no further incidents," he said. "And also inquire about Miss Graham." She told him that Sylvia was making a good recovery and invited him into the cottage.

She made some coffee and took Sylvia a cup. "Inspector Merlin says he'll drive the car if you want to take it all the way to town. There's plenty of petrol."

There was the flicker of an amused smile around the actress's mouth. "You certainly won't come to much harm, my dear, if that young man can help it."

Leslie was furious to find herself blushing. However, Sylvia accepted Merlin's offer, declaring that she would be relieved to have someone else at the wheel for the journey through the outer suburbs.

When Leslie went downstairs again, Merlin was reading the morning paper. "By the way, I took the liberty of having a look round the boathouse on my way here, just to see if there was anything in the nature of a clue," he said casually. "No luck, though."

"That may have been because someone else had been there before you," she suggested.

"You mean you've been there?"

She took the piece of cufflink from her bag and passed it to him. "What do you make of that?" she asked.

He whistled softly to himself as he turned it over in the palm of his hand. Then he looked up suddenly and said: "I suppose you're wondering if 'M' stands for Merlin."

"That possibility had occurred to me," she admitted.

He laughed and pulled back his jacket sleeve. "I can't have you getting ideas like that," he said, and showed her that his cuffs were buttoned. "I was wearing this shirt yesterday – look, there's the blood on it from the scratch on my cheek." He indicated a spot of blood which had been concealed by his tie.

"I quite forgot to inquire after your injuries," she said.

He fingered the scars somewhat cautiously. "They make it rather painful to grin," he told her.

She invited him to stay for lunch, but he said he had arranged for a meal at the inn.

He returned promptly at two-thirty, ready to drive them to town, and Leslie noticed once again that suspicion of a smile from Sylvia as she suggested that Leslie might prefer to sit beside the driver. In a somewhat remote tone, Leslie replied that she would sooner travel in the back of the car. This did not deter Merlin from conducting a steady conversation with them.

For the first half of the journey, they speculated upon the identity of the man in the boathouse. Merlin asked the two women to think of all the people they had seen during the weekend, and presently Leslie told them of her encounter with Peter Hamilton on the bridge at Maidenhead.

"I wonder if old Monty Midget really was going to Henley?" said Sylvia thoughtfully.

"Who's Monty Midget?" demanded Merlin. "Why, Peter Hamilton, of course. Montague Midget is his real name. He changed it when he became a highbrow producer because it sounded like a circus act. I still call him Monty when I'm feeling particularly catty."

Merlin glanced over his shoulder and caught Leslie's eye. She knew at once what he was thinking. Did that mysterious "M" on the cufflink stand for Midget? The conversation languished as they sped through the inner suburbs, and Merlin steered through the stream of traffic at Shepherds Bush.

He dropped Leslie at the house in Chelsea. As she entered the hall, Keith Everest was descending the stairs. He seemed much more cheerful; she noticed he had paint on his hands and walked with only a single stick.

"Have you been working?" she asked.

He nodded. "First time since -." He broke off and indicated the kitchen door. "Come in here a minute."

Somewhat puzzled, she followed him into the empty kitchen, and he closed the door behind them. "There's a patient of yours called to see you," he informed her. "I told him you were in Wolverhampton and I didn't know when you'd be back, but he insisted on waiting. I put him in the living room."

She moved towards the door, but he held up a hand to restrain her. "Just a minute, Leslie," he said. "There's something a bit queer about this fellow. Perhaps I'd better come in with you, just in case ..." She was a little touched by his concern but refused the offer and assured him that she had never experienced any difficulty with patients.

"Anyhow, I'll be in here. You've only to yell out, and I'll hobble along as fast as I can."

She nodded her thanks and went along to the living room. When she first opened the door, the room appeared to be empty. Then she realised that there was a man buried in the armchair with his back towards her. He turned as she came into the room, and she recognised him at once,

It was the man who called himself Clive.

8

The young man rose as Leslie came into the room, but it seemed to be a nervous movement rather than one of politeness. Her professional experience enabled her to judge at a glance that he was in a nervous condition. As Keith Everest had said, there was a wild look in his eye and a nerve at the side of his mouth twitched disagreeably every few seconds.

Leslie judged him to be in his early twenties, but the strain he was undergoing had made him look older than his years, and a single lock of silvery grey hair that was brushed back from the centre of his forehead accentuated that impression. He had unbuttoned his worn mackintosh to reveal a shabby suit; his shoes were cracked across the insteps and badly needed a polish.

It was when he spoke that any doubt about the fact that he had been her mysterious caller on Saturday night disappeared, for Leslie recognised the jerky voice that was always on the verge of a stammer. "I had to see you," he said in low tones, crossing over to the door to make sure it was closed. She followed his movements curiously and felt vaguely reassured by the fact that Keith Everest was within easy call.

"You could have seen me last night," she said at last. "I kept the appointment. That was the third time you haven't turned up."

"I know," he said, and there was a note of desperation in his voice. "You don't understand how difficult things are for me. I'm a marked man." He took half a cigarette from his pocket, and lighted it without asking permission. "I've tried to be there," he said jerkily. "Every time I tried. Last night, I was only fifty yards from the boathouse when I saw your policeman friend."

"You mean Inspector Merlin? What was he doing?"

"He was going in the same direction. Naturally, I thought you'd told him you were meeting me, though I asked you not to. I've got to keep clear of the police at all costs."

"I hadn't told him anything," Leslie assured the young man, who had slumped into his chair again and was puffing nervously at his cigarette. "Did you hear any sound from the boathouse?"

"No. As soon as I saw Merlin, I went off in the opposite direction. I can't afford to take any chances."

Leslie regarded him curiously. Why was he so desperate to avoid the police? "Then you know nothing about the attack on Sylvia Graham?"

He seemed to be more on his guard than ever. "Sylvia Graham?" he repeated. "I know nothing about her."

Leslie went on with her questioning. "If you didn't murder Andrea –"

"Of course I didn't murder her. I keep telling you, we were in love with each other."

"Then why are you so scared of the police?"

He sighed and threw his cigarette stub into the grate. "I'd better tell you all about that. It's partly the cause of this trouble." He looked at Leslie for several seconds, as if he were trying to make up his mind. "I suppose I am what the probation officers would describe as a psychological case," he said presently. "Being a doctor, you'll appreciate that. I was badly spoiled by my mother until she died, then soon after that I was called up. At first, I thought that was going to solve all my problems – my lack of money, boredom and loneliness. But I very soon discovered my mistake. I simply couldn't stand up to army life. I hadn't the stamina, the ballast, the capacity for making the best of things. I was a complete and utter misfit, so I ran away."

"You mean you deserted?"

Clive nodded. "That's what they call it. I've been on the run now for two years – expecting the police to pounce at any moment, rarely sleeping two consecutive nights under the same roof, mistrusting everybody – with not a friend in the world since Andrea died."

"But how do you manage to live?" queried Leslie curiously.

He shrugged. "Chiefly by petty crime, of course."

"How did you meet Andrea?"

"It was the first time the police really got track of me. I was being followed along Shaftesbury Avenue by two plain clothes men, and I suddenly caught sight of a police car approaching from the opposite direction. I should have been cornered, so I dodged down the alley at the side of the Viceroy Theatre. I went through an open door and straight along a corridor. It happened to be the stage door. I walked along to the end of a passage and into an empty room."

"You certainly had a nerve," said Leslie.

"I was quite desperate. After I had been in the room for ten minutes, Andrea came in. She didn't seem surprised or frightened. At first, I think she took me for somebody else, but I blurted out the whole story, and she was terribly decent. She let me stay there, and eventually smuggled me out of the theatre and brought me back here to this house."

"You mean you actually stayed here?"

"I stayed all that night. No-one else saw me – they were all in bed when we got back." While he was talking, Leslie was striving to assess this strange young man who had so unaccountably aroused her sister's sympathies. "After that, Andrea became the centre of my life," went on Clive. "Since my mother died there had been no-one I could go to. Andrea took her place. Of course, we had to meet in all sorts of strange places and under assumed names but being with Andrea tended to distract suspicion from me. I daresay the hotel people occasionally suspected that we weren't married, but it never occurred to them that I was wanted by the police. Andrea gave me a new lease of life, just when I was getting really desperate. I owe her everything."

Leslie noticed there were tears in his eyes now. She tried to bring him back to the subject of her sister's murder. "Did

Andrea tell you of any troubles she had?" Leslie asked. "And were they serious?"

He nodded. "They were so frightening that I was usually more worried about her than about myself. We were always trying to figure some way out, but the only real solution seemed to be to get out of the country. We never had enough money for that, though there was always a chance that Andrea might get a tour in Canada or South Africa."

"You haven't told me anything about Andrea's troubles," said Leslie. "I did hear she was mixed up with drug distribution, but I haven't got all the details."

"Andrea was being blackmailed," Clive assured her excitedly. "That was the cause of the murder. She was always saying she would refuse to go on with the dope racket, and I believe this blackmailer murdered her."

"But what about Judy Everest? She was murdered too. Was she being blackmailed?"

"It's possible. I never met the girl."

"I should have thought Andrea might have given you some clue about this man," said Leslie. "Haven't you any idea as to his identity?"

Clive got up from his chair and walked across to the window. After a moment he turned and said: "I have a very good idea who he is. I'm waiting until I've got absolute proof. Then I shall go straight to the police."

"Even though it will mean your own arrest?"

"It's the least I can do for Andrea," he replied quietly. "Nothing else seems to matter now. But it's important that I shouldn't get dragged back into the army before I can produce the final proof."

"Surely if you went to the police and explained –" began Leslie, but he quickly shook his head.

"I've got to go my own way," he argued. "If the killer thought I'd contacted the police then my plans would be ruined."

He told Leslie that he suspected that the blackmailer already realised that he was on the right track, hence the attempts to prevent his meeting her. Leslie tried to persuade him to tell her more about the evidence he was compiling about the suspected killer, but he remained adamant, arguing that she would be in danger of meeting Andrea's fate if she interfered. However, he eventually agreed to contact her the moment he discovered anything really important.

When Clive had departed, Leslie went into the kitchen to make some tea. The room was empty, but she soon heard Keith Everest's heavy tread on the stairs. He came into the kitchen and told her that Mrs. Miller was taking a half-day off.

They had tea together in the living room, and he seemed more at ease than she had known him since she arrived. She put it down to the fact that he was immersed in his work again. She was tempted to ask him what he had been doing at Sylvia Graham's cottage late on Saturday night, and just how much he knew about Andrea being involved in the drug racket. But it would mean admitting to him that she had told him a lie about going to Wolverhampton, and she also had a feeling that he would calmly deny the whole thing.

After he had picked up a book and started to read, she found her thoughts straying to the weekend at the cottage. She felt strangely restless and began to wonder what was happening to Sylvia. Why had she gone down to the boathouse at that late hour? There was still a lot to be explained.

On the spur of the moment she told Keith Everest that she was going along to the theatre. He merely nodded abstractedly and returned to his book.

*****

Leslie bought a seat at the back of the stalls and settled down to watch the play. She had to admit that Sylvia Graham was giving a very smooth performance. If she was suffering from the strain of the weekend's events, she betrayed not the slightest sign of it; every movement was assured and polished to the last degree. Nor was it in any way a mechanical performance; there was a depth of feeling in the acting that held Leslie's interest through every scene right up to her magnificent exit about ten minutes before the play ended. It was a particularly good house for a Monday evening, and Leslie was certain they would give Sylvia an enthusiastic reception.

She waited with some impatience after the curtain slowly descended on the final scene. There was a longer delay than usual, but it eventually rose again on a line-up of the company and Leslie noticed at once that Sylvia was missing. The others seemed a trifle uncertain of themselves, and she saw one or two of them glancing doubtfully offstage. There was only one more curtain, then the lights went up.

It took Leslie a few minutes to extricate herself from the throngs of patrons crowding towards the exits. She was uncertain as to the whereabouts of the pass door from the auditorium to backstage at the Viceroy, so she eventually came out of the front entrance and pushed her way through the crowds on the pavement towards the stage door alley. As she was turning the corner, she saw a police car pull up with a jerk, and before it had stopped a door was flung open and a familiar figure emerged.

Detective Inspector Merlin saw her at once. "Hello, what are you doing here?" he queried hurriedly as they walked down the alley.

"I'm on my way to see Sylvia Graham," she replied.

"So are we," said Merlin grimly, and there was something in his tone that made her look up sharply.

"Is anything wrong?" she demanded.

"Plenty! We got a call at the Yard ten minutes ago. Sylvia Graham was murdered – stabbed with a knife as she was sitting in her dressing room waiting for the final curtain of the play." They had just reached the stage door. Leslie drew back. She felt as if she were going to be violently sick. Merlin caught her arm. "Come on," he said. "You'd better see it through now."

Leslie followed Merlin into Sylvia's dressing room and stood in the doorway, while he went over and took a quick glance at the still figure that lay on the divan. A plain clothes man was focusing his camera on one side of the room, and another was busy tracing fingerprints.

Merlin took immediate command and asked to see the stage door keeper. In the little cubby-hole, the man showed him the record of visitors he kept in a special book, with the time they called and the person they saw. "I see that nobody called during the last twenty minutes," Merlin said, referring to the book.

"No, sir. It's been a bit quiet tonight."

"Are you sure you were here all the time?" The man looked worried. "Don't you ever slip out for a drink about that time?" suggested Merlin, whose experience had taught him something of the habits of theatre staffs.

83

"Well –" the door keeper began to hedge. "I only went to the pub on the corner of the alley, and Albert always looks after the door."

Merlin questioned Albert the callboy, but without any success. The boy admitted that he had been asked to keep an eye on the door, but he had had to go out twice on errands for members of the company. The inspector returned to Sylvia's dressing room, and was asking Leslie how she happened to be at the theatre on this particular evening when there was a knock on the door, and they saw a uniformed constable outside with a young man in shirtsleeves.

"This young feller says he saw something suspicious," announced the officer importantly. Merlin beckoned them inside and closed the door.

The man in shirtsleeves was a stagehand named Lawrence. "I never thought about it at the time, sir," he said. "A young fellow knocked at Miss Graham's door quite casual like, and just walked in."

"When was this?"

"Just after she'd come off the stage. She gets lots of gentlemen friends popping in and out, so I never thought much about it."

"Had you ever seen this man before?" asked Merlin.

Lawrence shook his head. "No, never."

"How can you be sure of that?"

"Because if I'd seen him once I'd have remembered him," said Lawrence emphatically. "He'd got a streak of grey hair pushed back off his forehead."

9

Leslie hoped that Inspector Merlin had not seen her start of surprise when the stagehand described the man who had entered Sylvia Graham's dressing room. She immediately glanced in Merlin's direction, and noticed the keen grey eyes were regarding her shrewdly.

However, he said nothing to her but turned to the man and queried: "I suppose you know most of the people who are allowed backstage?"

The man hesitated a moment, then said: "As a matter of fact I'm new here, sir. I only started today. Of course, I know the company by sight and the stage staff."

"And you're positive it was none of them?"

"Quite certain, sir."

Merlin turned to the plain clothes detective who had come in a few minutes previously. "I'd be glad if you'd take this man's private address, Sergeant Jukes, just in case we need him at short notice. And you might get him to repeat full particulars as far as possible."

At that moment there was a tap at the door and the police surgeon walked in, nodded to Merlin, and put down his bag. Lawrence and Sergeant Jukes went out, quietly closing the door behind them. The police surgeon glanced questioningly at Leslie, and the inspector said: "This lady is a doctor – she was in the audience."

The police surgeon nodded vaguely at Leslie and mumbled to himself as he knelt down to examine the body. "Life extinct about half an hour," he went on mumbling. "Quite a small wound, very narrow, some sort of dagger I should imagine." He looked up at Merlin. "Any sign of the weapon?"

"It hasn't turned up yet."

The police surgeon nodded and went on with his examination. He was just concluding it when there were rapid footsteps in the passage outside, and the door opened to admit Peter Hamilton. The producer stood for a moment in the doorway, his glance roving round the room.

He licked his lips nervously. "This is awful, inspector. The stage door keeper just told me – it's ghastly! The play will have to come off. It's the end of everything."

"Now don't panic, Mr. Hamilton," said Merlin slowly. "Just think carefully and see if you can call to mind a youngish man with a streak of grey hair brushed back from his forehead. An individual answering to that description was seen to enter this room just before Miss Graham was murdered."

Hamilton wrinkled his forehead into a thoughtful frown, but finally shook his head. "I once knew an actor named Solari who had a streak of grey hair, but I'm pretty sure he's dead. It's certainly no-one connected with this theatre." He hesitated. "Now wait a minute –" He rubbed his right hand thoughtfully across his chin. "It's coming back to me," he murmured. "I once saw Andrea Lake with a young fellow answering to that description. They were just coming out of a news theatre in the Strand."

Hamilton nodded to himself as he recalled the details of the incident. However, he did not know Andrea's companion on that occasion, and she had never mentioned the young man to him.

When the ambulance arrived, Merlin left Detective Sergeant Jukes in charge, telling him to phone the Yard if there were any further developments. Then Merlin turned to Leslie. "I think a cup of very black coffee would be just the thing for both of us."

He took her to a shabby little café in Old Compton Street which was practically deserted, and as they sat at one of the metal-topped tables drinking coffee out of thick cups, he said: "Don't you think you'd better own up, doctor? I saw you catch your breath when that stagehand mentioned the man with the grey streak."

Leslie went on drinking and did not reply immediately. Could she in fairness withhold such important information? She knew instinctively that if she did so she would get no further co-operation from Inspector Merlin in tracing her sister's murderer. Finally, she put down her cup, and in a carefully guarded voice told him all she knew about the deserter Clive, who had been in love with her sister. "All the same, I don't think he had anything to do with the murder of Andrea or Sylvia Graham," she concluded.

Merlin thoughtfully stubbed out the cigarette he had been smoking. "It seems pretty definite that he was in the theatre tonight, and that he went into Sylvia Graham's dressing room."

Leslie shook her head helplessly. "I can't understand it," she confessed. "His whole life is concentrated on keeping out of the public eye. He's terrified the police will catch him before he can follow up his clue to Andrea's murder."

"That may be all bluff," suggested Merlin. "Anyhow, you must be on your guard, because he's almost certain to try to get in touch with you again." He hesitated a moment, then rested his elbows on the table and looked into her eyes. "You must promise faithfully to telephone me the moment you hear from him."

Leslie considered this for a moment, then nodded. "All right," she agreed, "providing you promise not to hand him over to the military police until we've discovered the murderer."

He nodded, glanced at his watch, and decided it was time to go. She was a little surprised when he insisted on accompanying her back to Chelsea. "I'm getting very worried about you," he told her as they sat there in the semi-darkness of the taxi. "The more you get mixed up in this affair, the more precarious your personal safety. A nice girl like you should steer clear of this sort of thing."

"I think I've told you before, inspector, that I'm accustomed to all sorts of unpleasantness. It's part of my daily routine."

"Yes, but in the present circumstances there's danger to yourself. That's what worries me."

Leslie laughed. "Now you're being melodramatic, inspector. I like your tough policeman act much better."

The taxi jerked to a standstill before Merlin could think of a retort. He paid the driver, then said: "Do you mind if I come in with you for a minute? Just to make sure your mysterious friend isn't waiting in the hall?"

Leslie nodded, and opened the door with her latchkey. The house was quiet and in darkness, save for a faint glow through the half-open study door. Leslie peeped inside and saw that the electric fire had been left on, though the room was empty. "You'd better come in here – it's warmer," she called over her shoulder to Merlin. I expect Mr. Everest has forgotten to switch the fire off."

Merlin settled himself in a comfortable armchair. "You know," he began, "you look less like a doctor every time I see you."

"Does that mean I'm gaining the patient's confidence?" she smiled.

"Your patients are certainly very lucky," he murmured with what sounded like a note of envy. "I'm going to miss you when your month's holiday is over. Although you've got me worried stiff at times, it's been nice having you around."

"Are you hinting I should apply for a job as police surgeon?"

"The saints forbid! You're worth something better than that." He seemed about to enlarge upon this, but the door opened to reveal Keith Everest standing there in his dressing gown.

"I thought I heard voices," he said. "I've been doing a few odd jobs up in the studio. I was interrupted by that patient of yours – you know, the chap with the streak of grey hair. He was very upset about something and wouldn't wait a couple of minutes even."

"Didn't he leave any message?" asked Leslie quickly.

"Not a word. He just vanished into the night almost before I could turn round."

Inspector Merlin leaned forward in his chair. "Mr. Everest," he said quietly, "is this young man with the streak of grey hair the same person that called here before?"

"Yes, of course he is," replied Everest somewhat brusquely.

"What time did he call?"

"It would be just before ten. I remember when I came in here the ten o'clock news was just starting. That was about a minute after he left."

Merlin looked worried. Leslie realised he was trying to work out how Clive could have been in Chelsea at a few minutes before ten and in Shaftesbury Avenue at almost exactly the same time. Everest asked them to have a drink, and when they refused, he helped himself to a generous half-tumbler of whisky. It was obviously not his first. As he gulped it down, Leslie told him about the murder of Sylvia Graham.

"It's the same swine who murdered Judy!" he rasped. "I'm certain of it." He swung round and turned on Merlin. "When is it all going to end?" he demanded. "Week after week this case goes on, and you're no nearer to finding the murderer. What's the matter with the police in this country?" Everest paced restlessly up and down the room. "Haven't you any clue? Don't you suspect anybody?" he demanded.

"We suspect a lot of people," replied Merlin equably.

"Including me, I suppose," said Everest sardonically.

Merlin shrugged and picked up a paper knife from the desk beside him. "This looks quite valuable. Where did you get it?" he asked, anxious to change the subject.

"As a matter of fact, it is fairly valuable. It's a Venetian stiletto – sixteenth century, I believe. I bought it in Paris."

Merlin admired the elaborate scrollwork on the handle, then ran his thumb along the narrow, finely tempered blade. "It could be a very nasty weapon," he said softly.

"I suppose it could, considering that was what it was made for," replied the artist. "Personally, I use it as a paper knife."

Merlin replaced the knife on the desk without any further comment, and after a further few minutes of desultory conversation announced that he must be going. Leslie accompanied him to the front door. "That Venetian dagger," she whispered. "It could have been the weapon used to kill Sylvia Graham."

"That would make your landlord a pretty strong suspect if he were not physically disabled. And if he did kill Sylvia Graham, he'd hardly leave the weapon in full view like that."

She shook her head doubtfully. "Keith Everest is a very strange person," she said quietly. "Of course, if he opened the door to Clive at ten o'clock it's difficult to see how he could have been at the theatre."

"We've only his word for that," put in Merlin. "But I feel somehow he's telling the truth. Something tells me this fellow Clive isn't very far away." He clasped her hand as they said goodnight. "Remember your promise to telephone me the moment that chap appears on the scene," he reminded her. She nodded and softly closed the front door.

For a moment Merlin stood at the top of the short flight of steps to accustom himself to the darkness. He was just about to descend, when he saw a movement in the shadows of an alley between two houses almost directly opposite. He realised almost at once that there was a man lurking there, a watcher who was anxious to see who had been leaving the house.

The inspector came briskly down the steps as if to cross the road, and the silent figure promptly disappeared into the shadows. Merlin changed his mind and did not cross the road after all, hoping that the watching man had not detected his involuntary start of recognition. Instead he walked briskly down to the Kings Road and swung round the corner as if he were returning to the West End. After walking ten yards or so, he stopped and retraced his footsteps.

He sidled quietly past the shop front and stood in the doorway, which gave him an excellent view down the street. There was a lamp about ten yards beyond Keith Everest's house, and Merlin stood rigidly in the shop doorway concentrating upon the pool of light.

A couple of empty buses rushed past on their way to the garage, and a small group of men and women in evening dress carrying balloons and streamers came noisily down the Kings Road. There was still no sign of life down the side street.

Merlin began to wonder if the hidden watcher had crossed the road and entered Everest's house during the short space of time when he had not held it under observation.

The minutes dragged slowly by. Late night stragglers passed on either side of the road. If they saw Merlin, they gave no sign. He began to brood over the murder of Sylvia Graham, and his mind wandered almost at once to Leslie, who had been so deeply involved in this chain of tragic events and might at this moment be in considerable danger herself. He was just beginning to debate whether he dare light a cigarette before settling down for a long vigil, when he saw the shadow of a man move from the shelter of a house opposite Everest's.

The man crossed the road, mounted the steps that Merlin had just recently descended, and was about to press the front doorbell when he heard the voice of Merlin ten yards away. "Just a minute!"

The moment he spoke, Merlin noticed the figure at the top of the steps stiffen. His hand dropped to his side but he did not turn to face Merlin, who had now reached the foot of the steps. "What d'you want?" asked the man at the front door in thick, indistinct tones.

"I'm a police officer. I'd like a word with you."

The man slowly began to turn towards Merlin, but before the inspector could catch a glimpse of his face he took a flying leap and Merlin found himself lying in the gutter with all the breath knocked out of his body. The impact had dislodged the shabby felt hat the young man was wearing, and the inspector caught sight of a streak of grey hair as his attacker ran madly towards the Kings Road.

It was a second or two before Merlin could recover his breath, and when he eventually regained his feet, he could see his quarry just turning the corner into the main road. Merlin reached the corner in time to see his man cross the road in front of a bus and leap a low wall that fronted a bomb site. After that, Merlin did not see him again.

He searched the piece of derelict land and explored every cranny around the crumbling walls, but there was no sign of the fugitive. After stumbling over piles of masonry for some ten minutes, Merlin realised that his quarry had probably vanished into the network of side streets at the rear of the bomb site.

Somewhat disgruntled the inspector returned to the road, and after walking nearly to Sloane Square managed to get a taxi back to New Scotland Yard. His only consolation lay in the thought that the nocturnal visitor would not readily return to Everest's house if he suspected it was under observation by the police.

At the Yard, the duty sergeant told him that there had been a telephone message from Sergeant Jukes, who had been left in charge at the theatre. He was anxious to get in touch with Merlin as soon as possible. The inspector nodded wearily and went up to his office to telephone the theatre.

There was a note of suppressed excitement in the sergeant's voice when it came over the wire. "Something's turned up, sir. I'd rather not tell you over the phone – just in case." Merlin said he would be round at once and slammed down the receiver.

There seemed to be an eerie atmosphere about the silent theatre, as Merlin made his way down the deserted alley to the stage door. He found Sergeant Jukes in the little office usually occupied by the stage door keeper. "I thought there'd be no harm in taking a look through the dustbins just outside the door here, sir," said Jukes, "and I came across something I think will interest you."

He fumbled in the dispatch case at his feet, and presently drew out a shabby brown wig, which was rather crumpled. For a moment Merlin was a trifle mystified. Then he turned the wig over and saw that in the front of it was a lock of grey hair.

10

Inspector Merlin thoughtfully smoothed the wig over the back of his clenched fist, as he called to mind the details of the play in which Sylvia Graham had been appearing. He was positive that none of the male actors had that distinctive streak of grey hair.

"Of course, the wig could have been planted in that dustbin," murmured the sergeant thoughtfully, rubbing his chin.

"You mean the murderer deliberately put it there to lead us to believe that he hasn't a grey streak, though he really has in fact?" Merlin pursed his lips. "This is becoming rather involved," he mused.

The inspector noticed that the wig bore the makers' names Forsythe and Terrell, and early next morning he visited their shop in Shaftesbury Avenue. An obliging assistant looked up the wig for him in a register, and informed Merlin that it had been sold to an actor named Chris Layton, who was at that moment touring in South Africa.

Merlin pushed the wig into his overcoat pocket and went round to the Viceroy Theatre, where he found a rehearsal had been called for ten o'clock so that Sylvia Graham's understudy could have a run-through with the company. When the actors arrived, he arranged to interview them separately in the stage manager's office.

He showed the wig to each of the five men and it was not until he reached the last, a middle-aged character actor named Thompson, that he noticed a gleam of recognition. "I certainly had a wig like that," said Thompson. He took it and examined the lining. "Yes, this is mine all right. I got it from a chap named Chris Layton when I was in rep with him at Southend. He never wore it, and I bought it cheap."

They went to Thompson's dressing room and searched his property basket. There was no sign of a wig with a grey lock of hair. Merlin told him where the wig had been found, and asked if it was he who had placed it in the dustbin. "Of course not!" replied Thompson indignantly. "It's a perfectly good transformation. Why the devil should I throw it away?"

"Does anyone else know you have the wig?"

"Practically the whole company, I should think. I wore it at the first dress rehearsal, but Hamilton made me change it. Said it made me look a bit of a freak."

"Is that usual, to buy other people's wigs?"

"We do it sometimes. A new wig costs a lot of money."

As a precautionary measure Merlin sent for Lawrence, the stagehand, who stated quite definitely that Thompson was not the man he had seen leaving Sylvia Graham's dressing room. Feeling somewhat disgruntled, Merlin sat in the stalls while the company assembled on the stage. Then Hamilton gave his final instructions, and the rehearsal began. After watching it rather moodily for ten minutes, the inspector walked out through the front of the house and returned to the Yard.

*****

When Leslie came down to prepare breakfast that morning, she saw a little pile of letters lying behind the front door. Picking them up, she ran through them quickly and found one addressed to herself. Opening it, she read:

I have just heard about the Sylvia Graham murder. I had nothing to do with that, I swear it. I can prove this to you if you'll meet me. I can't show myself in daylight, so I shall be in the back stalls of the Elite Cinema in Tottenham Court Road all afternoon. If you come, I will tell you everything I know. Please don't say anything about this to anybody. – Clive

In Merlin's barely furnished office, Leslie passed over the letter she had received from Clive. He seemed to take rather a long time reading it, and she got the impression that he had not slept much the previous night. At length he put the note down on the table and said quietly: "I'm glad you've shown me this."

"What do you want me to do?" she asked.

He traced an involved design on his blotting pad. "You can keep the appointment, if you're not scared," he replied presently.

"Does that mean you don't think Clive killed Sylvia Graham?" she asked.

"It seems unlikely." He went on to tell her about the discovery of the wig.

"So, you're writing Clive off the list of suspects?" she queried when he had finished.

Merlin shook his head. "It still remains to be proved that he had nothing to do with either of the other murders," he told her. "I propose to keep a close watch on that young man."

"Then you've no objection to my keeping the appointment?"

"That's what I said. Unless you're scared, of course."

"I'm not afraid of Clive. I think he's a weak character with very little moral stability, but I've handled more awkward customers in my time."

"Anyhow, there'll be a couple of my plain clothes men within call, just in case there should be any trouble."

"And what am I supposed to do if Clive turns up?" she demanded curiously.

Merlin gave a little shrug. "There isn't very much you can do – except listen to what he has to say. But be very careful not to let him know he may be under observation. And you might wear that light raincoat, so that my men will·be able to identify you in the dark."

She rose to go, and Merlin escorted her to the front door. He held her arm for a moment and turned her towards him. "Don't worry, Leslie," he said quietly. "We shan't be far away."

*****

During lunch Leslie became conscious that Keith Everest was discreetly pumping her as to how she had spent her morning. When she admitted she had seen Inspector Merlin, he wanted to know at once if there had been any development since the previous evening. Leslie said there was nothing of importance.

He rose painfully and hobbled across the room. "I'm damned if I couldn't do better than that myself," he muttered. "They don't seem to use their imagination! Surely there must be somebody at that theatre who saw the murderer? It's only a question of sifting the evidence in the right way. I've a good mind to go to the theatre myself and take a look round."

"Why don't you?" said Leslie, humouring him.

The artist went out of the room muttering to himself, and ten minutes later she heard the front door slam. Through the half-open window she saw him hail a taxi, and heard him order the driver to take him to the Viceroy Theatre.

*****

Leslie had to inquire as to the whereabouts of the Elite Cinema from a friendly bus conductor. It proved to be a third-run hall, midway between Goodge Street and Warren Street, with decaying stucco front relieved by a framework of naked electric bulbs. A seat in the back stalls cost one and sixpence and judging by the curling stills in the frames she concluded that the main attractions were westerns and gangster films.

As she watched a western, Leslie was conscious that a man was pulling down the empty seat on her left. The moment he spoke, she realised that it was Clive. "You're on your own?" he asked.

"Yes, of course." She could see him looking round cautiously in all directions.

"The police are after me," he whispered. "They nearly got me last night when I came to see you." He accepted a cigarette from her and bent down to light it so that his face should not be seen.

"I suppose you read in the papers that the police are looking for a man answering to your description, in connection with the murder of Sylvia Graham?"

"It must be somebody else."

"It was – somebody who wore a wig with a grey streak of hair. The police found the wig late last night."

He seemed to stiffen in his seat. "I was right," he said quietly, with a tense note in his voice. "I knew I was right!"

She looked at him questioningly, but he did not offer to enlighten her. "You can't go on forever living this sort of life," she said. "It's undermining your health, and it may affect your mind. You'd be better off in prison. If you give yourself up, I'll have a talk with the medical officer —"

But Clive did not seem to be listening and was apparently to all outward appearances absorbed in the action on the screen. Suddenly he leaned over and said: "I'm going to get some cigarettes from the kiosk. I'll be back in a moment." Before Leslie could stop him, he disappeared into the darkness.

Leslie sat watching the screen, where a western film of ancient vintage had just begun. The minutes passed by. Leslie stirred uneasily in her seat and looked round. There was no sign of Clive.

She got up and went out into the foyer, where she asked a plump woman in the kiosk if she had seen anything of a young man in a raincoat. The woman said he had bought a packet of cigarettes and gone out into the street. Leslie walked slowly to the front entrance and looked up and down the wide thoroughfare. There seemed to be no point in hanging around any longer. Clive had obviously disappeared.

She was just about to make for Warren Street Underground when a taxi drew into the kerb and she heard a familiar voice. "I came to collect you as soon as I could," Merlin told her. "We've had a bit more trouble down at the theatre."

She did not wait to hear about this, but quickly told him what had transpired with Clive. He patted her hand reassuringly. "You did very well, Leslie," he said. "The main thing was for us to get a sight of that young man. Don't worry now, there are a couple of my best men tailing him."

But Leslie still looked thoughtful. "I can't think why his whole attitude should have changed when I mentioned the wig," she mused. "I'm certain he knew something."

"We'll sort it out," Merlin assured her, as the taxi swung into Shaftesbury Avenue and pulled up at the Pandora Restaurant. "I haven't told you what's happened at the theatre yet, so you'd better come in and have some tea," he suggested.

They found a corner table and ordered tea. Then Merlin told her how he had received a call from Sergeant Jukes at the theatre, telling him that there had been an accident to the stagehand Lawrence, who had seen the murderer of Sylvia Graham. "It appears they were setting the scene for act two when a hundred-pound counterweight fell from the flies right on to the back of Lawrence's neck. He was rushed to hospital, but they don't expect him to live."

"But how could that have happened? Wasn't anyone responsible?" asked Leslie, somewhat mystified.

Merlin shrugged. "The counterweight wasn't properly tied off, and the man to blame for that was Lawrence himself — unless of course it had been tampered with."

Leslie looked across at him. "You think it might have been foul play?"

Merlin shook his head doubtfully. "We can't be sure. Of course, it's extremely convenient for the murderer that the man who might recognise him is now cosily out of the way."

There came into her mind a picture of Keith Everest opening a taxi door and calling out "Viceroy Theatre" to the driver. She tried to make her voice sound casual as she asked: "Did you see Mr. Everest at the theatre?"

"I didn't see him myself, but the sergeant said he'd been there, poking around and asking a lot of questions. Made rather a nuisance of himself, I gather. He said the police were thoroughly incompetent."

Merlin then looked up as a familiar figure came into the restaurant. The newcomer was Peter Hamilton, looking rather sorry for himself. He asked if he could join them and slumped dejectedly into a vacant chair.

"This damned play is bewitched!" he announced moodily, lighting a cigarette. "We're up to our eyes with bookings, we've lost the two best members of our cast, and now this new girl is driving me raving mad. She's just not suitable for Sylvia's part. I had to give them half an hour's break, or we'd have been running up the wall."

As Leslie gave him some tea, he turned towards Merlin. "By the way, your sleuth at the theatre wants to see you. There was a phone call that came through while he was questioning me about Sylvia."

"I'll phone him straight away," said Merlin.

After the inspector had gone, Hamilton became rather more voluble about his difficulties. "Your Mr. Everest has been a bit of a trial," he said. "He's been snooping round all afternoon. And all this on top of the accident to that poor chap Lawrence! It's been a hell of a day, and it isn't over yet. The mere thought of that third act brings me out in a cold perspiration."

As soon as Merlin returned, Hamilton glanced at his wristwatch and announced he must rush back to the theatre. As he stood up to go, he said: "Why don't you come in tonight and see this new girl? I'd like to think we have two friends in front!"

"I'll be around the theatre in any event," said Merlin, and looked questioningly at Leslie.

"I'd be most interested to see the new girl," she nodded.

101

"Good," said Hamilton. "You can have the management's box. I'll mention it as soon as I get back."

When he had gone, Leslie asked: "Was your telephone call important?"

"As a matter of fact, it was about your friend Clive. My man followed him to a dingy lodging house in Perrigo Street, near Euston Station. It seems he has stayed there for several nights. It's a drab neighbourhood, but ideal if you want to avoid attracting attention."

"What are you going to do now?"

"Keep him under observation for a day or two. I've got men shadowing him day and night. In fact, I'm pretty certain he could lead us to the man responsible for all the nylon murders."

*****

Leslie went back to Chelsea to change her dress, and she found Keith Everest in his studio moodily cleaning a canvas.

"Did you have any luck at the theatre?" she inquired.

He picked up a palette knife and scraped away some paint. "I discovered what fools the police are," he snapped.

"Did you see the accident to the stagehand?"

"I saw a lot of people running round in circles." He looked at Leslie and put the palette knife down on the table. "I suppose the fact that I was at the theatre makes me more of a suspect than ever," he said.

*****

At the theatre, the inspector was inclined to be restless all through the first act, which was hardly surprising, for the

102

newcomer to the company lacked both the technique and charm of Sylvia Graham.

"Any more news?" asked Leslie as soon as the curtain descended.

"I'm waiting to hear from the men up at Euston," he told her. "I've a feeling something will happen in that quarter fairly soon."

"It looks as if you'll soon be rid of me then," replied Leslie, watching the audience surging towards the exits.

"I sincerely hope not," he said earnestly. "In my job we don't make friends very easily, but you've been different somehow. I've never been able to talk to a woman before and feel I can trust her implicitly."

The door of the box opened, and a man stood in the doorway. Merlin obviously recognised the man, for he excused himself to Leslie and led the man out into the corridor. She could hear the two men talking in low tones outside the box. Presently the door opened again, and she heard Merlin say: "All right. Back to Perrigo Street, and see there's no mistake this time." He sank into the seat beside her, breathing rather heavily.

"Something wrong?" she asked.

"The confounded fool followed Clive to what was an obvious rendezvous, then let him slip out of the house by the back entrance."

"Have you any idea who lived there?"

Merlin turned and looked at her, then said slowly: "Yes. It's your friend the artist, Keith Everest."

11

Outwardly calm, Leslie contrived to conceal her doubts and fears at the news that Clive had been traced to Everest's house in Chelsea. She wondered if he had gone there to try to get in touch with her again, possibly to tell her of some new decision he had made.

But it seemed that Merlin had different ideas. "I must talk to Everest right away," he decided.

"What makes you think he knows anything?"

"The young man was in his house for some considerable time."

"I don't see how you can tell that, if your detective lost him. He might have walked straight through the house and out of the back door."

"Somebody must have let him in."

"Not necessarily. The front door is often on the latch."

"All the same, I think I'd better go right away while the trail is hot. There's always a chance Everest may have found out something."

"In that case I'll come with you," Leslie said, picking up her bag.

*****

The footlights were up, and the house lights had just been lowered as they left the box. "It'll be quicker this way," said Merlin, as they stood in the corridor. He indicated the pass door that led backstage.

Just as they were leaving by the stage door, they heard a familiar voice hail them, and saw Peter Hamilton approaching along the corridor. "Good Lord is it as bad as that?" he said dolefully. "I did think you'd manage to stick out a couple of acts."

Merlin explained tactfully that there had been a new development in the case which demanded his urgent attention, and that it was essential that they should leave at once.

"What did you think of the new girl?" Hamilton asked, as he walked with them out of the stage door. Leslie tried to be polite, but Hamilton would have none of it. "She's driving me crazy! Talk about a grey streak — my hair will be snow white before the night's out!" He waved to them rather wistfully, as they got into a taxi and drove off.

"Poor Peter Hamilton. He gets so intense about everything," sighed Leslie.

"When you've seen as much of theatre folk as I have, you won't pay the slightest attention," Merlin assured her. "Concentrate your sympathy on me for a change, because I want you to do me a favour."

"Well?"

Merlin swung round in his seat and faced her squarely. "I want you to leave Everest's place." He hesitated a moment, then added firmly: "Tonight."

"Any special reason?" she asked.

"Nothing definite. It's just that I've a hunch that Everest's house is a danger spot. I wouldn't be in the least surprised if something pretty violent happened there in the next forty-eight hours."

Leslie smiled. "And there I was, thinking I'd demonstrated to you that I am capable of taking care of myself."

He caught her wrist in his firm grasp. "Leslie, I'm very serious about this. Apart from your own safety, you might complicate things for me if you go on staying there."

"That's all very well," said Leslie. "But you don't seem to appreciate the position in London where accommodation is concerned."

"I've thought of that," he replied. "I could put you up at my place for a few nights, till this affair is settled."

She leaned back against the seat. "Well really, Inspector Merlin," she said, "if you think I'm in the habit of staying with bachelor gentlemen –"

"You know me by now, Leslie," he said quietly. "You can have my room. I'll fix up a shakedown on the settee for myself, that's if I'm not out on the job. You'll be quite safe there, and it will set my mind at rest."

Leslie considered the idea for a minute or two. "Well, I'd hate to impede the arm of the law," she said at last, "but I can't think Everest's house is such a danger spot as all that."

"Surely there's been enough evidence in that direction," he replied. "I'm by no means satisfied about Everest himself, and if we trace that young man Clive there again there's bound to be some sort of showdown."

"What will Everest say when he knows I'm leaving?"

"We can think up some excuse. No need to tell him you're coming to my place."

*****

When they arrived at the house in Walsingham Street, Leslie let them in with her latchkey. The house seemed very quiet, but they found Everest in the sitting room. He was slumped in an armchair, a decanter of whisky on a small table beside him.

He asked them to have a drink in a voice which was reasonably steady. Merlin accepted a small whisky, partly because he did not wish to alienate Everest if it could be avoided. Leslie refused, however, saying she must go to her room and pack.

"You mean you're leaving us?" queried Everest, eyeing her suspiciously.

She told him she had telephoned the hospital and had been asked to return to duty a week earlier, as a colleague was away ill.

When Leslie had gone upstairs, Merlin sat sipping his whisky and presently said casually: "So you had another visit from Leslie's patient this evening?"

Everest looked across at him somewhat stupidly. "Patient?" he queried.

"You know, the young fellow with the streak of grey hair who was here before."

Everest took a sip of his whisky, then said: "I haven't seen any young fellow this evening."

"That's very strange," replied Merlin smoothly, "because he came into this house just after seven o'clock."

"You seem very certain of that."

"One of my most reliable men saw him come in. Apparently, he slipped out the back way – unless he is still in the house," added Merlin significantly.

"Of course he isn't in the house! He's never been near the place," snapped Everest testily.

Just as Merlin was about to reply, the telephone rang in the hall and Everest went out to answer it. Possibly the heavy drinking had made him careless, for he left the sitting room door open a couple of inches. "Speaking," said Everest, answering a query from the caller. "Yes, yes, he got it all right … Quite certain … I tell you I kept my promise … All right then, goodbye."

The receiver was slammed down rather heavily, and Everest muttered something under his breath that might have been an imprecation. Then he came back into the room. "I'm afraid I can't invite you to search the house – unless, of course, you have a warrant," he said brusquely.

"That's all right," nodded Merlin, apparently quite unperturbed. "I've no doubt the young man will turn up again in the near future."

At that moment Leslie came in again, having packed her cases. She thanked the artist for his hospitality, but Everest hardly seemed aware of what she was saying. He announced that he was going up to his studio to work.

As they walked towards the Kings Road, Merlin heaved a sigh of relief. "I can't tell you how thankful I am that you're away from that house," he said.

*****

Merlin's flat was at the top of a massive Victorian building in Holborn which had no lift installed. He carried Leslie's cases into the bedroom and returned with a pile of blankets to make a bed for himself on the settee in the living room.

"The first thing is to see about supper," he announced, dumping down the blankets.

"I'll do that while you fix the bed," she answered. "Of course, you'll have to take my word for it that I can cook."

He grinned. "You can't go far wrong, because there's only eggs and bacon in the fridge."

He was about to lead the way into the kitchen when the front doorbell buzzed sharply. Merlin went to answer it, while Leslie went into the kitchen, switched on the light, and closed the door behind her.

To Merlin's surprise, his visitor was Peter Hamilton. The stage director was profuse in his apologies for taking up Merlin's time. As he followed him into the sitting room, he explained that he had discovered the inspector's address by the simple expedient of looking him up in the telephone directory.

"Then why not telephone?" asked Merlin, who was annoyed to have his space invaded.

"Yes, I did consider it," nodded Hamilton, "but I thought perhaps we might be overheard."

"What's the trouble?" asked Merlin, indicating the most uncomfortable chair in the room. Hamilton ignored the hint and settled himself comfortably in an armchair.

"I think I've stumbled across what might be an important clue," said Hamilton. "When I was pacing up and down, waiting for the third act to end tonight, I started chatting with the stage door keeper. We got talking about the murder of course, and he suddenly recollected that Sylvia Graham had received a visitor earlier in the evening before the show started."

"Why didn't he tell us that when we questioned him?"

"Because he'd forgotten all about it. He's well into his seventies, and his memory isn't what it was. Also, it didn't strike him as being important, as it was so much earlier than the time of the murder."

"Did this visitor leave a name?"

"Yes, the old boy said he was a Mr. Fortescue. He described him as thick-set, average height, sandy colouring. He wore a soft hat and carried a briefcase."

"Does that convey anything to you?"

Hamilton shook his head. "Of course, he may have been an insurance agent or somebody quite harmless," he said. "But I thought you'd better know."

Any further speculations were cut short by the ringing of the telephone in a distant corner of the room, and Merlin went across to answer it. He lifted the receiver and recognised the familiar voice of Sergeant Jukes, who was speaking from New Scotland Yard.

"There's a message come through from the Albert Docks that the dock police have picked up our man," boomed Sergeant Jukes.

"You mean Clive?"

"That's right, sir. He was trying to stow away on board the Mombassa that sails tomorrow. They want to know if it's o.k. to take him to Canning Town or –"

"Tell them to hold him," snapped Merlin. "I'll be along there right away."

During the conversation Hamilton had apparently been interested in the collection of theatrical biographies on Merlin's well-stocked bookshelves, but the inspector wondered just how much of the conversation he had heard. The sergeant had a hearty voice that could quite easily be picked up at least ten feet from a telephone receiver.

"I didn't know the theatre was a hobby of yours," said Hamilton. "We must have a talk about it sometime."

"I shall be delighted," Merlin replied mechanically. "But I'm afraid I have to go out now."

"Something to do with this latest development in the case?" quizzed Hamilton.

"It could be."

"In that event, I won't detain you." Hamilton picked up his hat.

"How did the play go tonight?" asked Merlin, as they moved towards the door.

"Pretty grim," replied Hamilton with a shrug. "I give it two more weeks, perhaps three."

"Tough luck," sympathised Merlin.

Hamilton paused for a moment in the doorway. "The theatre's a tough place," he murmured. "Some poor devil is always on the way out." He paused to adjust his hat to exactly the right angle, then wished Merlin goodnight.

As soon as he heard Hamilton descending the stone stairs, Merlin went into the kitchen. "Hold everything!" he ordered. "We're going out." Leslie, with a large apron round her waist and a worried look in her brown eyes, was carefully beating eggs in a bowl. "I'm sorry, but we must go," he insisted. "The dock police have just picked up Clive. I want you to come and identify him."

"Where is he?"

"They're keeping him down at the docks till we get there. I don't want to lose any time."

They found a taxi at a nearby rank and were soon moving at a good pace through the deserted streets of the City. At the entrance to the Royal Albert Docks, they were met by a policeman who was obviously expecting them, and who immediately directed them to an office which was little more than a fair-sized army hut.

Clive had been locked in a room that was used as a temporary detention cell. As the door opened, he looked up from the plain wooden chair on which he was sitting near the window. There was an expression of utter dejection on his thin, colourless face.

"We found nearly two hundred pounds on him in pound notes," said the dock policeman who accompanied them into the room.

Merlin crossed to Clive and looked down at him. "Where did you get that money?" he demanded.

But Clive was looking at Leslie, who had tried to remain in the background. "So, you went to the police," he said accusingly in a harsh, strident tone.

Leslie took an involuntary step forward. "Clive, this is Inspector Merlin, a friend of mine. He'll try to help you – he knows you had nothing to do with the murders. If you'll only tell him –"

Clive shook his head. "Nobody's on my side – they're all against me," he muttered, almost to himself.

Merlin shook him roughly by the shoulder. "You're in a tough spot, my lad," he said. "That attitude isn't going to help you."

"Nothing's going to help me," replied Clive sullenly. "It's too late now."

"Don't be a fool!" snapped Merlin. "Tell us where you got that money from."

A wave of pity for the bewildered young man swept over Leslie. "Clive, I give you my solemn promise to see you get abroad and make a fresh start," she urged.

But Clive shook his head once more. "If I told you everything, he'd be waiting for me when I came out," he mumbled.

"Tell us everything, and he'll be hanged for murder," retorted Merlin brusquely.

"He always gets away," insisted Clive obstinately. "The police will never catch him. He's a devil ..." There was a look of fear in the young man's eyes.

Leslie glanced across at Merlin, and saw his chin tighten. She guessed he would shortly resort to rather less polite methods, and for Clive's sake felt she ought to make a last effort. She went and stood over him and said: "Clive, look at me." Reluctantly he lifted his head, his eyes meeting her steady gaze. "Clive, have you forgotten Andrea? When you first got in touch with me, all you wanted to do was to get even with the man who had killed Andrea. Have you forgotten that?"

His head dropped. She could see his lips quivering with emotion. "After all Andrea did for you," she went on, "after all she meant to you, are you going to let her murderer get away without making some effort?"

For over a minute he did not speak but sat there biting his lower lip. At last he said in a choked whisper: "All right. I'll tell you."

Then the tension relaxed. Merlin leaned on the rough wooden table. "That money you had on you – did you get it from the murderer? Did you blackmail him?"

"I wanted to get away and make a fresh start. I was desperate."

"Of course," said Merlin. "I understand. Now, tell us what you know about him."

Clive cleared his throat nervously. "The man you want is –" Before he could complete his sentence, they heard what sounded like a sharp rap on the window. Clive caught his breath, clutched at his chest and slumped forwards in his chair.

Merlin leapt over to the window. A neat little bullet-hole had been drilled through the glass. The inspector saw a man running towards the corner of an office building and vanishing into the shadows.

12

Leaving Leslie to look after Clive, Merlin rushed for the door and out on to the dock in the direction of the office buildings behind which the attacker had disappeared. He soon realised it was hopeless to look for him. He might be hiding in any of a thousand odd corners, or possibly by this time had escaped into the labyrinth of back streets.

Turning on his heel, he went back to the hut where he found that Leslie, with the help of a dock policeman, had laid Clive full length on the floor and bundled his coat to make a pillow for him. She looked up and shook her head as Merlin entered. "He's in a bad way," she whispered. "They've phoned for an ambulance, but I'm afraid it will be too late."

The inspector nodded and went over to kneel beside Clive, who opened his eyes and recognised him. "Is there anything you want to tell me?" Merlin said quietly.

Clive made a determined effort to speak. "He killed Andrea," he gasped. "He killed her when she fell in love with me and refused to take his orders any more. When he knew I suspected that, he began to throw suspicion on me ... I saw him that night at the boathouse ... The devil! I knew he'd get me ..."

"You were blackmailing the murderer?" queried Merlin softly.

"I was desperate ... I had to look out for myself ... It was my only chance to get away ... So, I went to Chelsea, and he gave me the money." Clive was breathing with great difficulty.

"You mean, Keith Everest gave you the money," persisted Merlin.

The injured man's eyes were half closed. "That's right. Everest gave me two hundred, then I slipped out the back … The devil must have followed me here … it's no use."

His eyes closed, and the voice trailed away into silence. There was the strident sound of an ambulance bell. Leslie picked up Clive's wrist. "You'll get no more information from Clive," she said quietly.

They slowly rose to their feet as the ambulance drew up outside. "Poor devil," said Merlin. "Maybe he's better off … But I should have taken more precautions. I'd no idea that the man we're after would be on the spot so quickly."

"You think he was trailing Clive?" asked Leslie.

"Either that, or he had an accomplice doing the job for him."

Two ambulance men came in with a stretcher, and Merlin and Leslie turned to go. Outside they found a police car had arrived, and the inspector commandeered it to take them back. Merlin told the driver to make for his flat in Holborn, and on the way, he persuaded Leslie to go there and finish cooking their supper, thinking this would at least occupy her mind.

"And what about you?" asked Leslie.

"I'm going on to Chelsea to have a word with Mr. Everest. I must strike while the iron's hot."

"You think he'll try to leave the country?"

"There's always that possibility." But there was a worried note in his voice, for he could not convince himself that Keith Everest had been the man he had seen running rapidly into the shadows. So, he told Leslie about his doubts, and asked her if she were quite certain that Everest was disabled.

"I never had reason to doubt that he was recovering from polio," she replied. "He never talked about it very much, but he had all the characteristics of the disease." She tried to recall any occasion which might have offered some clue to Merlin's problem, but could remember none. It was true that Everest had made some improvement during her stay, but she could not visualise him running as actively as a normal man of his age.

"There must be an answer somewhere," mused Merlin. "Maybe I'll find it tonight."

"Don't you think I should come with you?"

"Certainly not! You've run quite enough risks for one evening. Your job now is to concentrate on that omelette!"

*****

On arriving at Everest's house, Merlin posted a man at the front and one at the back. He could see a light at the top of the house and guessed that Everest was working in his studio. When he rang the front doorbell there was no reply, so he pressed the button again.

"You might give me time to get downstairs," protested Everest as he opened the front door. Then he recognised his visitor. "You police are having a busy evening," he said sarcastically.

"I must ask you to come back to Scotland Yard with me, Mr. Everest," began Merlin.

"Just a minute," interposed Everest. "Perhaps we'd better have a talk about this first. Come inside."

"I warn you the house is under observation."

"All right!" retorted Everest testily. "I'm not likely to try to escape. And I'd like to find out exactly where I stand in this business."

They went into the sitting room. Merlin noticed that the whisky decanter was now empty. Everest picked it up and set it down again, then slumped heavily into an armchair. "And what are you proposing to charge me with?" he enquired.

"That's soon answered," replied Merlin crisply. "I shall charge you with the murders of Sylvia Graham and your daughter Judy."

"Judy?" repeated Everest, obviously aghast. Watching him closely, Merlin could see that he was completely taken aback by this development. "I don't know what you're talking about," he said. "Judy was my only child — we were always devoted to each other."

"My information came from a young fellow named Clive, who was with you a little earlier this evening though you denied it."

"My word is as good as his. The fellow's lying."

"Dying men don't usually tell anything but the truth," retorted Merlin. "He's dead by now, and I think you know who killed him."

Everest licked his lips and looked round the room restlessly. "D'you mind if I have a drink?" he asked.

"Haven't you had enough tonight?"

"I've got to have something — since I stopped taking drugs."

"So, you were mixed up with the dope gang," said Merlin. "You'd better start and tell me about that from the beginning."

Everest heaved himself out of the chair and went to the sideboard, which he opened and took out a fresh bottle of whisky. He poured himself a generous three fingers then looked across at Merlin, who shook his head. "Not for me, thanks," he said in reply to the unspoken invitation. Everest drank the whisky neat and set down the glass somewhat unsteadily.

"Now," prompted Merlin. "About this dope racket. Who, exactly, was involved in it besides yourself?"

Everest returned to his chair and gazed moodily at the electric fire. "There was Andrea Lake – that was the reason she was living here – and Sylvia Graham. There was an actor who was supposed to have gassed himself a few months back, a night club dancer, and several others who distribute the stuff from time to time."

"And what about Clive?"

"He was nothing to do with it. He's just a young fool Andrea got herself mixed up with. The head of the whole outfit – call him X – told her to break it off, and they had a row about it. She threatened to expose the whole set-up, and X told her he couldn't have anyone working for him who wasn't one hundred per cent."

"So, Andrea was eliminated?"

"That was the start of all the trouble. I was against it at the time, but X is absolutely ruthless. It upset Sylvia Graham, and she began to get scared that she might be the next. That's why she took Leslie into her confidence – I suppose she felt she had to talk to somebody. Anyhow, X got wind of it and I was told to go and see Sylvia at her cottage and warn her that her supply would be cut off if there was any nonsense."

"Was it you who attempted that murder in the boathouse?"

Everest shook his head. "That must have been X. He probably found out that Sylvia had ignored the warning. I told you, he's quite ruthless."

Merlin shifted uneasily in his chair. He realised that the artist was scared and was convinced that he was still holding something back. "You talk a lot about this mysterious X," he said. "You've no proof of any of these statements. You could have murdered those girls yourself."

Everest rose painfully and went over to the bureau. From a drawer he took a small black diary. "I found this only last week in Judy's room. It was her private diary. I think you'll find evidence there who killed her."

"Then why haven't you told the police before this?"

"I've been trying to make up my mind," replied Everest slowly. "You see, she was killed by X. There's no doubt about that now. They were very friendly, in fact she was infatuated with him, and I knew nothing about it. You'll find it all there in the diary."

Merlin took the little book and turned the pages. They were written in a neat girlish hand, full of cryptic comments so typical of girls in their teens. There was silence except for the ticking of the clock, as the inspector carefully read through the last month's items in the book. He looked up at last and said: "The only man mentioned besides yourself is this Peter ..."

"That's true," nodded Everest.

"It refers to the photograph he gave her ..." Merlin whistled softly. "Good Lord! Peter Hamilton!"

"That's right," nodded Everest wearily. "Peter Hamilton. He gave Judy a photograph but daren't sign it himself, that's why he forged Sylvia Graham's handwriting."

Merlin got up and stood with his back to the fireplace. "Are you quite certain about this?" he demanded.

Everest nodded. "Hamilton has been running the whole outfit. He had us where he wanted us. But I didn't know what was going on between him and Judy, or I'd have taken her away – to Italy, America, anywhere."

"Why should Hamilton offer her any encouragement? I should hardly have thought she was his type."

"You don't know him. The idea of corrupting a young girl would fascinate him. And he probably thought it would give him an even stronger hold over me. He knew I'd stopped taking drugs for a time last year and thought I might give it up again."

"But you surely had some suspicion that Judy was going around with a man?"

"I've told you time and again, I hadn't an inkling. He must have coached her into keeping it a secret from me. You know what young girls are – they enjoy these little conspiracies." He seemed sincere enough now. "If I'd suspected for a moment that he killed Judy, I'd have strangled him with my own hands," he went on.

But Merlin was intently reading the last page of the diary. "According to this, Judy found him out. This was written on the day she was murdered, and she says she was going up to the theatre to have a showdown with him." He closed the book and pocketed it. "Poor kid," he said quietly.

"By God, I'll get even with the swine!" said Everest.

"There are two ways of doing that," suggested Merlin. "In the first place, you can tell me everything else you know about him."

"I don't think there is much more," replied Everest.

"There's all this business with Clive," Merlin reminded him. "You were here when he came, weren't you?" Everest nodded. "You gave him that two hundred pounds?"

"Yes, on Hamilton's instructions," said Everest sullenly. "I simply did as I was told. It seems that Clive had discovered something about Hamilton, who had been throwing suspicion on him and had shown his hand too plainly for once. So, he had to shut Clive's mouth, at least for the time being."

"And now he's shut it permanently," said Merlin, silently reproaching himself for allowing Hamilton to overhear that telephone conversation with the sergeant, which had obviously prompted Hamilton to follow them to the Albert Docks.

"He never makes a mistake, even when he's in a tight corner. When he decides to get rid of anyone, there's no escape. Sylvia Graham cheated him for a day or so, thanks to Leslie, but he got her in the end. He came here the same night and boasted about it – then left the stiletto he'd used on my desk when my back was turned."

"Well, all you have to do now is tell me where to find him and leave the rest to me," said Merlin.

"I'd do so with pleasure if I knew," replied Everest grimly. "But none of us ever discovered where he lives – I've a suspicion he moves around. He always contacted us by telephone and arranged a rendezvous. Often it was at his room in the theatre."

"Is it all right for you to telephone him and say you want to see him?"

"I wouldn't know where to find him at this time of night, unless –" He hesitated. "Sometimes he spends the night at the theatre. There's a bed in his office, and he switches the telephone through."

"No harm in trying," decided Merlin. "Tell him you've somebody with you who will pay anything for a supply of drugs."

Everest nodded and went to the telephone. Merlin watched intently to see that he could convey no warning to Hamilton. From his side of the room Merlin could hear the ringing tone very faintly, and presently a click as the receiver was lifted at the other end. But whoever received the call spoke in a very low voice that was audible only to Everest.

"You know who this is?" said the artist. "I've someone here who wants some of the stuff urgently. He'll pay a good price. Yes, of course. No, no, it's all right. I'll bring him to the theatre ... about half an hour. Goodbye."

He slowly replaced the receiver and returned to the inspector. "I'm to meet him at the theatre in half an hour. He's arranged with the nightwatchman to let me in. There'll be no trouble in that direction."

Merlin went to the telephone and rang Scotland Yard. He gave brisk instructions for Flying Squad cars to be at the Viceroy Theatre in half an hour's time. They were to be particularly careful not to attract attention, he added. All the theatre exits were to be covered, and no-one allowed to leave without being challenged. Six men were to be armed, in case of any emergency.

Everest went to put on the black cloak he often wore, and Merlin joined him in the hall. Then the artist went back to the sitting room to switch off the light, but Merlin did not see him pick up the Venetian stiletto that lay on the writing desk.

*****

In the police car on the way to the theatre, Everest was silent for some time. Then, as they swung round the corner to Sloane Street, he said: "This business has got to be handled carefully, Merlin. He's as slippery as an eel."

"You don't have to tell me that," replied Merlin.

"Perhaps I could make a suggestion." Merlin half turned, and looked at him by the uncertain light of the passing street lamps. He seemed to have sobered down almost to normal now. "I suggest you come into the theatre with me and we go to Hamilton's room. I'll go in alone and make sure he's there. When you hear me talking to him, you can give the signal to your men through one of the dressing room windows – flash a torch or something – for them to close in. You can't afford to take any chances, as Hamilton knows every nook and cranny of that theatre."

"You think he might hear more than two people come in and try to make a bolt for it?" queried Merlin.

"It would be better not to take any chances. He always seems to be on the alert, and I'm not sure the nightwatchman isn't one of his men. He could easily telephone through from the stage door keeper's office while we are on the way up if he suspected anything."

"All right, we'll do as you say," decided Merlin, after weighing up the pros and cons of the plan.

*****

When they arrived at the theatre, Merlin gave the necessary instructions. Two police cars were in the car park behind the building, while two more were some thirty yards away in Shaftesbury Avenue. Men in raincoats and trilby hats stood unobtrusively in shop doorways, and they could see a large police van just round the corner of Wardour Street.

After a last word with the officer in charge, Merlin walked with Everest down the familiar alley to the stage door of the Viceroy Theatre. A chilly wind swept along the passage, carrying odd scraps of paper and empty cartons with it. There was no-one at the stage door, which was open, and they could see a dim light at the far end of the corridor that led to the stage.

Everest led the way up a flight of stairs to the row of dressing rooms on the first floor. "It's the farthest door," he whispered.

Merlin felt for the torch in his left hand coat pocket, and the revolver in his right. "Shout out at the first sign of trouble," he said quietly, and Everest nodded.

Merlin opened the door of the room adjoining Hamilton's and stood in the doorway, while Everest knocked at the next door and entered in response to the muffled invitation. Merlin could hear voices at once, so crossed to the window and flashed his torch several times. From about forty yards away there was a brief answering signal.

He moved back to the doorway, and suddenly heard the voices from the next room raised in anger. There was a shout from Everest, and the report of a revolver shot. Merlin leapt to the door, pushed it open, then stumbled across the body of Keith Everest which lay just inside the room. He was clutching the Venetian stiletto and had been shot through the head.

Apart from Everest the room appeared to be empty. Then Merlin noticed a curtain flapping in a far corner and realised that this concealed an emergency exit. With his finger on the trigger of his revolver, Merlin moved over to the doorway and stood there for a couple of seconds. He imagined he could hear footsteps and guessed that this was the exterior staircase attached to every theatre.

Cautiously he put his head round the door and looked out. A quick downward glance satisfied him that there was no-one on that section of the staircase. Then he traced its upward curve, and imagined he caught sight of a shadowy figure somewhere near the top. Carefully he began to climb the iron staircase, flattening himself as far as possible against the side of the building. He reached the small platform at the top of the next flight and tried the door which opened out on to it but found it could only be opened from the inside. Merlin tackled the next flight and discovered another door. That too was bolted.

There seemed to be no doubt that Hamilton was on the roof of the theatre. Merlin promptly signalled to the men below, and two minutes later heard footsteps behind him on the fire escape. There was a blaze of light, as a powerful spotlight from a police car below came into action and focused on the roof. As Merlin came over the parapet, he heard the crack of a revolver and ducked instinctively. He saw his hat go swirling down and wondered if it had been dislodged by a bullet or the jerk of his head.

"You all right, sir?" came a voice.

Before Merlin could reply, there was a metallic clatter and a sudden loud oath from a few yards away on the flat roof. Concluding that Hamilton had stumbled over something, Merlin seized the opportunity to edge over the parapet and lie full length, while he tried to get accustomed to his surroundings. Silhouetted against the glare from below, he saw the outlines of two large ventilating shafts and a chimney stack a little farther away.

Merlin heard a movement behind him. It was one of his men trying to clamber on the roof. Almost simultaneously the inspector saw an arm come round a ventilator twenty feet away, and there was the flash of a revolver. Merlin took hasty aim and fired at the arm.

It was a lucky shot. There was an exclamation of pain, and Hamilton's revolver clattered on to the roof. The next moment two men had joined Merlin, who was quick to press home his advantage. He indicated the ventilator behind which Hamilton was hiding, and they advanced towards it.

When they were about six feet away, Merlin called: "You'd better come out, Hamilton."

But Hamilton had other plans. Almost before they realised it, he had broken from cover and was running full speed for the edge of the roof.

"My God, he's going to jump!" cried one of the detectives.

Hamilton's objective was the roof of the next building, about nine feet across the stage door alley. He cleared the gap with a foot to spare, but the parapet where he landed was old and weather-beaten and proved unequal to withstanding this sudden impact.

Hamilton's feet seemed to slide from under him, and for some seconds his hands clutched at the crumbling masonry. Then, with a terrible gasping cry, he fell into the darkness.

*****

Wearing an attractive dressing gown over her pyjamas, Leslie was watching Inspector Merlin devouring an omelette with considerable relish, pausing occasionally to answer the volley of questions she had never stopped asking since his return to the flat.

"I'm glad it's all over," she said at last, with a sigh of relief.

"Yes, it's been a hectic business," agreed Merlin. "You'll be pleased to see the back of the lot of us, I dare say."

There was a smile round the corners of her mouth, but she did not reply.

Presently Merlin pushed back his chair and lit a cigarette. "That was certainly the best omelette I ever tasted," he announced. "It was good of you to get up at four in the morning specially to make it."

"Doctors are accustomed to being wakened in the middle of the night."

"Anyhow, it's shown you the worst side of life with a policeman," he said.

"There must be a better side too," she suggested enigmatically, as she poured him a second cup of coffee. "It might be interesting to find out."

"Leslie!" he exclaimed, catching her free hand and holding it in his. "Do you really mean –?"

She laughed. "If you care to rephrase your proposal rather more romantically, I'll give it my best consideration," said Dr. Leslie Sanders.

THE YELLOW WINDMILL

Published in the *Sunday Dispatch* in eleven parts, 17 January – 28 March 1954

This was never published as a book in the UK, but an adapted German version appeared as *Die gelbe Windmühle* in the magazine *Bild und Funk*, in eleven instalments, 1965-66.

THE YELLOW WINDMILL

1

It was a mild spring day, warm enough for Mary O'Reilly to sit on a seat near the gates of Regents Park and read a letter from her brother in County Down. It never occurred to her that she was neglecting Susan, as the child seemed happy enough making friends with a poodle from one of the nearby flats.

A car which had been crawling along outside the railings suddenly stopped, and the man sitting beside the driver got out. He approached the little girl, knelt on one knee, and began to talk to her about the dog. After a short while, the man produced a little yellow windmill.

Five-year-old Susan Kelford was always receiving small gifts from her many casual acquaintances, and Mary O'Reilly merely nodded and smiled when the child rushed up to her with the bright yellow toy. Susan ran back in the direction of the car, the tiny sails of the windmill whirring merrily.

As Susan approached the car, the man in the front seat looked round casually to make sure that there was no-one within easy distance. Then he called to the child, and she ran forward to meet him. He opened the door, and with a sudden movement swept the child into the back seat. The man's hand came out of his pocket, and there was a stifled cry as the chloroformed pad was clapped over the child's mouth. The door slammed almost simultaneously, and the car moved off. The incident had passed unnoticed by the few stragglers around the park gates.

It was not until the frantic nursemaid had been answering questions for nearly an hour that she remembered the yellow windmill.

*****

"So, you've checked everything?" queried Superintendent Elder three days later, sitting back in his chair and looking out of the window of his office at Scotland Yard.

"Everything," replied Detective Inspector Mike Houston, doodling a series of chains across the corner of his notepad.

"Nothing more to be got from the nursemaid?"

"The poor girl's practically on the edge of a nervous breakdown," put in Detective Inspector Loman, who had been sharing the investigation with Houston.

"You're certain that Kelford hasn't had a ransom note or anything like that?"

"He's never mentioned it."

"I suppose it might have come through the post – he has half a dozen different addresses," mused the superintendent.

"That's true," agreed Houston. "And it certainly would be a big temptation for him to pay up and say nothing to the police."

"In which case he wouldn't be telephoning the Assistant Commissioner twice a day," pointed out Loman shrewdly. "Sir

Cedric's a big man. He can pull a lot of strings, and he's centred everything on this child since his wife died."

Houston nodded. "Well, I don't see what else we can do," he said. "We've dragged Regents Park canal, questioned everybody living within sight of where it happened, broadcast two appeals, checked on every crook with a kidnapping record ..."

"There's simply no factual evidence to start with," said Loman. "The child apparently went into the park and completely disappeared."

"Could have been one of these cranky women who lure kids away because they're so lonely," mused Houston. "That would account for there being no ransom note."

"There have been such cases," conceded Elder, polishing the bowl of his pipe on his sleeve. He sighed. "Then I take it there's nothing whatever to report the next time Kelford telephones?"

Houston shook his head. "I'm terribly sorry for Kelford," he said. "That's one reason why I've worked night and day on this case. I put myself in his shoes and imagined how I'd have felt if anything had happened to either of my two kids when they were that age."

"How are your youngsters getting on, Mike?" inquired Elder, glad to change the subject for a couple of minutes.

Houston's face lit up. He was a widower in his late forties, and his children were easily his favourite topic of conversation. "Dennis is plugging along in his steady job – the Central Bank, you know ..."

"Isn't Sir Cedric Kelford the chairman of that outfit?" asked Elder, irresistibly drawn back to the case.

Houston nodded.

"And your daughter?" pursued Elder. "Didn't she go on the stage?"

"Yes, she's finding her feet. There was a piece about her in the paper yesterday." He took a cutting from his wallet and passed it over to his superior.

"Only twenty-two, and playing the lead in a new television play?" Elder read aloud.

"It's on Sunday."

"Got herself engaged to the author too, I see."

"That's all exaggerated," said Houston hastily, "although they're quite friendly of course."

"I take it you don't like this chap Knight?" said Elder with a smile.

"I've nothing against him," replied Houston uneasily. "He's supposed to be very clever, and Rona's been seeing quite a lot of him at rehearsals and so on."

The superintendent shook his head. "You widowers who have to be father and mother to your kids," he murmured, "have got your hands full. Anyhow, we'll make a point of seeing that play, eh, Loman?"

"Looking forward to it," Loman assured him.

"And talking of widowers," went on Elder, "you'd think Kelford with all his money would manage to keep an eye on his one solitary chick."

"His money makes him all the more vulnerable," pronounced Mike Houston wisely.

"It certainly looks like it," agreed Elder. "Well, let's get back to the job and comb through these reports just once more."

The three men worked in silence until there was a tap at the door, and a uniformed sergeant brought in a small package. "Just arrived by registered post, sir," he said, handing the package to Houston.

Houston turned the parcel over. It was addressed to him in block capitals and tied with brown string. Inside the brown paper was a small cardboard carton, tucked into the folds of which was a half-sheet of notepaper. On it was scrawled: *I can give you the tip-off on the Kelford case. You'll see from what's inside this box I know what I'm talking about. Meet me in The Skipper's Haunt in Chatham, seven o'clock Sunday night. Nobbler Williams.*

Houston passed the note over to the superintendent, then slowly lifted the lid off the small cardboard box. It contained Susan Kelford's little yellow windmill.

"What d'you know about this man Williams?" asked Elder, carefully examining the windmill.

Houston wrinkled his forehead, deep in thought. "I managed to get him let off lightly in a bank job at Hammersmith. He only got twelve months, with the usual remission. I haven't heard much about him since he came out – I think he's been working on some coastal vessel."

"That would explain Chatham," nodded Elder, glancing at the note. "Well, I'll leave you two to check up on the windmill."

"Do you think we should tip off Chatham C.I.D.?" asked Houston.

"I'll decide about that later. In any case you'd better keep the appointment, Mike."

"Yes, sir. I'll take Loman too, just in case there's trouble."

"It might be a good idea if you got down there early and had a talk with the local boys. They might know something about this chap Williams." The superintendent pushed the toy windmill across the desk. "Now you'd better run along and see that nursemaid," he said.

*****

Houston found Mary O'Reilly, as usual, on the verge of tears. When she saw the little yellow windmill, she recognised it at once, and began crying in earnest. But she could add nothing to what she had already told the inspector at their previous interview.

It was well after nine when Houston arrived home. Dennis looked up from the magazine he was reading and asked: "Any news in this Kelford case, dad?"

Houston paused in the act of filling his pipe. "You know I never talk out of school," he said.

"But the poor kid's been missing for days. Aren't the police doing anything?"

"The police are very busy indeed," replied Houston stiffly. "At least, I can tell you that much."

Dennis shrugged. "Sorry, dad. But I've got a sort of personal interest in this case. Remember, she's my chairman's daughter."

Houston nodded. "I know that," he said, "but remember we don't discuss police business here, any more than your customers' overdrafts."

At that moment Rona came in, looking very smart in a new tweed outfit. Houston noticed that there were tiny wrinkles under her eyes. She dropped into an armchair. "Ten hours' rehearsal, off and on," she announced. "Carl's driving us mad with his alterations to the script."

"Well, you would go on the stage," said Dennis seriously. Rona looked across at her father and grinned. It was a joke between them that Mike had gone to great lengths to discourage his daughter from following her career, but now that she had settled down to it and was taking it so seriously no-one was more proud of her than her father.

"How's the play coming along?" Houston asked.

"I think it's going to be good. I'll admit Carl's alterations are all improvements, but I wish he'd made them earlier. I do hate having to learn fresh lines and forget old ones."

"Does he write all the new stuff at rehearsals?" asked Dennis.

Rona shook her head. "It wouldn't be so bad if he did," she said. "But he keeps popping back to his flat."

"Still, I suppose if this play is a success it will do you both a lot of good," mused Houston. "They say millions of people look in every Sunday."

She shivered. "Don't remind me. Millions of eyes watching for the slightest mistake – it's terrifying!"

He patted her shoulder. "You'll be all right once it starts," he said.

Dennis put down the magazine and went up to his room, where he was studying for a secretarial examination. Rona went into the kitchen and made some coffee, then she and her father sat gossiping for half an hour.

For Houston this was the best time of the day, but tonight there was obviously something at the back of his mind. "Tell me," he said presently, "are you and Carl Knight engaged?"

She hesitated a moment, then said: "Don't you like Carl?"

Houston shifted uneasily in his armchair. "Well ... he's a bit theatrical ..."

Rona laughed. "Darling, we're all theatrical – or at least we seem so to outsiders. But Carl is different underneath. He's quite a thoughtful sort of person."

"You haven't answered my question."

"About our being engaged?" She held out her left hand, which was bare of any rings. "Satisfied?"

"Up to a point," he said. "But you're still young, my dear, and I don't think you ought to tie yourself down just yet awhile."

She gave his arm a little squeeze. "You policemen always expect the worst to happen," she said lightly. "Carl and I are fond of each other, but at the moment we're both too het up about the play to find time for much else." She poured him a second cup of coffee. "Will you come round to the studio on Sunday evening?" she asked. "It would be nice if you were there, and you could see the play in the viewing room."

He shook his head reluctantly. "I'm afraid I've got a job on hand."

"You mean you won't see it at all?" she exclaimed in disappointed tones. "But daddy, it's my first real chance."

"I'm sorry, dear, but I've an appointment out of town that I must keep. It's urgent."

"What a shame," she said, but cheered up almost at once. "Anyhow, you'll be able to see the repeat on Thursday."

"I expect your boyfriend will be there on Sunday to give you his moral support."

"No, he's much too nervy about the whole thing. He says he's going to watch the play in his flat behind locked doors."

"He's certainly a very intense young man," commented Houston. "If ever you two get married, life will be one long drama."

*****

On Sunday Rona went off to Lime Grove immediately after breakfast, while Dennis and his father spent the morning, as usual, tidying their large garden. Dennis mentioned that he was playing tennis in the afternoon but would be home in good time to see the television play in the evening.

Mike Houston went over to Putney immediately after lunch to pick up Loman, who drove them to Chatham. They arrived just before teatime and went straight to the police station, where they had a long chat with the C.I.D. inspector. However, apart from directing them to the public house called The Skipper's Haunt, he was unable to help very much.

The hostelry in question lay between the docks and the centre of the town. It was small, and not very noticeable apart from its protruding sign. The public bar was the larger of the two and was comfortably filled. The two Scotland Yard men ordered beers and manoeuvred themselves into a position which gave them a good view of the street outside. The clientele of The Skipper's Haunt seemed to consist of a few seafaring men, a number of local tradespeople, and one or two furtive types who did not appear to fit into either category. However, on the whole, Houston decided that the place seemed harmless enough.

Just after seven o'clock, Houston caught sight of a familiar figure on the opposite pavement. As usual, Nobbler Williams was wearing an overcoat two sizes too large for him and a shabby felt hat pulled towards his right eye. He walked with his hands in his pockets, apparently deep in thought. To Houston's surprise he walked past the public house for about fifteen yards, then turned casually to cross the road.

Houston was just about to mutter an intimation to Loman, when he saw the car. It was a powerful American saloon, and when Williams stepped off the kerb it was twenty yards away but seemed to accelerate like a rocket. Williams made a dash for the opposite pavement, but then hesitated. Houston saw the driver pull the wheel over and drive straight at Williams. There was a screech as the car swerved, then it straightened out and accelerated again, leaving a limp figure incongruously sprawling in the gutter. Both Scotland Yard men rushed into the street, to find that a small crowd had already gathered around the inert form. Houston sent Loman back to the public house to telephone for an ambulance.

A policeman came running up and pushed his way through the crowd. "Are you Inspector Houston, sir?" he asked.

Houston nodded.

"I got the number of the car, sir."

"You did? Then for goodness' sake write it down."

When Loman returned from the public house, they decided there was no point in trying to move Williams, and a few minutes later an ambulance arrived. The two Scotland Yard men accompanied it back to the hospital, where the house surgeon examined the unconscious figure.

"Think there's any chance he'll come round, doctor?" asked Houston.

The doctor shrugged. "You never can tell," he said. "But I should say the odds are heavily against." He proved to be correct, and at nine o'clock that evening the broken body of Nobbler Williams lay in the mortuary.

*****

As they drove back to London, Loman suddenly turned to Houston and asked: "Did you see anything of the fellow driving that car?"

"It wasn't a very good light, and he had a scarf round his chin and a hat pulled over his eyes," said Houston.

"You've got that number all right?"

Houston passed a slip of paper to him. "There it is. The local people have already broadcast it, but you might check the registration as soon as you get back to the Yard. I think I'll go straight home. I'd like to be there when my daughter gets back from the television studios."

Loman stuffed the slip of paper into his coat pocket. "I'll have the car traced at once. If it looks interesting, I'll phone you at home."

Houston sat silently frowning at the winking headlights of the cars rushing towards London on their way back from the coast. His mind was brooding over that ominous figure at the wheel of the car that had so ruthlessly run down Nobbler Williams. The set of the hat, the way the man had worn the scarf, reminded him of someone. Someone he had seen quite recently. Suddenly he knew. He was thinking of the young man his daughter had brought home several times in the past few weeks. But Carl Knight would be watching his play on television. What on earth would he be doing in Chatham? With an involuntary shake of the head Houston dismissed the idea and took out his cigarette case.

*****

After the first impact of deflation owing to the absence of applause and curtain calls, Rona Houston suddenly felt wildly happy as she removed her make-up in the dressing room at the television studios.

The play had been a success. She felt it in her bones. After they had got over that dismaying technical hitch at the very beginning, the whole thing had gone like a dream. No-one had forgotten a single line, and all the effects had been perfect.

138

"Has Carl phoned yet?" asked Mavis Long, who shared a dressing room with Rona.

"Not that I know of. Maybe he passed out when we had the breakdown at the beginning."

Mavis giggled. They were all inclined to be a trifle irresponsible after the ordeal they had been through.

As they left the dressing room they bumped into Terry Smith, who had produced the play. "What's happened to Carl?" he asked. "I thought he'd have phoned by now."

"Rona thinks he might have passed out when we had the technical hitch," said Mavis.

"More likely drunk himself into a stupor," grunted Smith. "Well, I've got a train to catch. Post-mortems in the morning. Goodnight, girls." He went out, swinging his rolled umbrella.

Mavis ran off to catch a bus, and Rona stood hesitating in the hallway for a few moments. She asked the commissionaire if there had been any telephone message for her, but he shook his head. "No, nothing, Miss Houston."

Acting on a sudden impulse, she asked him to telephone for a taxi. When she went out, she noticed the gutters were running and the rain coming down fairly steadily. She gave the driver Carl's address and settled back in the cab. "Nasty night," commented the driver.

"I haven't noticed the weather for the last ten hours. Has it been raining long?"

"Couple of hours. Fair teeming down – not far short of a cloudburst, I reckon."

Rona rang the bell twice at Carl's flat, but there was no reply. She was just about to turn away when she heard the light click on in the hall. A moment later the door opened.

Carl stood before her in a dark green dressing gown. His hair was ruffled, and he seemed ill at ease. "Oh, it's you, Rona," he said nervously.

"Are you expecting someone else?"

"Well, no … at least I don't think so …" He hesitated a moment, then said: "Do come in, darling." He led the way into the drawing room.

"Carl, you're not worried about the play, are you?" she asked, sitting on the arm of a chair.

The muscles of his face jerked abruptly. "The play? No, no, that was wonderful. You were superb."

"You thought the opening went well?"

"Perfect."

A sudden feeling overwhelmed her. Carl had not seen the play. She felt sure she was right, as apart from the fact that he hadn't noticed the technical hitch he apparently had nothing whatever to say about the individual performances. Rona was completely bewildered. They had talked so much about the play during the past weeks, discussed so many aspects of it, she had imagined that there was nothing on earth that would prevent Carl from seeing tonight's performance.

A little hurt, she refused a drink. "I'm very tired, Carl," she said. "It's been a great strain. I'd like to get home."

Carl nodded and took her by the arm. He hesitated for a moment as if about to say something, but he changed his mind and led her towards the door.

On her way through the hall, her hand brushed against something damp. It was Carl's mackintosh.

*****

Ever since Loman had dropped him in Putney and he had caught a bus home, Mike Houston had been worrying over the death of Nobbler Williams. He realised only too well that the superintendent was pretty much on edge just lately, with all the pressure being brought to bear by Sir Cedric Kelford. He would probably consider that they had bungled what had looked like a promising clue to the Kelford kidnapping. The only clue so far, in fact.

Yet Houston failed to see what other action he could have taken. Some instinct born of long years of police experience told him that there was probably far more to this Kelford case than the abduction of a little girl. After all, there had still been no ransom note. He had an uneasy feeling that there was something big in the offing, that this was perhaps the first shot in a sinister campaign against Kelford.

He fitted his latchkey in the lock, noting that the house was in darkness. It was only just eleven, and Rona probably wouldn't be home for half an hour or more. As he closed the front door behind him, he was surprised to hear a taxi stop outside and Rona's quick footsteps up the path. He opened the door for her.

"You're back sooner than I expected," he said. "How did the play go?"

"Oh, it was all right," she replied rather wearily.

He was about to ask another question, when he noticed that the light was on in the drawing room. "Hello, Dennis has gone to bed and left the light on!" he exclaimed, opening the drawing room door. The television set was also switched on, and an armchair was drawn up in front of the set which faced the door. Dennis appeared to have fallen asleep in it, with one arm dangling over the side of the chair.

Houston was just about to call to him when he stopped abruptly and caught his breath. He turned to Rona, who was standing in the doorway. "Get the doctor!" he said, in a harsh voice that he hardly recognised.

"What's the matter, daddy? Is he ill?"

"He's been shot," said Houston. "Get on to the doctor right away." But even as he stooped to examine the bullet wound in his son's left temple, he knew it was too late.

The inspector slowly straightened himself and went over to switch off the television set. He could hear Rona dialling at the telephone in the hall. With one hand on the switch, he hesitated as something caught his eye. Just above the screen, on the woodwork of the set, was a neat little crayon drawing.

It was a sketch of a yellow windmill.

2

After what seemed an age, Houston was suddenly aware of Rona standing in the doorway, her face white and strained. "There's no reply from the doctor," she said.

"Get the hospital. Ask them to send an ambulance."

She went back to the telephone, while her father methodically examined the room for any trace of an intruder. He found the bullet that had killed Dennis, buried in the upholstery of the armchair. Presumably, it had been fired from behind the television set.

He sent Rona up to her room and sat alone waiting for the arrival of the ambulance. He could never remember feeling so depressed. What possible motive could there be for killing his son, a harmless conscientious bank clerk? And what did the yellow windmill mean on the television set? Was there some connection between Dennis Houston and the kidnapping of Sir Cedric Kelford's child?

The telephone shrilled out in the hall, and as if in a daze he went to answer it. "Is that you, Mike?" came the familiar voice of Loman. "Chatham have just been through. They want one of us to go to the inquest on Nobbler Williams."

"I'm afraid you'll have to go," said Houston heavily, and told him the reason. Loman was aghast at the news, and immediately began asking the same questions that Houston had been putting to himself. They had been talking for nearly ten minutes when Houston heard the ambulance stop outside. He told Loman he would have to ring off.

"Before you go, there's just one thing. I've checked the number of the car that ran down Williams. It had false number plates."

"I'm not surprised," said Houston quietly. He replaced the receiver and went to open the front door.

*****

The next twenty-four hours assumed a strange unreality for Mike Houston. Looking back on them, he recalled vaguely a conference at Scotland Yard the following morning; then there was the inquest on Dennis in the afternoon, when he gave formal evidence of identification and discovery of the body. The coroner had appeared unduly curious, but he had eventually returned a verdict of "Murder by person or persons unknown".

It was not until he was sitting opposite Rona late in the afternoon that his brain seemed to clear a little. Skilfully prompted by Rona, he began to tell her what had happened at Chatham the previous evening.

"Didn't you see the man driving the car?" she asked.

"I only caught a glimpse of him – I was too busy watching Nobbler Williams."

"Then you can't remember anything distinctive about the driver that might help?"

He frowned. "I didn't really see his face. But he was wearing a soft hat and a scarf round his chin, rather like your friend Carl Knight."

His tone was casual, but Rona could not repress a sudden start. However, she said nothing and hoped that her father had not noticed her reaction. But she could not erase from her mind the scene in Carl's flat on Sunday night, when she had been overwhelmed with the certainty that he had not seen his television play. "What do we do now?" she asked, passing him a second cup of tea.

"Carry on as usual, I suppose," he sighed. "I saw the Assistant Commissioner and he offered to let me back out of the case, but I told him I'll never have a night's rest until I find out who killed Dennis. The main thing is to keep going in the normal way. We mustn't arouse the murderer's suspicions that we're on the alert."

"Then it's all right for me to do the repeat of the play on Thursday night, in spite of all the fuss in the papers?"

"If you feel equal to it."

"Of course."

Before they could discuss any further plans, there was a ring at the front doorbell and Houston went to the door. A distinguished looking man in his late forties was standing on the doorstep. "Sir Cedric!" exclaimed Houston.

"May I come in, inspector?"

The inspector led him into the drawing room and introduced him to Rona. Sir Cedric Kelford was obviously

144

impressed by Rona Houston and made a considerable effort to be charming to her. Finally, he turned to Houston. "The Assistant Commissioner told me about your trouble, and said he was suggesting that you should withdraw from the case. I sincerely hope you won't do that, inspector."

"Have you a particular reason for wishing me to stay on the case, Sir Cedric?" enquired Houston, wondering if there were new developments.

"I'm confident that your son's death is in some way connected with my daughter's abduction," replied Sir Cedric, "and the link is the yellow windmill."

"I appreciate that," said Houston quietly.

"I'm sure you're the man who has the best chance of solving this mystery," said Kelford emphatically. "I can be quite certain this won't be just a routine job with you."

"You can rest assured of that, Sir Cedric," said Houston grimly. "But I ought to tell you that I'm as much in the dark as ever."

"You've no idea what that yellow windmill on your television set may have meant?"

"I've lain awake for hours figuring out dozens of theories, but none of them really makes sense."

"If there's any way I can help, don't hesitate to mention it."

"There is just one thing you might do for me," Houston said slowly. "I'd like you to use your influence as chairman of the bank to make a few enquiries about Dennis."

"Certainly, though I don't suppose I'll be able to tell you anything about your own son you don't already know. I had his dossier turned up this morning, and it seemed to me completely normal."

"It's surprising how little I really knew about him," said Houston quietly. "Of course, I'm away all hours, but he seemed to live the average life of a young bank clerk. He played tennis, studied for exams, and had no special girlfriends. He had only one hobby, philately, and one fairly close friend - Bob Harridge who's in the same branch of the bank."

"Perhaps Miss Houston knows a little more," suggested Kelford politely.

"I'm sorry, I can't help," replied Rona. "We were very good friends, of course, but we never confided in each other."

"You see?" said Houston helplessly. "There's nothing at all in the least suspicious."

"What about this Bob Harridge? Have you tackled him?"

"He looked at me as if I'd gone out of my mind," said Houston. "I got the impression that he regarded Dennis as a nice chap but a bit of a stick-in-the-mud."

"I'll get two of our best intelligence men on the case," promised Sir Cedric. "I'll have them question everybody who was in contact with your boy, and you can read their reports yourself."

"I'd be very grateful, Sir Cedric. I take it there's no more news of your daughter?"

Kelford shook his head. "Not a word, apart from that business you looked into at Chatham."

"I'm following that up," Houston assured him. "The local C.I.D. are having a comb-out down there."

Sir Cedric turned to Rona again. "I'd almost forgotten to compliment you on your performance on Sunday," he said. "It took my mind off my troubles for the first time. I'd no idea you were the inspector's daughter until I read it in the papers." His manner was so genuinely sincere that Rona, accustomed to compliments, felt slightly embarrassed.

As he rose to go, he shook hands with both of them. "I have a feeling we're going to make some progress on this case at last," he told them.

Rona saw him to the front door and watched him enter the grey Rolls. Somehow, she felt much more reassured about the outcome of the case. But she was still worried about Carl Knight.

*****

The following morning, Rona had a telephone call from a local garage to tell her that her small car had now been repaired, so she decided to use it to attend a special rehearsal of the television play. Driving up to town, she resolved that in view of the developments that had arisen since Sunday she must have a showdown with Carl.

But Carl was not waiting for her at the little mission room off Baker Street where the rehearsal was to take place. Terry Smith, the producer, and all the cast were most sympathetic about Dennis. Yet Carl, who must have read the report in the papers, had not even troubled to telephone her, nor had he turned up at the rehearsal to offer his commiserations.

Despite her colleagues' efforts to cheer her up she felt more and more depressed, and when the tea break came, she avoided the others and slipped out to a nearby cafeteria. Dropping her gloves and the play script on a chair at a vacant table, she went to the end of a line of people queueing along the counter. When she returned to her table, a man and a girl were sitting there.

"Bob Harridge!" she exclaimed.

The man jumped up at once. "Why, it's Rona Houston. Haven't seen you for ages." He pushed an unruly lock of dark brown hair from over his eyes. When she was studying at R.A.D.A. Rona had been to the cinema several times with Bob, but within recent months she had lost touch with him.

Bob turned to introduce his companion. "Rona, this is Mary Latimer."

The dark girl with the large mouth and deep-set eyes stretched out a slim white hand. "I've been hearing about your brother, Miss Houston. I'm terribly sorry for you." There was something in her speech that irritated Rona.

"The bank's let you out early today, Bob," said Rona as she sat down.

"I've been in the personnel department all afternoon, telling them what I could about Dennis."

Rona felt a sudden impulse to ask him what had transpired, but the presence of the other girl suddenly restrained her. Something made her mistrust Mary Latimer. She wondered how a man like Bob Harridge had become acquainted with a girl who seemed so exotically out of place in a cafeteria.

"Mary met Dennis at one of the staff dances," said Bob. "She was most upset when I told her the news." He seemed torn between the excitement of Dennis's murder and the presence of his stimulating companion.

Mary Latimer did not talk much. She just sat and watched them, occasionally casting a quick glance round the room. Bob Harridge was telling Rona that he had seen her in the television play, when she felt a hand on her shoulder.

She turned and looked up. Carl Knight was standing by the table. "I thought I might find you here," he said quietly.

148

Rona noticed an unusual tenseness about the muscles of his face, and his eyes looked as if he had not been sleeping well. She introduced him to Bob Harridge and Mary Latimer and was a little puzzled by the cynical smile that flickered for a moment round the girl's mouth as they shook hands. She could not help wondering if they had met before but was not very anxious to proclaim the fact.

Bob Harridge glanced at his watch and announced that they must go. Carl made no effort to detain them. He hardly waited until they were out of earshot before he said: "I went over to your home this morning, specially to see you. Your father was there, and he told me about Dennis. Of course, I'd already seen it in the papers. Your father seems to think it's all mixed up with that Kelford case. Is that really true, or is your father over-wrought and just imagining things?"

"Of course not," she replied, wondering why Carl should appear so anxious. She told him how they had discovered Dennis and the sketch of the yellow windmill on the television set.

Carl sat clutching a newspaper, until the whites of his knuckles showed. When she had finished, he asked her no more questions but lit a cigarette. Rona noticed that his hand was shaking as he replaced his cigarette case. To relieve the tension, she asked him to get her another cup of tea and suggested he bought one for himself. Somewhat reluctantly, he obeyed.

When he sat down again a few minutes later, she said calmly: "Now, Carl, I've answered your questions. Suppose you answer one or two of mine."

Carl frowned, with a tiny pulse throbbing near his temple. "Well?" he said.

Rona took a deep breath. "Are you quite sure you saw the play on Sunday?"

"Of course."

"You never commented on the breakdown or anything else. And I noticed a wet mackintosh hanging in your hall. Are you sure you weren't out in the rain that night?"

"Quite sure. If you must know, a friend of mine dropped in and returned a raincoat that he'd borrowed a week ago. He stopped and looked at the play."

"Can you tell me who he was?"

"I could, but I don't see why I should. If you don't choose to believe me, there's no more to be said." He now appeared to be unconcerned, as if his mind were busy with something quite different.

Rona was completely at a loss, and finally she asked: "Are you coming back to the rehearsal?"

He shook his head.

*****

At the mission room, she met Terry Smith in the entrance hall. "We shan't be needing you again today, Rona," he informed her. "Go home and put your feet up, dear."

She managed to smile wanly. "All right, I think I will," she agreed. "See you tomorrow."

Still very worried about Carl, she went out to her car. Had she been fair to him, she wondered. After all, his private life was really no concern of hers. And how could he possibly be connected with her brother's death? He was probably brooding over the plot of a new play, which simply made him seem remote and detached from the actualities of life.

As she turned the car into Baker Street, there seemed something familiar about the slightly stooping shoulders of a man who was standing with his back to her, talking to a girl in a shop doorway. She looked at them again as she passed. It was Carl Knight and Mary Latimer, deeply engaged in conversation. They did not even look in her direction. Suppressing an impulse to stop the car, Rona drove on towards Oxford Street. So, she had been right about Carl and Mary Latimer – obviously, they knew each other.

She steered the car into the park and across to Knightsbridge, hardly conscious of her surroundings. She had received the impression that Mary Latimer was going out for the evening with Bob Harridge. How had she contrived to get rid of him and meet Carl? Or had it been just a chance encounter?

Her mind was still busy with these speculations as she crossed the Albert Bridge. Suddenly she was conscious of a light lorry coming towards her at a good pace. Half way across the bridge it seemed to be out of control, as if the driver were having difficulty with the steering. A second later, Rona saw it coming straight at her. She took the only chance that was open to her. Twisting the wheel, she pressed the accelerator and mounted the pavement, missing the oncoming lorry by a matter of inches. Luckily there were no pedestrians in her path, and she swung back on to the road in about twenty yards.

Turning in her seat, she expected to see that the lorry had stopped or possibly crashed into the parapet, but it continued across the traffic lights and disappeared into Oakley Street. Feeling considerably shaken, Rona stopped for some minutes, wondering if someone who had witnessed the occurrence would come up to her. But there had been no pedestrians in the middle of the bridge, and the motorists were apparently too intent on their own affairs.

It was not until she had driven another two miles that a sudden thought crossed her mind. Had the lorry been deliberately driven at her car? She tried to dismiss the idea, but it persisted until she reached home. There was a note from her father, asking her to pick him up at Scotland Yard at about eight o'clock.

She was preparing a meal for their return when the telephone rang. To her surprise she recognised the voice of Mary Latimer. "I must talk to you," said the voice. "I've got some very important information about Dennis –"

"Don't you think you should phone my father at Scotland Yard?" suggested Rona.

"No, I must speak to you first. You'll understand why when I see you."

Still very suspicious of Mary Latimer, Rona agreed to meet her the following morning at the same cafeteria. She was quite convinced now that Carl was in some way connected with her brother's murder and the abduction of Susan Kelford.

*****

When Houston came out of Scotland Yard, Rona noticed how tired he looked. There were dark rings under his eyes, and he was stooping slightly. He asked her to take him to an address in Wimpole Street.

"Has something happened?" she asked as they climbed into the tiny car.

"Yes," he said. "We've traced the car that knocked Nobbler down. It was abandoned in a field the other side of Hertford."

152

"You know the owner?"

"Yes, it's a Dr. Spedro at an address in Wimpole Street. Of course, there's a big chance it was stolen."

When they arrived at the house in Wimpole Street, Rona had to draw in behind an ambulance. Her father was half out of the car when the front door of the house opened, and a swarthy little man came out. He gave rapid instructions in broken English to two white-coated attendants who carried a stretcher.

The driver of the ambulance climbed out and opened the back doors. The two attendants began to lift the patient inside. As the stretcher passed between the car and the ambulance, Rona leaned forward. She gave an involuntary gasp.

"What's the matter?" said Houston sharply. "D'you know that person on the stretcher?"

"Yes," said Rona softly. "It's a girl named Mary Latimer."

3

Mike Houston closed the car door again, to make sure their conversation could not be overheard. "What do you know about this girl Mary Latimer?" he demanded.

"I met her for the first time this afternoon – she was with Bob Harridge. Later this evening when I got home, she telephoned and said she must see me. She sounded rather upset, and said she had some information about Dennis."

The swarthy little man gave final instructions to the ambulance men and went back into the house. Just as the men were closing the back doors of the ambulance, Houston got out of the car and went up to them. "Would you mind telling me where you are taking your patient?" he asked.

They looked at him suspiciously for a moment, but when Houston told them who he was the elder of the two said: "I suppose there's no harm in telling you, sir. We're taking her to a nursing home in Martineau Road, St. Johns Wood."

"Do you happen to know what's the matter with her?"

The man shook his head doubtfully. "The doctor says it's a heart attack. We have to be careful moving her. That's all I know."

Houston thanked him and returned to Rona. "Wait here for me," he said, and went to the front door of the house. He rang the bell and was admitted almost at once. He gave the receptionist his name and said that he wished to see Dr. Spedro on an urgent private matter.

After a few moments, Houston was ushered into the consulting room. He had entered scores of such rooms in the course of his professional duties, and he immediately noticed that there was something a little different about this particular one. True, there were all the customary furnishings – the long couch, filing cabinet, a desk, and two large mahogany boxes which presumably contained instruments – but the room had a different atmosphere which the inspector found difficult to define.

Dr. Spedro had risen from his desk and was motioning Houston to be seated. "What can I do for you, inspector?"

"It's about your car."

"Oh, yes, so you have found it at last?" exclaimed Spedro. "It is now almost a week since I notified the police."

Houston quickly realised that it was necessary to take the initiative and fired off a series of questions about the car and how it had been stolen. Spedro answered the questions in an offhand manner, twice assuring Houston that he had already given the police full details at the local station. According to

154

the doctor, the car had simply disappeared from outside a surgical firm's headquarters in Bloomsbury – but when Houston mentioned that the car in question had been used to run down Nobbler Williams, the doctor's manner noticeably changed.

"You don't know this man Williams?" persisted Houston, giving a brief description.

"I do not know anyone named Williams. You are not suggesting that I was driving the car?"

"Can you account for your movements on Sunday evening?"

"Certainly. I was staying with some friends near Epping. Would you like their address?" He scribbled on a notepad, tore off the sheet and handed it to Houston.

At that moment the receptionist came in to ask Dr. Spedro if he would take a telephone call upstairs. While he was away Houston walked slowly round the room, examining its contents more closely. He was particularly intrigued by a number of small ornaments on the mantelpiece. There was a tiny model of the Eiffel Tower, another of the leaning tower of Pisa, a musical chalet from Switzerland – and a small, neatly carved yellow windmill. Houston was about to pick up the windmill when he heard the doctor approaching. Instead he turned and stood with his back to the fireplace.

The doctor apologised for his absence, declaring that the call had been from his nursing home in St. Johns Wood. "You may have seen the ambulance outside, inspector. It was a young lady I have been treating for heart trouble."

"Is her name Mary Latimer?"

Spedro looked surprised. "You know her?"

"My daughter has met her, and she caught a glimpse of her being carried into the ambulance. The young lady seemed to be in a very bad way."

"Yes. I'm afraid she collapsed right here in my consulting room. I have been expecting it for some time, but she would not go for treatment." The doctor shrugged. "Now, maybe it is too late."

"I'm sorry," said Houston. He hesitated a moment, then said: "I think perhaps my daughter would like to visit her."

"I doubt if that will be possible," frowned Spedro. "But if you telephone me in the morning, maybe we will have some news then."

The inspector could not help noticing that the doctor's attitude was now much more friendly. Indeed, he almost seemed anxious to prolong the conversation and Houston had no difficulty in switching the subject to the souvenirs that lined the mantelpiece.

Spedro told him that each of the souvenirs was a reminder of a visit to a foreign city.

"And the little yellow windmill?" put in Houston.

Spedro's eyes seemed to narrow the merest fraction. "The windmill? Ah, yes, that came from Amsterdam."

The receptionist entered and whispered to the doctor that his next patient had arrived. Houston took this as a fairly broad hint that his interview was over. He told Spedro that he would have his car returned the following day, wished him good evening, and followed the receptionist out into the hall.

As the receptionist went ahead to open the front door, Houston hesitated for a fraction of a second outside the half-open door of the waiting room. He imagined he had caught sight of a familiar figure. As he hesitated, the man half turned.

156

Houston moved on quickly, wishing the receptionist goodnight, and closing the front door behind him.

But he knew he had made no mistake. The next patient waiting to see Dr. Spedro was Sir Cedric Kelford.

*****

Houston told Rona that he wanted to stay in the neighbourhood to make some enquiries about Dr. Spedro and his nursing home, so they had a light meal at a little restaurant in Devonshire Street. She told him in low tones all the incidents of the afternoon, except the narrowly averted accident on Albert Bridge. She found it hard to believe that this had been a deliberate attempt on her life and was anxious not to worry her father any more than she could help.

"It's strange that Mary Latimer should know Carl Knight," said Houston. "I wonder if Carl knew Dennis a great deal better than we realise?"

"They hardly ever exchanged more than a dozen words," said Rona.

"Not so far as we know. But there are other aspects of the case, remember." He finished his coffee and paid the bill. As he was uncertain how long his investigations would take, he told Rona to go home and get a good night's sleep in readiness for her strenuous camera rehearsals and the repeat of the television play.

It was just after ten when Rona arrived home. She decided to go to bed at once and had one foot on the stairs when she heard a car stop outside the house. A few seconds later, there was an urgent knock at the front door. She was a trifle nervous after her experiences of the day, and took the precaution of opening the door on the chain.

Then she heard a familiar voice. It was Carl Knight. As she opened the door wider and he came into the hall, she could see that he was desperately worried. "I'm sorry I was so rude this afternoon, Rona," he said. "I've had so much on my mind lately, and it's nearly driven me crazy."

He sank his chin into his hands and looked so desperately miserable that she was tempted to forgive him. Feeling that their misunderstanding should be thoroughly ventilated, she made a reference to his meeting with Mary Latimer. Instantly he was on guard, and she saw his jaw muscles stiffen. "You must have made a mistake," he said. "I'd never set eyes on the girl till you introduced me. And I went straight back to the flat after I left you this afternoon."

Rona said no more. It was true she had been passing in a car, and his back had been half turned towards her. There were hundreds of men of the same build, so she might have made a mistake. As Carl went on talking, the words blurred on her consciousness. Suddenly she realised he had mentioned her brother.

"You must persuade your father to give up the Kelford case," he was saying. "He'll be in terrible danger if he doesn't. You can't afford to lose him too."

"He has already been offered the opportunity to withdraw from the case," said Rona softly. "He told them he'll see it through if it takes the rest of his lifetime."

Carl picked up his hat. "In that case," he sighed, "I suppose there's nothing more we can do. Unless you could persuade him —"

"Why should I? I'd do exactly the same in his place. In fact, I'm more than ready to help him if there's anything I can do." To relieve the tension a little, she offered him a drink, but he shook his head. "I wish you'd tell me the real reason why you came all this way," she said wistfully. "Maybe I could help."

"I simply wanted to warn you."

"But why should you, Carl? You've nothing to do with this case. Why should you want me to persuade my father to give it up?"

"I – I can't go into all that," he said wretchedly. "It's just a sort of intuition."

"Well, I'm sorry you've had your journey for nothing," she replied, as they stood at the front door.

"Let's forget the whole thing," he retorted abruptly. "Maybe everything will straighten out. See you tomorrow at the studio." He wished her a curt goodnight and strode off into the darkness.

Rona stood looking after him for some seconds, then slowly closed the front door. The clock in the hall struck eleven, and she decided not to wait up for her father.

She passed Dennis's room on the way to her own. The door was closed. She had not been inside since the night Dennis was murdered, but she knew exactly what was inside the room – the school photographs, the writing desk with the secretarial correspondence courses stacked in neat piles, the plain oak bedstead and reading lamp. It was all so ordinary, so innocuous. Who could possibly gain by killing a harmless young man like Dennis?

Though she felt exhausted by the events of the day, she found it difficult to sleep. When at last she fell into an uneasy doze, it seemed she had only been asleep a few minutes when she heard the sound of a door closing. Rona switched on the bedside lamp and looked at her watch. It was a quarter to two. Anxious to hear what her father had discovered about Mary Latimer she slipped on a dressing gown and went downstairs.

But there was no sign of Houston, and she climbed the stairs again. She hesitated for a moment outside Dennis's room, and heard the unmistakable sound of some object falling to the floor. She pushed open the door and fumbled for the light switch. Before she could find it, two hands closed round her throat.

Rona struggled and screamed. She could hear a man's heavy breathing. The grip grew tighter, despite her efforts to tear his hands away. She screamed again, and the blood surged through her ears as she clawed desperately at the man's hands.

Suddenly a door banged down below, and there was a sound of quick footsteps. The intruder flung Rona to the floor and rushed over to the window.

"Rona! Where are you?" called her father from the stairs.

The rush of cold air from the open window revived her. Houston heard her gasping for breath and ran into Dennis's room, switching on the light. Still lying on the floor, she pointed to the open window. "I'm all right ... he went through there."

Houston went to the window and looked out, then he ran downstairs, picking up his torch from the hall table. Outside he searched the garden thoroughly, but without any result. Under the window of Dennis's room, the soft soil had been disturbed, but there was no clear indentation of footprints. Presumably, the visitor had stopped to obliterate them.

Houston returned to the house and found Rona downstairs, sipping a small glass of brandy. "What the devil's been going on?"

She told him all she knew.

"Then you didn't see him at all?"

160

"It was dark in Dennis's room. I didn't get a chance to switch on the light."

Houston discovered that Dennis's room had been thoroughly searched, but as far as he could ascertain nothing had been taken away. He looked round, and saw Rona standing in the doorway. "Who on earth could it have been?" he wondered.

"All I know is that the visitor was a man," she told him.

"Probably just a small-time crook out for what he could lay his hands on," mused Houston. "I shouldn't let it worry you too much. Try to get some sleep now. You're due at the studios in less than eight hours."

At her bedroom door, she stopped and called to him: "What did you find out about Dr. Spedro?"

"Nothing very much. It seems he is a heart specialist, one of those birds with a strange degree. The local boys couldn't help about the nursing home either. Seems he only converted it recently."

"And you discovered nothing about Mary Latimer?"

He came and patted her shoulder. "All in good time. Now try and forget the whole thing, take a couple of aspirins and let yourself relax. I'm looking forward to seeing you give a first rate performance tomorrow night."

*****

Rona came down just as Houston was finishing breakfast. He asked if he could use her car and arranged to call for her at the television studios – arriving, he hoped, in time to see the play.

The post arrived just as he was leaving, and he came back with a large envelope addressed to Rona. As she opened it, she exclaimed: "It's my script! I must have left it in that café yesterday afternoon."

"Then it was good of somebody to send it straight back. I wonder how they discovered your address."

"From the telephone directory, I daresay."

He nodded and went out to get the car. Rona started her breakfast and glanced at the morning paper. She heard the car leave, poured herself some more tea, then took the script out of the envelope to refresh her mind on the cuts that had been made.

She turned the first sheet, which listed the cast and rehearsal arrangements, then suddenly caught her breath. Scribbled across the top of the second page were the words: *There will be a third death unless your father abandons the Kelford case.* And underneath, there was a crude sketch of a yellow windmill. Rona examined the writing closely but could not recognise it. She was certain it was not Carl Knight's, unless he had disguised it very effectively.

*****

Since she had some time in hand before the rehearsal, Rona decided to visit the cafeteria off Baker Street. It was almost empty when she got there, and she asked for the proprietor. It did not take long to find out that he knew nothing about the script. It had obviously been picked up by someone who had followed her at the table.

Twenty minutes later she was at the studios where she managed to get a word with Terry Smith, the producer. He too knew nothing about the lost script, and as soon as he saw the envelope, he assured her that it had not been returned by the B.B.C. Resolutely, Rona put the whole incident from her mind and concentrated fiercely on the camera rehearsal. It was a relief to lose herself in the world of make-believe.

After the transmission, she changed quickly and found her father waiting for her in the viewing room. He was chatting to one of the attendants but came over as soon as he saw her. "I was proud of you," he said quietly.

"You saw it all?"

"Except the first few minutes. I've had a busy day. Things seem to be happening."

Rona came back to the world of reality. "Let's go and have supper somewhere, daddy. I want to talk to you." She was anxious to tell him about the returned script, with its strange warning.

"The car's just up the road. I've got plenty to tell you. Come on," he said.

She quickly said goodnight to the producer and several members of the company, and they went out into Lime Grove. The night air was chilly after the heated studios. Houston made one or two commonplace comments on the play. When the light from the street lamps caught him, she thought he looked tired and haggard. Undoubtedly, he had aged noticeably during the past week.

In less than five minutes they reached the cul-de-sac where he had parked the car. It was badly lighted, with decaying Victorian terraced houses towering on either side.

"I know a little place in Hammersmith where we can get a decent meal," said Houston, his hand on the door handle. He was suddenly conscious that there was a considerable weight pressing against the door. He looked up and down the deserted street, then said quietly: "Stay on the pavement, Rona. I think there's someone in the car."

As he spoke, he opened the car door and braced himself to take the weight of the human body that sagged heavily against him. It was a woman, and he leaned over and switched on the dashboard light. He recognised her immediately, although he had only seen her once before when she was being lifted into an ambulance.

"It's your friend Mary Latimer," he said to Rona. "Can you come and give me a hand?"

They managed to prop the girl upright against the front seat of the car. "There's blood on her face," whispered Rona.

But Mike Houston was not looking at the dead girl's face. He had just caught sight of the object she was clutching in her left hand. It was the model of the yellow windmill that he had seen in Dr. Spedro's consulting room.

4

Rona suddenly felt faint and clutched at the projecting driving mirror to steady herself. She soon recovered in the cool night air and said nothing to her father. Whatever Mary Latimer had been anxious to tell her, they would never know.

Houston looked up and down the deserted cul-de-sac, then he told Rona to telephone the police station for an ambulance. When she had gone, he picked up the model of the yellow windmill and carried it to the nearest street lamp.

"Where did you get that?" Rona asked, when she returned to find him still examining it.

He flicked the tiny sails with the tip of his finger. "Mary Latimer had it in her hand," he said. "I've seen one that's identical."

"Where was that?"

"On the mantelpiece in Dr. Spedro's consulting room."

164

At that moment, the ambulance turned the corner, and further conversation was impossible. Houston introduced himself to the police sergeant who accompanied it, the girl was lifted on to a stretcher, and ten minutes later Houston and Rona were on their way home.

"What was Mary Latimer doing in my car?" asked Rona, as Houston maneuvered into the traffic across Hammersmith Bridge.

He shrugged. "Waiting for one of us, perhaps," he suggested.

"I can't think how she escaped from the nursing home. She was supposed to be seriously ill."

"We've only Dr. Spedro's word for that," he reminded her. "I shall be interested to learn what the post mortem reveals."

"How could anybody murder her in an open street?"

"Not so difficult," he insisted. "Somebody obviously followed her, watched her get into the car, came up behind her with some sort of stiletto, and there you are. A pretty straightforward sort of job for a determined type."

After they had crossed the bridge, Rona said: "What were you going to tell me – you know – just after the show?"

"Only that I paid another visit to Dr. Spedro's nursing home this afternoon and found Mary Latimer had gone. The matron told me that she had made a remarkable recovery."

"So that explains how she came to be wandering around Lime Grove."

He nodded, then glanced at the clock on the dashboard. "I'll have to put a move on. I've asked Bob Harridge to look in about ten. It's turned twenty to."

"Bob Harridge?" she repeated, mystified.

"Yes. Loman has been making a few more enquiries. He discovered that Dennis saw Mary Latimer quite a number of

165

times, and that Bob Harridge first introduced them. I thought Bob might be able to throw a bit more light on the business."

As they approached Roehampton Lane, Rona decided to tell him about the mysterious message on the returned manuscript. "That's the third warning we've had asking you to give up the case," she recalled.

He turned and smiled at her reassuringly. "I've had a lot of warnings like that in my time," he said. "They usually mean that the other side is getting a bit jumpy. I've never taken them very seriously." He hesitated a moment, then went on in a rather more anxious tone: "All the same, I'm not very happy about this young fellow Carl Knight. I'd rather you didn't see him again just yet awhile. In fact, I think it might be a very good idea if you took a little holiday at Aunt Kit's. That Dorset air would do you the world of good."

She shook her head decisively. "I'm not leaving you on your own in the middle of this business. After all, Dennis was my brother, and if there's anything I can do I'm not running away. I said as much to Carl."

Houston looked interested. "And what did Carl have to say to that?"

"He seemed very upset. Then he hinted that your being on the case had already caused one death in the family, and that there might be another."

"Did you ask him what made him suggest that?"

"He wouldn't tell me."

Houston patted her hand. "You're a plucky kid," he said. "Your mother would have been as proud of you as I am. Don't worry, we'll get clear of all this before long."

*****

When they reached home, Bob Harridge's open two-seater was drawn up to the kerb and Bob was standing on the front doorstep. Houston jumped out and apologised for keeping him waiting. "It's all right, sir," said Bob quietly. "I've only just arrived."

Houston led the way into the drawing room, switched on the electric fire and pulled the curtains. Rona went out to take off her hat and coat. When she returned, Houston had just broken the news of Mary Latimer's death.

Bob Harridge seemed very upset. "What's going on, Mr. Houston?" he was saying in agitated tones. "What's behind all this?"

"That's why I asked you here, Bob," said Houston easily. "I thought you might help me to throw some light on it."

"I wish I could, sir," said Bob fervently, "but I'm completely in the dark. The bank people have been asking me all sorts of questions, but there's nothing much I can tell them. I met Mary Latimer at the same time as Dennis, at a staff dance. I gathered he saw quite a lot of her afterwards, but I wasn't particularly interested in the girl. Not my type at all."

"Did you see her again?"

"We made a four to go the theatre once or twice. I took a girl named Cynthia Harper – she's in our West End branch. But I don't suppose I ever talked to the Latimer girl for more than a couple of minutes at a stretch."

"Then why did you meet her in the café?" asked Rona.

Bob Harridge frowned. "Yes, that's another blessed mystery. She phoned me at the office and asked me to meet her. Said she had something important to tell me about Dennis. As you know, Rona, we met at that cafeteria, but she never said a word about Dennis while you were there. Then, after you'd gone, she suddenly got very agitated, said she'd forgotten something very important, and went off in a flash. Just left me there high and dry."

"Was it you who returned my script?" asked Rona.

Bob Harridge looked surprised. "I didn't see any script," he said. "You left it in the café?"

"I can't be sure. There's always a chance that I might have dropped it in the street."

Houston stirred restlessly in his chair. "Then you can't throw any more light on this girl Mary Latimer?" he asked. "You don't know if she had a job?"

"She never said anything about it. I somehow got the idea that she was rather an irresponsible type. That's why I was rather surprised that a steady fellow like Dennis should have been interested in her."

"Maybe that was why he never brought her home," mused Rona.

"I was always a bit suspicious about Dennis where she was concerned," said Bob. "You see, most of the fellows in the bank are only too eager to boast about their girlfriends. Dennis hardly ever mentioned her. It used to make me wonder if —"

"Yes?" prompted Houston.

"Well, if she had some sort of hold over him," said Bob uncomfortably. "It might have been nothing particularly sinister, but I often wondered. Dennis could be very close you know, sir. You must have realised that, if only from the fact that he never mentioned the girl to you."

"He was a shy person," said Rona. "He didn't like to intrude his private affairs on us."

"Well, I've told you all I know," said Bob Harridge, rising to his feet. "I'm only sorry I can't be of more help. But the more

168

questions I answer, the more mysterious the whole affair seems."

"All the same, I'd be grateful if you'd keep your ears open, Bob," said Houston. "Let me know anything that sounds in the least promising." He walked along the hall and opened the front door.

"I'll do that, sir," Bob Harridge assured him.

*****

The superintendent shuffled through the pile of reports on his desk and gazed uncomfortably at Mike Houston. "I've been through these reports very carefully, Houston, and I feel bound to say —" He hesitated.

"You're trying to say that it looks as if Dennis was in some way connected with the organisation that you suspect kidnapped Kelford's little girl?" said Houston calmly.

"There are several facts that seem to point in that direction. Are you sure you want to go on with this, Houston?"

"Never more sure of anything in my life. After all, if it's anything connected with Dennis, I'm in a good position to investigate."

The superintendent nodded. "I know we can rely on you, Mike. I just wanted to spare your feelings if it should be anything unpleasant."

"It's very kind of you, sir. But if I'm taken off this case, I'll resign from the force and follow it through off my own bat."

"All right, Houston. No need to get dramatic. You're still with us."

Ten minutes later Houston was on his way to see Dr. Spedro, with whom he had taken the precaution of making an appointment. He was shown into the waiting room, and rather to his disappointment the doctor joined him there, instead of taking him into the consulting room.

Houston went to the point at once, and asked how it was that Mary Latimer had been well enough to leave the nursing home the previous afternoon, though she had had to be carried there on a stretcher less than twenty-four hours before.

Spedro shrugged. "One can never tell with heart cases, inspector."

"She wasn't under the influence of any drug when she was taken to the home?"

"Certainly not. I told you she collapsed right here in my consulting room."

"If she was that ill, why did the matron let her leave?"

"I understand she slipped out without anyone being aware of it. But you know quite well, inspector, that we have no power to compel a patient to remain in the nursing home if she chooses to go."

Houston had to admit that the doctor's answers were plausible enough. But there was a certain evasiveness in Spedro's manner that made him suspicious. "Would you mind telling me how she came to consult you?" he asked.

"Certainly. She was recommended by another patient, Sir Cedric Kelford."

Something clicked inside Houston's brain. "Was she a friend of Sir Cedric's?" he enquired.

"I have no idea. No doubt he would give you that information."

"How long has he been coming to you?"

"About three months. Just lately he has paid me several visits. No doubt you know his little girl was kidnapped – the worry has aggravated his heart condition quite considerably."

170

A telephone rang in the consulting room, and Spedro went to answer it. Houston followed him out into the hall. Suddenly the door of the consulting room opened and Spedro said: "Scotland Yard want to speak to you."

When he walked to the telephone over by the window, Houston tried to conceal his eagerness to glance across at the mantelpiece. He heard Spedro close the door, and he turned instinctively. The yellow windmill was still there. Obviously, it could not be the same one that Mary Latimer had been clutching at the time she was murdered.

Inspector Loman was at the other end of the line, and he told Houston that Sir Cedric Kelford wanted to see him urgently. After Loman had rung off, Houston did not immediately replace the receiver. He was gratified to hear a click in the earpiece, which betrayed the fact that someone had been eavesdropping on an extension.

When he went out into the hall, Spedro was just descending the stairs. Houston told him that his evidence would be required at the inquest on Mary Latimer and gave him details of the time and place.

Houston was still very uneasy in his mind about Dr. Spedro, as he drove round to Eaton Place. The post-mortem on Mary Latimer, of which they had had a report, revealed that she had indeed suffered from heart trouble.

He was shown into Kelford's study at once, and it was obvious that the banker was excited. "I've got some news for you, inspector!" he exclaimed, indicating a single sheet of notepaper that lay on his blotting pad. Houston guessed it was the long-awaited ransom note and stooped to look at it without picking it up.

The typewritten message ran: *Your daughter is alive and well. If you want to see her again, leave £7,000 in one pound notes in the telephone box at the end of Oasthouse Lane, Haydock Green. Saturday night. Ten o'clock. Wait near the telephone box. Do not get in touch with the police or the child will not be returned.*

Pulling on his gloves, Houston examined the envelope in which the letter had been delivered. It was postmarked Penge. He carefully returned the letter to the envelope. "Leave this with me, sir. I'll get in touch with you again later on today. I take it you haven't mentioned this to anyone else?"

"Certainly not. But I'm relying on you, Houston. There must be no slip-ups. I'm giving you this chance because I know you want to get the man who killed your son. But I'd sooner pay the money – and double as much – rather than take the slightest risk of losing Susan."

"I quite appreciate that, sir," replied Houston tactfully. "You can rely on me to take care of everything."

*****

Houston went straight back to the Yard and handed over the ransom note to the fingerprints department. Just as he was telling Loman the latest developments, the telephone rang.

It was Rona, who sounded very excited. "I'm just coming into town," she said. "Carl telephoned to tell me that Ambrose Wyler is interested in the television play, and he wants to see me about playing my original part."

"That's fine," said Houston.

"I thought I'd let you know I won't be at home for lunch."

"As a matter of fact, I'll be in town all day."

"That's all right then."

He wished her luck with her interview and was about to ring off when something occurred to him. "By the way, Rona,

172

do you happen to have a letter or anything that's been typewritten by your friend Knight?"

"What on earth …?" she began when he cut in briskly.

"I'm serious, Rona. This could be important."

There was silence for a few seconds, then Rona said: "Yes, I believe I've got a film story somewhere that he asked me to read. He told me he'd typed it himself."

"That'll do admirably. Can you drop it in at the Yard for me after you've had your interview? Put it in a sealed envelope addressed to me personally. Then you can leave it if I should be out."

"I'll bring it along right away if it's as urgent as that. I'm not seeing Wyler till lunchtime."

Rona found the script and put it in an envelope. When she got to New Scotland Yard her father was out, but the hall sergeant said he had left her a message to meet him at Danilo's Restaurant at seven o'clock. Rona thanked the sergeant for the message and handed over the envelope.

Ambrose Wyler's offices were in St. James's Street, and since Rona was ten minutes early for her appointment, she walked up to the second floor and into the comfortably furnished reception room. She was glancing through the pages of a magazine, when the outer door opened and a man in a chauffeur's uniform entered and politely enquired: "Miss Houston?"

"Yes," said Rona.

"I'm sorry, Miss Houston, but I'm afraid your father's met with a slight accident."

Rona felt a constriction in her throat which prevented her from speaking.

"It's nothing serious, but he particularly asked for you. Could you possibly –?"

173

"Yes of course," said Rona, jumping up.

"I have a car outside. It won't take ten minutes."

Rona followed him downstairs, her heart pounding so madly that she found it difficult to breathe. As they walked down the last flight, she did manage to ask: "You're sure it isn't serious? I'd sooner you told me."

"The doctor assured me there was nothing to worry about," he said politely.

A large black Cadillac was drawn up to the kerb, and it was not until the chauffeur had closed the door behind her that she saw the man sitting in the far corner. As the car swept away, the little man leant forward. "I don't think we've been introduced, Miss Houston," he said quietly.

At that moment she recognised him. It was Dr. Spedro.

5

The car swung round the wide curve at the foot of St. James's Street, and edged its way into the narrow opening at the side of the palace.

"Your father may have mentioned me – I'm Dr. Spedro," said the swarthy little man, but Rona could only nod. "I must apologise for this subterfuge. Please don't look so upset. Your father is perfectly well, to the best of my knowledge."

"What do you want with me?" asked Rona angrily.

"Just a little talk, Miss Houston. We will drive round the park for ten minutes. That will be ample." As the car moved into the Mall, Spedro said: "Your father seems to be under the delusion that I am involved in the murder of a man called Nobbler Williams."

"I'm afraid my father doesn't discuss the details of his cases with me."

"But surely this case is an exception," he persisted. "Didn't I understand him to say that Mary Latimer was a friend of yours?"

"Hardly that. I gather she knew my brother."

"I am only too anxious to help the police," he continued. "I have told them all I knew about Mary Latimer, which was little enough. Has your father any clue at all as to who killed her?"

Rona assured him that she was not in her father's confidence, but the little man went on asking questions about Mary Latimer as if he were anxious to vindicate himself.

"Are you interested in this murder simply because the girl was your patient?" demanded Rona shrewdly.

For answer, he passed her a copy of the mid-day edition of one of the evening papers. The name of Mary Latimer was splashed across the front page. Underneath was a dramatically written resumé of the case, suggesting the importance of the yellow windmill which the dead girl had been clutching. Somehow or other, the writer of the story had also discovered that there was a sketch of a yellow windmill on the television set that Dennis Houston had been watching.

"Your father was very curious about a yellow windmill in my consulting room," went on Spedro. "I was quite mystified at the time, but now I have read that report of course I can understand the reason."

"Then why not tell him all you know about the yellow windmill?"

"My dear young lady, there is nothing to tell. My model of the yellow windmill is merely a souvenir of a short visit to Amsterdam. I wish your father would realise that I am a firmly established doctor with a reputation to consider. I simply could not afford to get mixed up in any nefarious affair."

Spedro seemed so very much in earnest that Rona hardly knew what to reply. "My father is always very cautious before making accusations," she said at last. "But I'll certainly tell him what you say."

"Thank you, Miss Houston. And I do hope you'll forgive this little ruse to get you into the car. As you see, it was quite harmless."

The car had drawn up again outside the offices in St. James's Street. As the chauffeur came round and opened the door for Rona to descend, Dr. Spedro politely raised his hat. Rona stood watching the car for a moment, then turned into the entrance. She would be just on time for her appointment with Ambrose Wyler.

She was about to ring for the lift when she heard a quick footstep behind her. A hand grasped her elbow. She swung round and saw Carl Knight. He looked pale and tense. "Whose car was that?" he demanded.

For a moment she was so taken aback that she could not frame an answer. Then she said: "It belongs to Dr. Spedro."

"Who's he? What d'you know about him?" he said tensely.

"Practically nothing. He has a house in Wimpole Street. He was Mary Latimer's doctor, so he wanted to know if my father had discovered anything about her murder."

Carl forced a smile. "I'm sorry, Rona," he said apologetically, "but you should be careful about taking a lift from strangers." He glanced at his watch. "We're keeping the great impresario waiting," he said.

*****

After reading the experts' report, which stated that the letter to Sir Cedric Kelford and the film story by Carl Knight had been typed on the same machine, Houston spent a busy afternoon trying to find the playwright. He telephoned his flat several times, but there was no reply.

As an afterthought, he also phoned Wyler's office and was told that Carl Knight had been there around lunchtime. Then Ambrose Wyler himself came on the line and said that Knight had mentioned visiting one of the outlying film studios, but he could not remember which one. Houston gave it up for the time being and went off to Marylebone to make further inquiries about Dr. Spedro.

He was ten minutes early for his appointment with Rona at Danilo's Restaurant, so he went into the call box and rang up Sir Cedric, with whom he had been constantly in touch all day. There had been no further approach from the kidnappers. He arranged to call on Sir Cedric in an hour's time to complete their plans.

Houston thought that Rona was looking rather pleased with herself when she came into the restaurant. "Well, have you had any more requests for me to give up the case?" he asked, after they had ordered a meal.

"Not exactly a request, but a pretty strong hint – from Dr. Spedro." She told him what had happened in Spedro's car and could see that he appeared uneasy. "Have you discovered anything new about Dr. Spedro?" she asked.

"That's just the tantalising part about it. I don't like the look of the fellow, and he's so evasive. I've spent best part of the afternoon checking on him, but there's nothing really suspicious in his record. One or two big men at the hospitals spoke very well of him. At the moment, I'm rather more interested in your friend Carl Knight."

"Carl?" she repeated, slightly surprised. "But I saw him in Wyler's office at lunchtime. He was awfully nice and insisted that I should have the part if the play goes on."

"That's fine," nodded Houston. "I'll keep my fingers crossed."

"And after that," she went on, "Carl took me out to lunch, and we were on top of the world."

"Did he say where he was going afterwards?"

"He had an appointment at the film studios at Shepperton. Why?"

"I've been trying to get hold of him all afternoon."

"Is anything wrong?"

"We thought he might be able to enlighten us on one or two points. Loman's going round to his place in the morning."

Rona looked worried. "It sounds like those carefully worded police appeals, when they say they think a certain person can give them information that will lead to the murderer. Everybody knows that person is the one they're after for the crime."

Houston laughed. "It isn't as bad as that. We're not making any public announcements."

After they had finished their meal, Houston was waiting for Rona in the somewhat restricted vestibule of the restaurant when Bob Harridge bumped into him.

"I'm glad to have seen you, inspector," said Harridge. "I've some news that might interest you. It's about Mary Latimer." They moved to a corner of the vestibule where they were less likely to be overheard. "I was having lunch in a pub called The Rising Sun, just off Cheapside, when I happened to hear the barman talking to some of the regulars. They'd been reading about Mary Latimer in the lunchtime edition. The barman said she often used to call in there, though he never knew her name. One or two of the regulars remembered her as well. I don't know if that's any help to you, sir, but I thought you might follow it up somehow - I mean, she might have been going there to meet somebody."

"I'm glad you told me," nodded Houston.

"Oh, here's the man I'm having dinner with. I'll give you a ring at home, sir, if I hear anything else."

"Thanks, Bob," said Houston.

*****

After Rona had driven her father round to Eaton Square, he told her to go on home. He expected to be some time with Sir Cedric.

Rather to his surprise he was shown into the drawing room, where Sir Cedric was talking to a striking looking woman whom Houston judged to be in her middle forties. Two empty liqueur glasses stood on a small table. The woman was wearing a light outdoor coat.

"Come in, Houston, come in," said Kelford affably. "Mrs. Spedro, may I introduce Inspector Houston?" If Houston was a trifle startled at the familiar name, he showed no sign of it. They chatted for a few minutes, then Mrs. Spedro declared that she must leave.

After she had gone, Sir Cedric turned to Houston. "So, you've met Dr. Spedro?"

"Yes."

"He's a queer bird, but a brilliant man in his own particular field. Mrs. Spedro, of course, was a very old friend of my wife."

"So that's how you came to consult him?"

Sir Cedric looked up sharply. "How did you know I was going to him?"

"He happened to mention it. He also told me you'd recommended Mary Latimer."

"That name's familiar."

"It's in all the evening papers."

"Oh, yes. Yes, of course! She was the girl who was found murdered."

"Then you don't know her?"

"Certainly not."

"And you didn't recommend her to Dr. Spedro?"

Sir Cedric looked faintly annoyed. "I assure you, inspector, I'd never heard of the girl till I read today's papers. How could I possibly send her to Spedro? He must have made a mistake." He seemed to regard the affair as trivial and was obviously anxious to pass on to something more important. "Have you made any arrangements about tomorrow?" he demanded impatiently.

"We need your co-operation, Sir Cedric," Houston told him. "We want you to follow the instructions exactly, draw the money from the bank and leave it in the telephone box at Haydock Green. You're prepared to do that?"

"Yes, of course. But I only hope you have every contingency covered, inspector."

"We are taking elaborate precautions. Of course, it's absolutely vital that you tell no-one else about the ransom note."

"You can rely on me, inspector."

*****

When Houston left the house and strolled into Eaton Square, he thought he saw a familiar figure approaching. She came into the glare of the street lamp, and he recognised Mrs. Spedro.

"It was such a lovely evening, I've been walking round the square," she told him.

He had a feeling that she was making conversation and had been waiting to get an opportunity to speak to him. "Will you walk to the end with me, inspector? I can pick up a taxi there."

She strolled very slowly. Presently he demanded curiously: "Did you want to say something to me, Mrs. Spedro?"

She hesitated a moment. "I know your family rather better than you think, inspector," she said quietly. Houston was surprised but did not betray it. "Dennis used to tell me all about you."

"You knew Dennis?"

"Very well indeed."

"I'm beginning to think I never really knew him," admitted Houston. "Hardly a day goes by without my coming across some friend of his whom he'd never even mentioned to me."

"It's a wise father …" she quoted absently.

"You're not trying to tell me you can throw any light on Dennis's murder?" he suggested, but she shook her head.

"No, but I'm worried about your daughter."

"Why?"

"I think she's in grave danger," she replied simply. "Can't you persuade her to go away for a little while?"

"I've already tried to do so. She refuses to leave me." Mrs. Spedro sighed. "A lot of people seem to be anxious for me to give up this case," continued Houston. "Whether it's anxiety for my safety or their own, I have yet to find out. Only today your husband hinted to my daughter that she might persuade me to stop worrying him. It's all very involved, Mrs. Spedro."

Their footsteps echoed on the pavement of the deserted square. As they reached the corner, he asked: "How did you get to know Dennis?"

"That's easily answered. I taught him economics at the London Central. He was my favourite pupil."

"Really, I had no idea," he said somewhat lamely.

"You're thinking I don't look the type," smiled Mrs. Spedro. "I assure you I've got quite a good degree. You can look it up for yourself. I thought Dennis showed great promise. At the end of the course, I gave him a little book of mine that had just been published, called *Economics in a Post-War World.*

At that moment, a taxi swung round the corner, and Houston hailed it. After she had entered the taxi, he stood with one foot on the step. "If your husband wants to talk to Rona again, I'd be glad if he'd refrain from melodrama," he said quietly.

"You'll have to overlook today's little episode. He told me about it at tea-time. He's a very excitable sort of man, you know. But I'll see it doesn't happen again."

*****

When Houston reached home, Rona was in the kitchen. He took off his coat and hat, then changed into an old alpaca jacket and slippers. An appetising smell of coffee floated out of the kitchen, as he sat in his armchair and scanned the evening paper.

Rona came in carrying a tray and set it down on a small table. "Carl Knight was on the telephone just before you came in," she informed him.

Houston looked up from his paper. "What did he want?"

"He said your Inspector Loman had been trying to get in touch with him. He wondered why."

"Did he seem put out at all?"

"He didn't sound like it. Apparently, he has even offered to go round to Scotland Yard, and Loman told him that would be more convenient. He'll be there in the morning at ten sharp."

Houston returned to his paper. Somehow, he could not get the image of Mrs. Spedro out of his mind. He found himself curious about the book she had written. What was it called – *Economics in a Post-War World*?

As he sipped his coffee, his eye ranged along the shelves at the side of the fireplace level with his armchair. A lot of the books were Rona's - classical plays, textbooks on acting, some modern novels. If it was still in the house, it would probably be in Dennis's room.

Houston set down his cup and saucer and went upstairs. There were three shelves of books in his son's room, and he ran his eye along the titles. There were three economics textbooks, but no sign of Mrs. Spedro's.

Finally, he found the book he wanted, at the back of a drawer in the writing desk. It was a fairly slim volume, with an inscription on the flyleaf: *To Dennis from Margarita Spedro*. That was all. Houston idly turned the pages. Several words and phrases that he did not understand caught his eye. It was obviously a somewhat advanced publication.

As he flicked back the pages, he realised that a section in the middle of the book was uncut. But there was something unusual about it. A neat little square, measuring about two inches, had been cut from the centre of each page, forming a pocket which had clearly been intended to conceal a small object. But the pocket was empty.

Then he heard his daughter calling him, and he walked thoughtfully downstairs and showed her the book. She had never seen it before, nor had Dennis ever mentioned it to her. Houston was puzzled. Did Mrs. Spedro know anything about the pocket in the middle of the book? Why had she mentioned the book to him?

Houston always enjoyed a cigarette with his coffee, and he remembered that he had a fresh packet in his overcoat pocket. He went out into the hall and lifted his overcoat off the hall stand. As he pulled the packet of cigarettes out of his pocket, a flimsy piece of paper fell to the floor. He picked it up and smoothed out the creases. It was a half sheet of cheap paper, such as typists use for taking carbon copies. He took it nearer the light and read: *Kelford has ignored our stipulation about going to the police. The appointment is cancelled.*

And underneath the message was drawn a small yellow windmill.

6

Houston took the slip of paper into the drawing room and showed it to Rona. While she read it, he tried to figure out how the note could have found its way into his overcoat pocket.

"Did you leave your coat anywhere?" Rona asked as she passed back the note.

"In the cloakroom at Danilo's Restaurant." He recalled that Bob Harridge had been emerging from the cloakroom when he bumped into him. "It might be Bob Harridge," he said slowly.

"I think Mrs. Spedro is a much more likely suspect," said Rona. "She could easily have slipped it into your pocket."

"That's true," he had to admit. "Though there are several other possibilities." He took the original ransom note from his wallet and compared it with the latest message. They had clearly been typed on the same machine, and when he explained this to Rona she said: "So that's why you wanted that script of Carl's."

Houston nodded.

"And was it his typewriter?"

"There seems to be no doubt about it."

She paced restlessly across the room. "What are you going to do about it?" she enquired presently.

Houston shrugged. "That depends on what Mr. Knight has to say for himself tomorrow morning."

* * * * *

While they waited for Carl Knight in Superintendent Elder's office, Loman and Houston discussed with Elder the latest developments and examined the book that Houston had found in Dennis's room. They were unable to decide what the neatly cut pocket had concealed. "Maybe that was what your visitor was after the night Rona found him in that room," suggested Loman.

"If only we knew what it was," said Elder. "I've a feeling it would put us right on the track."

They went on to examine the note Houston had found in his overcoat pocket, which had already been tested for fingerprints without result. The two notes now lay side by side on Elder's desk. "Do you think there's any point in going through with this Haydock Green job?" asked Houston.

"Certainly," replied Elder crisply. "There's always a chance that the second note wasn't from the kidnappers at all. We can't afford to take any chances. We'll let Sir Cedric go down there, and we'll patrol the roads as arranged."

"But if the note isn't from the kidnappers, then who could —" Loman was beginning when the telephone rang. It was the hall sergeant to say that Sir Cedric Kelford urgently wished to see the superintendent.

When Sir Cedric arrived, he was plainly very perturbed. "The whole plan is off," he announced in agitated tones. "Somebody here must have given everything away." He flung a slip of paper down on Elder's desk, and the three Yard men bent to examine it. It was an exact duplicate of the note Houston had found in his coat pocket. "This came by the morning post," said Kelford.

"Have you got the envelope?"

Sir Cedric fumbled in his pocket, and eventually produced a manila envelope. The postmark was London W.1. The three men looked at the exhibits for a minute or two without speaking. Then Kelford could contain himself no longer. "Don't you realise my child may be murdered?" he said desperately.

"Are you sure you never told anybody else about this?" asked Elder.

"Not a soul outside this building," insisted Sir Cedric. "It's leaked out from here somehow. Now they'll probably never give me another chance."

"Don't worry, Sir Cedric," said Elder calmly. "The kidnappers obviously want money. They'll be quite ready to take another chance, knowing they've given you a thorough scare."

Kelford took out a handkerchief and mopped his forehead. "You really think so, superintendent?"

"The next note will demand at least ten thousand pounds, if my experience is anything to go by," replied Elder imperturbably.

"I'd pay double as much!"

"I wouldn't advertise that fact if I were you."

Sir Cedric Kelford looked from one to the other in the little group. "Then you think Susan is still alive?" he asked.

The superintendent nodded. "I'm quite convinced she is," he said quietly.

Sir Cedric looked rather more reassured, and presently took his leave. As soon as he had gone, Elder picked up the telephone.

"You're having him trailed, sir?" asked Loman.

"Of course. When he gets another note he won't say a word to us. He'll just hand over the money."

"But how on earth did it leak out?" asked Houston. "I'll swear it wasn't at this end. He must have told somebody."

"Probably – he'd be too obstinate to admit it." The telephone rang again, and the hall sergeant announced the arrival of Carl Knight. "Send him up in a couple of minutes." Elder put down the telephone and turned to Houston. "I'm worried about this man Knight," he said. "What's more, I've a feeling he's likely to try to exert some sort of influence over your daughter. It may even be more dangerous than that."

Houston was once more overwhelmed with that cloud of apprehension that had never been far distant since the death of Dennis.

"I've asked O'Donovan to keep an eye on your girl, Houston. He's one of our best men. She'll never spot him, and there's no need to say anything to her. What's more, he may come across something that will give us a valuable lead. Any objections?"

Houston shook his head. "I appreciate it, sir," he replied. "She travels around a lot, and I'll feel much easier if I know somebody is within call."

There was a knock at the door, and Carl Knight came in. Houston noticed at once that he was much more carefully dressed than usual. Instead of flannel trousers and a sports jacket, he was wearing a dark blue suit and a fancy waistcoat.

Superintendent Elder lost no time in coming to the point. He showed Knight the note that Kelford had given him. Houston noticed that Carl did not remove his gloves when he picked up the note. Elder then handed him the film story which Houston had got from Rona. It was obvious that Carl recognised the manuscript.

"Would you agree that the same typewriter was used in each case, Mr. Knight?" Elder asked.

"Yes, of course, said Knight frankly. "It's my old Mercury. It was a dependable machine, and I often wish I'd never sold it."

"You sold it?" repeated Elder sharply.

"Several weeks ago. I had a cheque for some foreign royalties, so I treated myself to a new machine."

"Did you sell the Mercury privately?" asked Houston.

"No. I took it to Elcocks – in Conway Court, just off Fleet Street. They do a big trade in reconditioned machines. You shouldn't have any difficulty in tracing it." He picked up his hat and looked round the room rather jauntily. "Is that all you want to know?" he asked.

Superintendent Elder leaned on his desk and focused his keen grey eyes on Carl Knight. "There are many more things we want to know," he replied deliberately. "The question is, Mr. Knight, how much can you tell us?"

Knight was immediately on the defensive. "What are you referring to?" he asked.

"Among other things, the disappearance of Susan Kelford and the murder of Mary Latimer."

"What should I know about them?" There was a note of uncertainty in his voice.

"I'm giving you this opportunity to tell us," replied Elder unemotionally.

"Are you suggesting that I am implicated in these crimes?" challenged Carl Knight. "Remember you are speaking before two witnesses."

"I'm suggesting that it might make matters a lot easier for yourself if you told us what you know, instead of leaving us to find out. When we do find out, things could be decidedly unpleasant for you."

"I neither like your tone nor your attitude, superintendent," said Knight. "If you want me, you know where you can find me." In spite of this arrogance, Houston thought Knight looked quite pale and had clearly been shaken by the interview.

*****

Houston could see that the incident had irritated the superintendent, so he went back to his own office and telephoned Dr. Spedro. The doctor himself answered the telephone and seemed faintly surprised when Houston asked to speak to his wife.

"I'm afraid she is visiting some friends in the country, inspector. Is there anything I can do?"

Houston said the matter could wait until Mrs. Spedro returned, then went on to ask the doctor about Mary Latimer.

"You told me that she had been introduced to you by Sir Cedric Kelford. He says he had never heard of the girl until he saw her name in the newspapers."

Spedro began to talk very fast and his foreign accent became more noticeable. "I do not wish to contradict Sir Cedric. Possibly I have made a mistake ... I have so many patients ... I will get my wife to turn up the file at the nursing home when she returns, if you really think it is important."

"I think it's most important," retorted Houston with some emphasis. "I must ask you to remember that this is a case of murder, Dr. Spedro. The more I can discover about the dead girl, the better chance I have of arresting her murderer."

Dr. Spedro began to apologise profusely but Houston, somewhat out of temper, cut him short and said he would be in touch with him again as soon as Mrs. Spedro returned. With a feeling of frustration Houston slammed down the receiver and told Loman that he was going home to lunch.

It was rather late when he arrived, and he found that Rona had not waited for him. He carefully refrained from immediately mentioning Carl Knight's visit, and she asked no questions. Instead she was chattering about a proposed visit to a theatre that evening, with an actress friend who had managed to get tickets for one of the West End shows.

"I must go and do some shopping first," she said, standing in front of the mirror and tying her scarf.

"Yes, a trip to the West End might take your mind off everything," nodded Houston. The thought struck him that O'Donovan was going to have a fairly busy evening tailing Rona around the West End.

"What are you doing for the rest of the day?" she asked, carefully adjusting her scarf.

"Making the rounds – fairly routine stuff as far as I know. By the way –"

She turned from the mirror. "Yes?"

"Can you remember when Carl Knight sent you that film story?"

"It must have been quite six months ago." She hesitated a moment, then said: "Did you ask him when he sent it to me?"

"Not directly. He says he sold his old typewriter some weeks back, and it sounds as if he was telling the truth. I'll check up with the shop just in case."

"Was there any trouble – with Carl, I mean?"

"No trouble at all. He seemed to know all the answers."

She looked relieved. He felt there was no point in telling her that the superintendent was far from satisfied and was checking up very closely on Carl Knight. "You run along and do your shopping now," he said. "Take a walk across the common. You need some fresh air after all the excitement of last week."

After she had gone, Houston went to the window and watched her turn down the avenue towards the shopping centre. A thick-set man, whom Houston recognised as Sergeant O'Donovan, strolled across the road and followed about thirty yards behind her.

Houston walked briskly to the nearest tube station and went to The Rising Sun in Cheapside. The lunch hour rush was over, and he had no difficulty in having a few words with the landlord, who acted as his own barman. He remembered Mary Latimer at once. "She wasn't the usual sort we get in here," he explained. "That's why I noticed her."

"Did she come very often?"

The landlord frowned. "Perhaps once a week," he hazarded. "She seemed to meet a young fellow – studious

191

type, untidy hair and horn-rimmed glasses. I thought maybe he was a student at one of the hospitals. I must say he didn't look the sort you'd expect a girl like that to fall for."

After the landlord had promised to find out what he could about the young man, Houston took a bus heading for Fleet Street. He was not surprised when the proprietor of the typewriter shop turned up the transaction relating to the purchase of Carl Knight's Mercury, as Knight would hardly have lied about this unless he were stalling for time.

But the typewriter was not in the shop. "We sold it again almost at once, as soon as we'd cleaned it up a bit," announced Mr. Elcock, peering at his ledger through pebble lenses. "It was bought by a Mr. A.P. Arnold, of 29 Ainsworth Court in Bloomsbury."

"Do you remember him by any chance?" asked Houston.

The old man frowned. "From what I can recall, he was quite a youngish fellow. He wore horn-rimmed glasses, and his hair kept falling over his eyes when he tried the machine."

Houston took a note of the address and thanked the man. He walked thoughtfully in the direction of Bloomsbury, pondering upon the possibility of the young man who bought the typewriter being the one who met Mary Latimer at The Rising Sun.

*****

Ainsworth Court proved to be a huge block of flats just behind Euston Road. When Houston walked in, the entrance hall was deserted. He found that number 29 was on the first floor.

He pressed the bell, and plainly heard it ringing. As no-one answered it, he rang again. There was no sound of any movement inside the flat, but he could hear a radio blaring forth a popular dance tune. He hesitated again, then lifted the neat brass knocker on the door and rapped several times. As he did so he felt the door give slightly, and when he pushed gently it opened. Someone had pulled back the tongue of the Yale lock and pressed the catch.

Houston looked round cautiously, then went into the narrow entrance hall and closed the door behind him. He rapped with his knuckles on the door of the lounge, where the radio was playing, but again there was no reply. He put his head inside, and saw the room was empty.

After a moment's hesitation he returned to the entrance hall and tried the door opposite which opened into a bedroom. Here, a quick glance told him that something was wrong. The bedclothes were partly on the floor, and the dressing table stool lay on its side with a hairbrush just beside it.

Houston moved carefully across the room, taking in all the signs of disorder. There had clearly been a struggle, but it was not until he came to the foot of the bed that he saw the body of a woman lying on the floor. It was Mrs. Spedro.

Houston knelt beside the still form and picked up her left wrist. There was no pulse. She had been strangled with a silk scarf. Mechanically he began to release the scarf from the dead woman's neck. As he did so, a wave of apprehension sent the blood surging to his ears. He examined the scarf closely, holding it up to the light.

There was no doubt about it. It was the scarf that Rona Houston had worn.

7

Houston stood looking down at the body of Mrs. Spedro, running the scarf through his fingers. He found it hard to believe that Rona had played any part in the death of this woman. What possible motive could she have had? Could there be any link between his family and the yellow windmill murders?

He went out into the lounge and looked round for the telephone. It was standing on a small bureau in a far corner. He dialed the Yard and spoke to Loman. As he talked, he slid back the lid of the bureau, revealing a small typewriter standing beside a neat pile of quarto paper.

Houston replaced the receiver and turned his attention to the machine. It was a Mercury. He slipped in a sheet of paper and laboriously copied a line from the first ransom note, which he had extracted from his wallet. Though he was no expert, he was confident that this was the machine which had been sold by Carl Knight.

Before the Scotland Yard squad arrived, Houston made a quick examination of the flat. There was nothing in the least suspicious. He pushed the scarf inside his coat pocket, and when the others arrived, he told the sergeant in charge not to remove the body until he returned. Then he went out to the police car, and half an hour later was letting himself in at his own front door.

He was just turning the latchkey when he saw a shadowy figure at his front gate. Houston turned and called: "Is that you, O'Donovan?"

"Yes, sir."

Houston went out to the gate. "Get inside the car for a minute," he said.

"Have you lost track of Rona?" asked Houston, when they were both sitting in the back of the car.

"No, sir. She's here."

"But she was going to the theatre."

The sergeant shook his head. "She hasn't been near a theatre, inspector. After she had been shopping this afternoon, I tailed her to a flat in the Cromwell Road." Carl Knight's flat, thought Houston. "She stayed there about an hour, and got back here around seven o'clock."

"You're quite sure she didn't call anywhere else, if only for five minutes?"

"I never lost sight of her," O'Donovan assured him.

Houston considered this for a few moments. "What time do you go off duty?" he asked.

"Eleven o'clock, sir, unless you want me to stay."

"I'll let you know later."

*****

Houston got out of the car and went into the house. Rona was sitting on the settee in the drawing room, her legs tucked under her, reading a play script. "I thought you were going to the theatre," he began rather abruptly, a note of challenge in his voice.

Rona looked up in some surprise. "After I got back from shopping, I had an urgent message from Carl. He wanted me to go and see him right away, so I phoned Sheila and put her off."

"Was it as important as all that?"

"Of course. It was about the play."

"Oh, the play," murmured Houston, conscious of a certain anti-climax.

195

"Ambrose Wyler is definitely going to put it on, but he wanted some alterations made. That's why Carl asked me to go and see him."

"How long were you there?"

"About an hour, I should think. Carl had lots of new ideas, and –"

"What has happened to the scarf you were wearing when I last saw you?" he interrupted. "Did you wear it when you went to Carl Knight's flat?"

Rona looked puzzled for a moment. "Yes, I think I must have left it there, now you come to mention it. I remember now – I draped it over that little head of Nero that stands on the hall table."

"Why didn't you pick it up as you came away?"

She looked bewildered. "I don't know. We were probably talking about something or other, and I forgot. I've often done it before. Is it as important as all that?"

He took the scarf from his pocket. "Is this it?"

"Yes, of course. Where did you get it? Have you been to Carl's?"

"No," he replied curtly, taking the scarf and pushing it back into his pocket. "I'll explain about the scarf later. In the meantime, you mustn't set foot outside the door. Push the bolts across after I've gone, and fasten all the windows."

After giving O'Donovan instructions not to let Rona leave the house, Houston climbed into the police car and told the driver to take him to Dr. Spedro's nursing home in St. John's Wood. When he arrived, one of the nurses told him that the doctor was making his evening round of the patients, and was reluctant to be interrupted except in the case of an emergency.

"This is an extreme emergency," retorted Houston sharply. "Kindly tell him so at once."

In spite of Houston's remark, Spedro kept him waiting five minutes. "I am very sorry, inspector," he began when he finally put in an appearance, "but I am unable to give you any information about Mary Latimer until my wife returns."

"I am afraid I have very bad news about your wife," said Houston quietly. "Your wife will not return – she was found dead this afternoon."

Spedro took a step back, obviously stunned. "But it isn't possible. My wife went to some friends in the country for the day."

The inspector shook his head. "She was found in a flat in Ainsworth Court, Bloomsbury," he said softly. "Perhaps you'll be good enough to come along there with me right away."

Spedro nodded and took a brandy decanter from a corner cupboard. He poured himself a generous measure. "I have never heard of this Ainsworth Court, inspector."

"You have no friends there?" The doctor shook his head. "The flat belongs to a Mr. A.P. Arnold," went on Houston. "Does that name suggest anything to you?"

"I don't think so. My wife, of course, knew a lot of people – professors, lecturers and so on. But I have never heard her mention anyone called Arnold."

Five minutes later, the doctor had recovered sufficiently to accompany Houston to the police car. At the flat they found the sergeant inside, chatting to a uniformed constable. Apparently, the owner of the flat had not returned.

Houston took Dr. Spedro into the bedroom, where he identified the body of his wife. Though he was accustomed to the sight of death, Spedro was obviously very upset and considerably shocked. "She has been strangled," he muttered

197

almost to himself. He swung round and faced Houston. "Who has done this? Who brought her here?"

"That is what I'm trying to find out," replied the inspector imperturbably. "And I think it's high time you told me all you know."

"But I don't know anything about this," protested Spedro. "What can I tell you?"

"There are still a lot of questions about Mary Latimer to be answered, and then there is your wife's acquaintance with my son Dennis."

"I know nothing of that. Besides, what connection could it possibly have with this?"

"I'm here to ask questions, not to answer them," said Houston. "I suppose you were aware that your wife had a book on economics published?"

"Of course."

"You knew she gave my son Dennis a copy?"

"I believe she gave copies to several of her students."

"In my son's copy, there was a pocket which had obviously been used to conceal some small object. Have you any idea what that was?"

"Of course not. This is wasting time, officer. You should be looking for her murderer."

"I think I'm the best judge of that, doctor. And I ought to warn you that unless you're more co-operative you are going to find yourself in very serious trouble."

The blood mounted to Spedro's face. "I don't know what you're talking about. I have told you before that I have a responsible position, an established reputation. You are talking to me as if I were a criminal."

Houston was about to make an impatient retort, when there was a tap on the door and the sergeant came in.

"Fingerprints have just returned Mrs. Spedro's handbag," he informed Houston. "I found this inside." He handed the inspector a small silver pocket-knife with a neat little cigar cutter at one end. Houston turned it over and examined it closely. At the opposite end to the cigar cutter were the initials "C.K." "Rather an unusual sort of knife to find in a woman's handbag, sir," commented the sergeant.

Houston passed it to Spedro and asked if he had seen it before. Spedro gazed at it for some moments, then admitted reluctantly: "I think it belongs to Sir Cedric Kelford."

"C.K. ... of course," murmured Houston, wondering if Spedro would have acknowledged it if there had been no initials. He asked the sergeant to leave the knife with him, and to telephone him at home the moment Mr. A.P. Arnold returned to his flat.

He took Dr. Spedro back to Wimpole Street in the police car, questioning him relentlessly all the way. But the doctor insisted that he knew nothing more about Mary Latimer, that he had never met Carl Knight, never heard of Dennis Houston, and knew very little about his wife's relationship with the Kelfords. When he got out of the car, Spedro seemed to be completely dazed. He leaned heavily on the rail beside the steps leading to his front door.

As he watched him disappear, Houston wondered if he had been too severe with him, yet he still felt that Spedro was withholding information. He curtly ordered the driver to take him to Carl Knight's flat in the Cromwell Road.

The door of the flat was opened by Carl himself, who looked startled for a moment but then assumed his customary nonchalance. "Hello, inspector. Something turned up about the typewriter?" he asked, inviting Houston inside.

"I'm following that up," Houston told him. "What interests me more at the moment is the question of Rona's scarf."

"What the devil has that got to do with anything?" demanded Carl, apparently quite mystified.

"Never mind. She was wearing it when she came here this afternoon, wasn't she?"

"Yes, I believe she was. I happened to notice it because she doesn't often wear one in town."

"And she left it here?"

"I don't think so. You're at liberty to search, of course."

"She says she put it down in the hall."

Carl Knight led the way into the hall. They looked behind the table on which stood the Nero's head. This was the only possible place where the scarf could have been mislaid. Houston did not tell Knight that the scarf was at present in his pocket. He was waiting to see if the author would make even the tiniest slip.

"What's all this about anyway?" asked Knight.

"A woman has been found strangled with a scarf exactly like Rona's," said Houston bluntly. "It probably happened around the time Rona was here, or just after."

"Good Lord! You're not suggesting that Rona —"

"I'm suggesting that someone used Rona's scarf to throw suspicion on her."

Carl stepped back a pace and leaned against the wall. He seemed to have turned pale, and there was a note of apprehension in his voice. "Hadn't you better tell me the name of this woman?"

"She was a Mrs. Spedro. Do you know her?"

There was a pause, then Carl Knight said slowly: "The name means nothing to me."

200

It was obvious that Houston would gain no further information, so he left and picked up a taxi in the Cromwell Road. As they drove through the deserted streets, he surveyed the day's events. It had been a stroke of inspiration on the part of Superintendent Elder to have Rona kept under observation. She had an alibi as far as the death of Mrs. Spedro was concerned; that was the main thing.

It was after midnight when he got home, but he found Rona sitting by the radio. "I kept some coffee for you," she said, and he followed her into the kitchen. "Did you discover anything about my scarf?" she demanded anxiously, as he sat stirring his coffee.

He shook his head and told her of his visit to Carl Knight's flat. "I'm certain I left it there," she said. "Just as I was taking it off, Carl was called to the telephone."

"Why didn't you look for it as you came out?"

"I don't quite know. Maybe I did, sort of subconsciously. I'm sure if it had been where I left it I would have seen it and put it on again. It simply couldn't have been there."

"Then presumably somebody took it. Was there anyone else in the flat?"

"I didn't see anyone. We seemed to be alone all the time." She hesitated a moment, then asked: "You don't think Carl is mixed up in this murder?"

"There's no proof of it. But your scarf will have to be produced in evidence, and you'll be called on to identify it."

Their speculations were cut short by the telephone ringing. Thinking it was the sergeant reporting the return of the mysterious Mr. Arnold, Houston lifted the receiver. A soft, pleasant voice said: "Inspector Houston? I thought you'd like to know that Sir Cedric Kelford has had another note about his daughter. This time the demand is for ten thousand pounds.

201

The money is to be taken to Leach's Farm near Petworth tomorrow night. Of course, he won't tell the police this time, but I thought you'd like to know, inspector."

The line went dead. Houston had the call traced at once, but it had come from a public call box in Hammersmith.

*****

At a short conference in Superintendent Elder's room the next morning, it was revealed that the elusive Mr. Arnold had yet to return to his flat. Elder decided that Houston must see Sir Cedric Kelford about the silver pocket-knife. Meanwhile, Loman telephoned the Sussex Police to inquire about the farm near Petworth.

Houston had some difficulty in tracing Sir Cedric, who had been moving around his various business headquarters. He eventually found him in his office at the Central Bank and had to wait nearly half an hour before Kelford could see him.

Sir Cedric was in an uncommunicative mood, but when Houston produced the knife, he identified it at once. "I mislaid it some weeks ago. Where did you find it?" Houston told him. "I can't think why Mrs. Spedro should have been carrying it around. Maybe I dropped it when I was at the doctor's, and she was intending to return it to me."

His explanation seemed genuine enough. "Is there any other news, Sir Cedric?" asked Houston, offering him an opportunity to mention the second ransom note.

Sir Cedric rather pointedly looked at his watch. "No, nothing else, inspector. So, if you'll excuse me, I'm already ten minutes late for an appointment."

Houston returned to the Yard, confident that Sir Cedric had received the note and proposed to comply with the terms.

Loman told him that the local police had given him some information about the farm near Petworth. It was, in fact, little more than a smallholding, rented by a man named Len Milford.

"They say the place has completely gone to seed," continued Loman, "and there can't be a living in it. But Milford is never short of money, and they've often suspected he's up to something but there's never any proof. Anyhow, they've sent a plain clothes man to keep an eye on the place until we get down there."

The police cars had a little difficulty in finding Leach's Farm that night. It stood on an unmade road that was little more than a lane. They had to stop some distance short of the house, which stood about thirty yards from the road at the end of a narrow drive overgrown with weeds. A sullen moon came from behind a heavy bank of clouds and made the house visible for a few minutes. It had once been white, but badly needed repainting. There was a room on either side of the front door, and a light in one of them behind a drawn blind.

Houston and Loman made a round of four strategic points, where men were posted to cover every approach to the farm. Then they moved cautiously along the weedy drive. In a little paddock they found a spot which offered excellent cover and also a perfect view of the front door. Somewhere at the back of the house a dog howled dismally, so Houston decided that anyone approaching the back door was bound to attract the animal's attention, and there was no need to keep a close watch on that quarter.

A cool wind from across the downs rustled through the overhanging wisps of hay. There was no sign of life outside the farm. Loman and Houston stood shivering in the night breeze for nearly an hour. Then, just as a distant clock was striking ten, they heard a car stop near the entrance to the drive. It stood there for a moment, then turned into the drive. The dog at the back of the house began barking furiously.

In front of the door the car stopped with a jerk, and a man emerged from the driving seat almost immediately. In the half-light from the moon, they could see he carried a large case. "It must be Kelford," whispered Loman, but they could not see the visitor's face. The man rapped briskly on the front door of the house. There was a pause, then a shadow crossed the blind and the lighted room went dark. As the caller knocked again, the door opened almost immediately.

Houston and Loman found themselves moving cautiously forward.

8

Loman blew a short blast on a whistle he had taken from his pocket, as a signal for the police to close in on the farmhouse. The moon had disappeared behind the clouds again, and they could barely see the shadowy outline of the buildings.

Walking carefully along the weed-covered drive, Loman and Houston approached the front door. When they were a few yards away they could hear raised voices from inside the house, and Loman clutched his colleague's arm, pointing to the window which was open about four inches at the top.

"I tell you I know nothing about any girl," said an unfamiliar voice, presumably Len Milford's.

"Is this a trap of some sort?" came the voice of Sir Cedric.

"All I know is that I am to take charge of a case with ten thousand quid inside -" Sir Cedric was about to protest again, when the man cut in: "It's no use talking to me, mister. I'm only doing as I'm told."

Houston made a sign to Loman, and they moved towards the front door. Loman blew his whistle again, and the two men prepared to put their shoulders against the door. However, it was not locked, and they found themselves in a stone-flagged hall. A moment later, they were confronting Kelford and Len Milford.

The farmer made a dash for the door on the other side of the room, but Loman had moved across to intercept him and grabbed his arm. Sir Cedric stood quite still near the fireplace his left hand pressed against his heart. "Are you all right, Sir Cedric?" asked Houston. Kelford nodded without speaking.

Milford tried to shake off Loman's firm grip. "Who the devil d'you think you are, breaking into a private house?" he shouted.

"You know who we are, Mr. Milford," replied Houston curtly.

"I don't know what you're talking about. You get out of here."

"We'll get out presently," Loman assured him. "And we'll take you with us."

"You'll get nothing out of me," was the reply.

Houston went over to Kelford, who had now sunk into a chair near the fireplace. "Then you did get another ransom note, Sir Cedric," he said quietly. Sir Cedric took a slip of paper from his pocket and passed it to Houston. The note was typed with the same machine, and in the same terms as its predecessors demanded the sum of ten thousand pounds. "Have you seen any sign of the little girl?"

Kelford shook his head, and Houston swung round on Milford. "What about it?" he snapped. "If you're hiding the child here, you'd better own up. The place is surrounded, and it will be searched."

"You'll find nobody here," grunted Milford.

Houston went over to the table and picked up the case containing the notes. Policemen were pouring into the house from back and front doors. The dog was barking furiously. "Come along, Milford," said Houston, handing the bag back to Sir Cedric.

"You can't charge me with anything," protested Milford uneasily.

"We'll see about that," said Houston, and turned to Kelford. "I think you'd better come along too, Sir Cedric, just in case there are any queries."

"All right, inspector," said Kelford heavily. "I'll follow you in my car."

They led the still protesting Milford out to the waiting police car in the lane. When they were in the charge room at the local police station, Houston motioned to Milford to sit down and had an extra chair brought in for Sir Cedric.

"Now, Milford," Houston began, "let's get this clear. I can very easily bring a charge against you." The man looked sullen and made no reply. "On the other hand," went on Houston, "if you decide to tell us all you know ..."

"All right," Milford said after a long silence. "But you got to get one thing straight. I ain't in on this set-up. I only work for 'em now and then, do as I'm told and ask no questions. Like I was doing tonight."

"You mean the yellow windmill people?"

"That's right."

"Is it a big organisation?"

"I'm not sure. I think so."

"What's their line?"

Milford hesitated for a moment, then answered quietly: "Blackmail. They gather information about people, then put

206

the black on 'em. They did the same to me. Found out about a job I did at the end of the war, and -"

"All right, we won't go into that now," put in Houston, to reassure him. "What about tonight? What were your instructions?"

"I had to take the case to Victoria Station and leave it in the left luggage office. Then I had to post the ticket to this address." He took a grubby envelope from his inside coat pocket and passed it to Houston. The address was: Mr. A.P. Arnold, 29 Ainsworth Court, London W.C.1.

"Have you seen this man Arnold?" asked Houston. Milford shook his head. "What about this little girl of Sir Cedric's?"

"All I was told was to collect the money," Milford persisted doggedly. "I didn't even know who would be bringing it."

"You are telling us you've never met anyone in this organisation?" demanded Loman.

"It's that sort of set-up. They do all their work over the phone or through the post. You can't pin 'em down. Somebody's on the watch all the time. They'll probably have somebody waiting at the farm now. I daren't go back."

"All right, Milford. I'll arrange for you to stay here for a few days." Houston made the arrangements with the station sergeant, then turned to his companions. "We'll get back to town," he decided. "As you're carrying a lot of money, Sir Cedric, perhaps I'd better come with you."

He instructed the driver of the other police car to keep them in sight. After dropping Kelford in Eaton Square, Houston went to the flat in Ainsworth Court, where the sergeant in charge told him that Mr. A.P. Arnold had still failed to put in an appearance.

Houston went down to the basement and introduced himself to the porter on duty. He was a talkative Irishman, and he gave Houston an elaborate description of the man Arnold, which tallied with that which had been supplied by the landlord of The Rising Sun and the proprietor of the typewriter shop.

Houston eventually reached home at six in the morning. He slept for a couple of hours, and then decided to take a bath. Rona was waiting for him when he came out of the bathroom; she had already made coffee and was cooking the breakfast.

After breakfast he telephoned the Yard, to make sure there were no further developments, and told them to expect him towards mid-day. He was skimming through the morning paper when there was a knock at the front door, and Rona brought in Bob Harridge.

"Why, Bob, I thought you'd be at the bank by now," said Houston curiously.

Harridge looked very pleased with himself. "Ah, that just shows the police don't know everything," he declared facetiously, accepting a cup of coffee from Rona. "In me you see the latest representative of good old private enterprise!"

"Do you mean you've left the bank?" cried Rona.

Bob was clearly in an expansive mood. "That's right. I've seen it coming for some time, so I've been working up a cosy little connection as an insurance agent, assessor, valuer, and anything that comes along. I've got a snug little office in Tooting, and I roll in at ten or later." He smiled. "I thought I'd pop round and see if you've got any news about the case."

"What news did you expect?" said Houston shrewdly.

"Well, I thought you might have checked up on my tip about Mary Latimer and her visits to The Rising Sun."

"Yes, I looked into that and I'm very grateful for that bit of information. It might prove extremely useful. Now, while you're here, you might be able to help me with one or two other little queries."

"Anything I can do, of course," nodded Bob, lighting a cigarette and settling himself comfortably in his armchair.

"Have you ever heard of a man called A.P. Arnold?"

"Arnold? No, I don't think so. Afraid I can't help you there, inspector."

"You never heard Mary Latimer speak of anyone of that name?"

"I'm quite sure I didn't. I think I told you I never had much to say to the girl." He suddenly leaned forward in his chair. "By the way, didn't I read that you are in charge of this Bloomsbury murder case?"

"That's right."

"A woman named Spedro, wasn't it?"

Houston nodded. "Did Mary Latimer ever refer to her?"

"No, I don't think so." Bob flicked the ash off his cigarette. "Afraid I'm not much use to you this morning, inspector."

Bob Harridge finished his coffee and rose to go. Rona accompanied him to the front door. "What about having dinner with me one evening, to celebrate my escape from the bank?" he asked.

"I'd love to, Bob. But I may have to start rehearsing fairly soon."

"Make it tomorrow night," suggested Bob promptly. "See you at Danilo's – eight o'clock suit you?"

"I'll be there," Rona promised.

*****

Houston finished the morning papers, then set off for the Yard. The first person he saw was Loman, who told him that they had persuaded Carl Knight to allow them to take his fingerprints.

"Any news from Ainsworth Court?" enquired Houston.

"Nothing there in the way of fingerprints."

"And what about Arnold?"

"Still no sign of him."

Houston went off to report to Superintendent Elder concerning the events of the previous evening. Loman had already given him a rough outline of what had happened, and he was anxious to discuss one or two theories with Houston.

Elder was particularly intrigued with the silver penknife belonging to Kelford and was now suspicious that Sir Cedric knew far more than he cared to admit, particularly in view of the fact that he had concealed the information about the second ransom note.

"You need to make some allowances for him, sir," said Houston. "He's a very desperate man."

At that moment there was a knock at the door, and a sergeant came in with a cigarette case. "This was found in Mrs. Spedro's coat pocket, sir," he informed Elder. "We showed it to her husband. He confirmed that it belonged to her, but he didn't know where she got it."

The superintendent turned the case over in his bony hands. It was a slim and expensive-looking case with initials in one corner. "Are those her initials, M.S.?" he asked Houston, passing the case to him.

"That is so," replied Houston, taking the case over to the window. When he came back with it, he pointed out to Elder that the letter S had been changed from an R.

"You sound very pleased with yourself," commented Elder, eyeing him curiously.

"It proves a theory I'd worked out. I'll tell you later, there's no immediate hurry," said Houston.

*****

Rona complimented Bob Harridge on what was obviously a new suit, when she met him in the vestibule of Danilo's. He looked very gratified and murmured something about dressing the part now he was his own boss.

Over dinner Bob became very confidential. "Now I've left the bank, Rona, I feel at liberty to mention something that's been worrying me ever since Dennis's death," he said. "It might have some connection, but on the other hand it might not."

He paused to fill her wine glass, then went on: "Of course, this is all in absolute confidence, but a few months back we had a bit of trouble at the office. Information about customers' private affairs kept leaking out to trade rivals. Several of them came in with definite complaints. If there had been only one case the leakage might have been through other channels, but the fact that there were several pointed to the bank staff as suspects."

"Dennis never said anything about this."

Bob Harridge looked faintly surprised. "I thought perhaps he might have mentioned something, yet it's understandable that he didn't. Well, as a matter of fact, suspicion fell on Dennis. He was closely questioned, and I believe he was watched for quite a time but nothing was ever proved."

"Sir Cedric never said anything about this," said Rona.

"Of course, there was nothing on Dennis's report because they never proved anything."

"Why are you telling me this?" she demanded.

Bob, who had noted her paleness, sounded worried now. "I was only trying to help. It occurred to me that Dennis might possibly have got mixed up with some queer people and refused to do as they asked him."

Rona nodded. It was the most likely explanation of her brother's death she had heard so far — indeed, the only plausible explanation. She made up her mind to speak to Sir Cedric Kelford about it at the earliest opportunity.

*****

It was half past eleven when Rona arrived at Eaton Square, and she was taken up immediately to the large drawing room on the first floor. Sir Cedric was wearing a smoking jacket and slippers and appeared quite pleased to see her. He took her hand and led her to an armchair beside the fire.

"I have been meaning to telephone you for some time about that television play," he told her. "I might be able to introduce you to one or two people who could be interested in putting some money into it." She told him about Ambrose Wyler, and he listened attentively. "You can't do much better than Wyler," he commented. "He's pretty sound from the financial point of view." He stood with his elbow on the mantelpiece and looked down at her. "Now, what's this about your brother?"

Without mentioning Bob Harridge, she told Sir Cedric that she had heard that Dennis was suspected of betraying professional secrets.

Sir Cedric rubbed his chin thoughtfully. "It's true there was a serious leakage at that branch, and your brother came under suspicion," he replied frankly. "I had the whole business thoroughly investigated twice over — it was highly

212

complicated. But I can tell you that there was never any proof that your brother was implicated."

Rona did not say anything, but he could see she was still worried. "As time went on," he continued, "we began to direct our suspicions into quite a different quarter. Any day now, we're hoping to find some definite proof."

"But I thought the leakages had stopped."

He shrugged. "It is very difficult to say when the information actually passes in such cases."

"Then you're quite sure that Dennis wasn't mixed up in it?"

He patted her shoulder reassuringly. "Absolutely. You see, we have every reason to believe —"

The telephone rang abruptly, and he went across to the side table and picked up the receiver. Immediately he heard the voice on the other end, his expression changed. He gave a little gasp and clutched his left lapel. "Susan! Susan!" he exclaimed in a curious, strangled whisper. "Are you there, Susan?"

Then his voice changed. Someone else had clearly taken over at the other end of the line. Rona could hear the faint crackle of a man's voice. "Yes, the case is still here," said Sir Cedric. "That's right ... the money is just as you said ... very well ... I quite understand."

He replaced the receiver and wiped the perspiration from his forehead. Then he turned to Rona and said desperately: "Miss Houston, you've got to help me." He seemed to find some difficulty in getting his breath.

"Aren't you feeling well?" she asked in some concern.

"I'll be all right in a minute." He took a tablet from a small green bottle on the mantelpiece, then swallowed half a glass of water. After that he sat back in an armchair with his eyes

213

closed. "My little girl is still alive," he said softly. "I heard her voice. The man who is holding her came on the line and said that she would be returned if I handed over the ten thousand pounds at once."

"You agreed to that?"

"Of course, but that isn't all. They know that you are here with me, and they insist that you should deliver the money." A cold wave of apprehension swept over Rona. "They want you to take the money to Wimbledon Common," said Kelford.

"Couldn't we telephone my father?" she suggested.

"No, we daren't take the risk," cried Kelford, unable to conceal the desperation in his voice. "They may have the line tapped. Please, Miss Houston, you must help me! You can't let anything happen to that child – you'd never forgive yourself. I swear you'll come to no harm."

She hesitated a moment, then: "All right," she said quietly. "Tell me exactly what they want me to do."

9

Sir Cedric went to the cocktail cabinet and poured a glass of brandy for Rona. She noticed his hand was shaking as he passed it to her. Her own was none too steady!

"Do I have to go there entirely alone?" she asked.

"That's what the man on the phone said. He warned me that this was my last chance. You do realise that I daren't take any more risks?"

"I quite understand," she nodded, some of her confidence returning. "Hadn't you better tell me what I have to do? There's no time to lose."

"It's quite straightforward," Kelford said. "You take my car and drive to Wimbledon Common. You pull into the car park near the Windmill and just sit there. The money will be in a large suitcase in the back of the car. They will bring Susan to the car, you will hand over the suitcase, and they will leave Susan with you. Then you bring her straight back here."

"How will they recognise me?"

"They know my car. And I doubt if there will be any others there at this time of night."

He pressed the bell beside the fireplace and instructed the butler to bring the large suitcase downstairs and place it in the back of the car. Rona stood up and began to put on her gloves, trying to conceal her nervousness by asking him questions about his car.

Five minutes later, she was driving cautiously but with increasing confidence in the direction of Sloane Street. The roads were fairly deserted, and soon she was cruising comfortably at just under thirty miles an hour. The car almost drove itself.

*****

Sergeant O'Donovan had followed Rona from the restaurant to Sir Cedric Kelford's house in Eaton Square. He had stopped his own taxi some thirty yards away, paid the driver, then strolled quietly past the house. He was not far away when the butler brought out the large suitcase and stowed it in the Rolls which stood at the front door. But he felt a trifle conspicuous and was careful to avoid giving the impression that he was watching the house.

He stopped to admire a rakish cream sports car that stood ten yards from the nearest corner, then he moved on again, turned and strolled past the house in leisurely fashion. He turned just in time to see the front door open, and Rona and

Sir Cedric coming down the steps. O'Donovan watched her get in the car and drive off. Sir Cedric stood looking after her for a minute, then went back inside.

As he heard the door slam, O'Donovan was suddenly conscious of the fact that the big car was just disappearing from sight round the far corner of the square. His instinct told him that there was something afoot, and it was important to keep Rona in sight. He moved swiftly over to the sports car and noting that the driver had failed to remove the ignition key he opened the door and climbed behind the wheel. The car started at the first touch, and he was on the tail of the saloon as it crossed Sloane Street. Without very much effort, he kept the big saloon in sight.

O'Donovan waited until Rona was inside the car park near the Windmill, gave her a couple of minutes, then drove in himself. He came to a standstill as unobtrusively as possible, behind two other cars which were parked about twenty yards away. Rona saw the sports car enter the deserted car park. It looked vaguely familiar to her, but she could not recall where she had seen it before.

So far, there had been no sign of life in the car park. Rona sat in the Rolls, wondering what she would do if there were any sort of unpleasantness. When she first heard the footsteps, they seemed to come from the opposite side of the car park from where the other cars were standing. The man was standing beside the car almost before she realised it.

He tapped gently on the window beside the driving seat, and she lowered it at once. He wore a hat pulled down over his eyes, a mackintosh, and a scarf over the lower half of his face. "Will you get out of the car please?" His voice was gruff, and obviously disguised. She did as she was told. He turned his head away from her and asked: "Where is the case?"

"In the back of the car," she replied.

"Stay there," he ordered, and opened the back door of the Rolls. She watched him snap open the catches and push back the lid of the case. After a brief examination of the contents, he closed the lid again and hauled the case out of the car.

"This way," he said curtly.

Rona followed him to a narrow side road off the car park.

A small saloon car was standing there, concealed by a clump of bushes. He signalled to her to stop, set down the case, took a key from his pocket and opened the car door. He switched on the dashboard light, and by its subdued glow she could see the dim figure of a child in the back of the car. The man leaned over and opened the back door. "Come on, Susan," he said in a whisper. "The lady's going to take you home."

The child ran to Rona, who placed a protective arm around her. She took the child's hand, and almost ran with her back to Sir Cedric's car.

*****

O'Donovan had quietly left his car and moved to a point of vantage just behind the car parked some twenty yards from Sir Cedric's Rolls-Royce. He saw the man approach and take away the suitcase, accompanied by Rona. He was in two minds whether to follow them, then decided against it. When Rona returned with the child, O'Donovan went back to the sports car. He waited until the Rolls left the car park, then followed about fifty yards behind.

About a quarter of a mile further along the road, he suddenly noticed a car just about to emerge from a side turning. His powerful headlights picked out the figure of a man at the wheel. O'Donovan saw he had his hat pulled well down and a scarf around his mouth. It was certainly the man who had collected the suitcase, decided O'Donovan as he passed. He slowed down almost at once to let the saloon car pass him.

Was the man trailing Rona for any reason? O'Donovan switched off his headlights and decided to follow him. When the car stopped at the traffic lights in the Kings Road in Chelsea, O'Donovan managed to pull in just behind, in a position that gave him a good view of the driver. The man at the wheel took advantage of the delay to light a cigarette, pulling the scarf from his mouth as he did so.

The flame lit up his taut, lean features, and O'Donovan recognised him at once. He was a one-time notorious West End pickpocket called Fingers Phillips.

*****

In the Fulham Road, Rona caught sight of an empty telephone box and pulled up. She asked Susan if she would like to speak to her daddy and took the child into the box with her. Sir Cedric was overjoyed to hear that everything had gone off without a hitch, and that Susan was unharmed. Rona said: "Now would you do me a favour, Sir Cedric?"

"Yes, of course, anything."

"Would you please telephone my father and tell him what's happened? I think he's probably at the Yard, as he said something about working late."

Sir Cedric agreed at once, and Rona took Susan back to the car. By the time they reached Eaton Square, the little girl was fast asleep. Almost as soon as the car stopped, Rona saw the front door open and Sir Cedric running down the steps, followed by the child's nurse.

Rona switched on the roof light of the car so that he could see the child, then put her finger to her lips. "Take her straight to bed without waking her," she advised. Sir Cedric nodded, picked up Susan and handed her to the nurse.

As Rona switched out the light and climbed out of the driving seat, Sir Cedric caught her hand in his. "I can't begin to thank you …" he mumbled incoherently. He was still trying to find words when the police car swung round the corner and jerked to a standstill.

Before it had stopped, the door opened, and Houston emerged. He came running towards his daughter. "Are you all right, Rona?" he inquired anxiously.

When she had reassured him, they all went into the house. Kelford led the way into the drawing room, where he insisted on opening a bottle of champagne. As he was busying himself finding the glasses, Houston turned to Rona and said in a low tone: "Did you notice anyone following you?"

Rona wrinkled her forehead in an effort to remember. "I don't think so," she said at last. "Why?"

"We've had Sergeant O'Donovan tailing you for days. We were expecting something like this."

"Wait a minute," she said quickly. "I remember seeing a cream sports car at the Windmill, and I caught sight of it once in the driving mirror on the way back. I thought it was just a coincidence."

"It might have been," grunted Houston. "I hope it was O'Donovan. He may have got on to something. I'd better dash back to the Yard right away, in case he's been on the phone."

After they had finished their drinks, Houston suggested that Rona should accompany him to the Yard, but Kelford insisted on taking her home himself. He refilled her glass and his own. "From now on I look upon Rona as one of the family," he told Houston, raising his glass to her.

*****

At the Yard, there was no message from O'Donovan. Houston telephoned Superintendent Elder at his home and had no sooner replaced the receiver than the bell rang. It was the hall sergeant, announcing the arrival of Bob Harridge. "Send him up," said Houston. He wondered what Harridge could want at that late hour.

When Bob arrived, he seemed a trifle nervous. "I tried to telephone you at home as soon as Rona left me," he said, "but there was no reply. Then I phoned here and they said they expected you back some time, so I thought I'd drop in on the off chance."

"Is it anything important?" asked Houston.

Harridge frowned. "I don't really know," he said candidly. "It might be. You see, I was very worried about Rona. She acted most mysteriously and dashed off almost as soon as we'd finished dinner. I wondered if you'd seen or heard of her since then."

Houston smiled. "She's all right, Bob. I saw her twenty minutes ago."

Bob Harridge looked extremely relieved, and Houston was just about to tell him of Rona's adventures since she left him but was prevented by the telephone ringing.

It was O'Donovan. "I'm speaking from a call box in Whitechapel Road," he said. "Is Miss Houston all right? Did she get back safely?"

"She's all right," replied Houston. "What happened to you?"

O'Donovan quickly described how he had followed the saloon car. "You remember Fingers Phillips, inspector? I've tailed him to a little tobacconist's shop in Malabar Street in Whitechapel. He's parked the car down a side entry and switched off the lights, so it looks as if he's there for the night. Incidentally, I should imagine he's taken the case in with him as it isn't in the car now."

Houston asked O'Donovan to repeat the address and made a note of it on his pad. "Get back there as soon as you can," he ordered, a note of excitement creeping into his voice. He replaced the receiver, then picked up the internal phone to make arrangements for the Flying Squad to collect him.

"Sorry I've got to dash off, Bob," he said. "But you needn't worry about Rona. We're keeping an eye on her."

*****

Ten minutes later, the squad cars were approaching Whitechapel through the deserted city streets. The driver of Houston's car knew Malabar Street, and Houston instructed him to park as unobtrusively as possible on the nearest bomb site.

The drivers remained with their cars, ready for a quick getaway. Two men accompanied Houston, and two more went off to explore possible means of egress at the back of Malabar Street. They found O'Donovan standing in a doorway almost opposite the tobacconists. "There's a light at the back of the shop and another upstairs," he pointed out in a whisper.

Houston waited a couple of minutes for the benefit of the men at the rear of the house, then crossed the road, taking O'Donovan with him. The detective pointed out the saloon car standing in an archway near the shop. Under this same opening was a side door, which apparently led into the living quarters. Houston went round and knocked sharply on the door. There was silence. He knocked again, and a second later they heard heavy footsteps.

A middle-aged man in shirtsleeves stood before them. "What is it?" he demanded in a surly voice. "Don't you know the place is shut?"

Houston looked at him for a moment, then said: "You remember me, George Waters? The safe deposit job that went wrong in Holborn, just before the war?"

Waters took a step back. "You can't pin anythin' on me," he said. "I been goin' straight for ten years now."

"We've got nothing against you – yet," Houston reassured him. "We're here to have a word with Fingers Phillips. If you aren't mixed up with him in this little job, then you're in the clear."

"I only let him a room. I don't know anythin' about him," protested Waters.

"All right then, where is he?"

Waters led them to the foot of the stairs and pointed to a door on the first landing. Houston nodded to O'Donovan to accompany him. "Don't try any tricks, Waters," he said over his shoulder. "We've got the house surrounded."

When Houston knocked sharply on the bedroom door, there was the sound of a scuffle followed by the slamming of a cupboard door. "Open up, Phillips!" snapped Houston.

"There's no lock on the door," came the reply from inside.

Houston turned the knob and went in. Phillips, who had been standing behind the door, immediately tried to escape as the police officers entered the room. There was a brief struggle, but Phillips was plainly out of condition. O'Donovan pushed him into a chair and stood over him while Houston began to look round the shabbily furnished room.

The most likely hiding place was a large cupboard near the window. He went across and found it locked. "Have you got the key?" he asked, turning to Phillips. "It'll save us breaking it open."

Reluctantly Phillips fumbled in his waistcoat pocket and produced the key. Houston opened the cupboard, and found the large suitcase hidden under a pile of old clothes and newspapers. He pulled it out, snapped back the catches, took a quick look inside and closed it again. "Anything you want to say?" he asked, turning to the man in the chair.

"I didn't know what was in it. I'm only collecting it for somebody," said Phillips sullenly.

"That's a lie for a start," said O'Donovan. "I saw you hand over the Kelford child."

"We know a lot more than you think, Phillips," said Houston smoothly. "You'd better open up, or things might get very tough for you before long."

Phillips was plainly beginning to lose his nerve. "I only did as I was told," he protested. "I collected the kid, handed her over and picked up this case."

"Where are you taking it?"

"I wasn't takin' it anywhere. He's goin' to call for it."

"When?"

"In the next day or two."

"And who is he?"

Before Phillips could answer, they heard the sound of quick footsteps running from the back of the house towards the stairs. Houston went out and peered over the banisters. A young man was standing with one foot on the bottom stair, looking up at him. They eyed each other in silence for some seconds, then Houston said slowly: "Were you looking for something, Mr. Knight?"

10

Carl Knight made no immediate reply to Houston's question. The inspector walked slowly down the stairs. Carl watched him approach, but made no effort to move.

"I had no idea you were familiar with this part of the world, Mr. Knight," continued Houston deliberately. "What exactly are you doing here?"

Suddenly Knight's pale features split into a sardonic grin. "I should have thought you'd have guessed that, inspector. I'm an author, looking for local colour."

"But what brings you to this particular address?"

Carl Knight shrugged. "Maybe I shouldn't answer that, inspector. It might get Waters into trouble. After all, his shop has been closed about five hours."

"What are you getting at?" snapped Houston.

"Just that George Waters lets me have a couple of packets of cigarettes at the side door after he's closed. It's against the law, I know, but I hope you won't hold it against him. He's sorry for chain smokers like myself."

"Have you seen him tonight?"

"No, he doesn't seem to be about."

"Stay where you are for a minute," ordered Houston, then called to O'Donovan to bring Fingers Phillips down. The detective had taken the precaution of slipping the handcuffs on Phillips, and Houston saw that Carl Knight noticed this. As they reached the bottom of the stairs Phillips suddenly seemed to recognise Knight, who looked straight past him.

O'Donovan took his prisoner out to the police car. Another officer came through the side door, went upstairs and returned with the large suitcase.

"Is this a police raid of some sort?" asked Knight in a puzzled tone.

"Did you know that man who passed you just now?"

"Never seen him before in my life. Why was he handcuffed?"

"He's involved in the kidnapping of Sir Cedric Kelford's daughter."

Knight seemed genuinely astonished. "Good Lord! I'd almost forgotten about that."

"Scotland Yard has a very long memory," said Houston curtly. "I hope for your sake you're telling the truth when you say you don't know that man."

Knight was about to protest once again, but there was a sound in the darkened shop and the shirt-sleeved figure of George Waters emerged. "I got nothing to do with this, inspector," he said hoarsely. "Fingers Phillips asked me to fix him up with a room, and that's all I know."

"You don't know this gentleman, by any chance?" queried Houston.

Waters' eyes narrowed, and just as Carl Knight seemed about to speak, he shook his head. "Never seen him before, inspector. Is he a pal of Phillips?"

"That remains to be seen," said Houston grimly.

"But you've been selling me cigarettes for weeks now," protested Knight desperately.

Waters obstinately shook his head. "I don't remember," he persisted.

"You'd better come along to the station, and we'll find out just how much you do remember," said Houston. He turned

225

to Carl Knight. "Perhaps you'd look in at the Yard tomorrow morning, Mr. Knight. I hope we'll have a little more of this business sorted out by then."

*****

When Houston looked in at the police station early next morning, he was greeted by a very worried station sergeant.

"Trouble?" asked Houston at once.

The sergeant nodded. "Afraid you won't get anything else out of Phillips. He's dead."

"How the devil …?" began Houston angrily.

"He had a capsule hidden on him somewhere."

"But surely he was searched?"

"He must have had it concealed in his mouth."

Houston began to pace impatiently up and down the sergeant's office. "Just when we've really started to sort things out, this has to happen," he said savagely.

"I'm sorry, inspector. Is it any use your having a talk to Waters?"

Houston nodded, and Waters was brought in. Houston questioned him for half an hour without eliciting any real information. He was particularly insistent that he had never seen Carl Knight before.

When Houston got back to the Yard, he found that Superintendent Elder had already been acquainted with the events of the night before. "That settles the Kelford side of the case, thank the Lord," said Elder. "But we've quite a way to go yet, Houston. Did you get anything out of Fingers Phillips?"

Houston told him of Phillips's death. "He wouldn't have done a thing like that if he hadn't been guilty of something more than acting as an agent," mused Elder.

226

"He might have been scared," suggested Houston. "In fact, I'm pretty sure he was completely terrified of the head of this set-up."

"That may well be," nodded Elder. "Though I don't see how anyone could get at him while he was in custody. Still, the fact remains that he's dead and there's no alternative but to write him off. Anyhow, the Assistant Commissioner will be pleased the Kelford case has made some progress. By the way, he's called a special meeting for this evening. He wants to discuss recent developments."

"I'll be there," said Houston.

*****

The evening conference, over which the Assistant Commissioner presided, was not such an ordeal as Houston had anticipated. The Assistant Commissioner complimented him on getting Sir Cedric Kelford's ransom money back, then went on: "It would be a help, Houston, if you could give us some indication of your theory about who is behind this set-up."

"I think it's a little early to say, sir," replied Houston, "though there are signs that we should make an arrest fairly soon."

"Don't you think it's about time you did something about this man Knight?" demanded Superintendent Elder. "We have suspected him of being involved in the murder of your boy and Mrs. Spedro."

"It isn't easy to prove anything against him," said Houston. "In fact, I very much doubt that he killed Mrs. Spedro. I've discovered that she was a kleptomaniac, and she had several stolen articles in her possession when we found her. I think she stole my daughter's scarf when she visited Knight's flat. She was wearing the scarf when she visited the mysterious Arnold, and someone strangled her with it."

"Knight could have followed her there and murdered her," persisted Elder.

"That's possible," agreed Houston.

"It looks to me as if Knight may well be this mysterious Arnold," grunted the superintendent.

The Assistant Commissioner closed the files. "All right," he said. "But I want you to keep me in touch with every development. Telephone me at home if necessary."

*****

Big Ben was chiming ten o'clock as Houston left the Yard, and he decided to take a short walk along the Embankment on his way home.

He was suddenly conscious of a man standing under a light in the Embankment wall and gazing aimlessly across the river. His hands were thrust deep in the pockets of his overcoat, his hair was dishevelled for he wore no hat, but there was something familiar about the set of his shoulders.

As Houston came closer, he saw it was Dr. Spedro. The doctor looked up as Houston approached, and did not seem at all surprised. "Hello, inspector," he said in a listless tone.

Houston looked at him curiously. "You wanted to see me?"

"I had to see you," said Spedro, a note of desperation creeping into his voice. "I'm so terribly worried. I want to tell you," he said slowly, "about the yellow windmill."

The inspector regarded Spedro keenly, but it was not easy to see him clearly in the light from the street lamp. "Do you

228

want to talk here, or shall we go back to the Yard and take an official statement?" asked Houston.

Spedro hesitated for a moment, then replied quietly: "We will go to the Yard, if you don't mind."

"Yes, of course," Houston readily agreed. He took Spedro back to his office, gave him a cigarette, and telephoned for a sergeant to take shorthand notes. The sergeant came in and settled himself unobtrusively behind Spedro. He nodded to Houston, to signify he was ready.

"Just over ten years ago, when I first came to this country, I was very hard up," Spedro began. "My studies were expensive, I had to live, and I had only a very small income from part-time hospital work. I desperately needed two hundred pounds, and I became involved with a money-lender. He suggested an easy way for me to earn the money, but of course it was against the law."

"You accepted?"

Spedro nodded. "Yes, I accepted," he said quietly. "I went to a large country house in Hertfordshire and met a strange young man who asked me to supply him with certain drugs. I was able to steal the drugs from one of the hospitals."

"I understand," answered Houston. "Go on."

"Some years later, when I was established in Wimpole Street, a young man came to see me. He reminded me that we had met before."

"You mean he blackmailed you?"

"It's been going on for years now," nodded Spedro. "At first he simply demanded money, then when he realised my finances were limited he began to make use of me in other ways."

"Do we know this young man?"

229

Spedro hesitated for a moment, then said: "His name is Carl Knight."

Houston leaned forward. "Why didn't you come to us?"

Spedro drew his hand wearily across his forehead. "I was well established in London by this time. As long as Knight's demands were not too excessive, it seemed simpler to obey them."

"So, he began to employ you in other directions," prompted Houston, while the sergeant busily turned a page in his notebook.

"Yes. He would frequently borrow my car, which used to worry me because I had no idea what he wanted it for. He took it the night that man Nobbler Williams was killed."

"I had a hunch it was Knight," murmured Houston.

"After a time," continued Spedro, "my wife could see I was deeply concerned about something and she began to get suspicious. Eventually she discovered I was being blackmailed by Knight. She was a very forthright person, and she immediately tackled him about it. He told her that he was only the tool of another man named Arnold, who had a flat at Ainsworth Court. He suggested that she should tackle Arnold, and she agreed to do so. When she got to Ainsworth Court, Carl Knight was waiting for her."

"You mean that he was the mysterious Mr. Arnold?"

"There's no doubt about it. When he'd been drinking one night, he boasted to me about the dance he'd led you over a typewriter that he'd sold and bought back in the character of Mr. Arnold."

"So Mr. Arnold was just a myth," mused Houston. "Carl Knight certainly has a lively imagination. What was his connection with your patient, Mary Latimer?"

"He was having an affair with her, and she was madly in love with him. Eventually he grew tired of Mary, and became a shade frightened because he'd told her so much. Also, she realised that he was interested in your daughter, and this made her more dangerous than ever. There was only one way out for Carl – he made me take her into my nursing home."

"But she absconded," Houston reminded him.

"Yes, she recovered from the effects of the drug I had given her and managed to get away. She went straight to the television studios to warn your daughter against Knight, but unfortunately, he forestalled her. He murdered Mary Latimer and hid her body in your car."

"And what about the yellow windmill she was clutching when we found her?"

"That was stolen from my consulting room. I missed it after he had been to see me to arrange about Mary Latimer."

"But I saw it there when I came to question you."

Spedro shook his head. "What you saw was one exactly like it that I had taken from my wife's room. I had an idea that Carl was going to throw suspicion on me, so I took steps to thwart him."

Houston nodded. "Now, let's go back a step further," he said, "to the kidnapping of the Kelford girl. Are you suggesting he was responsible for that too?"

Spedro stubbed out his cigarette. "I've no proof, but I'm fairly certain that he was. He took my car about that time."

"It's surprising that a busy young man like that ever had time to write a play," commented Houston drily.

"He didn't. It was written by Mary Latimer." Houston whistled softly. "You see how much she was under his spell," went on Spedro. "He told her that the play would stand a much better chance if it were presented under his name. That gave him a new 'front' – the busy author. He made a great show of re-writing scenes, but it was Mary who actually did the work. I managed to get that out of her myself."

Spedro nervously plucked at his lapels. "You can take it from me, inspector, that Carl Knight is the man you're looking for, and I must admit I won't be sorry when he's in custody." He mopped his forehead with a large handkerchief.

Houston asked him several more questions but was unable to find any flaw in his story. He picked up the telephone and gave instructions for a warrant to be made out for Knight's arrest, then he telephoned Sergeant O'Donovan and told him to stand by with a police car.

*****

On the way to Carl Knight's flat on the Cromwell Road, Houston briefly outlined to Sergeant O'Donovan the salient facts of Dr. Spedro's statement. They called at the local station and picked up two extra men who were well acquainted with the topography of the neighbourhood. When they arrived at their destination, Houston sent them to the back of the house.

The house appeared to be in darkness, and the outer front door was closed. Houston rang the bell twice, and presently they heard shuffling footsteps. When the caretaker opened the front door, it was obvious she had slipped on an old coat over her nightdress.

"Is Mr. Knight at home?" demanded Houston.

She indicated the front door of Carl Knight's flat, and retired downstairs. Carl answered Houston's knock almost immediately. He was fully dressed, and the inspector noticed a raincoat flung across a chair in the hall.

"This is rather a late call, inspector. I was just in the middle of packing." He led the way into the lounge.

"Going away?" asked Houston, noticing that Knight looked rather paler than usual.

"I'd planned to take a few days off."

"This is my colleague, Sergeant O'Donovan," said Houston. "We want to ask you a few questions."

Knight leaned back against the sideboard, hands clasped across his elbows. "This seems to be a very solemn occasion," he said lightly. "Perhaps you'll tell me the reason for this visit?"

Houston did not move from the doorway. "I've had a long talk with Dr. Spedro," he said quietly. "As a result of that conversation, I am charging you with the murders of Mary Latimer and Margarita Spedro. There'll probably be further charges, but we won't go into that now." He added the routine caution, then said: "You'd better get your hat and coat, Mr. Knight."

Carl Knight moved away from the sideboard and crossed the room. "This is sheer melodrama," he protested. "That man Spedro must be mad. I suspected as much the last time I saw him. The fellow's got some sort of kink, inspector. Surely you could see that for yourself?"

"On the contrary, I'm quite certain he was telling the truth," retorted Houston.

"I shall need one or two things from my bedroom, if you can give me five minutes."

"Make it two," said Houston, "and leave the bedroom door open."

Knight nodded, then went into the bedroom, which overlooked the street. Houston saw him pick up a spectacle

233

case, then move over to a small table. Suddenly there was a tinkle of glass, and Knight's hand went to his mouth.

Houston rushed into the bedroom. Before he could reach him, Knight had collapsed. "He's taken a capsule," cried Houston, as O'Donovan followed him into the bedroom. "Better get the men up from below, in case we have to carry him down."

The sergeant went running out of the flat, and Houston crossed into the hall and telephoned for an ambulance. As he put the receiver down, he heard O'Donovan blow his whistle as a signal to the men below. He went back to the bedroom and was immediately conscious of a gust of night air stirring the window curtains.

The room was empty. Carl Knight had vanished.

11

Houston looked quickly round the room and noticed that the curtains, which had been drawn across the window, were stirring. He strode over and pulled them aside.

The French window opened outwards on to a balcony. He stepped out, and the first thing that caught his eye was the beam from a powerful torch shining from below. Houston followed the beam and saw that it was focused on a figure clinging to the wall some twenty feet from him. Carl Knight had climbed along the decorative stone cornice that ran round the building and was presumably trying to escape through one of the other flats.

As Sergeant O'Donovan came out of the front door, Houston leaned over and called to him to keep Knight under observation. Then he ran quickly out of the flat and on to the landing. He rang the bell of the next flat, and when a somewhat dishevelled young man answered it he rapidly explained the position.

The young man quickly led the way to a room at the end of a short passage, and they ran over to the window which looked out on to the street. Houston expected to see a silhouette loom across the window. "Don't switch on the light," he said to the young man. However, when he got to the window and looked out along the building, there was no sign of Carl Knight. Nor was the torch focused in his direction. Instead it shed a concentrated pool of light into the area thirty feet below. O'Donovan and a constable were just running down the stone steps.

Houston leaned out of the window and called to O'Donovan to ask what had happened. "The stonework gave way under him," was the reply.

"Is he unconscious?"

"Yes, sir. Pretty bad fall – caught his back on the railings."

"I'll come down."

Two minutes later, Houston could see at a glance that Carl Knight would be in no condition to answer questions for some hours. He was still unconscious when the ambulance arrived. The house surgeon who accompanied it took one look at the inert figure and shook his head. The inspector gave him his home telephone number and asked him to ring if Knight recovered consciousness.

Houston then returned to the flat with O'Donovan and searched it from top to bottom. He sorted out a number of letters and papers which appeared to have some bearing on Knight's nefarious activities and stuffed them into a briefcase to examine at his leisure.

They left a constable in charge of the flat, and O'Donovan drove Houston home in the police car. "Looks as if we might be able to close the case pretty soon," said O'Donovan, when he pulled up at the front door.

Houston shook his head dubiously. "There are quite a lot of questions to be answered yet, sergeant," he said. He wished O'Donovan goodnight, picked up the briefcase and went inside. He took the case into the drawing room, where he found Bob Harridge talking to Rona.

"Is there any more news?" asked Rona.

Houston briefly outlined what had happened an hour before. Bob Harridge seemed very interested. "I'll hand it to you, inspector," he said at last. "You've been moving pretty fast these past few days. I suppose this clears up the yellow windmill mystery?"

"I'm afraid not, Bob," said Houston. "But I expect more developments fairly soon."

The telephone rang, and Houston went out into the hall to answer it. It was the doctor at the hospital. Carl Knight had recovered consciousness, but his injuries were very serious and he was not expected to survive.

As Houston was talking, Bob Harridge came past, silently mouthing goodnight to him. When the front door closed, Houston replaced the receiver and said: "Carl Knight is asking for you, Rona."

Her eyes widened. "Why should he want to see me?"

"The doctor seems to think there's something on his mind. They don't expect him to last the day out."

For a moment she seemed to be at a loss, then she suddenly announced: "I'll go, of course. It may be something important."

Houston nodded. "I'll take you," he said. "Better get a warm coat – it's turned very chilly now." Rona went upstairs to change, and Houston returned to the drawing room.

When Rona was coming downstairs a few minutes later, the front doorbell rang, and she answered it. Bob Harridge was standing there. "I'm terribly sorry to bother you again," he said, coming inside, "but I'm afraid I went off with the wrong briefcase."

They went into the drawing room and Houston rose from an armchair, in which he had been meditatively sipping a small glass of whisky. Harridge explained about the briefcase, which proved to be almost identical to that which Houston had brought from Carl Knight's. Bob picked up his own case, which had apparently fallen to the side of the settee, and they went out into the hall with Rona explaining about their visit to the hospital.

* * * * *

Houston drove Rona's car through the quiet streets at a good pace, and they were at the hospital in less than half an hour. He waited for her, while a sister conducted her into the ward where Carl Knight lay. When she came back, she was obviously upset, and Houston did not speak until they were out in the car once more.

"Why was he so anxious to see you?"

"He was most eager to deny that he had anything to do with Dennis's death. He told me about the others – Mary Latimer, Mrs. Spedro and Nobbler Williams – and about Susan Kelford's abduction. He took the blame for all of them, but he kept saying time and time again that he didn't kill Dennis."

"Why did he kill Nobbler?"

"Because he discovered that you had once done Nobbler a favour, and he was frightened that Nobbler might turn informer – which, of course, he did."

Houston nodded. "And did he explain about the yellow windmill?"

"Yes, he had to attract the little girl's attention with some toy or other, and he picked on a yellow windmill because he knew that Dr. Spedro had one on his mantelpiece. He also knew –"

Houston interrupted: "That if the car was identified and Spedro was interviewed, we were almost bound to see the yellow windmill and suspect the doctor." Rona nodded. "He seems to have thought of everything," said Houston grimly, "but do you think he was telling the truth about Dennis?"

"I'm certain of it. What point would there have been in his lying to me?"

"Yes, I'm inclined to agree with you, particularly in view of some other evidence that's come along."

It was just then that Rona noticed that he was driving in the direction of Eaton Square. "I've got to see Sir Cedric right away," he informed her somewhat cryptically.

"But at this time of the morning?"

"An hour one way or the other might make all the difference."

*****

The first pale streaks of dawn were beginning to break over the city when Houston rang the doorbell of the Euston Square mansion. Sir Cedric was down in a few minutes, waving aside Houston's apologies. "I'm always up at six-thirty – before breakfast is my favourite working time."

He took them into a small morning room and switched on the electric fire. "Now, inspector, what's the trouble?"

Houston opened his briefcase and took out several sheets of paper, which he passed to Sir Cedric. The banker gave them one glance and caught his breath in a little gasp of surprise. "They're photocopies of the plans for the Cranfern-Raydown merger. We're still trying to discover how that leaked out."

"Presumably, you had the originals in the possession of the bank?" queried Houston.

"Yes, of course. The scheme was put up to us by both groups. Somebody got the advance information and brought off a big coup on the Stock Exchange, but we always thought the leakage was at the companies' end." He hesitated a moment, then asked: "Can you tell us where these copies came from?"

"They were in the possession of an ex-employee of yours called Bob Harridge. I removed them from his briefcase when he took mine in mistake for his own. He's probably discovered they're missing by this time, which is why I had to call on you so early."

Rona, who had been looking from one to the other without speaking for some minutes, suddenly said: "Has this any connection with Dennis?"

"It's almost certainly the reason Bob Harridge killed him. Dennis was obviously going to give the game away."

Instead of calling the butler, Sir Cedric accompanied Houston to the front door himself. "I didn't want to upset Rona," he said, "but we've had a very thorough investigation. We've taken the matter to Scotland Yard — not your department, of course — and they've pretty well pinned it down to Harridge and Dennis."

"Thank you for telling me, Sir Cedric."

"You won't say anything to Rona yet?" queried Sir Cedric anxiously. "She rather idolised her brother, and she's had far too much worry lately."

"You're very considerate."

"Not at all. I'm eternally in her debt. What's more, I greatly admire her. She's a fine girl, inspector, with far more character than most. It would upset me very much to see her hurt in any way."

*****

On the way back to the Yard, Houston began to figure things out. Somehow Dennis had obtained those photocopies, then had hesitated about handing them over to Bob Harridge. He may even have decided to destroy them or give them to the police. Obviously Harridge had determined to prevent that happening at all costs.

He had called on that fatal evening when Dennis was alone watching Rona's play on television. He had asked for the photocopies which Dennis had refused to hand over. After killing Dennis, Harridge had scrawled the yellow windmill on the television set, guessing it would almost certainly be linked with the crimes since attributed to Carl Knight. Then he had searched Dennis's room, but without finding the photocopies – they were hidden in the secret pocket of the book given by Mrs. Spedro to Dennis.

Later Harridge had returned when Rona had surprised him. That attempt too had been abortive. He had been hanging round the house ever since the murder, presumably paying attentions to Rona but actually on the alert to search Dennis's room yet again.

At the Yard, Houston took out a warrant for the arrest of Bob Harridge whose address he found on a card Bob had given him recently in connection with his insurance business. It was now nearly seven o'clock, and he knew that Harridge would be sure to make a bolt for freedom as soon as he discovered that the photocopies were missing from his briefcase. However, the police car lost no time in getting down to Richmond.

Accompanied by one of the Flying Squad men, Houston went up the steps of the Victorian mansion where Harridge lived. They rang twice before the door opened, to disclose an elderly woman with her hair in grips. When Houston asked about Bob Harridge she shook her head. "He went about five minutes ago," she replied.

"Have you any idea where he was going?"

"No, sir. He took all his things and paid what he owed."

"Did he go by car?"

"No, he's sold that. He went off in a taxi."

Houston went round to the nearest cab rank and found three drivers assembled in the shelter. They told him there had been a call from Harridge's address, to take a passenger to Victoria Station.

The police car headed for Victoria right away. Houston leapt out of the car almost as soon as it had stopped and grabbed the arm of the nearest porter. "Is there a train due out now?" he snapped.

The porter looked puzzled for a moment, then said: "Boat train's just leaving – platform six."

Houston called to the other two men, who were just getting out of the car: "Search the other platforms! I'll look after platform six." He was through the barrier before the startled ticket inspector could challenge him and flung himself into the last compartment of the boat train as it slid smoothly along the platform.

He sat down for a moment to recover his breath, then he went into the corridor and began to walk slowly along the train, stopping at each compartment to scrutinise the occupants. When he reached the final coach, he was beginning to suspect the flash of intuition that had told him that Harridge would be on this train. Halfway down the coach a compartment door suddenly slid open, and he saw Bob Harridge quickly withdraw into the compartment.

Houston took three quick steps along the corridor and pulled back the door. Bob Harridge was facing him in an empty compartment. "Better stay out of here, inspector," said Harridge backing slowly towards the outside door. He had shaved off his moustache, revealing thin, narrow lips.

"Now don't be a fool, Harridge!" exclaimed Houston. "You can't possibly hope to escape now that —" As the inspector advanced into the compartment, Harridge fumbled for the catch of the door with his left hand. His right slid into his inside pocket.

"You don't get me that easily, inspector," he said, and Houston found himself looking into the muzzle of a revolver. Harridge's left hand found the catch of the door at the moment the train lurched over a set of points.

Houston made a low dive at him. Harridge was so taken by surprise that the revolver fell from his hand, but he recovered sufficiently to catch Houston a glancing blow on the side of the head with his left fist. Houston clutched desperately at his opponent, realising the odds were against him, for Harridge was twenty years younger and sturdily built.

At length Harridge broke free and grabbed at the revolver which had fallen on the seat. Houston clutched his arm and they struggled for some seconds, then the train gave another lurch which sent Houston reeling away from Harridge, who caught him square under the chin with his right fist.

As Houston collapsed on the seat, Harridge pushed the revolver in his pocket and pulled back the catch of the door. The train was travelling at a good speed now, but Harridge poised himself ready to jump. The rush of air revived Houston, who immediately made a grab at Harridge's nearest leg. Harridge quickly brought up his other knee into the pit of Houston's stomach, kicked himself free again – and jumped.

Houston just caught sight of Harridge's head disappearing down a steep embankment. The inspector was badly winded, and it was a minute or two before he could stagger to his feet and reach for the communication cord.

An hour later, a small search party discovered the body of Bob Harridge in a culvert at the foot of the embankment. His neck was broken.

*****

In a small drawing room at Sir Cedric Kelford's house in Eaton Square, Houston sipped his second glass of sherry as he watched Rona playing with little Susan.

"You must feel very relieved it's all over, inspector," said Sir Cedric, leaning against the mantelpiece and sipping his sherry.

"It's certainly a weight off my mind," admitted Houston. "I was more worried about Rona than anything else. Now she'll be able to concentrate on her stage work again."

"I'm not worrying about that, darling," said Rona, squeezing his arm affectionately. He noticed for the first time that she was wearing a diamond ring on her engagement finger.

Houston looked from Rona to Sir Cedric, somewhat taken aback. "What's been going on here?" he demanded.

Rona laughed. "It's all right, darling," she reassured him. "I'm just tackling a completely new role – that's all."

THE MAN WHO BEAT THE PANEL

Published in *TV Mirror* in six parts, 16 April – 21 May 1955

This is by far the shortest of the four novellas, and it is the weakest. One can only speculate that Durbridge was having to observe stipulations by *TV Mirror* regarding word count and overall length, and that this prevented him from displaying his usual flair for multiple twists and turns and a genuine "whodunit?" element. Indeed, to speculate further, it is quite likely that Durbridge was not satisfied with this story himself – because seven years later he revised and expanded it almost beyond recognition, and his new version appeared in Germany as *Mitten ins Herz* in the magazine *Bild und Funk*, in nine instalments, 1962-63.

There is no evidence that the new version has been published in English, nor is it likely to appear because newspapers and magazines today are woefully deficient in their publication of fiction. Information from Dr. Georg Pagitz, the foremost expert on Durbridge in German, reveals *Mitten ins Herz* to be a very different story from *The Man Who Beat the Panel*. Although a few of the original characters appear, most of the others are re-named or entirely new – and the plot revolves around a different type of crime syndicate, with alterations to the murder victims, murder methods, and even the perpetrator!

THE MAN WHO BEAT THE PANEL

1

Michael Lance pushed back his soft felt hat a couple of inches, and sat waiting for the commissionaire to open the gates of the Commodore Film Studios. "What goes on, Fred?" he asked, as the car drew level with the man in uniform.

"They're still busy on the picture, Mr. Lance. That Swedish girl started work yesterday."

"Thanks for the tip, Fred," replied Michael solemnly, slowly releasing the clutch and steering his car towards the largest of the sound stages. A tiny frown wrinkled his forehead, as he tried to recall what he had read about this new actress.

Her name was Carel something-or-other, and after her hit in a sensational Swedish film the Commodore Studio had offered her a supporting role in their current epic. He silently reproached himself for not remembering more about the girl. The trouble was that his heart was not in this job of glamourising the entertainment world. He had been doing it for five years and needed a change. But his show business feature had become quite a success, and all his pleas to the editor of the *Evening Comet* had so far been fruitless.

Michael Lance yearned for the sordid realities of life and was frankly bored with the artificial extravagances he reported week after week. He had always wanted to be a crime reporter. During the three years he had spent at Oxford, he had read widely on the subject of criminology and it still fascinated him. But there was no vacancy for a crime expert on the *Evening Comet*. An elderly journalist named Ben Dickens had held this job for over twenty-five years and looked good for another quarter of a century. Ben was a rule-of-thumb reporter, using only facts passed on to him by the police.

Michael felt this was an old-fashioned approach and was insistent that the modern crime reporter should bring to the job all the imagination and unorthodox initiative of the professional criminal investigator. But he had no wish to leave the *Comet*, as he liked the editor and had a number of close friends on the staff. Moreover, his job was not exacting, as he was only expected to turn in his weekly Show News and an occasional article or news story.

Chester Lyle, the studios' publicity man, was waiting for Michael and took him directly on to the set. There he had a word with Harvey Gray, who was directing the picture, and a brief interview with leading lady Jean Maybury. He was so busy absorbing the studio gossip that he forgot all about the Swedish actress, until he went into the canteen with Lyle.

He saw her almost as soon as he stepped through the door. She was sitting by herself at a corner table and looked up at him as he passed by. "Just a minute," said Lyle. "I'd like you to meet Carel Helvin, who has quite a nice little part in this picture."

Carel Helvin raised her dark blue eyes. "Little is right," she said in a strange, unemotional tone. "Two scenes and a close-up."

Lyle pulled out two chairs from a nearby table. "Maybe we can think up a story about you for Mr. Lance's column," he suggested.

The girl shrugged. "I have told you all there is to tell," she said softly.

Michael was intrigued. An actress disdaining publicity! This was indeed an unusual state of affairs. He fired a number

247

of questions at her, but she answered quietly and in a deprecating tone and lit a cigarette. As she flicked her lighter, he noticed she was wearing an unusual ring. It was quite large without being ostentatious and had the head of a falcon designed on a gold background. He guessed that it was of foreign origin.

When they returned to the studio floor, Lyle apologised for Carel's behaviour. "Sorry there was nothing for you there," he said. "She's been the same with three of the other press boys. I thought perhaps you might be luckier, but obviously she's just plain dumb."

"On the contrary," said Michael quietly, "I've an idea there's a very good story behind those eyes – a very good story."

He saw no reason to change his opinion when he watched Carel Helvin act a short scene with Jean Maybury. The Swedish girl made the star look like a recruit from an acting academy. Every tiny movement, each twitch of the mouth or lift of the eyes, conveyed the exact meaning of her lines and redoubled their intensity. Michael would have liked to continue his talk with her, but as soon as the scene was over she went straight off the set, and since Lyle was anxious for him to interview the male lead Jeff Dixon he made no attempt to follow her.

*****

On his return to town, Michael sorted out the stills he had brought back from the studio and selected a photograph of the Swedish girl with Jeff Dixon. He carefully cut the "heart-throb" out of the picture, then added the caption *Star to Watch – Carel Helvin*. He surveyed his handiwork with considerable satisfaction. The picture was far more effective than the snappiest gossip paragraph.

It took him just over an hour to type the rest of his feature, then he carefully placed the cover on his machine and took the article to Barry Ford, the features editor. As usual, Barry was sucking peppermints and looking very worried. He flung Michael's copy into his in-tray without even looking at it. "You're the chap who fancies his chance as a crime reporter," he said.

"I can dream, can't I?" retorted Michael.

"Well, it looks as if your dream's come true. Ben Dickens has had a heart attack and will be away for two or three weeks at least. Do you want to see if you can make crime pay?"

"I can do it all right," said Michael. "And my own column too, providing you let me down lightly on the diary jobs."

The features editor nodded. "We'll give it a trial for a week or so. If it doesn't work out, maybe I can arrange for you to have some help."

"Suits me," said Michael, looking very pleased with himself.

Barry Ford smiled, as he knew this was the chance Michael had been waiting for. "Hope you have a wonderful crime, Mr. Lance," he said.

*****

Soon after eleven the next morning, Michael was scanning the early edition of the paper. He was very pleased with his column, which had come out rather well, especially the picture of Carel Helvin.

He was reading the column for the second time, when the telephone rang. "This is Carel Helvin," said a voice at the other end of the line. "I want to thank you for the excellent publicity you've given me."

"I thought you didn't like publicity," said Michael, smiling to himself. The little laugh at the other end encouraged him to ask if she was speaking from the studio.

"No, I'm free until Tuesday."

"Then why not lunch with me?"

"Today?"

"There's no time like the present, Miss Helvin," said Michael. "Suppose we meet at Pinellio's at one o'clock?" She hesitated for a moment, then accepted his invitation.

But although Michael enjoyed his first "date" with Carel Helvin, she seemed strangely reluctant to discuss her activities. Apart from the fact that she lived alone in a small flat in Notting Hill Gate which she had taken for six months, and had no plans following the completion of her present film, he learned little of importance about her.

For the next two days, Michael could not get Carel Helvin out of his mind. Suddenly, acting on impulse, he telephoned her flat to invite her to accompany him to a theatrical first night, but there was no reply. Somewhat reluctantly, he went to the theatre by himself. It was a musical play which seemed to be peppered with romantic loopholes and feeling distinctly bored he drifted into the bar at the earliest opportunity.

The bar was crowded with the usual first-nighters and Michael was moodily sipping a gin and tonic when he caught sight of Carel at the far end of the bar. Her fair hair fell loosely on to her shoulders; she wore a blue frock and was talking in animated fashion to a heavily built man in a dinner jacket. Michael noticed that the jacket had a shawl collar and velvet cuffs. There was something about his gestures and facial expressions that stamped him as a foreigner.

Michael was a trifle startled to find himself experiencing a pang of jealousy. He told himself that it was absurd. He had only met the girl twice. Besides, the man was probably her agent or an executive of a foreign film company.

He hesitated to intrude on their conversation, but presently the bell went and Carel and her escort came towards him. He waited for her to catch his eye, and when they were level with him, she suddenly looked up. To Michael's amazement, she deliberately turned her head away and went on talking to her companion. They were speaking a language Michael could not distinguish. He watched them disappear into the foyer, then he turned abruptly and drained his glass.

The incident left him so completely baffled that he found great difficulty in concentrating on the last act. Carel Helvin had fooled him, yet he could have sworn she was not the type of girl to cut even the most casual acquaintance.

He was still puzzled when he lay in bed that night, pondering upon the identity of Carel's companion. Eventually he fell into a restless doze and dreamed that Carel was telephoning him night and day, and that he was refusing to take the calls. Suddenly, he woke with a start. The telephone at his bedside was ringing.

He looked at his wristwatch. It was four-thirty. As soon as he lifted the receiver, he heard the voice of Hammond the night editor. "Barry Ford left your phone number with me – he said you were to handle any crime job that turned up."

"That's right," agreed Michael sleepily.

"Then off you go to Ronway Mansions, laddie – it's in the Bayswater Road."

"What's happened, Mac?"

"A girl's been murdered. Nothing else known yet. Phone through a paragraph for the first edition as soon as you can."

Michael was lucky enough to find a cruising taxi in the Kings Road and was at the Bayswater flat ten minutes later. There was a little group of police and reporters in the lobby, and he was surprised to see an old Oxford friend.

"Well, well," said Detective Inspector Jack Gaylord. "What brings you out at this time of night, Michael?" Michael and Jack Gaylord had often compared notes on criminology during their Oxford days, and since then they had met several times for a meal or a drink. "This is going to be rather different from reporting studio gossip," said Gaylord rather grimly, as he led the way into the bedroom of the flat. "I'm afraid the poor girl has been so beaten up that we can't even identify her."

"Who owns the flat?"

"According to Bert Howard, the head porter, it's a man named Eric Shroeman. He's in Holland on business – that's why Howard was so startled when he heard the girl screaming, as the flat's supposed to be empty. The porter telephoned the local station, they came and forced the door, and that's what they found."

He indicated the inert figure on the bed. A towel had been thrown over the girl's face, and the inspector did not offer to remove it. "Well, now you know as much as we do, Michael," he said, "so you can go right ahead and try out those theories you were always airing at Oxford."

Michael did not reply. He picked up the girl's left hand, carefully examined it and then let it fall lifelessly on to the bed. There was no mistaking the ring the girl was wearing. "Would it interest you if I could identify this girl?" he asked.

"It most certainly would!" exclaimed Gaylord. "But how the devil –"

"Her name is Carel Helvin," said Michael Lance.

*****

Michael invited Gaylord back to breakfast, and told him all he knew about Carel Helvin. "She sounds a mysterious customer," mused Gaylord. "We've got to do our damnedest to get hold of this fellow Shroeman. I've been on the phone to Amsterdam, and the Dutch police are checking their records."

Michael saw the inspector out, then returned to his desk and started work on his first crime story. There were eighteen cigarette stubs in the ashtray before he completed it.

Although he was constantly in touch with Gaylord during the next two days, the Yard still had no news of the elusive Mr. Shroeman. Michael spent a whole morning at the Yard, looking through dozens of photographs in an attempt to recognise a likeness of the man he had seen at the theatre with Carel Helvin, but although he hesitated once or twice he could not be certain.

When he put his head round the door of Barry Ford's office at the end of the week, to see if there were any further assignments, the features editor beckoned him inside. "What about this new parlour game on television tomorrow night?" he asked.

"You mean *Guess My Birthplace*?"

"That's right. Let us have a couple of hundred words on it."

*****

Sunday afternoon was damp and foggy, and Michael was not sorry to have an assignment which compelled him to remain indoors.

He telephoned Jack Gaylord and invited him round for a drink. They drew the curtains on the thick fog outside and settled down with their drinks in front of the fire, chatting about the Bayswater murder case.

At eight o'clock Michael switched on the television set, in order not to miss the new parlour game. They were just in time to hear the chairman introducing the panel, and for some fifteen minutes they watched in silence. The new game appeared to be slick and full of possibilities.

After the celebrity spot, Michael went over to the sideboard to refill their glasses. He turned with an exclamation, as he caught sight of the challenger on the screen.

"What's the matter?" asked Gaylord.

"I could swear I know that man," said Michael. As he spoke, the camera switched abruptly to a close-up. There was no doubt about it – the challenger was the man he had seen at the theatre with Carel Helvin.

2

When Michael Lance told Jack Gaylord the identity of the challenger, the detective was inclined to be incredulous. "You told me that the man at the theatre looked like a foreigner and was speaking another language," he argued. "This fellow hasn't any accent."

The man, whose name had been given by the chairman as Victor Vorse, was answering the questions easily enough. After eight questions they had narrowed down his origins to the county of Cornwall, but failed to guess his native town, which he gave as Fowey. "Mr. Victor Vorse is the first challenger to beat our panel," announced the chairman amidst considerable applause. "He wins one of our special birthplace plaques." He handed over a medallion the size of a tea plate to the successful challenger, who bowed to the panel and in the direction of the audience.

"I'm positive that's the man," declared Michael. "Can't we do something?"

"What do you suggest? After all, it's no crime to go to the theatre with a woman who is afterwards murdered."

"Couldn't we go round and see him?"

"We'd never get there in time, with the fog this thick. No, I think you'd better leave it to me. I'll get his address from the television people. It'll be better if he doesn't see you."

The panel game continued, but as it turned out Victor Vorse was the only successful challenger. After Gaylord had gone, Michael settled down to write his two hundred words of comment about the new game, but found it extremely difficult to concentrate. How did Victor Vorse come to be at the television studios? Was there any significance in it? Would a man who had committed a murder dare to show his face to ten million viewers? The next morning, the same face was paraded before five million readers of the *Daily Pictorial* with the caption – *The Man Who Beat the Panel*.

Jack Gaylord telephoned Michael at the office and said he would have some news for him if they could meet for lunch. And soon after twelve-thirty Michael made his way to the oak-panelled dining room of a public house near Whitehall. Gaylord was standing against the small bar, finishing his usual glass of light ale. He ordered two more, and they carried them to a secluded table.

"Well, I've seen your Mr. Vorse," smiled Gaylord.

"You mean you've been down to Cornwall?"

"No, you ass! That was his birthplace."

"So he said."

"I got his address from the television people. He lives at Ealing and runs a dancing school with a woman named Connie Halliday. She was on the programme last night."

"Yes, I remember her," said Michael. "A platinum blonde."

The detective nodded. "Yes, that's the girl – and I can't help thinking she reminds me of someone. Anyhow, he went along to the studio with her last night, and when a couple of challengers didn't turn up on account of the fog, the producer persuaded Vorse to step into the breach."

"Well, I've been looking at his picture in the *Daily Pictorial*," said Michael. "I still think it's the same man."

"You may be right. If so, the fact that he stuck his neck out by challenging the panel last night rather points to his innocence."

"I'm not so sure about that," said Michael. "He may be under the impression that no-one noticed him with Carel Helvin that night."

"He says he's never heard of Miss Helvin," said Gaylord bluntly. "And he didn't particularly strike me as a foreigner. He answered all my questions without any fuss. I'm having his background checked, of course, but there's nothing against him in the records."

After they had ordered lunch, Michael remembered the missing owner of the flat where Carel Helvin was murdered, and asked: "Any news of Eric Shroeman?"

"None at all. If he went to Holland, as Bert Howard the porter says, he seems to have disappeared."

"Did the porter say Carel Helvin had ever visited Shroeman?"

"He was most emphatic that he had never set eyes on her. He says he didn't even see a girl go into the flat the night she

256

was murdered. He reckons she must have entered by the fire escape."

* * * * *

When Michael got back to the office, Barry Ford the features editor was looking more worried than ever. "I'm taking you off the show page for the time being," he told Michael. "Samson will take it over. Just show him the ropes. You'll carry on as crime reporter."

"What's wrong?"

"Ben Dickens died at half past seven this morning," said Ford softly. "You'd better move into his room."

Michael nodded, and went off to the pokey little room at the end of the corridor where Dickens had typed his crime stories for over twenty years. The wall was lined with maps — the Metropolitan Police divisions, the Thames-side areas, a detailed hand-drawn map of the square mile around Piccadilly.

Michael looked down at the cheap little desk that was still littered with piles of newspaper cuttings, files and odd scraps of copy paper. It occurred to him that there might be some of Ben's personal possessions in the desk. He found a large piece of brown paper and began to turn out the drawers. There was nothing of any real value.

He was still fumbling at the back of the top drawer when he came across what looked like a small brochure. He turned it over and saw that it was an advertisement for the Victor Vorse School of Ballroom Dancing at Lansdale Grove, Ealing. There was a picture in one corner of Victor Vorse who was described as the winner of the British Area National Waltz Competition in 1951.

257

On a sudden impulse Michael picked up the telephone and gave the number that was on the brochure. A woman's voice answered him, artificial and excessively polite, particularly when he said he was enquiring about a course of dancing lessons. "When did you wish to start?" she asked.

"As soon as possible."

"We've had a cancellation this evening, if that's convenient – seven-thirty?"

"That'll be fine."

"What was the name, please?"

Michael gave his name, then hesitated a moment before asking: "I take it Miss Connie Halliday will be the instructor?"

"That's right," said the voice. "I am Miss Halliday. I'll expect you at seven-thirty."

Michael went along the corridor and into the general office, where he spoke to an elderly typist named Miss Derwent, whom he knew helped Ben Dickens when he had any secretarial work. "Does this mean anything to you, Miss Derwent?" he asked, showing her the brochure. "I found it in Mr. Dickens' drawer."

She turned the pages slowly, then shook her head. "He never said anything about it to me," she said sadly. "But Mr. Dickens was always saving up odds and ends." Now we'll never know, reflected Michael, as he thanked her and tucked the brochure into his jacket pocket.

However, he had to admit that there was nothing particularly sinister about the Victor Vorse School of Dancing, as that evening, he promenaded somewhat cautiously around a fair-sized studio to the music of a radiogram. He recognised Connie Halliday from seeing her on the television screen, though she looked slightly older at close quarters. There was a slight hardness about the mouth, which the lines around the eyes accentuated.

While she was putting on a couple of fresh records, she asked him how he had heard of the school. "I read an advertisement a little time ago, then seeing you on television last night brought it to mind," he replied glibly.

"It was certainly a wonderful advertisement," she nodded. "We've had over twenty phone calls today."

"Do you ever get any enquiries from actors and film people?" he asked casually.

"Very occasionally."

"It's surprising how many of them are clumsy dancers," he went on. "I was talking to a film actress just lately who was asking about some lessons. A girl named Carel Helvin." By this time, they were dancing, and he could feel the muscles of her left hand tighten involuntarily. "Have you ever come across her?" he asked.

"No," she replied tonelessly. "I've never heard of the girl."

At that moment the door opened, and a man came in carrying a large red diary. Michael recognised him at once as Victor Vorse. Vorse apologised for interrupting the lesson and drew Connie to one side, apparently querying some entry in the diary. While they talked, Michael stood a few yards away eyeing the man carefully. He was now quite convinced that this was the man he had seen with Carel Helvin at the theatre.

*****

On the way home Michael bought an evening paper and found that it contained a photograph of Victor Vorse – *The Man Who Beat The Panel*. He was staring at the photograph when it suddenly occurred to him that it might be a very good idea to visit the flat on the Bayswater Road.

Bert Howard, the porter, was on duty and recalled Michael's previous visit on the night of the murder. "Any news of Mr. Shroeman yet?" asked Michael, offering him a cigarette.

"Not a word, sir. There's something very fishy about this business, if you ask me."

"There often is about murder," said Michael, taking the evening paper from his pocket and folding it back so that Vorse's picture was revealed. "Did this man ever visit Mr. Shroeman, by any chance?"

Howard seemed to hesitate, but finally shook his head. "So many people come here," he said a trifle brusquely. "I can't remember half of 'em."

"No, of course not," replied Michael smoothly, stuffing the paper back into his pocket.

"I saw this chap on television last night," went on the porter. "If I'd recognised him as a friend of Mr. Shroeman's, I would have phoned the police. They asked me to tip 'em off about anything like that."

Michael nodded and wished Howard goodnight. He got back to his flat just after ten and had turned on the water for a hot bath when the telephone rang.

At first, he did not recognise the voice, then suddenly he realised that it was Connie Halliday speaking. "How much are you interested in Carel Helvin, Mr. Lance?"

"I'm very interested indeed," said Michael quietly.

"That's what I thought."

"Then you do know her, after all?"

"I couldn't tell you at the time – we might have been overheard. But I'm ready to talk now if we can meet."

"Tonight?"

"Why not tonight?"

"Could we meet in town?"

"There's a little restaurant in Soho called the Espadalo. I'll be there about eleven. Do you know it?"

"No, but I'll find it," said Michael.

"It's in Melkin Street, a turning off Poland Street."

"I'll be there at eleven," he promised, and put down the receiver.

*****

A night breeze was stirring scraps of paper in the gutter, as Michael stood at the entrance to Melkin Street. It proved to be a narrow one-way thoroughfare between high buildings. There was no footpath, and hardly room for a small car to pass down. He stood at the corner under a lamp and looked along the street. There was no sign of a lighted restaurant.

He walked along the street somewhat warily. The high buildings had a gloomy, foreboding aspect. There was no sign of life in the street, and he was nearly half-way down when he was conscious that a car had turned the corner and was following him. Although it was overtaking him, the driver appeared to be in no great hurry.

Powerful headlights were suddenly switched on, and he found himself instinctively recoiling against the wall of a warehouse. The car came on. Michael began to walk again, looking for some opening where he could find shelter. Suddenly, a feeling of panic swept over him. The car engine roared, and Michael began to run.

As he came towards the end of the street, the car's headlights picked up a small opening that was clearly a back entrance to the warehouse. Michael flung himself into the opening. The door was locked, but the recess gave him momentary protection from the relentless glare of the oncoming headlights.

He crouched in the shadows as the car roared past. From the back window there was a spurt of flame, and a bullet whistled past his head. Michael crumpled up in what, he hoped, was a realistic manner and sank to the pavement.

He heard the car slow down and wondered if the man with the gun would shoot again.

3

The car had stopped with the engine running. Then it seemed to be backing towards him with a steady purr. With a gentle squeak of the brakes, it stopped. The back wheels seemed to be level with Michael, but he dared not move. He was conscious of a torch being flashed at him, then the engine suddenly accelerated and the car drove off.

As it swung round the corner it passed under the street lamp and he caught a momentary glimpse of the driver. He could not see the man's features clearly, but there was something about the set of his shoulders that reminded him of Victor Vorse.

Michael lay there until he could no longer hear the car, then he cautiously rose to his feet, still keeping in the shadow of the wall. As he was dusting off his clothes, there was a sudden sound of running footsteps from the far end of the street. A man in white overalls appeared; he was a foreigner, obviously from a nearby café. "You heard a gunshot, mister?" he called to Michael.

"I heard nothing."

The man shook his head. "I don't like this street. You're a stranger here, ain't you?"

"Not exactly," said Michael. "I live about a mile away."

Another man came running up. He was wearing evening dress under his overcoat and might have been a dance musician on his way to an engagement. "What's goin' on 'ere?" he demanded in cockney tones.

"I heard the shots," said the foreigner.

The newcomer eyed Michael curiously. "Did you hear anything?" he asked.

"Well, it might have been a car back-firing," hedged Michael.

The man in evening dress looked up and down the street. "There doesn't seem to be anybody about," he said.

"I telephoned for the police when I heard the shots," said the foreigner excitedly. "They will soon be here."

"I'll have to be getting along," Michael told them. "I'm already late for an appointment."

The foreigner seemed about to protest, but Michael curtly wished them goodnight and made for the corner of the street. He had no wish to be involved with the police at this juncture. Later there would probably have to be an inquiry, but first he was anxious to learn who it was that wanted him out of the way.

In Wardour Street he picked up a taxi and sank somewhat breathlessly into the back seat. The events of the past half hour surged through his mind like an endless kaleidoscope. He had been a fool to keep that appointment, as clearly it had been a trick on the part of Connie Halliday or Vorse to get him quietly out of the way. Did that mean they were implicated in the murder of Carel Helvin?

When the taxi stopped for traffic lights, a police car drew up alongside. Michael was suddenly aware that a man in the back of it was making signs to him - it was Jack Gaylord. He paid off his driver, and quickly climbed into the back of the police car. "What the devil are you doing in these murky parts?" asked Gaylord. "Investigating another murder?"

"As it happens, I very nearly played the part of the victim," Michael told him, then went on to relate the incident in Melkin Street.

"Well, this is all very interesting," murmured Gaylord. "You seem to have got under somebody's skin all right, Michael."

"What do you think I should do next?"

"You might try quite a number of things. But I think your safest bet would be to turn up for another dancing lesson and try to find out why this woman Halliday telephoned you. It would be interesting to know if she's the moving spirit, or just acting on orders."

"Of course, somebody might have overheard the conversation," Michael pointed out.

"In that case, why didn't Miss Halliday turn up at the rendezvous?"

"She could have been scared off by the shots."

"That's possible. But it's my bet she won't admit she phoned you. In fact, I'll lay a level ten bob –"

He was interrupted by the short-wave radio in the car. "Calling Detective Inspector Gaylord in car WZ2387. Please proceed to Hammersmith Station immediately. A murdered man has been found in the river."

Gaylord leaned forward, pressed a switch and acknowledged the instructions. Then he turned to Michael. "Where can I drop you?" he asked.

"Hammersmith Police Station," replied Michael pleasantly. "I'm a crime reporter now, remember?"

Gaylord frowned for a moment, then his face cleared. "You're a glutton for punishment," he replied. "But I warn you, it's probably a very routine job that'll mean weeks of boring inquiries."

"A murder's a murder," said Michael, offering him a cigarette.

As Gaylord lit it, he asked: "You've no idea if it was a man or woman who fired at you tonight?"

"I didn't see any woman. But the man driving the car certainly looked rather like Vorse, though I can't swear to that."

"You haven't had a very profitable evening so far," grinned Gaylord.

"At least I've learned that someone is out to get rid of me."

"Yes, I suppose that's worth something," mused the detective. "I hope you'll be on your guard in future."

They drove through the quiet streets, to the little mortuary used by the river police. It was a disused chapel, with the distemper flaking off the walls as a result of the damp. A sergeant in uniform pulled back the blanket that covered the solitary corpse lying in a corner near the door.

Michael gripped Gaylord's arm. "It's Bert Howard!" he exclaimed.

The sergeant eyed him curiously. "You can identify this man, sir?"

"We can both identify him," replied Gaylord. "He's a man named Howard, caretaker of a block of flats called Ronway Mansions in Bayswater. Wasn't there any means of identification on the body?"

The sergeant shook his head, then thoughtfully rubbed his chin. "Ronway Mansions," he repeated. "Wasn't that the place where a girl was murdered – a film star called Carel something or other?"

"Quite correct, sergeant."

"D'you think there's any connection between the two jobs, sir?"

Gaylord shrugged. "That's one of the little things we have to work out. Better get round to Ronway Mansions and see what you can find there. Let me know if anything turns up."

Gaylord and Michael went round to the police station and had a chat with the local inspector, who was unable to throw any light on the murder. Gaylord quickly scanned the report of the finding of the body, then turned to Michael. "Let's go into the canteen for a cup of coffee, then we'll see if anything's come to light at the flat."

They went down to the canteen, which was almost deserted, and Gaylord fetched two huge mugs of coffee. "Well, it's high time we began to get one or two things sorted out," ruminated Gaylord, as he stirred his coffee and produced a packet of cigarettes.

"You think this business may have some connection with the murder of Carel Helvin?"

"What's your opinion?"

"I only know that I had a feeling Bert Howard was lying to me when I tackled him about the mysterious Mr. Shroeman and the visitors to his flat. He said he'd never set eyes on Victor Vorse and I didn't believe him. There was something very suspicious about Howard – by the way, did you ever check if he had a criminal record?"

Gaylord grinned. "Now don't get too smart, Michael. You're taking this new job of yours a bit too seriously. By the way, aren't you going to telephone a report?"

"Plenty of time for that later, after we've checked up at Ronway Mansions," said Michael. "Then I can let them have a full report."

Gaylord sipped his coffee and smiled indulgently. "You know, Michael, I've a feeling you've an idea that you can walk into this set-up and put your finger on the murderer by cool, calculated deduction. But it doesn't work that way. For deduction you need facts, and finding the right facts is our biggest headache. These things may look all right on paper, but there's a lot more to it than that. Theory only takes you so far."

Michael nodded, and stirred his coffee. "Anyhow, there's one theory I'm going to try out – and incidentally take you up on that bet. I'm going to arrange another dancing lesson as soon as possible."

*****

A strange woman's voice answered Michael when he rang up the Victor Vorse School of Dancing. She told him that Miss Halliday could not come to the telephone, but that he might have a lesson that afternoon at three-thirty. He thanked the girl politely and replaced the receiver.

He was a little surprised when the door was answered by Victor Vorse himself. Vorse did his utmost to cover his own surprise but could not conceal the widening eyes and slight twitch of his jaw muscles. However, he conducted Michael into the studio without comment and introduced him to a slim brunette whom he addressed as Miss Jackson.

267

When they were alone together, Michael asked the girl: "What has become of my former instructor?"

"You mean Miss Halliday? She's had to go up to town on urgent business. I always take over for her." She busied herself with the gramophone. Michael was a little worried. Obviously, Connie Halliday was afraid to face him.

The lesson went smoothly enough. In fact, Miss Jackson was a rather more sympathetic teacher than Connie Halliday had been. But although he gave her several opportunities to talk about her employers, she somehow contrived to by-pass all his hints – and Michael came to the conclusion that she had been warned.

He returned to his flat without any further incident. When he had tried to make another appointment for a further lesson, Miss Jackson had been extremely vague and suggested that he should telephone. On the way home he bought a paper, and saw that the death of Bert Howard was dismissed in a dozen lines, chiefly because there were no more facts available other than those which had already been discovered.

Wondering whether he should telephone Gaylord, he fitted his latchkey in the lock and swung open the door of his flat. As he closed it, he saw a crumpled note sticking through the letterbox. He smoothed it out carefully and saw that it was written on blue notepaper in a feminine hand. The note read: *It is imperative that I see you. Meet me in the tube station at Piccadilly tomorrow morning at eleven. Please come alone and tell no-one. I am relying on you. C.H.*

He slowly refolded the paper and went into the lounge. Was Connie Halliday genuinely anxious to see him? Had she any information about the Bayswater murder or the death of Bert Howard? Of course, it could be another attempt to get rid of him, reflected Michael. But surely, she would have chosen a less public meeting place than the Piccadilly Underground.

He felt bound to give her the benefit of the doubt. After all, she may have been ignorant of the attempt on his life in Melkin Street. Once or twice he moved to the telephone, to get in touch with Gaylord and ask his advice. Once he even picked up the receiver, but after a moment's thought he replaced it. Michael decided he would say nothing to anyone about this appointment but would simply do as she asked.

*****

It was five minutes to eleven when Michael approached the underground station from Shaftesbury Avenue. There was no sign of Connie Halliday. He hesitated a moment, then caught sight of the reassuring stolid figure of a policeman by the ticket barrier.

He ventured into the open promenade and began walking slowly in front of the display windows. No-one appeared to take the slightest notice of him. Five minutes later he was strolling past the long line of telephone boxes, all of which were occupied, when he caught sight of a girl whose back view seemed vaguely familiar. What really attracted his attention was the fact that the girl was not using the telephone at all, but simply standing in the box looking into the small mirror. Yet she was not looking at herself but using it to survey the people who walked past.

Suddenly, he was conscious that their eyes had met, and she turned swiftly. The door of the box opened, and the girl stepped out. She came towards him, with a tiny smile of recognition playing round the corners of her mouth.

It was Carel Helvin.

4

Michael's first impression of Carel Helvin was that she looked pale and distressed. She smiled faintly as she came up to him and said in her husky voice: "I am so glad you could come."

Michael found his tongue at last. "I − I − thought ..." he stammered.

"You thought I had been murdered?" She stood there, swaying slightly on her high heels and looking somewhat apprehensively to right and left.

He pulled her into a little niche between two display windows. "Was it you who sent me that note asking me to meet you here this morning?" he demanded.

Her eyes widened. "But of course! Who did you think sent it?"

"As a matter of fact, I thought it was a girl named Connie Halliday," he said slowly.

She shook her head helplessly. "I do not know that name. Who is this Miss Halliday?"

"Never mind her now. What about you? Don't you know there have been reports of your murder in all the newspapers? Scotland Yard have worked night and day investigating it! And yet here you are, as large as life." He was at a loss for words.

"I do not wish to talk here," she replied nervously. "I am afraid I will be recognised. Can't we go somewhere else?"

"Yes, of course." He took her arm, and they walked up the steps. They emerged at the Regent Street exit, where he quickly picked up a taxi. Michael gave the address of his flat, as he held the door for the girl to enter. When the cab had started, he closed the glass panel and turned towards her.

"The police found the body of a girl wearing a ring exactly like yours. Who was she?"

Carel Helvin shifted uneasily. "I will explain that later."

"But I can't understand why you let the police go on thinking it was you. It simply doesn't make sense – what was the point?"

"Later … later I will tell you everything," she said softly.

They hardly spoke for the rest of the journey, sitting in their respective corners. When they arrived at the flat, he settled her in a comfortable armchair and crossed to the cocktail cabinet. "It's early for a drink, but I think we both need one pretty badly," he said.

She asked for a small gin and vermouth, and he poured himself a whisky and soda. Then he switched on the electric fire and settled himself on the arm of the settee. Carel sipped her drink and looked round the room.

"Well?" said Michael at last. "I'm waiting to hear everything."

"May I have a cigarette?"

Michael nodded, took out his cigarette case and flicked his lighter.

"You are quite sure no-one will hear us talking?" she asked.

"Absolutely certain."

"I'm sorry to be so cautious, but I've been so terribly worried. My nerves are – how do you say it? – on edge. I am a stranger in this country, and do not know anyone really well. Time and again I have tried to think of some person I can turn to, someone who would be sympathetic." She paused and flicked the ash off her cigarette. "Then suddenly I remembered you. How you told me all about yourself at lunch that day, about your ambition to be a crime reporter."

"I am a crime reporter now," he said.

Her eyes lit up. "You are? Then I was right, because something told me you were the best person to advise me. I knew you would be sympathetic."

Michael sipped his whisky. This was all very gratifying, but she had not satisfied his curiosity.

"Night after night I have paced up and down my room, trying to think of some way out," she said.

"Where are you living now?"

"In Canterbury Road, St. John's Wood. My room looks on to a little chapel. In desperation I have actually stood and counted the rows of tiles on the roof."

"Yes, but what about this murdered girl?" he broke in impatiently. "Do you know who she was?"

Carel nodded. "Yes, I know," she said quietly. "She was my sister, Paula."

"Your sister!" Michael exclaimed.

"She looked very like me, and sometimes she got a job as my stand-in for films in Sweden. But she was usually dismissed before the end of the picture." Carel Helvin sighed. "You see, Paula was unreliable. She had good looks but little talent, and she liked a gay life. So, there was often trouble."

Michael looked at the sad Nordic features, the high cheekbones, the large and expressive mouth, and suddenly he felt very sorry for her. "You were fond of your sister?"

"I always looked after her. We had no mother since we were children. I was a year older, and she depended on me to get her out of trouble. But she was always annoyed that I should make good money in films when she thought she was a much better actress. She did not appreciate that if it had not been for me, she would have had no work at all."

"It must have been a great worry for you."

272

"I was used to it. I could usually manage her – that is, until Lengaard came on the scene. He seemed to put a spell on her, and after that I was helpless."

"Who was this Lengaard?"

"I think he was a crook of some sort. He started Paula taking drugs and used her in all sorts of ways. I guessed she was mixed up in a smuggling case, but fortunately they never traced anything to her. Then one night they had a terrible row, and Paula came into my room sobbing that she had killed Lengaard."

"Had she?"

"I never found out the details. As it happened, I'd recently had an offer of a small part in a British picture, so I caught the next plane to England, bringing her with me."

"Had you always intended to bring her to England, or was it a sudden decision because of what had happened?"

"It was a sudden decision," answered Carel. "I just couldn't leave her behind."

"Didn't you hear any more about Lengaard?" asked Michael.

"He wasn't the sort of man the police would make a fuss about. We never saw anything in the papers. Maybe the police were glad to see the end of him, or maybe Paula hadn't really killed him. We didn't talk about it."

"Was she afraid the police would try to trace her?"

"Not so much the police –"

"Then who?"

"Lengaard's friends. He had contacts all over Europe."

Michael drained his glass and set it down on the mantelpiece. This affair was becoming even more involved than he had imagined. All the same, if he could check up on some of these facts it would certainly make a very good story for his paper.

"What happened when you got to England?" he asked.

"We lay low for a time. I did my work at the studios and came straight back to Paula. She hardly went outside the flat for two or three weeks. We ordered most of the things by telephone, and she seemed to enjoy herself cooking and keeping house. She was quite good at that when she gave her mind to it. Then suddenly she began to get restless. I recognised the signs at once, and I was afraid."

"You mean she wasn't staying at home when you were at the studios?"

"She was sometimes out when I got back in the evening. She began to get mysterious phone calls, and I suspected she was mixing with the same sort of people she had known at home. It was even more worrying because we were so alike in appearance, and she was occasionally mistaken for me. It had often led to complications before."

"Then that was it!" exclaimed Michael suddenly. The incident in the theatre bar had leapt to his mind. The girl who had ignored him on that occasion must have been Paula. He told Carel of the incident, and she recalled that on that particular evening Paula had received a telephone call from a man who had invited her to the theatre.

"I remember, because I was worried at the time. I answered the telephone, and thought I recognised the voice. It sounded like a man Paula had been friendly with in Stockholm. I listened to the conversation, but she did not address him by name, and she wouldn't say anything about him. I guessed there was something going on, but I couldn't keep her at home."

There were tears in Carel Helvin's eyes, as Michael took her glass and poured her another drink. "Have you ever come across a man named Victor Vorse?" he asked.

Carel shook her head. "I do not know anyone of that name."

He gave her a brief description of Vorse, but she did not seem to recognise him. "This man didn't bring your sister home from the theatre?"

"If he did, she didn't invite him inside," replied Carel. "That also made me very suspicious. She usually asked her friends in for a drink after they had been out for the evening."

"Did you notice anything unusual about her that night?"

"She seemed very excited. Her eyes were unnaturally bright, and she was extremely gay. Of course, she might have been drinking."

Michael frowned. "I'm still rather puzzled about Vorse," he admitted. "Maybe you could identify him if you saw a picture. I daresay I could get one from the office if you –"

He was cut short by the telephone ringing, and he went over and picked up the receiver. "Jack Gaylord here," said a voice.

"That's a bit of luck," said Michael. "I was just going to telephone you. There's an amazing development in the Bayswater case."

"You don't have to tell me," interrupted Gaylord. "I know exactly what you're going to say."

"But you can't possibly –"

"You are going to tell me that Carel Helvin is still alive."

"Yes, but how on earth -?"

"You're also trying to tell me she's in your flat at this very moment."

"Now look here, Gaylord –"

275

"There's no time to argue," cut in Gaylord urgently. "You're in a tough spot, Michael, and you've got to act quickly, otherwise you'll be mixed up in something really serious. Now, listen to me. Make an excuse to Carel Helvin and get out of the flat as quickly as you can. Meet me right away outside the post office in Sloane Square."

There was a click as the receiver was replaced, then Michael turned to Carel. "I'm afraid I've got to report to the office right away," he said quietly, wondering if by any chance she could have overheard the conversation. But Carel seemed to be lost in her thoughts, staring into the fire.

"I'm sorry about this," he went on. "Will you wait here for me? Make yourself at home – there's plenty of food in the fridge if you feel hungry." He picked up his hat. "I won't be more than an hour."

*****

It was more than ten minutes after Gaylord's call that Michael arrived at Sloane Square, and he was surprised to see no sign of the inspector. After waiting nearly a quarter of an hour, he went into a call box and dialled New Scotland Yard. He was connected with Gaylord's office straight away, and to his amazement the inspector answered the telephone himself.

"What's going on?" demanded Michael. "Why the devil didn't you meet me in Sloane Square?"

"Why on earth should I?"

"But you practically ordered me to come here –"

"My dear chap, I haven't spoken to you since yesterday."

"You mean to say you didn't phone me half an hour ago and tell me Carel Helvin was still alive and –"

"I most certainly didn't!" exclaimed Gaylord. "Suppose you enlighten me for a change?"

Michael rapidly gave him the gist of the previous telephone conversation. "It sounds to me like a trick to get you out of the flat," decided the inspector. "There's something going on there? I'll be round right away – you get back as quickly as you can." Michael suddenly saw the force of his reasoning and rushing out of the call box he hailed a passing taxi.

He did not wait for the lift, but leapt up the stairs three at a time, fumbling for his latchkey as he came to his landing. When he reached the door, however, he hesitated. If Gaylord's deduction was correct, there might be someone in the flat besides Carel – someone who was by no means friendly disposed, and quite possibly armed.

Should he wait for Gaylord? But the thought of what might be happening to Carel Helvin spurred him to sudden action. He fitted the key into the Yale lock as silently as possible, cautiously opened the door and stood listening. He moved a step or two along the hall and saw that the door of the lounge was ajar. With a sudden movement, he flung it open and stood clear. Again, there was no sound. He put his head inside and looked round.

The room was empty.

5

Michael went quickly through the other rooms of the flat. There was no trace of Carel Helvin. He returned to the lounge and stood for a few moments in complete bewilderment. It was almost as if he had dreamt the whole episode of his meeting with Carel.

An insistent buzzing of the front doorbell brought him back to reality. He went to the door, and found Gaylord standing there. "Are you all right, Michael?" Michael nodded and beckoned him inside. "What's been going on?" asked the detective.

"I wish I knew. I simply came back and found the flat empty."

"You mean this girl Carel Helvin had gone?"

"That's right. She promised me she'd wait and tell me the rest of her story, but it looks very much as if somebody called while I was away and got her out of here."

Gaylord looked rapidly round the flat, and over by the fireplace he paused. There was a faint smell of perfume. "You should have told me about that note, Michael," he said abruptly. "Then we could have arranged to have had the place under observation. You've got a lot to learn yet."

Michael grinned somewhat ruefully. "I'll remember next time," he promised. He sank on to the arm of the chair, deep in thought. The life of a crime reporter was proving very different from the fascinating affair he had envisaged. But he had never contemplated being so closely involved in a murder case as he was in this, his first.

Gaylord was speaking again. "Did you keep that note she sent you?" Michael took it from an inside pocket, and Gaylord smoothed it out. "She doesn't give any address, I see," he said at last.

"Good Lord, that reminds me – she did tell me where she was living! It was somewhere in St. John's Wood – Canterbury Road, that's it! She took a room there after the –"

"After the murder. So that's why we could never find anyone at her flat."

"Surely you hardly expected to, if she'd been murdered?"

278

"On the contrary. It was obvious that she had been sharing it with another girl, but we couldn't discover who this girl was. It seems that Miss Helvin must have covered her tracks when she went back to pack."

"I'm sure she said Canterbury Road," mused Michael.

"Canterbury Road happens to be just over half a mile long. And she's probably using a false name."

"You can get a picture of her from my office, and very soon get her landlady to identify her."

Gaylord smiled. "You have your moments, Mr. Lance."

Michael ignored his remarks, and suddenly snapped his fingers. "Wait now, there's something else. She said her room looked on to a chapel. I distinctly remember that."

"H'm, that's more like it. We should be able to go straight there. But we'll collect that photo from your office, just in case there's any difficulty."

*****

Half an hour later, they were knocking at the front door of 83 Canterbury Road. It was opened by a dumpy middle-aged woman with a noticeable north country accent.

She recognised Carel Helvin's photo at once. "Why, that's Miss Sterne – she's got my two top floor rooms. Nice little flat, all self-contained. She's very comfortable up there and keeps herself to herself."

"Could I speak to her?" asked Gaylord.

"As a matter of fact, she went out soon after ten this morning and I haven't seen her come back."

"Couldn't she have come in without your seeing her?"

"She might have," conceded Mrs. Prothero.

"Perhaps we could go up and make sure? It's very urgent."

The landlady hesitated a moment, then turned and led the way up four flights of stairs. Outside the top flat, she stopped to get her breath. It was then that she noticed that the outer door of the flat was ajar. "That's funny," she murmured. "Miss Sterne always locks that door."

The first room they entered was simply furnished as a kitchen-living-room, with gas stove and sink screened off in one corner. It was somewhat untidy, and there was a faint smell of perfume. Michael went over to the window. There, sure enough, was the chapel Carel had told him about.

Suddenly he stiffened. There was somebody moving around in the bedroom. He looked at Gaylord, who had also heard it. They moved quietly over to the bedroom door. Gaylord motioned to Michael to stand clear, and with a sudden gesture flung it open.

A girl, who had clearly been searching the bureau under the opposite window, swung round and confronted them. "Connie Halliday!" exclaimed Michael.

Gaylord turned to Mrs. Prothero, who was standing just behind them. "Did you know she was here?" he asked.

"No, sir, she must have slipped in while I was busy downstairs."

"Have you seen her before?"

"Never set eyes on her."

Gaylord nodded to Michael to enter the bedroom, and when they were inside, he carefully closed the door. "You know this lady?" he asked Michael.

"Yes, of course. It's Miss Halliday from the dancing school. I told you about her."

"Would you care to explain what you're doing here, Miss Halliday?" asked Gaylord politely.

"I happen to be a friend of Miss Helvin's, that's all," she replied with a self-possessed air.

"I'm afraid I'll have to contradict that," interposed Michael. "A couple of hours ago Carel Helvin told me that she had never heard of you."

"She might have been saying that for a special reason."

Gaylord perched on the edge of the divan and regarded Miss Halliday thoughtfully. "If you're a friend of Miss Helvin's, perhaps you can tell us where she is at this moment," he suggested.

"How should I know that?" Connie looked at the two men a trifle uncertainly, then her tone changed. "You mean she has disappeared?"

"I didn't say so," replied Gaylord evenly. "Anyhow, never mind her for a minute. Tell us more about yourself. Why the dance routine?"

"I don't understand you."

"I think you do, *Miss Wilding*."

There was a tense silence for a few seconds, then Michael demanded: "What's all this?" He turned to the girl. "Is your name Wilding?"

She shrugged but did not reply.

"You're unlucky, Miss Wilding," said Gaylord. "I have a memory for faces, and last year I saw you giving evidence for an insurance company."

"You mean she's a private detective?" stammered Michael.

"Don't look so shocked, Michael – you'll meet all sorts in this crime racket." He turned to the girl again. "Well, Miss Wilding, don't you think you'd better tell us about this job?"

Julia Wilding, alias Connie Halliday, shrugged once more.

"It's an offence to enter a stranger's room and conduct a search," Gaylord reminded her.

She walked to the door and opened it to see that no-one was listening, then she returned and sat in the only chair. "I'm still working for Staten Investigations," she told them.

"The American firm? How do they come to be interested in Miss Helvin?"

"We're retained by a Swedish insurance company who have had to pay out heavily on stolen jewellery in the past year or two. They said some of the stuff had been broken up over here and thought they might get a lead from this end."

"What has all this to do with the dancing school?" asked Michael.

She ignored the interruption and said quietly: "For a long time I went on without a clue of any sort, and I was on the verge of giving up the job. I admitted as much to my old friend Ben Dickens, the crime reporter – your predecessor, who told me that he'd been tipped off by one of his pals in the underworld that a certain Mr. Victor Vorse had some hot jewellery from abroad. Ben thought it might be worth following up, so I went down to the dancing academy that Vorse was running as a cover. Vorse interviewed me, and I got a job as an instructor. I'm keen on dancing as it happens – won a couple of amateur championships, so it seemed a pretty good prospect."

"And did you get any evidence?" asked Gaylord.

"Nothing really cast iron. But I'm quite convinced Vorse is the agent of the Swedish gang."

"What makes you so certain?"

"Just one or two conversations I overheard. A dancing school is an ideal cover for a man of that type, because we get a constant flow of strangers through the place without

282

arousing any suspicion. But just as I was really on to something, Vorse discovered who I was."

"So why did you telephone me to meet you in Melkin Street?" asked Michael.

"I was anxious to tip you off about Vorse, but he must have been listening when I made the call."

"But surely he couldn't prevent you from keeping the appointment?"

"That's exactly what he did. He locked me in the one room at the studio that has a barred window. Of course, he thought you were deeply involved in this business – a sort of confederate of mine. He didn't realise we had only just met."

"Then you knew it wasn't Carel Helvin who had been murdered?" asked Gaylord.

"I suspected it. I knew that her sister, Paula, was mixed up with a man named Lengaard who was head of this set-up in Sweden. From reports I've heard he certainly had a motive for getting rid of Paula."

"That seems to agree with what Carel Helvin told me," nodded Michael, "except that she said that her sister Paula had told her that she had murdered Lengaard, and that she must get out of the country. But there has been no report of any such murder. Now, I wonder if –" He broke off, as a new idea occurred to him.

"Now what is it?" asked Gaylord, but before Michael could reply there was a tap at the door. "Who's there?" called Gaylord sharply.

"It's me, sir, Mrs. Prothero." Gaylord opened the door. "I'm sorry to bother you, sir, but there's a foreign gentleman downstairs asking for a Miss Helvin. He says she lives here, and he won't go away."

"Did he tell you his name?"

"Yes, sir," said Mrs. Prothero. "It's a funny sort of name –
sounded to me like Lengaard."

6

Detective Inspector Gaylord moved over to the door,
hesitated a moment, then turned to Julia Wilding. "Did you
know Lengaard was in this country?" he asked.

"It's news to me," she said.

"Are you sure you've never seen this man?" he asked Mrs.
Prothero.

"Quite sure," said the landlady. "He's never been here
before."

With his hand on the doorknob, Gaylord said: "All right, I'll
go down with Mrs. Prothero and see if I can bring him back up
here." He nodded to the landlady to accompany him
downstairs.

Michael Lance and Julia listened to their receding
footsteps in silence, then Julia said in a low voice: "If it's really
Lengaard he might be dangerous. I suppose neither of you has
a gun or –"

"Don't worry, we can deal with him if he gets tough,"
Michael assured her.

They could hear footsteps ascending the stairs, then the
sound of a man's voice. Julia and Michael shot a quick glance
at each other as the door opened. There could be no mistaking
that voice.

"Come inside, Mr. Lengaard," said Gaylord.

Julia Wilding made an involuntary step forward as she
caught sight of the visitor. "But this isn't Lengaard," she said
in a shrill whisper.

"Of course not! It's Mr. Victor Vorse, the man who beat the panel," said Michael pleasantly.

Vorse turned and looked round as if seeking a way of escape, but Gaylord was standing with his back to the closed door. There was a moment's silence, then Vorse said: "I called to see Miss Helvin. Where is she?"

Michael pushed a chair against the back of his legs, so that he sat down abruptly. "Miss Helvin will be here presently," he replied. "Meanwhile, you can help us to clear up one or two little matters, Mr. Vorse."

Vorse looked round the group, plainly ill at ease. "Has she been telling lies about me?" he demanded sullenly, indicating Julia.

"If she has, this is your chance to put things right. And first of all, you might tell us why you gave the name Lengaard."

"It's no business of yours."

Michael stood over him threateningly. "Your affairs have concerned me quite a lot, Mr. Vorse, since you tried to murder me in cold blood. That was one of your less successful jobs." Vorse half rose to his feet, but Michael pushed him back into his chair. "I haven't forgotten that night in Melkin Street, so don't tempt me to get tough with you," he said softly. "Now, perhaps you'll tell me why you used the name Lengaard."

Vorse licked his lips nervously. "I had to see Carel Helvin, and I thought she'd want to meet Lengaard."

"Because she was under the impression that her sister Paula had killed this man Lengaard?"

"That's right."

"Why were you so anxious to see Carel Helvin? Was it you who imitated Inspector Gaylord's voice on the telephone, in order to get me out of the way while Carel Helvin was in my flat?"

"I wanted to see her on business," was the sullen reply.

"I suppose that business wouldn't have any connection with a valuable necklace," suggested Michael softly.

"What the devil do I know about necklaces?"

Michael stood looking down at him, his hands thrust deep into his trouser pockets. "You know more than most people," he replied quietly. "You're a highly skilled man at breaking up jewellery and getting rid of it to the right people. What's more, you'd had the tip from Lengaard about Paula getting her sister to bring her over from Sweden with that necklace. When you contacted her, you found she wouldn't hand it over, so you got tough and murdered her in that flat which was supposed to belong to a Mr. Shroeman.

"She had bribed Bert Howard, the porter, to give out that the owner of the flat was a Dutchman. But it didn't fool you, Vorse. You searched the flat after you'd murdered the girl, and you went back again for another search a few days later. When Bert Howard tried to stop you, there was another murder."

Vorse swung round and confronted Gaylord. "He can't prove any of that!" he stammered.

"You'll be surprised what I can prove before we've finished with you, Mr. Vorse," said Michael easily. "I've been ferreting around in your past quite a bit – and incidentally, you didn't beat the panel fairly in that parlour game on television. You were born much nearer Cracow than Fowey."

"I'm not staying here to listen to any more of this rubbish," snapped Vorse, and jumped to his feet.

Gaylord laid a restraining hand upon his arm. "I think it would be an even better idea if you came along to the Yard and told us what you do know about this business," he suggested.

With a sudden heave, Vorse pushed Gaylord aside and made for the door, running down the short flight of steps that led from the flatlet. Michael was very close behind however, and as Vorse reached the landing he flung himself forward and gripped his ankle. Vorse overbalanced and fell heavily against the wooden balustrade.

There was a sound of splintering wood, and Vorse's leg was jerked convulsively out of Michael's hand as the dance instructor crashed down into the well of the stairs. The others raced down the stairs and reached Vorse at the same moment that Mrs. Prothero appeared from the lower regions.

"Better not try to move him," advised Gaylord, noting the peculiar twisted position in which Vorse was lying. He seemed to be unconscious but opened his eyes for a moment and muttered a few words. Michael thought he caught the word "necklace" but could not be certain.

"I'll get the police car to run to the hospital," decided Gaylord, opening the front door.

When he went over to the police car, the driver said: "There's a message just come over the radio, sir. They said there's a Miss Carel Helvin ...." He consulted his notebook in which he had written down the name. "... waiting to see you at the Yard. They want you back right away."

Gaylord hesitated a moment, then said: "Please go into the house and stay with the man who's lying in the hall. I'll send round an ambulance. And ask Mr. Lance to come to the Yard with me."

The driver got out, and Gaylord took his place behind the wheel. A minute later, Michael climbed in beside him. The inspector decided that it would be quicker to telephone for an ambulance than to visit a hospital, so they stopped at the first call box then went on to the Yard.

*****

Carel Helvin was sitting in Gaylord's office, her hands clasped over her handbag, looking quite self-possessed. Michael went over to her quickly. "I am glad you're all right," he said warmly. "Whatever made you run away like that?"

She gave a tiny shrug. "After you had gone, I started thinking," she murmured. "All sorts of things came into my mind – I thought perhaps the telephone call was a trick to get you out of the way, and the more I thought of it the more likely it seemed. So, I thought of a trick myself and decided to go out the back way, down the fire escape."

"That was pretty smart," said Michael, smiling at her.

"But that's not all. I went back and stood in the doorway of a shop, where I could keep an eye on your flat. Soon a man arrived, and I recognised him. I had seen him twice before with my sister Paula, and he was just like the man you described to me when you saw her at the theatre that night.

"I was undecided what to do, but I waited, and after a while the man came out again and went away. Then you yourself came back, and I was just about to run across the road when I saw a police car stop outside the flats. Then I was scared. I changed my mind and jumped on a bus.

"I went for a long, long ride, and tried to make up my mind what to do. Then I decided to come back and make a clean breast of everything, so I came straight here and asked for your friend, Inspector Gaylord."

Now he was up to date with Carel Helvin's story, the inspector decided to revisit the flat where Paula's body had been found. "Maybe you'll see something that might give us a clue about the missing necklace," he told Carel. "Nothing has been touched since the murder. In fact, the landlord's getting a bit impatient, and we'll have to release the place soon."

Twenty minutes later, the three of them stood in what had been Paula Helvin's bedroom. They examined the room exhaustively, but without any success. Michael, who had been searching a corner cupboard, suddenly produced a neat little japanned box.

"Paula's make-up box — it was a present from me," cried Carel. Michael lifted the lid and revealed a row of greasepaint sticks, two or three small boxes of carmine, mascara and an assortment of eyebrow pencils. He was about to close the box, when Carel stopped him.

"Wait a moment!" she exclaimed. "I've just remembered something." She took the box and pressed a little ridge of metal between the two hinges. "This box used to have a secret drawer. I wonder if — look!" She lifted out the top section containing all the make-up, and in the space below lay a diamond necklace.

Michael ran the slippery stones through his fingers. "Miss Julia Wilding will be delighted to hear about this," he said.

"She isn't the only one," said Gaylord. "This seems to be the key to the whole mystery."

As they were leaving the flat, Michael said to Carel: "I think this calls for a celebration. Do you think you could dine with me this evening?"

"But of course!" she smiled.

"What about you, Jack?" asked Michael, turning to Gaylord.

The inspector shook his head. "I've a lot to clear up yet. And I must go round to the hospital right away, in case Vorse has recovered consciousness."

As the hospital was in a different direction, Gaylord said goodbye to them outside the flat and they hailed a taxi. As the taxi swung into the Bayswater Road, Michael turned to Carel. "I'm very pleased that you asked for my help in this business," he said.

"You were the most trustworthy man I could think of," she replied simply.

*****

Two hours later, Carel Helvin was sitting in a small office in Fleet Street watching Michael finish his report.

Suddenly the telephone rang, and Michael recognised the caller's voice. It was Geoffrey Frame, a television producer friend. "Michael, I'm in a spot," said the familiar voice. "Can you come along to the studios?"

"What's the trouble?"

"It's my new programme, *Personal Appearance*. Lewis Bailey was filling the crime spot, but he's been rushed off to Paris on some job or other. Could you fill in?"

"But I've only just started in the crime racket."

"All the better," replied Frame eagerly. "You can give us a completely new angle – show business to crime."

"No, I don't think so, Geoff – though, wait a minute." He covered the receiver and turned to Carel. "How'd you like to go on television tonight?" he asked her.

Her eyes widened. "Tonight?"

Michael grinned and uncovered the mouthpiece. "All right, Geoff," he said. "It's a deal – on one condition."

"What's that?"

"My future wife comes in on the same contract."

Michael Lance put down the receiver, picked up his report on the Vorse case, and turned to Carel. "That just about ties everything up," he said. "Including you and me."

THE FACE OF CAROL WEST

Published in the *News of the World* in eight parts, 9 August – 27 September 1959

This was never published as a book in the UK, but an adapted German version appeared as *Sie wußten zuviel* in the magazine *Bild und Funk*, in ten instalments, 1963.

THE FACE OF CAROL WEST

1

The floodlights that lit up the vivid blue water of the swimming pool outside The High Dive roadhouse were rarely switched off before midnight. It was often two in the morning before the last car roared away in the direction of London.

The management of The High Dive was in the competent and well-manicured hands of Victor Johnson. Johnson was just under six feet tall, with a delicately trimmed moustache and an all-the-year-round tan that seemed more suitable to Las Vegas than London. He had the type of figure on which tailors love to hang clothes – plus a weakness for fancy waistcoats and flamboyant neckwear.

Every morning before breakfast, no matter how late he had gone to bed the night before, he took a brief dip in the swimming pool. Now, in the pale sunlight of a June morning, exotically attired in maroon striped bathing trunks, Johnson looked younger than his thirty-eight years as he stood poised on the diving board. For a few seconds he looked round as if seeking an audience, then he entered the water with a neatly-executed dive.

As he usually did, he had a bet with himself that he would reach the other side of the pool without surfacing. But he was about two-thirds of the way across when his left hand encountered something solid that was ice cold to the touch. Momentarily startled he rose to the surface, then quickly dived again. This time his eyes and hands told him that the object on the floor of the pool was the body of a woman.

Johnson pulled the body to the side of the pool. The face was that of a girl in her late twenties, and there were several heavy abrasions near the eyes and the forehead. Her clothes appeared to be expensive – black cocktail frock, sheerest nylons, black satin sandals. Johnson examined the rest of the girl's face and saw that the mouth and lower jaw were tightly bound with waterproof adhesive tape.

*****

Victor Johnson took exception to Detective Sergeant Raine's tone right from the start. The detective's questions seemed to contain an unpleasant hint that The High Dive was in fact a low dive, capable of harbouring any sort of crime.

"You're quite sure you've never seen this girl before?" persisted Raine. It was the fourth time he had put the question.

Johnson shook his head impatiently. "This pool is only twenty yards from the main road," he snapped. "Someone could have dumped the body there in the small hours, and no-one would be any the wiser."

293

"I quite see that, sir," returned Raine smoothly. "On the other hand, some of your customers may have been larking about after drinking too much."

"I don't encourage that sort of thing," replied Johnson acidly. "If she had fallen into the pool by accident, someone would have been sure to raise the alarm. Besides, how can you account for the tape on her face?"

"I can't," said Raine shortly.

A uniformed constable came into the office, and placed a dark blue handbag on Johnson's desk, at which Raine was sitting. "We found this in the pool," said the constable. "It's some sort of plastic – practically waterproof."

Raine opened the bag and turned the contents on to the desk. There were two lipsticks, a heavy gold powder compact, a nail file, a wallet containing four five-pound notes, and a diary bound in leather. Raine opened the diary and read in the space for the owner's name and address: Carol West, 8 Dorchester Close, St. John's Wood, N.W.8.

He showed this name and address to Johnson. "This mean anything to you?" he asked. Johnson shrugged and shook his head.

Feeling that Johnson had by no means told him everything yet realising that he was unlikely to say more at the moment Raine went to take a final look at the swimming pool. He put the handbag and its contents into his raincoat pocket.

"Looks like murder, sergeant," said the constable, as they stood beside the pool.

Raine sniffed. "We'll have to wait for the doctor's report of course, but there doesn't seem to be much doubt about it," he said. "The girl was either thrown into the pool when she was unconscious, or else she was forcibly drowned."

Superintendent Max Christian read carefully through the file on Carol West and came to much the same conclusions as Raine. His opinion was reinforced further by the doctor's report. He closed the file and picked up the handbag, which was the only other tangible evidence apart from the dead girl's clothing.

Christian had arrived at his present position the hard way, but in a comparatively short while. Three years on the beat in Coventry and two with Birmingham C.I.D., then promotion to detective sergeant at Scotland Yard for two years' experience with the Fraud Squad, followed by four years as a detective inspector. His thoroughness was a byword at the Yard.

Having carefully scrutinised Carol West's beauty aids, he began to make a thorough examination of the dead girl's diary. As far as Christian could see, it was confined to notes of appointments at dress shops and hairdressers. Near to the end, he came to a page set aside for telephone numbers. There was only one number, scrawled slantwise in pencil across two columns. Christian stared at the diary in astonishment, then suddenly dropped it down on the desk in front of him. He half rose in his chair, then changed his mind and sat down again.

For several minutes, and with a gradually deepening frown, he sat staring at the dead girl's diary. He was puzzled and had good reason to be. It was his own telephone number in Carol West's diary.

Though Superintendent Christian had been visiting mortuaries for many years, he had never overcome his aversion to the experience. On such occasions his manner was noticeably more brusque than usual, and he never stayed a minute longer than was necessary.

There were three bodies in the bare room in which Christian now found himself. He dismissed the attendant with a nod, after he had pointed out the one Christian sought. He then went over and pulled back the sheet which covered Carol West. He stood looking at her for a full minute. Then, dissatisfied with the light from the distant electric bulb, he took the pencil torch he always carried and focused its concentrated beam on the lifeless features.

This time he did not hurry out of the mortuary. He covered the girl's head and then stood beside the body, deep in thought. The wrinkle between his brows deepened into a furrow. Christian had a phenomenal memory for faces, and he racked his brains to try to remember where he had seen this girl before. He shook his head irritably, as his mind ranged over a mental picture gallery of women – criminals, socialites, prostitutes, actresses, showgirls, debutantes, social acquaintances. But the face of Carol West remained nothing but a vague and intangible recollection.

Impatient with a memory so rarely at fault, Christian walked out of the mortuary. He told the driver of the waiting police car to take him to Dorchester Close in St. John's Wood. Fifteen minutes later, he was ringing the bell of number eight.

The woman who opened the door was about forty-five, plumpish and attractive. Her blonde hair obviously owed its appearance to skilful bleaching. She wore a silk floral-patterned housecoat. Christian felt a surge of inner relief as he remembered where he had seen her before. "Aren't you

Mary Aylestone?" he asked as soon as he had introduced himself.

The woman looked surprised but not displeased. "That's right," she said.

"I thought so. I saw you in a revival of *Ghosts*."

She smiled. "That's quite possible. I played in it about five years ago," she said.

"Are you still on the stage?"

She tucked a stray tendril of her hair into place. "No, I gave it up when I married. I'm Mrs. Fredericks now," she explained. "My husband died three years ago."

"What can you tell me about Carol West?" asked Christian.

"I told the other officer who called this morning that I know very little about her," she replied. "She came about three months ago, when I advertised for a paying guest. I've never let the room before, but as it was empty, I thought I might as well make it into a bed-sitter."

"I see," said Christian. "She had a job of some sort, I take it?"

"Oh, yes. She was a secretary at the Apex Insurance Company in the City – Cannon Street. She was rather a quiet girl, you know – kept very much to herself. I was hoping she might be company for me, but she used to shut herself in her room for hours."

"Didn't you wonder what had happened to her, when she didn't come back here to sleep?"

"No," said Mary Fredericks. "She said she often had to go away on business for two or three days at a time. She said she'd phone me from the office when she got back."

"Perhaps I could take a look at her room?" suggested Christian.

Mary Fredericks led the way upstairs, to a room at the end of a short corridor. The room had a strangely impersonal look about it, like a hotel bedroom that is rarely used. There was a small pile of books on a table in the middle of the room, but no sign of any personal possessions except for a photograph by the side of the divan bed.

Christian glanced at the photograph, which depicted a group of four girls standing outside a chalet in Switzerland. Their attitude was one of carefree gaiety. Christian made a mental note of the fact that Carol West was not one of them.

"May I use the telephone?" he asked.

Mary Fredericks nodded. Her dramatic instincts were clearly responding to the possibilities of the tragedy, and she listened eagerly as Christian spoke to the personnel manager of the Apex Insurance Company.

The man told Christian that no-one by the name of Carol West worked for his company, and none of his staff was missing.

*****

Christian went back to Scotland Yard, and worked on the case until about seven-thirty. Then he decided to call it a day and return to his flat for a bath and a meal. He occupied the top floor of a house in a mews in Kensington. It was comfortable and tastefully furnished, but on days like this he envied his married colleagues who found a drink poured out and a meal cooking in the kitchen at the end of a day's work.

Christian sighed gently and felt for his latchkey. As he fitted the key into the lock, he could hear the telephone ringing. He lifted the receiver and gave his number.

"Would you mind telling me who you are, sir?" asked a man's voice on the other end.

"My name is Christian – Max Christian."

"And is that your home number?" asked the caller.

"Certainly it is," said Christian. "Anything wrong with that?"

"Could you give me some more details about yourself, sir?"

"Suppose you tell me who you are," countered Christian sharply.

"Yes, of course, sir. I'm Detective Sergeant Ingram, C.I.D. Belhampton."

"The devil you are! Well, I'm Max Christian and I'm a superintendent at Scotland Yard." Christian's voice was curt. "Now, perhaps you'll do a bit more explaining, sergeant."

The man at the other end hesitated. "I think it would be better if you came down here, sir," he said. "It's only half an hour or so by car."

"Is this really urgent?" asked Christian. "I've had a hell of a day, and I'm tired."

"I think you should come over – in your own interests, sir," said the sergeant carefully.

"All right, I'll be over right away." Christian hung up and went over to the cabinet in the corner. He took out a bottle of whisky, picked up a siphon, and poured himself a sizeable drink.

*****

At Belhampton police station, Christian was shown into the office of Detective Inspector Wayne. Sitting at another desk in the corner was Ingram, the young detective sergeant who had telephoned him.

"I hope we haven't brought you on a fool's errand, sir," said Wayne, "but I think you'll agree this business is rather odd. Tell him about it, Ingram."

The sergeant described how, late that afternoon, he had been called to St. Julian's, a boys' preparatory school on the outskirts of Belhampton. Robin Lane, one of the masters, had been found unconscious in a gas-filled room. But for the prompt action of the housekeeper, who had smelled the gas, Lane would undoubtedly have died.

"Any doubt about it being attempted suicide?" asked Christian.

Ingram shook his head. "Not as far as we know, sir. But this was on the mantelpiece in Lane's study." He passed over a small scribbling pad. On the top page were several doodles that all seemed to point to a small circle. In the middle of the circle was written a Kensington telephone number.

"So that's where you got my number," said Christian thoughtfully. "You should have checked first with the directory inquiries people."

"I thought it would be quicker to dial," said Ingram apologetically.

"Well, there's no harm done," said Christian, glancing at a plain clothes detective who had just entered the office.

"Ah, Roberts," said Inspector Wayne, "did you find out anything else about Lane?"

The plain clothes man nodded, then looked across at Christian.

"It's all right," said Wayne. "This gentleman is from the Yard."

Roberts took a slip of paper from his inside pocket and said: "About an hour before Lane tried to gas himself, he went to the local post office and sent off this telegram."

Wayne read the copy of the telegram, and just perceptibly raised his eyebrows. His face was expressionless as he handed it to Christian. The telegram said: *Beckson, Queen's Hotel, Birmingham. Am worried about Christian Stop He'll remember her face.*

2

Inspector Wayne of the Belhampton police watched Superintendent Christian, as he read the slip of paper that contained Robin Lane's telegram. It looked as if there was more to this business than a simple case of attempted suicide.

"Did you know this man Lane?" asked the inspector, when Christian passed the copy of the telegram back to him.

Christian shook his head. "I don't know anyone of that name." He noticed that the three other men in the room — Wayne, Sergeant Ingram and a plain clothes man — were eyeing him with curiosity faintly tinged with suspicion.

Wayne nodded a dismissal to the plain clothes detective, then he turned to Christian again. "I'm afraid we can't enlighten you very much," he said. "It seems this chap Lane has been at the school for only about six weeks. Of course, it's just possible you may have known him under some other name."

Christian nodded. "That's possible."

"Perhaps it would help if you could tell us about the woman whose face he refers to in the telegram," suggested Sergeant Ingram.

Christian did not reply for a moment, then he said deliberately: "I can't answer that for certain, Ingram, but it seems likely that he means the face of a dead woman called Carol West. I'm investigating her murder."

"You mean the girl found in the swimming pool?"

"That's the one."

"And did you remember her face?" asked Ingram eagerly.

"I've seen her somewhere before," replied Christian, "but I can't place her."

"Perhaps it would be a help if you went up to the hospital, and had a chat with this chap Lane," suggested Inspector Wayne.

"That's just what I was thinking," said Christian, but as he turned towards the door the headmaster of St. Julian's, the prep school which employed Lane, was announced.

The headmaster, Jonathan Corbett, was a somewhat nondescript looking man in his late fifties. "I hope there won't be any unpleasant publicity," he said nervously as he entered. "Parents get very worried, you know. I'm sure you understand."

"Of course," said Christian.

"It's all very distressing," went on the headmaster. "I'd no idea when I engaged him that the young man was in any sort of trouble."

"He never confided in you?"

Corbett shook his head. "No."

"Do you know anything about his background?"

"Very little, I'm afraid. Staff are not easy to get, and he had a very good degree - very good, that is, for a teacher in a prep school of this size."

Christian nodded. "I take it that he lived in?"

"Oh, yes – it was in his own bed-sitter that we found him. The boys were out at games, but luckily the housekeeper smelt gas. If only she hadn't sent for the police –." He broke off in confusion.

"Did Lane ever get any visitors?"

The headmaster frowned in an effort to remember. "Not that I recall," he said. "He seemed to keep very much to himself."

"No lady friends at all?"

Corbett shook his head. "No, but someone did come to see him last week – rather a flamboyant sort of man. I told him Lane was taking the boys to the sports field, but rather to my surprise Lane said the man was there on urgent family business and asked to be excused his sports duty. I took the boys myself, and Lane was still talking to this man when I got back."

"What time did the man leave?"

"About five."

"And Lane didn't say what he wanted?"

"No. Of course, I hardly know him well enough to discuss family matters."

"Can you describe this man?" asked Christian.

Corbett thought for a moment, then said: "He was in the middle thirties, I should think, and rather loudly dressed – check coat, yellow waistcoat. He had what my generation used to call a Ronald Colman moustache."

"Well, I think that's about all for now, sir," said Christian. "You can rely on me to see that the affair gets as little publicity as possible."

*****

From his hospital bed, Robin Lane eyed Christian with undisguised hostility. He was about twenty-four - a pallid, hollow-eyed young man with tousled black hair, a receding chin and a weakly effeminate mouth.

Christian knew at once that he was up against a difficult proposition, and so it proved to be. Lane was sullen and awkward from the very first question. "The whole thing was an accident," he snapped petulantly. "Please let's have as little fuss as possible."

"If it was an accident," returned Christian smoothly, "can you explain why your curtains were drawn in broad daylight, the windows tightly closed, and a rug stuffed under the door?"

"I told you it was an accident," repeated Lane. "Now will you please leave me alone?"

Christian moved a little closer to the bed and said: "Take a good look at me, Mr. Lane. Are you quite sure we haven't met before?"

"Go away!" said Lane violently.

"I can't remember ever seeing you before," went on Christian imperturbably, "yet my telephone number is on your notepad. How do you account for that?"

"I don't account for it," said Lane sullenly. "It must have been a mistake."

"I suppose your telegram to Birmingham was another mistake?"

"I haven't sent a telegram to anyone for months."

"And you haven't heard of a girl called Carol West?"

Lane raised himself a little from the pillows and shot a look of concentrated venom at Christian. "Are you going, or do I have to ring for the nurse?"

Christian picked up his hat. "I'm going," he said, "but you'll see me again, Mr. Lane."

Christian called at the police station on his way back from the hospital and found Inspector Wayne still there. "Any luck?" asked Wayne.

"Nothing definite," replied Christian, "but I'm pretty sure there's rather more in this than meets the eye." He paused for a moment, undecided how much to tell Wayne. Then he made up his mind. "I'd appreciate your co-operation, inspector," he went on. "I'm convinced Robin Lane is concealing something, and I'd like you to see what you can uncover about him locally. Find out if he's been meeting anybody in cafés or pubs around here and let me know if he has any visitors at the hospital."

Wayne nodded. "I'll be in London tomorrow. I'll drop in to the Yard and tell you what I've managed to dig up."

Christian said goodnight to Wayne and went through to the outer office. He stopped at the switchboard. "Could you get through to Birmingham fairly quickly?" he asked the constable on duty.

"Should do at this time, sir," replied the man. "What number d'you want?"

Christian fumbled for the little black notebook he always carried and asked the constable to get through to the private address of Ralph Stoner. Stoner was a C.I.D. inspector in Birmingham, and an old friend of Christian's.

He was through to Stoner in less than a minute. "A little job for you, Ralph," he said. "Check on someone called Beckson at the Queen's Hotel – I want to know all about him. Got that?"

"Right away," said Stoner. "I'll ring you at your flat tonight."

On the way back to London, the forcible realisation came to Christian that he had not eaten since lunch. A signpost told him that he was one mile from The High Dive, the roadhouse where Carol West's body had been found.

The roadhouse, brilliantly bathed in light, seemed to offer an expensive welcome. Christian sat in his car for a few minutes, absorbing the surroundings. He found himself trying to reconstruct the death of Carol West. This girl had drowned, her mouth and jaw tightly bound with adhesive tape, clutching a handbag containing a diary with his telephone number inside it. What, Christian wondered, had Carol West known about him? For the hundredth time he cudgelled his brains in an attempt to remember where he had seen the girl's face before.

He was just about to open his car door, when a man and a woman came out of the back door of The High Dive and began to cross the car park. He did not recognise the middle-aged man, but the flashily-dressed woman was undoubtedly Mary Fredericks, Carol West's landlady. When they had driven off in a large American car, Christian walked towards the restaurant. He was wondering if Mary Fredericks was merely a casual patron, or if she were a close friend of Victor Johnson, the manager of the roadhouse.

Christian found a vacant table in a corner of the crowded restaurant and studied the menu. When he had ordered his meal, he asked the waiter if he could see the manager and presently Johnson came over to Christian's table, nodding amiably to selected members of his clientèle on the way.

Johnson was suave and charming, and his dinner jacket became him like a faultless uniform. He said: "Good evening, sir. What can I do for you?" His voice, like the rest of him, was smooth.

Christian detected a certain lessening of Johnson's bonhomie, when he introduced himself and asked the manager to take the vacant chair. Johnson fingered his moustache a trifle uneasily, as he said in a low voice: "I suppose it's about the girl who was murdered."

"Indirectly, perhaps," said Christian casually. "First of all, though, I wondered if you'd ever come across a schoolmaster by the name of Robin Lane?"

Johnson's eyes, Christian noticed, did not quite meet his own. "I meet a lot of people," he replied evasively. "I might possibly know him by sight."

"But not by name?"

"Not that I can recall."

Christian sipped his drink. "I just saw a middle-aged couple leave here," he remarked. "The lady was a Mrs. Fredericks. Does she come here regularly?"

Johnson shook his head. "No," he said shortly. "I'm not even sure that I know her."

"She used to be on the stage – as Mary Aylestone."

Johnson wrinkled his forehead. "I may have seen her in a film once," he said, "but I'm pretty sure she doesn't come here very often. I expect she just dropped in for a meal." He smiled suddenly, with a flash of white teeth. "Or perhaps she's one of those women with a morbid interest in the murder. We've had quite a few of them, you know."

"It wouldn't be surprising if she was interested in the murder," said Christian deliberately, "considering she was the dead girl's landlady."

Johnson raised his eyebrows. "Really?" he said. "Well –er – I expect that explains it." He rose from his chair. "And now, if there are no more questions, perhaps you'll excuse me?"

"There are quite a lot more," said Christian pleasantly, "but they'll keep." And he turned his attention to the large steak which had just been placed in front of him.

*****

It was approaching midnight when Christian drove his car into the garage at the end of the Kensington mews where he lived. There was no moon, and the mews was only dimly lighted.

As he came out of the garage, some instinct prompted Christian to duck, so the cosh whistled past the side of his head and he took the blow on his left shoulder. He lashed out with his right fist, and the jarring impact in his right arm told him he had connected between his assailant's eyes.

Christian's experience in Birmingham street brawls as a young constable had taught him that the Queensberry Rules play little part in fights of this sort, and to observe them is to risk being permanently injured. He therefore defended himself by raising his right knee, but not before the other man had landed a vicious uppercut to his mouth.

Christian heard the man gasp, as he leapt at him in the darkness and twisted the hand that held the cosh. The man swore and lashed out with his right foot as the cosh fell to the pavement. Christian retaliated with a rugby tackle, and the two men rolled on the ground together. The man finished uppermost and drove his fist into Christian's mouth. Christian struggled to a sitting position, dragged the man to his feet and hit him with a cruel driving right. The man doubled up, but as Christian drew back his fist again, he drove his right foot into the superintendent's groin. As Christian fell backwards, he heard the man running down the deserted mews.

Christian lurched unsteadily up the stairs to his flat. Clutching his stomach with one hand, he fumbled for his latchkey with the other. There was a drumming in his head, a burning pain in his right leg, and continuous waves of nausea swept over him.

He staggered into the living room, switched on the light, and stumbled towards the small bathroom. He looked at himself in the mirror above the washbasin and saw, with difficulty, that one side of his face was a mass of cuts and a bruise was beginning to form near his right ear.

He was dabbing his hand with iodine when the telephone rang. "That you, Max?" came the familiar voice of Ralph Stoner. "I've inquired at the Queen's Hotel about Beckson."

"Well?" said Christian, finding he had some difficulty in speaking.

"She checked out last night."

"She?"

"That's right. Middle-aged woman, blonde, probably bleached. Plumpish, just over average height, fairly attractive, rather flashily dressed in mauve."

"Thanks," said Christian tersely.

Stoner sounded a trifle mystified as he rang off, but the superintendent did not offer to enlighten him. He was thinking of the mauve dress Mrs. Fredericks had been wearing that evening, and Stoner's description which fitted Mrs. Fredericks exactly.

Still nursing his jaw, Christian returned to the bathroom. It was then that he noticed the drawing and stopped dead in his tracks. Someone had sketched a face on the bathroom wall. It had been crudely drawn with a ballpoint pen, but Christian recognised it immediately.

It was the face of Carol West.

3

Christian stood looking at the drawing for a full two minutes, lost in thought. Then he took a quick look round his living room and bedroom. He opened a few drawers, but as far as he could see nothing had been touched.

His front door was of unusual design, and Christian decided that the intruder must have been a clever lock-picker unless he had somehow gained possession of a key. He went to the rear of his flat, and found the back door unlocked. It was then that he remembered he had left it unlocked himself, earlier in the day.

He winced as he felt several of his bruises stiffening. His mind went back to the attack on him in the mews earlier that evening. Suddenly the prospect of a hot bath seemed infinitely desirable. As he twisted the taps, he was conscious of the sore knuckles on his right hand; he must have landed a very nasty blow on his assailant's cheek, probably somewhere around the eye.

Christian lay full length in the almost unbearably hot water and gazed at the drawing of Carol West on the wall through the clouds of steam. Where, he asked himself for the hundredth time, had he seen her before? Like frames of film clicking through a projector, his orderly mind turned over the strange chain of circumstances since the discovery of Carol West's body in the swimming pool of The High Dive roadhouse. There were, he thought ruefully, far too many unanswered questions.

What was Robin Lane, the young schoolmaster, trying to conceal? How did he come to have Christian's telephone number? Why had he sent that telegram to Birmingham? And why was Mrs. Fredericks, Carol West's landlady, staying at a hotel under the name of Beckson?

Christian decided that Mrs. Fredericks certainly knew more about Carol West than she had told the police, and he resolved to see her first thing in the morning. As he towelled himself gingerly, he wondered whether the drawing on the bathroom wall should be removed. He picked up a bottle of cleaning fluid and then, changing his mind, returned it to the cupboard. Perhaps the drawing would strike a chord in his memory sooner or later.

*****

The weather had turned cold during the night, and Christian had some difficulty in starting his car the next morning. He was just turning out of the mews when a taxi stopped at the entrance. A striking blonde girl, wearing a mink jacket and emerald green beret, got out.

As Christian's car drew level with the taxi, she suddenly looked him straight in the face and her mouth opened fractionally in what might have been surprise. After a casual glance, he turned away and concentrated on the traffic in the main road. But there was something about this girl's expression that puzzled him. Should he have known her? The alarming thought came to him that his well-nigh infallible memory for faces, which had helped to win him such rapid promotion, might be deserting him.

He worried at the problem all the way to St. John's Wood but was no nearer to any solution when he rang the front doorbell of Mrs. Fredericks's house. She opened it at once; apparently, she was on her way out shopping. After a momentary hesitation, she invited him inside.

"Is there any news about Carol West?" she inquired eagerly, as she led the way into her drawing room.

"There are certain developments," replied Christian enigmatically. "I'm hoping you may be able to throw some light on them. At the moment we're very interested in a man called Robin Lane. Does that name mean anything to you?"

She pursed her lips for a moment, then shook her head decisively.

"You're quite sure you never had a telegram from him which was addressed to a Mrs. Beckson at the Queen's Hotel in Birmingham?" Christian persisted.

"Beckson? Birmingham?" Mary Fredericks sounded completely bewildered. "What on earth should I be doing in Birmingham, and who's Mrs. Beckson?"

"A woman answering to your description was staying at the Queen's Hotel in that name," said Christian deliberately.

She smiled. "But there must be millions of women who answer to my description. I don't flatter myself that I'm unique."

Christian shrugged. "I'm sorry if I've made a mistake. But you understand that we have to follow up every line of inquiry, however vague it might seem."

As Christian picked up his hat and moved towards the door, she suddenly seemed much more at ease. In the hall, he asked: "Have you ever been to the roadhouse where Carol West's body was found?"

"Yes," she replied casually. "As a matter of fact, I was there last night. I felt rather morbidly curious about it, so I rang up Eddie Porter."

"Who's he?"

"He owns The High Dive and has several other places. Eddie's an old friend of mine – he backed a play I was in years ago. He took me down there for dinner."

"Did he introduce Victor Johnson, the manager, to you?

She shook her head. "No. While I was in the powder room, Eddie went into the office to see Johnson on business."

"I suppose you discussed the murder with Porter?" suggested Christian.

"Well, naturally I did. After all, the dead girl was my boarder."

"And could he suggest any solution?"

Suddenly much more self-assured, Mary Fredericks smiled. "He was more concerned with how it would affect business. He was delighted to see that apparently it hadn't done any harm."

Christian nodded thoughtfully and opened the front door. "I expect I'll be seeing you again, Mrs. Fredericks."

"Any time," she said. Her manner was slightly theatrical, even mildly flirtatious. "Only too glad to help."

Christian had a feeling that Mrs. Fredericks could have told him much more.

*****

Back at the office he found his assistant, Detective Sergeant Hale, carefully indexing the file on the Carol West murder. "What d'you know about Eddie Porter, Tom?" he asked.

Hale looked up in surprise. "Porter? Is he in on this?"

"He could be. He owns The High Dive."

"I know that, sir, but he hasn't been near the place for a week or two – I checked that."

"He was there last night," said Christian. "We've never had anything on him, have we?"

"Nothing," said Hale. "Eddie's a cute bird, you know – started as a barrow boy and came up the tough way. Done all right, too – he owns nightclubs, a couple of striptease joints, and half a dozen roadhouses. But he's too fly to get caught on the wrong side of the law. I used to see him quite often when I was on the beat in the West End."

"Find out when he can see me," ordered Christian.

Hale picked up the telephone and asked for a number. Two minutes later, he replaced the receiver. "Porter's up in Manchester for a couple of days," he said. "He's putting on some new show at his club there. They expect him back tomorrow."

"Thanks, Tom," said Christian.

*****

After two hours of concentrated desk work, Christian decided to walk to a restaurant near Victoria Station where he often went for lunch. It was a large oak-panelled room with substantial furnishings and was rarely overcrowded. A table was usually kept for him.

As he was about to sit down, he saw a blonde girl sitting by herself near the window. On her head was a bright green beret, and her mink jacket was carelessly flung over a chair. She was staring at Christian with a tense expression but dropped her eyes at once when she saw he was staring back.

He picked up the menu and studied it. He shot an occasional glance at the girl, but apart from the fact that she was the girl he had seen getting out of the taxi earlier that morning, he could not recall her face.

As Christian was drinking his soup, he suddenly noticed a man three tables away who was moodily stabbing at his food with a fork. This man, too, was clearly interested in the girl by the window. He turned slightly, and Christian saw that there was a cut near his right eye which was discoloured.

Christian looked away quickly, as he knew this man at once. He was puzzled why a small-time crook called Denny Winters should be watching this girl, who in turn appeared to be sufficiently interested in himself to have discovered his favourite restaurant.

The girl cut short his speculations by suddenly getting up and walking out. Almost immediately, Winters called for his bill and followed her. Christian restrained an impulse to rush after them. After all, Winters was breaking no law in following the girl as long as he did not make a nuisance of himself. Christian wondered if the girl knew she was being followed. Would she have come across and spoken to him if Winters had not been there? Winters's black eye posed yet another problem, and Christian thoughtfully rubbed the knuckles of his right hand and wondered.

As soon as he got back to Scotland Yard, he turned up the file on Denny Winters. It was a melancholy record of small robberies, two of them with violence. Winters had already spent more than half of his adult life inside prison walls. If only Christian could have been sure that Winters was the man who attacked him the night before, he would have pulled him in and grilled him relentlessly.

He was just wondering if it would be worthwhile putting a man on to tail Winters, when the telephone rang. A girl's voice, slightly husky, asked if he were Superintendent Christian. "I tried to talk to you in the restaurant," she said. "It's about Carol West."

"Are you the girl in the mink jacket?" he queried.

"That's right. I missed you at your flat this morning, but I could call this evening. It's terribly important."

"Nine o'clock suit you?"

"Yes, I'll be there."

"I'll be waiting for you," promised Christian. "By the way, you didn't tell me your name."

"When I see you," she said. He heard the click of her receiver being replaced.

Christian wondered what made the girl so scared. Was she making the call under duress, with Denny Winters standing over her with a knife or gun? Christian pressed the buzzer on his desk, and Detective Sergeant Hale came in. Christian pointed to the file on Winters. "Heard anything about this character lately?"

Hale grinned. "I sent Denny down a couple of times, so he steers clear of me now. But I've heard from a couple of the boys that he's picking up some steady money."

Before Hale could enlarge on the subject of Denny Winters, the telephone rang and Inspector Wayne from Belhampton, where they were handling the case of schoolmaster Robin Lane and his attempted suicide, was announced. Christian remembered that in well-cut plain clothes Wayne looked more like a prosperous businessman than a policeman. "Giving the wife a day in town," he explained. "There's a bit of news about Lane, so I thought I'd drop in and let you know."

"How is he?" asked Christian.

"Much better now. In fact, he had a visitor at the hospital this morning, and I've reason to believe that she was the Mrs. Beckson he sent that telegram to in Birmingham. She was with him for about ten minutes, and my man got a good look at her."

"Are you sure it was Mrs. Beckson?"

"That's the name she gave at the desk."

"Any description of her?"

"My man says she was a very attractive blonde, about twenty-seven, wearing a mink jacket over a pale grey suit - oh, yes, and she had a bright green beret."

Christian's expression betrayed no hint of surprise. He slowly unscrewed the cap of his fountain pen and made a note. "Thank you, inspector," he said quietly. "That's very interesting."

*****

Christian was restless in his flat that evening. He skimmed through the evening paper, made himself an omelette, and debated in his mind whether to ring up Inspector Ralph Stoner in Birmingham to make sure that there had been no mistake about the recipient of the telegram. Then he realised that, in the event of any such mistake, Stoner would certainly have telephoned him. The inescapable fact remained that a plump middle-aged woman had been staying at the Queen's Hotel under the name of Mrs. Beckson, and her detailed description tallied exactly with that of Mrs. Fredericks.

At nine o'clock there was still no sign of the girl. At twenty minutes to ten, Christian poured himself a whisky and soda and tried to concentrate on an American textbook on forgery that he had been trying to read for weeks. Two hours and three whiskies later, the girl still had not turned up and Christian was having some difficulty in keeping awake.

Then the ringing of the telephone jangled through the room, and he grabbed the receiver. Instead of the expected husky voice of the girl, Christian heard the matter-of-fact tones of Detective Sergeant Hale. "Glad I caught you, sir," he

317

said. "They've just fished the body of a woman out of the river at Hammersmith."

"Well, what's the idea of telling me that?" demanded Christian irritably.

"I thought you'd like to know about it, sir. You see, she's all bruised about the face and her mouth is taped up – just like Carol West."

"I see," said Christian. "Where are you speaking from?"

"Carter's Wharf, Hammersmith. The body's now in a warehouse, and we're just waiting for the ambulance."

"Tell 'em to hold on," said Christian. "I'll be there in a quarter of an hour."

On the way to Hammersmith, he brooded over the blonde girl who had been too terrified to contact him. He wished now that he had gone over to her in the restaurant and heard her story. Then at least he could have arranged for her to have police protection, but now it was too late. Christian felt a sudden surge of anger that a beautiful and vital young woman should now be a bedraggled and dripping corpse.

Hale was waiting for him at the entrance to the wharf and took him along to the warehouse where there were three police cars and an ambulance waiting. He nodded a greeting to a couple of men from the river police, with whom he had worked on several previous occasions.

They went into a night-watchman's cabin, just inside the main warehouse. Under the inadequate light from a grimy electric bulb, a doctor and two policemen stood beside a rough table on which the body lay.

Christian stooped and picked up a sodden green beret from the floor under the table. Water and slime were dripping all around him. He straightened up and forced himself to look at the dead woman. One of the policemen pulled back the

318

large white handkerchief which had been thrown over her face. He caught his breath sharply, then pulled aside the old mackintosh that had been flung over the dead woman's clothes. He looked at the battered cheeks, the cruelly bruised forehead, the repellent mass of sodden hair.

"Can you identify her, sir?" asked the local police sergeant.

Christian nodded. "Yes," he said slowly. "It's a woman called Mary Fredericks."

4

The little group of police on the Thames-side wharf were silent, when Superintendent Max Christian identified the body of the woman taken from the river as that of Mrs. Fredericks. All except his assistant, Detective Sergeant Tom Hale, who gave an exclamation of surprise. "You mean Carol West's landlady?" asked the sergeant, who had never seen Mrs. Fredericks before.

Christian nodded. "That's her," he said. He examined the green beret, reflecting as he did so that it was the last type of hat which a woman like Mrs. Fredericks would have worn. "Was this hat found in the river?" he asked the local sergeant.

"Yes, sir," said the sergeant, "but the dead woman wasn't actually wearing it."

Christian fingered the beret thoughtfully. It was sodden with water, but so far as he could judge it was very like the one worn by the girl with the mink coat whom he had seen in the restaurant, and who had failed to keep the appointment she had sought with him.

The ambulance attendants carried away the body of Mrs. Fredericks, and Christian walked slowly back to his car with Hale. As they drove through the deserted streets, Christian told the sergeant all about the girl in the green beret who had seemed so anxious to pass on some information.

"You naturally thought she was the woman who had been picked out of the river?" hazarded Hale.

"I did," said Christian, "but I'm very relieved I was wrong. I've got a feeling this girl may have quite a lot to tell us."

"It certainly looks as if Mrs. Fredericks could have thrown more light on the Carol West murder," said Hale.

"I've suspected that for some time," agreed Christian, "but now it looks as if she was just one of the minor stooges – someone who had to be quietly removed after she had done her job."

Hale nodded, and lit a cigarette. "Talking of stooges," he said, "I've been doing a bit of checking on Denny Winters."

"What did you find out?"

"It seems my first guess about him was wrong. Denny isn't putting the black on anybody – he's on Eddie Porter's payroll. The boys tell me he's around one of Eddie's clubs in the West End most nights."

"Doing what?"

"No idea but knowing him I should think it's dirty work of some sort – he's not much good at anything else." Hale drew thoughtfully on his cigarette. "D'you think Porter's mixed up in this Carol West murder, sir?"

Christian frowned. "Well, he owns The High Dive, where the body was found. He was seen there with Mrs. Fredericks. It's beginning to look as if he's involved in some way."

"He's managed to keep his nose clean till now," commented Hale.

"Maybe he's never been caught up in a murder case before," retorted Christian. "Anyhow, we'll pick up Denny

Winters for a start and see if he's in the mood to tell us why he was tailing that girl."

"He'll tell you a pack of lies," prophesied Hale gloomily.

*****

Eight hours later, when Christian arrived at the Yard, the sergeant in the front hall was on the lookout for him. "There's a Mr. Eddie Porter to see you, sir," he said. "He's in the top waiting room."

Eddie Porter was about fifty years of age; a large, rather coarse-featured man of undoubted presence and personality. His clothes, Christian noticed, were good and expensive. In the uncertain world of night clubs and roadhouses, Mr. Porter was clearly doing well for himself.

He was in the act of taking a cigarette from a gold case when Christian came into the room. He spoke with a trace of cockney accent. "Hello, super. Any news about Mrs. Fredericks's murder?"

"Nothing definite yet," replied Christian. "Perhaps you wouldn't mind coming into my office?"

He led the way along the corridor. When they were in Christian's office, Porter said: "This is a shocking business. Why, I only saw her this week – she asked me to run her down to The High Dive, y'know, where that girl was found drowned."

Christian indicated a chair. "Won't you sit down, Mr. Porter?" he invited.

"You've got to get the man who did this!" exclaimed Porter as he sat down. "If there's anything I can do –"

"One thing at a time," interrupted Christian gently. "Did you know Mrs. Fredericks well?"

"Not all that well. We met about a month ago at a party and got on very well. She was a nice lady, a very nice lady. It looks as if she was murdered because she happened to know something about this girl Carol West."

"That could well be," replied Christian. He sat back and covertly studied his visitor. Porter, he decided, was a tough, clever and possibly dangerous individual. "When you took Mrs. Fredericks to The High Dive the other evening," went on Christian, "did she tell you anything about Carol West?"

"Nothing much. It appears this Carol West was a bit of a high-stepper."

"And what exactly d'you mean by that?"

"Boyfriends and so on. Seems they used to nip in and out of the house in the middle of the night."

"I see," said Christian thoughtfully. "You'd never been to Mrs. Fredericks's house yourself?"

"Only that time when I picked her up to take her to The High Dive – I didn't go in."

"What about Carol West? Had you met her?"

Porter looked at Christian through slightly narrowed eyes. "Why should I have met her?" he asked.

"She was found dead at your roadhouse."

"So what? Thousands of people I don't know come to The High Dive."

"Didn't your manager, Victor Johnson, know her?"

"Doesn't seem like it. He'd have said if he did."

"Then you think Johnson is to be trusted?"

Porter flicked the ash off his cigarette. "Vic Johnson's a good boy – best manager I've got. I could find room for half a dozen more of his sort."

"That wasn't exactly what I meant," said Christian.

322

Porter leaned forward. "Now look, super," he said. "You know Johnson couldn't have had that job if he'd been in any sort of trouble with the law. The police wouldn't have stood for it."

"Perhaps not."

"And anyway," went on Porter forcefully, "I don't employ people with criminal records."

"You employ Denny Winters," pointed out Christian quietly.

Porter's heavy eyebrows shot up. "Did he tell you that?"

"It's true, isn't it?" persisted Christian. "He's on your payroll."

"Denny does a few odd jobs around the club."

"What sort of odd jobs?"

"This and that," said Porter casually. "Sometimes he acts as chucker-out –"

"And sometimes he does a bit of shadowing," interposed Christian suavely. "You've kept him quite busy following Eve Beckson around." Christian clenched his right fist and turned the knuckles, still sore and bruised from the attack made on him outside his flat, in Porter's direction. "Another thing – Denny seems to have collected a nice black eye from somewhere."

Porter smoked nonchalantly. "I don't think I quite get you," he said evenly. "It's more than likely Denny has been doing some other work in his spare time. I can't keep a close check on all my employees."

"I have a feeling Denny won't be one of them for very much longer," said Christian, and rose from his desk. "Will you be at your club for the next day or two, Mr. Porter? I might need to get in touch with you."

Porter nodded. "Look in any evening," he said. "Always pleased to see our friends." He walked out of the office, leaving Christian staring thoughtfully after him.

*****

"Just what the hell are you getting at?" demanded Robin Lane indignantly.

Christian sighed. Since his arrival at the hospital where Lane was a patient after attempting suicide, the schoolmaster had been surly, evasive and belligerent in turn. He was wearing a dressing gown and sitting by the window in his private ward. His hair drooped untidily about his forehead, and his knuckles showed white as he clenched his hands.

Christian leaned back in his chair and folded his arms. "People don't usually try to take their own lives unless they're pretty desperate," he pointed out mildly. "I'm simply trying to find out why you did it, that's all."

"Then I'd be glad if you'd mind your own business," countered Lane acidly.

"I'm paid to mind the public's business," said Christian curtly. "I'm fairly sure this thing goes deeper than you'd like us to believe."

Lane jumped up from his chair and began to pace angrily up and down the little room. Christian waited a few moments, then he said: "I'll go over the facts once more, Mr. Lane. My telephone number was found on a notepad in your room. You also referred to me in a telegram which you sent to a Mrs. Beckson in Birmingham. This telegram, strangely enough, was collected by Mrs. Fredericks, who was murdered last night." Christian's voice suddenly took on a stern and authoritative

324

tone. "I think you'd better tell me what you know about this business," he said.

"I'll tell you nothing – nothing!" Lane's voice had risen to near-hysteria.

A nurse hurried in, taking in the situation at a glance. She settled Lane in a chair and prepared to give him an injection. "I told you not to excite him, sir," she said reprovingly. Deftly she slid the needle into Lane's arm. "Perhaps you'd better have a word with Dr. Fitzgerald as you go out."

Fitzgerald was lean-featured and Irish. He waved Christian to a chair. "I'm getting a bit tired of this patient of yours," confided Christian. "He doesn't seem to appreciate that I've got a murder case on my hands."

A wry smile flitted across the doctor's face. "I doubt if you're as tired of him as I am," he said, "but he's improving. You must bear in mind that he's a hopeless neurotic, and he's been taking drugs into the bargain."

"I'm sure you appreciate, doctor," said Christian, "that in a case of murder every hour that passes reduces our chances of finding the culprit. I'd be grateful if you'd talk to Lane and try to make him see sense."

"All right," said Fitzgerald resignedly, "but I'm not making any promises."

Christian was conscious of weary irritation as he left. He had the feeling that he could have made better use of his time at the hospital. Had Robin Lane been shamming hysteria to avoid his questions? Even if Lane had answered the questions, Christian concluded, the word of a drug addict could scarcely be considered reliable.

Suddenly Christian hesitated, and half-turned towards the road. He felt, rather than heard, the high-powered car driven at reckless speed, which bore down on him from behind. With a split second to spare, he flung himself sideways onto the grass verge. Lying on his stomach, he caught a fleeting glimpse of the headlong progress of the car. He rose to his feet, and gingerly felt himself all over. He appeared to have suffered no injury, but the nearside mudguard had actually ripped into the skirt of his raincoat.

Christian walked on. He knew nothing of the driver, except that he had worn a cloth cap and had unquestionably done his best to murder him.

*****

Back at his Kensington flat, Christian took a bath and poured himself an outsize whisky and soda. Someone, he thought grimly, wanted him out of the way – and quickly. The drink tasted good, and Christian relaxed in an easy chair.

The telephone rang and the voice of Sergeant Hale, who sounded more animated than usual, came over the wire. "A van driver called here at the Yard to see you, sir," said Hale. "I told him I'd pass on any information, and he came out with an extraordinary story of picking up an excited young woman in Hammersmith about forty minutes before Mrs. Fredericks's body was found. He says this woman offered him ten pounds to take her to Richmond."

"Can he describe her?"

"He's a bit vague, but it sounded very like that girl you told me about – Eve Beckson. According to this fellow, she looked as if she'd been in a struggle."

"Where's this van driver now?"

"Still here, sir."

"Well, send him round to my place. It shouldn't take him long."

Christian finished dressing and relaxed again. Then he heard the sound of a car engine in the mews outside. He looked through the window and saw a small green van. The driver proved to be a middle-aged man with heavy jowls and a prominent underlip, who introduced himself as George Hodges and repeated the story that Hale had recounted on the telephone.

Christian listened attentively. At length he said: "Did you notice if this girl wore an emerald ring on her left hand?"

Hodges thought for a moment. "Yus, I think she did, guv'nor," he said hoarsely. "A nice lookin' sparkler it was an' all."

"Can you take me to the address where you left her?" asked Christian.

"Take you there now if you like, guv."

"Just wait while I get my hat and coat."

Christian ran back to his flat, and immediately telephoned Hale at the Yard. "Listen," he said urgently. "This van driver is a phoney. Get a couple of squad cars round here at once."

Hale's voice was anxious. "D'you think you can hold him there, sir?"

"I'm not going to try," said Christian. "This is a trap, and I'm deliberately walking into it. This is going to be very interesting, Tom."

5

Detective Sergeant Hale was obviously shaken by his chief's matter-of-fact statement that he was walking into a trap. "Just a minute, sir," he said urgently. "Will you be going to that place the van driver mentioned, near Richmond?"

"We've only got his word for that," said Christian. "Just tip off the squad cars to be on the lookout for any change of direction."

Hale's voice was tense and concerned. "I don't like it, sir. It sounds tricky to me."

"It is tricky," retorted Christian testily, "but it's a chance we've got to take. Now, just do as I tell you – I've got to go now, or he'll be getting suspicious."

*****

"Nice jalopy, this," remarked Hodges, as they drove in the van through Putney. "When I gave that bird a lift last night, we touched seventy as easy as kiss yer 'and. Outside the built-up area, of course," he added hastily.

It was a clear night, and they did not need the van's somewhat indifferent headlights. Christian tried to find out more about the girl Hodges had picked up the previous evening, but the van driver's garrulous attitude quickly changed to one of uncommunicative silence. Christian got the impression that the man was thinking out some future course of action.

From time to time the superintendent glanced across at the van's driving mirror, but there appeared to be no sign of any car following. Either the squad cars were keeping well out of sight, or they hadn't picked up the van yet. They were skirting Richmond Park now, and still heading south-west. Christian glanced at the luminous dial of his wristwatch and saw that it was just after ten-twenty. "Are you sure we're on the right road?" he asked.

"'Course I'm sure." There was a surly note in Hodges's voice now. Christian took another quick look in the mirror, but still there was no sign of any lights behind.

Then Hodges suddenly swung into a side road, and soon took a left fork that proved to be a narrow country lane. There were no street lights and the surface of the road was rough. Hodges drove up the lane for half a mile, then stopped the van on a grass verge. "'Ere you are, guv'nor," he announced. "This is it."

Christian peered about him in the darkness. "I can't see any sign of a house," he said.

"No more could I last night," said Hodges, "but she said it was a cottage, half way across that there field." He pointed vaguely into the darkness. "She went through that white gate, and that was the last I saw of 'er."

"Where is this place exactly?"

"I told you, guv," said Hodges impatiently, "it's the other side of Richmond. I just followed 'er instructions. I've never bin 'ere meself."

Christian opened the van door and got out, feeling soft turf under his feet. He said: "You'd better wait here while I have a look round." His eyes soon became more accustomed to the gloom, and he could see the white gate. It swung open almost at a touch, and he found himself on a rough cinder road as he moved cautiously forward. He was carrying a torch but was reluctant to advertise his presence.

About thirty yards along the road, he suddenly caught sight of a cottage with whitewashed walls. He stepped on to the grass and walked on unhurriedly. Just as he was level with the cottage, he heard the engine of the van start and, turning, he saw its tail lights disappearing into the distance. He had walked into a trap all right. Well, that was just what he had meant to do.

There was no sign of life in the cottage, though the windows were curtained and the place did not appear derelict. He walked carefully round to the back, and found himself on a strip of brick yard. Cautiously he tried the back door, but found it locked. Then he moved round to a window and tried to look inside, but everything was pitch dark. He tiptoed round to the front of the cottage, in a silence that was becoming oppressive. He came to another window and, seeing nothing but blackness inside, felt for the catch.

He was in the act of lifting the catch when he heard quick footsteps behind him. Swinging round quickly, Christian switched on his torch. Almost at once his hand went numb from a sharp blow, and simultaneously the light flashed on the saturnine and unmistakable features of Denny Winters. Then another blow from a blunt instrument caught him squarely across the temple, and he almost lost consciousness.

In a red haze of pain, he felt himself being dragged along the ground. Then he heard the front door being kicked open and was immediately aware of the all-pervading smell of petrol. He was flung to the floor, and from what seemed to be a long way off he heard a voice mutter: "Matches!"

Then there was a sudden rush of heavy feet, a blistering oath from Denny Winters, and finally a merciful silence. Still dazed, Christian felt himself lifted by strong hands and carried into the open air. Then he opened his eyes and looked into the anxious face of Detective Sergeant Hale.

"Near thing, sir," said Hale.

Christian felt his head carefully. "I don't want it any nearer," he said grimly.

330

"Sorry we weren't quicker," apologised Hale, "but we didn't think he'd attack you outside the cottage."

"Did you get that van driver?"

"We were waiting for him at the end of the lane. He won't give us any more trouble for a while."

"It was lucky you managed to get so close behind us," said Christian. He gently fingered his throbbing head. "I couldn't see any sign of you at first."

"They had a nasty trap laid for you," said Hale. "Everything in there is saturated with petrol – one spark, and you'd have been fried."

"I certainly walked into that one," commented Christian sadly.

"Well, you told us you were going to do so, sir," said Hale reprovingly. "No wonder we couldn't find Denny Winters when we tried to pick him up – he was busy laying on this little reception for you."

"Very thoughtful of him," said Christian, and got to his feet somewhat uncertainly. "So let's get out of here, before it blows up."

*****

Christian slept late next morning and was eventually awakened by the persistent ringing of his front doorbell. When he opened the door, a telegraph boy thrust an orange envelope at him.

He tore open the envelope and read the message, then shook his head to signify there was no reply. He took the wire into the kitchen and spread the flimsy paper on the table. The telegram said: *Desperately urgent see you tonight your office ten o'clock. Eve Beckson.*

Christian poured himself a cup of coffee and sat looking at the message. Who was this girl Beckson, and why was she so eager to get in touch with him? If she was so anxious to see him, why hadn't she turned up the night before? And how did Eve Beckson, whoever she was, fit into the complex pattern of the murders of Carol West and Mary Fredericks?

The ringing of his front doorbell interrupted his speculations, and it was Hale. "How are you feeling now, sir?" he enquired with some concern, but Christian shrugged off this anxiety about his health and asked if there were any new developments.

"We've taken a statement from Hodges, the van driver," said Hale. "He says Denny Winters gave him a hundred quid to spin you the tale and lure you to that cottage."

Christian whistled softly. "Where would Denny Winters get a hundred pounds?"

Hale grinned. "Denny won't talk," he said, "but we shouldn't have to look very far for the answer to that one."

"You mean Eddie Porter?"

Hale nodded. "That's who I mean, sir."

"I think," said Christian grimly, "that we'd better have another talk with Mr. Porter."

"He's in Manchester," said Hale. "He flew up there last night, as it seems that one of his strippers assaulted a customer for getting a bit too friendly. But he'll be at The High Dive tonight."

"How d'you know that?"

"Denny Winters says he makes a point of going there every Friday to go through the accounts with Johnson, and he particularly asked that Eddie Porter should be told about his arrest."

Christian smiled grimly. "I'll be glad to pass on the good news," he said.

*****

A somewhat pugnacious waiter tried to bar Christian's way to the office at The High Dive. "Mr. Johnson, the manager, is in conference," he said, "and he can't see anyone."

Christian brushed past him. "He'll see me," he said abruptly, and turned the door handle. Immediately he could hear the sound of men's voices raised in heated argument, as he walked through a small outer office and into a private office the other side of a partition.

Johnson was sitting in an armchair at the top of a small oblong table. Eddie Porter was pacing up and down, beating his right fist into his left palm, and he turned sharply as Christian came in. "I quite thought the door was locked," he said pointedly. "We're very busy going over the accounts."

"I'm concerned with something more urgent than your accounts," retorted Christian brusquely. "I've got some news for you, Mr. Porter."

"Really?" Porter's voice was disinterested.

Christian said deliberately: "Denny Winters is in custody, on a charge of attempted murder."

Porter laughed. "Well, what d'you know about that? Poor old Denny – who was it this time?"

"Me," said Christian shortly.

But Porter shrugged unconcernedly. "Well, well, he's aiming high. A superintendent, too."

"He'll be lucky if that's the only charge," said Christian, conscious of his rising temper. "He's also involved in the murders of Carol West and Mary Fredericks."

Porter remained urbane. "Can you prove that?"

"I will," said Christian curtly.

Porter suddenly changed his tone. "I'm sorry about all this, super," he said, showing his teeth in a broad smile, "but I can hardly be held responsible for how my employees spend their spare time."

"I may want to know something about how you spend your spend time," said Christian coldly. "You still need to convince me that you aren't involved with Winters."

"Now come off it, super," said Porter deprecatingly. "You surely don't think I'd have anything to do with Denny's funny business, do you? I gave him a chance to go straight, and if he's let me down then it's just too bad."

Christian switched his gaze from Porter to Johnson, who had been watching them with obvious interest, and he wondered just how Johnson fitted into this peculiar set-up. "If I were you, Mr. Porter," he said levelly, "I'd be careful whom I engaged in future."

"I'll make a note of it," said Porter ironically. "But mine's a big organisation, you know. The small fish do get through the net now and then."

"Well, Denny Winters got himself caught in mine," remarked Christian.

"So it seems," said Porter. He tapped a cigarette on his gold case, then said suddenly: "How would you like to work for me, Christian?"

"Be your age, Porter," said Christian. "I don't see a lot of future in that."

Porter raised his eyebrows. "Don't you?" he said. "I'd say you could do a lot better for yourself. The screw you're getting now is chickenfeed – about fifteen hundred a year is my guess. I'd start you at three thousand and expenses."

"Very tempting," said Christian. "I'll have to think that over." He rose to leave. "Oh, and by the way, I think Denny Winters expects you to get him a lawyer – he's certainly going to need one."

*****

As he went through the outer office Christian wondered why Johnson, clearly not a retiring individual, had so little to say. He was giving this point careful thought, when he almost collided with a swarthy middle-aged man who came through the outside door. The man shot a swift glance at Christian, then hurriedly looked away again and went straight into the private office.

When he was walking across the car park, Christian remembered where he had seen the man before. He was a Dr. Hefton, who had been involved in a drugs scandal some three years previously. Christian had been friendly with Detective Inspector Sims, who had worked on the case and had since retired.

Christian sat in his car for a few minutes, recalling more facts in the Hefton case. There had been an attractive girl named Barbara Cummings mixed up in it, he remembered – she had acted as an agent, selling drugs which she bought from Hefton at a considerable profit. They had both received prison sentences, and Hefton had been struck off the register. As he pressed the starter, Christian wondered if Hefton were back at his old game.

*****

Back at Scotland Yard, Christian telephoned the records office for the Hefton file. It proved to be a bulky affair, and he spent some time browsing through reports.

He then turned to the photographs. There was one of Hefton, who had been sentenced to twelve months. The other was of Barbara Cummings, who got two years. But when he saw the second photograph, Christian caught his breath. This was the face that had been playing tricks with his memory ever since he had seen the body of Carol West! But he was still baffled, as this was not Carol West - the nose was very much longer, aquiline and prominent, and it was in fact the girl's worst feature. Yet there was that look about the eyes and the high forehead that was strongly reminiscent of the dead girl.

Christian took the photograph from the file and propped it against the inkstand in an attempt to see it from a different angle. Then he sat back in his chair and studied it again through half-closed eyes. Was it the face of Carol West, after all?

6

Christian thoughtfully returned the picture of Barbara Cummings to the file on the drug case. Then, struck by a sudden thought, he took it out again. He remembered a picture of several girls that he had seen by the side of Carol West's bed at her lodgings.

Barbara Cummings was very like one of the girls in the photo. Christian recalled the hairstyle and the upward sweep of the forehead. He went on turning over the pages of the file, until he came to the evidence of a well-known Harley Street specialist. That witness had evidently been anxious to do his best for Dr. Hefton, with whom he had worked for two years at the end of the war.

It appeared that the specialist had been very impressed with Hefton's prowess as a plastic surgeon. Hefton had performed brilliant operations on badly burned and disfigured airmen, and the specialist thought he should be given the opportunity to remain in practice. But Hefton had gone to jail nevertheless.

Christian telephoned the Yard's fingerprint department, wondering if he would get a reply at this late hour. He was relieved to hear the familiar clipped tones of Sergeant Cooper. "Sorry to trouble you so late in the day, Cooper," he said, "but this is urgent. You remember I asked for Carol West's prints?"

"I've got 'em," said Cooper at once. "They're here on my desk."

"Good. Now, I want you to go back to the Hefton dope case of three years ago." Christian gave Cooper dates and further facts and asked him to turn up the fingerprints of Barbara Cummings. "I'll be with you in five minutes," he added.

He closed the file and sat thinking for a minute or two. Then he got up and walked slowly through the quiet corridors to the fingerprint department. Cooper had the prints ready for him, and they compared them carefully.

"No doubt about it," said Cooper immediately. "They're identical, so you can bet your life that Carol West and Barbara Cummings were the same girl." He hesitated a moment, then added tentatively: "Does this upset all your calculations, sir?"

"I wouldn't say that," replied Christian enigmatically. "In some ways it simplifies matters."

He thanked Cooper for his help and went back to his own office, taking the fingerprints with him. The clock on his desk pointed to ten minutes past nine. It would soon be time for Eve Beckson to turn up for the interview she had herself sought with him.

Christian made a sudden decision and grabbed his hat and coat. He told the sergeant in the hall that he would be back in about half an hour, and that if a Mrs. Beckson arrived she was to be taken to his room. "See that someone stays with her till I get back," he ordered as an afterthought.

Then he went out into Whitehall and picked up a passing taxi. He told the driver to take him as quickly as possible to Soho. He stopped the taxi on a corner, paid off the driver, and walked briskly along a narrow street. The cafés and coffee bars were brilliantly lit, and the strident sound of juke boxes could be heard. He stopped outside a narrow-fronted shop and looked up at the name above the window. Then he opened the door and went in.

The old man behind the counter had changed little since Christian had last seen him, except that he was rather balder and appreciably more haggard – there was a tired and hopeless look about him. He peered short-sightedly at Christian through steel-rimmed spectacles. "We were just closing," he began, then a light of recognition flickered in the grey eyes.

"You remember me, Mr. Cummings?" prompted Christian. "I called to see you when your daughter –"

"Of course, it's Superintendent Christian," said the old man. He rested his elbows on the counter and shook his head dolefully. "Ah, that girl of mine! That drug case killed her mother, you know."

"Do you hear from Barbara at all?"

"Not a word for years," said the old man tonelessly. "Someone told me she was in Manchester, but I don't know – she never wrote me a line." He shrugged his thin shoulders.

"Why didn't you try to get her back when she came out of Holloway?" asked Christian.

The old man looked down at the counter. "My wife was dying, you see. She had a stroke through worrying about Barbara." The weak chin suddenly came up in a pathetic gesture of defiance. "Barbara killed her, just as if she'd stuck a knife in her. I said then she was no daughter of mine, and I still say so." He drew a heavy breath, and then murmured: "Have you come here to tell me she's in more trouble?"

"No," said Christian. "I just wanted to find out if she was ever friendly with a young chap called Robin Lane. He's a schoolmaster now, but I don't know if he's always been one."

"Schoolmaster, is he?" said Cummings with a wealth of contempt. "I remember him, all right. Barbara was always going round with him and his gang. Artists, writers and poets they called themselves, but if you ask me they were nothing but blasted layabouts. But it wasn't any good telling Barbara that – she always knew better. You couldn't tell her anything."

The old man took off his glasses and polished them with a grubby handkerchief. "I warned her she'd be in trouble with the police before she'd finished," he went on, "but she said the police were a load of dimwits who couldn't catch a cold. They caught up with her in the end, though, just as I told her they would."

"Do you remember anything about this man Lane?"

"Only his name."

"Was Barbara with him in Manchester?"

"I don't know and I don't care." The old man blinked at Christian. "She's no good, Mr. Christian. I was watching her at the trial, and she looked like a – a –" The old man's voice faltered for a moment. "Anyway, she won't ever change."

A woman came into the shop, and Christian waited while Cummings attended to her. When she had gone, Christian said: "I'm afraid I've got bad news for you."

"You mean she's dead?" The old man's voice was quite lifeless.

Christian nodded. "Maybe you read about a girl called Carol West, who was found murdered?"

"Don't get much time for reading, and my eyes aren't too good. But I did hear she'd changed her name."

"She also changed her appearance."

"That doesn't surprise me," said Cummings. "She was always talking a lot of eyewash about having her face altered – said it would change her personality." He sighed. "I'm here any time you want me," he said heavily. He looked straight at Christian, and his eyes were moist. "My wife was a good woman, super. She starved and scraped for that girl. Of all the ungrateful –" He broke off, rubbing the back of his hand over his mouth.

Christian turned to go, then hesitated. "If anything occurs to you that you think might help us to trace Barbara's murderer, I'd be very glad if you'd get in touch with me," he said.

"Then you don't know who killed her?"

"Not yet."

"It could have been anybody," said the old man. "She knew some terrible people."

"Such as who?" asked Christian expectantly.

But the old man suddenly seemed to dry up. "I must close up now," he said. He shuffled round the counter to see Christian out.

*****

Back at the Yard, Christian asked the desk sergeant if his visitor had arrived, only to be told that there had been no sign of Mrs. Beckson. It was still two or three minutes short of ten o'clock, so he went up to his office. Eve Beckson, he thought cynically, looked just the sort of woman who would be late for appointments — she was doubtless accustomed to keeping men waiting for her.

Christian surveyed the events of the past two days, trying to unearth a new angle on the murders. As was his inveterate habit, he began to jot down notes on a pad. Seeing things written down often sparked off new ideas. Then suddenly he threw down his pencil and began to think about Mrs. Beckson. She looked as if she might be a model or a showgirl. Was she, he wondered, connected in any way with Eddie Porter? Was she aware of the risks she was taking in coming to see him? After all, there had been three attempts on his own life.

Doggedly he returned to his pad and wrote: *Points common to the murders of Carol West and her landlady Mrs. Fredericks — both women drowned, with sticking tape over mouth.* He considered this for a moment. The tape was obviously a warning to other people involved that they must not talk.

Again his thoughts switched abruptly back to Eve Beckson. It was understandable that she should be scared. Christian could hardly blame her for not keeping her appointment with him if, as seemed possible, someone whom she could not shake off was tailing her. He picked up his pencil again and wrote: *Why did Mrs. Fredericks collect the telegram addressed to Mrs. Beckson? Why did Robin Lane send the telegram? Did he want to warn Mrs. Beckson or Mrs. Fredericks?*

It now seemed clear that whoever was responsible for Carol West's murder was afraid the victim might be identified as Barbara Cummings, thus providing a link with the drug case of three years ago. Christian remembered that Robin Lane was a drug addict.

It was half past ten, and Christian was about to write another note when the telephone rang. "This is the Radio Car Company," said a man's voice. "One of our drivers has just come through with a message for Superintendent Christian. Says it's urgent."

"What's the message?"

"A woman told this driver to ask you to go down the Embankment, cross Hungerford Bridge, and wait for the taxi on the corner by the Festival Hall." The man gave the number of the cab and rang off.

Christian rang the Yard switchboard operator and told him to get through to the Radio Car Company. When the same voice came on the line again, Christian explained that he was confirming the message.

"Good heavens," said the man in a faintly affronted voice, "you don't leave much to chance, do you, sir?"

"Not too much," said Christian. "Would you mind just repeating the message and the number of the taxi?" The man confirmed, and Christian replaced the receiver with a smile. Then he scribbled a brief note about his movements and left it on his assistant's desk.

Ten minutes later, he was waiting at the appointed spot. A taxi appeared, cruising slowly. The rear window opened, and a gloved hand waved to him. By the light of a street lamp, Christian could see it was the blonde he knew as Eve Beckson. The taxi slid to a standstill, and Christian got in. He caught a subtle wisp of perfume in the darkness. "I'm sorry to put you to all this trouble," said the slightly husky voice, "but I found someone was following me. I had to give them the slip."

"It couldn't be the man who was following you the last time I saw you," observed Christian, "because he's in custody."

"There are others," she said. "It's a bigger organisation than you may expect."

Christian smiled in the darkness. "I never underestimate my opponents," he said. He leaned forward and made sure that the glass panel was pulled firmly across so that the driver could not overhear their conversation. Then he went on quietly: "Supposing you tell me what you know about Carol West – or perhaps you knew her as Barbara Cummings?"

She sounded surprised. "So you know about that?"

"Let's call her Barbara Cummings for the moment, shall we? Was she a friend or a relative of yours?"

Christian heard the girl draw in her breath. "She was my brother's mistress," she said in an oddly flat voice. "He was always going to get a divorce so that he could marry Barbara, but he never seemed to get around to it. I'm afraid my brother is rather a weak character."

"Is he involved in this business?"

"Yes," she said. "I think you've met him. His name is Robin Lane."

7

For a few seconds there was no sound in the taxi, except for the steady throb of the engine. Then Superintendent Christian said: "I'm sorry. It can't be much fun to have close ties with a drug addict. Couldn't your husband help you?"

"My husband died seven years ago," replied Eve Beckson quietly.

Christian nodded. After a little while he said: "Then your brother knew Barbara Cummings at the time of the trial – long before she changed her name to Carol West?"

"Yes," said the girl. "She went to prison because she tried to get drugs for him. She was a very loyal and devoted person in some ways – she kept Robin's name out of it all through the trial."

"They weren't living together at the time she was murdered?" asked Christian.

"Only occasionally. As his health seemed to have improved, Barbara persuaded him to take a job as a schoolmaster. But the craving for heroin got the better of him again, and he became desperate."

"What happened then?" asked Christian.

"The organisation stopped the supply and demanded more money. Barbara pleaded with them, but it was no use. In the end she threatened to go to the police, and that's why she was murdered."

"But couldn't Dr. Hefton help her at all?"

"So you know about him?" The girl's voice sounded surprised.

"I know a certain amount about him," said Christian, "and I'd like to know some more."

"Hefton was working for the organisation," she confirmed. "It was under their orders that he did the plastic surgery operation on Barbara. Then they gave her a new name – Carol West – and put her to work for them."

"How did you find out all this?" asked Christian.

"Through my brother," she said. "He was so desperate for drugs that he begged me to go to Eddie Porter – you know, the man who owns all the clubs – and try to persuade him to help. I know now that was a mistake. I should have made Robin go into hospital."

"You didn't get on with Porter?"

She paused for a moment. "Frankly, I was terrified of him. He did his best to get me to join the organisation – he even offered to let me name my own terms."

"I shouldn't have thought Porter was quite your type," commented Christian.

"He's bad," said Eve vehemently. "He's bad, evil, rotten all through. I came straight back to Robin and told him to get in touch with the police at once. I remembered that Barbara had spoken well of you over the Hefton case, so I got hold of your telephone number and wrote it down for Robin."

"I've been wondering how he came to have it," said Christian thoughtfully, "but he never telephoned me. Do you know why?"

"Everything seemed to happen at once," said Eve. "Barbara was found murdered, and Robin was terrified that he might be associated with her. He jumped to the conclusion that the police would recognise her as Barbara Cummings, but apparently Hefton's plastic surgery had changed her face more than he realised. On top of all this, he was desperate for more heroin."

"He was certainly in a tough spot," remarked Christian. "So he sent you a frantic telegram at the Queen's Hotel in Birmingham, and we found the telegram. Tell me more about that."

"I had a telephone call from Porter. He said that a Mr. Smith would let me have a supply of heroin for two hundred pounds. I was to meet Smith at the hotel." Her voice faltered for a moment, and then became steady again. "Robin begged me to go – he was so ill." Her voice trailed away into silence.

"Go on," encouraged Christian.

"A friend of mine warned me not to go –"

"Who was this?"

She hesitated for a moment, and then said: "Mrs. Fredericks, the woman who was murdered."

"And you went to Birmingham in spite of her warning?"

"No," she said. "In the end she persuaded me not to go, by offering to go in my place. I'd known Mary Fredericks for years – I was on the stage for a time, and we'd been together in a touring company. She was quite a bit older than me, and I confided in her because I hadn't anyone else to turn to."

The girl paused for a moment, and Christian took out his cigarette case. In the flame of his lighter, he saw that her lower lip was quivering. She inhaled deeply and went on: "Mary Fredericks thought this Birmingham business was a trick of Porter's, an attempt to seduce me into the organisation – and she was right."

"But what would have happened if it hadn't been a trick?" asked Christian.

"Then she'd have simply seen this Mr. Smith and bought the heroin. She was registered at the hotel as Mrs. Beckson and I'd given her the two hundred pounds."

"So that's why the telegram was handed to her," said Christian. "Mrs. Fredericks certainly ran into a load of trouble."

Eve Beckson said: "Yes, and you can guess what happened. Porter turned up at the hotel and was absolutely furious when he discovered I wasn't there. He also jumped to the conclusion that Mary knew a great deal more about the murder than she actually did."

"Which was why we had the pleasure of picking Mrs. Fredericks out of the river," commented Christian. Eve nodded, and Christian drew ruminatively on his cigarette for a moment. Then he said: "Mrs. Fredericks seems to have known a lot about Porter and his associates. Did it ever occur to you that she might be working for them?"

After a slight hesitation she replied: "Yes, I knew all about it. She was blackmailed into acting as a go-between for them on several occasions. But she hated the whole filthy business – and that's why she was anxious that I shouldn't get mixed up in it. She was always a good friend to me."

"Have you any idea why they were blackmailing her?"

"Is there any point in going into that now? Anyway, I can assure you it has no bearing on this business – and after all, the poor woman's dead."

Christian decided to let it go at that. It was, after all, satisfactorily explained why Barbara Cummings had gone to Mrs. Fredericks as a boarder after changing her name to Carol West. The organisation seemed to have spread its tentacles very wide.

"It must have been a big worry for you, having to cover up for your brother," remarked Christian.

"I'm quite used to it now," she said quietly. "I seem to have been doing it all my life. If only he could have stayed with his wife – Barbara Cummings was quite the wrong girl for him."

"I'm beginning to see why you found it difficult to come to the police for help," said Christian.

"I was afraid," she said, "but I did pluck up enough courage to go to your flat one night."

"So it was you! But why didn't you wait for me?"

Eve Beckson smiled. "I'm afraid I got nervous – everything was so quiet. Then suddenly I had the idea of drawing a face of Carol West and writing her real name under it. I was just about to write the name Barbara Cummings when I heard a commotion in the mews outside. I panicked and got out as quickly as I could."

"That was the night that crook Denny Winters tried to rough me up," recalled Christian.

"He also followed me to the restaurant at lunchtime the next day," she said. "I was trying to have a word with you, but I just couldn't shake him off."

The taxi jerked to a standstill at some traffic lights, and a stream of after-theatre cars surged past. "By the way," said Christian suddenly, "what happened to that rather becoming green beret of yours?"

"It was stolen." She was clearly surprised by the question. "But why do you ask?"

"It was found floating near the body of Mrs. Fredericks. I recognised it at once – as was intended, of course. Somebody was doing their best to throw suspicion on you." The girl shivered. "So you see what ruthless characters we're dealing with," continued Christian.

"But surely you can arrest this man Porter now?"

Christian shook his head. "What makes you so sure that Porter's the top man in this organisation?" he said.

"I took it for granted."

"I'm not so sure," said Christian. "But one thing I am sure of – neither you nor your brother will be safe until we clean up this gang. Are you ready to help?"

"Of course," she replied without hesitation. "What is it you want me to do?"

Max Christian told her.

*****

348

Christian went into a public call box and looked up the telephone number of Eddie Porter's house in Chelsea. Porter himself answered the phone and sounded mildly surprised.

"I'd like to talk to you about one or two things," said Christian.

"Such as what?"

"The last time we met," said Christian, "you mentioned a certain proposition to me. You had the idea that I might be worth rather more than – er – fifteen hundred pounds a year. Remember?"

Porter said: "Yes, I remember. Where are you speaking from?"

"A public call box."

"Supposing you tell me what's on your mind?"

"I've got nothing on my mind," said Christian. "I've just been thinking over that proposition of yours, that's all. Three thousand a year and expenses, I believe you said. Incidentally, while I think of it, I've got a message for you from our mutual friend Denny Winters." Christian paused. "I'd prefer to talk at my flat – it's rather draughty in this phone box."

Porter said: "I'll be there in an hour. Give me the address." And Max Christian gave it to him, and he was smiling as he rang off.

*****

In his office at The High Dive, Victor Johnson finished counting two piles of banknotes and then carefully locked them in the safe. He was turning away from the safe when a waiter entered. "There's a woman to see you, Mr. Johnson."

"Who is she?"

"A Mrs. Beckson. I haven't seen her here before. She says it's urgent."

"Show her in," said Johnson.

Eve Beckson was wearing her mink jacket and had clearly gone to considerable trouble to make herself attractive. The effect was not lost on Johnson, and he eyed her appreciatively. "Do sit down, Mrs. Beckson," he invited.

Eve sat down in the chair he pushed forward. "I'll come straight to the point, Mr. Johnson," she said.

"Please do," said Johnson airily. "Would you like a drink?"

"No, thank you," she said. "I've been told that you can help me to obtain a supply of heroin for someone who is in desperate need of it."

Johnson regarded her through slightly narrowed eyes. "I don't quite understand you," he said.

"Don't you? I should have thought I'd made myself quite clear."

Johnson leaned back in his chair and folded his hands over his ornate waistcoat. "You don't seriously think that The High Dive is a centre for the distribution of drugs, do you?"

"Isn't it?" said Eve Beckson simply.

"Sorry, m'dear, you've come to the wrong shop," said Johnson amiably. "There isn't enough money in the world to tempt me into that particular racket."

"There are other methods of payment besides money," she said quietly.

Johnson looked up quickly. "Just what are you driving at?"

"I have some information which I think might interest you."

"Really?" said Johnson. "Perhaps you'd like to give me some idea what this information is about?"

"It's about a man called Eddie Porter."

Johnson leaned forward. "Eddie Porter happens to be a very good friend of mine."

"I wouldn't be too sure of that," she said. "In fact, I got a very different impression."

Johnson sat for a moment, staring at Eve Beckson. "All right," he said at last. "If your information is worth anything, I'll see you get the stuff. Now, where did you see Porter?"

"I was at his house this evening, for the same reason that I came here. He couldn't, or wouldn't, give me a definite answer - but just as I was about to leave, the telephone rang, and he started talking to a man called Christian." She looked at Johnson with a level stare. "Porter mentioned your name several times. He made you sound quite a notorious character. That's what gave me the idea of coming to you for the heroin."

"What did he say exactly?"

She shrugged. "I can't remember the details, but Porter arranged to go round to Christian's flat in about an hour's time to continue the conversation. I think they were going to discuss some sort of a deal."

Johnson got up from his desk and started to pace up and down the room. He was biting his lower lip.

"Well?" inquired Eve Beckson. "Do I get the heroin?"

"Yes," said Johnson slowly. "I'll see that you get it."

*****

Christian had put the lights out in his sitting room and was standing by the window, looking down the mews. It was just after midnight, and he expected Porter at any minute.

There was a flash of headlights, as a car swung into the mews and stopped almost opposite his flat. The lights were switched off, then the driver got out and crossed in front of the car. Christian saw him clearly for a second, by the light of the side lamps.

351

It was Robin Lane.

8

As Superintendent Christian watched the figure of Robin Lane walk towards his front door, his attention was momentarily diverted by a movement in the shadows of the garage. He waited to see if a figure would emerge, but there was no further sign. Then the front doorbell rang insistently.

Christian opened the door, and Lane hurtled through it. He was in a state of considerable agitation.

"Hello, Mr. Lane," said Christian. "What brings you here?" He was wondering how to get rid of the man before Porter arrived.

"I had to see you," blurted out Lane with a kind of desperate urgency. "I couldn't wait any longer."

Christian drew the thick curtains of the living room and switched on the lights. "It's a bit late, isn't it?" he said on a note of mild protest. "I'm often in bed at this time. When did you leave hospital?"

Lane brushed his untidy hair back from his forehead, and Christian could see his hand trembling. "Only this afternoon – I'm going back tomorrow," he said. "For my own peace of mind, the doctor suggested that I saw you and told you everything I know."

"A very good idea," commented Christian. "Your sister has told me quite a lot, but there may be one or two gaps you can fill in." He motioned Lane to a chair, and as he did so he noticed that Lane's facial muscles twitched nervously. The man seemed to have difficulty in controlling himself.

"As a matter of fact, I'm expecting a very important visitor," went on Christian, "so I'm afraid I'll have to ask you to leave in a minute or two. But while you're here, there is one problem you might help to clear up."

"And what's that?"

"I've heard the whole story of Barbara Cummings alias Carol West, and how she worked for this organisation to get drugs for you," said Christian. "There's just one more thing I want to find out. Did your girlfriend ever give you the idea that Porter was not the top man in this set-up?"

Lane rubbed his chin thoughtfully. "Carol always dealt with Porter," he said, "but once or twice I seem to remember her saying Porter wasn't the top man. I think he usually telephoned somebody else for instructions."

"Did she say where he telephoned?"

"Apparently no names were mentioned, but she got the impression it was the man at the roadhouse – Johnson."

"Nothing more definite?"

Before Lane could reply, there was the sound of a car outside. Christian switched off the lights and went to the window. He was in time to see a taxi draw up behind Robin Lane's car. Porter got out and paid the driver, then stood for a moment looking up at Christian's window.

Christian was about to leave the window, when he suddenly caught sight of a shadowy figure moving from behind Lane's car.

*****

Down in the mews, Porter swung round sharply as a voice came out of the darkness. "I want you, Porter," it said. It was the voice of Victor Johnson.

"What the hell are you doing here?" stammered Porter. "I didn't know you were invited!"

353

"I wasn't," snapped Johnson. He grabbed the lapels of Porter's coat and pushed him into the shadow of the nearby garage. Then he hit Porter a vicious blow across the mouth with the back of his hand, cutting the man's lip with his signet ring. "You double crossing swine!" he said between his teeth. "So, you thought you'd do a deal with Christian behind my back."

Porter wiped his lip. "Now just a minute, Vic," he protested. "He wanted to see me about Denny Winters. He said so on the telephone."

Johnson interrupted, speaking softly: "You always did like shooting off that big mouth of yours." There was no sign of the debonair club manager now. "You were planning to fix me and take over the outfit. Luckily for me, you were overheard."

"But he telephoned me from a call box," said Porter desperately. "There couldn't have been anyone at his end."

"There was someone at your end," sneered Johnson. "Eve Beckson. You've been doing quite a line with her for the past few weeks, haven't you? You fat slob. But little Eve knows a thing or two, and she came to me instead."

"I don't know what the hell you're talking about. I haven't set eyes on her all day."

Johnson tightened his grip. "You're a lousy liar, Porter. I told you to get rid of Carol West and dump the body on Putney Heath. But, oh no! You had to drown her in my swimming pool and throw suspicion on to me. You thought that was smart, but it wasn't smart enough."

Porter struggled. "Now look," he pleaded. "I've explained all this before. We had to put her in the pool because she was screaming like hell, and a police car —"

"Shut up! You talk too much, Porter." Johnson's voice was no longer the soft, caressing one his customers knew. "But you won't have any more cosy chats with your friend Christian."

As Johnson spoke, there was a sudden flash of a knife – and with a thin squeal Porter crumpled to the ground. He lay moaning softly for a moment, banging his clenched fists on the cobblestones. Presently there was complete silence in the mews. Johnson turned Porter's body over with his foot. Then, as he came out of the shadow of the garage, he heard the gonging of a police car. In a matter of seconds, the whole mews was ablaze with the powerful headlights from half a dozen squad cars.

Christian, who had seen Johnson emerge from the shadow of the garage, came running out of his flat. Johnson turned and went back swiftly along the mews. Christian crossed to intercept him, but Johnson lashed out with his foot, catching the superintendent on the kneecap. Christian supported himself against the wall, and through a red haze of pain he saw Johnson run to an iron fire escape which led to the roof of the flats.

Three policemen rushed past in pursuit of Johnson, who was almost at the top of the fire escape by this time. "Cover his getaway in Girton Street!" gasped Christian.

Girton Street was the main road at the end of the mews and had become a teeming mass of people. Johnson's figure could be seen silhouetted against the sky by a powerful spotlight from a police car. He vanished over a parapet, with two policemen clambering after him.

The entrance to the mews had been effectively cordoned off. Christian gave instructions to guard the exits from two other fire escapes. Then he hobbled along to the end of the cul-de-sac, and climbed the ladder with the idea of getting on to the roof and directing operations.

Christian negotiated the parapet successfully and found himself in eerie solitude. The roofs were flat, and he sat down on a ledge for a few moments to get his bearings. Then he heard the voice of one of the policemen on the roof; he could not catch what the man said, but it sounded like a warning. Cautiously he edged his way round to the far side of the building, just in time to hear a police car pull up with a screech of brakes in Girton Street. He was peering down into the street, when he heard footsteps behind him.

He turned, to see Johnson rushing towards him. The man's coat was unfastened, and he clutched a knife in his right hand. He had apparently doubled back on his pursuers and had stopped short the moment he caught sight of Christian. The spotlight swept across the distorted and wild-eyed face.

Still painfully aware of his throbbing knee, Christian shouted: "They're waiting for you down there, Johnson. Better come quietly."

Johnson said nothing, and the wandering spotlight suddenly flashed across the knife blade in his hand. He advanced a pace, and the light illuminated his face – white and tense, his mouth twisted. He was within four feet of Christian and the hand holding the knife was raised to strike, when there was the sound of approaching footsteps.

Johnson wheeled round, to see a burly policeman. He weighed up the situation at a quick glance, swung round to his left and took what was now the only means of escape – the roof of the flat next door. There was a narrow chasm between the two buildings. He took two long strides, a flying leap – and fell on the far side of the other parapet with inches to spare. A split second later, Christian heard the clatter of metal as the knife fell far below on the cobblestones of the mews.

As the beam from a spotlight swung across the rooftop, Johnson moved quickly under the lee of a parapet towards the far side of the roof. Christian suddenly realised that the fire escape on this building did not lead into Girton Street, where the police had transferred several of their cars, but into the mews. Johnson was already gripping the top of the steel ladder, which ended on the roof of one of the garages below. Christian retreated to his own fire escape, calling to the two policemen as he did so.

Meanwhile Johnson had got down to the roof of the garage, and he stood listening for a few seconds. The only police car remaining in the mews – the one with the spotlight – was some thirty yards away. He edged round to the side furthest from the mews and found a skylight. With some effort he levered it open. Breathing hard, he peered into the garage below in an effort to see if there was a car inside. It was too dark, so he pulled himself through the skylight and, hanging on to the framework with his hands, swung his legs to and fro. There was no obstacle, so he dropped the four feet to the concrete floor.

Johnson felt his way through the darkness to the wall ahead of him and followed it until he came to the sliding doors. They were closed, but not locked. Cautiously he edged them open a couple of inches and peered out.

There were still about twenty or thirty people in the mews, crowding round the police car, but they all appeared to be looking up at the rooftops. Johnson quietly pushed the doors open and squeezed through them. He calculated that if he could make his way to the end of the mews without being seen, he might still make a getaway.

In the distance he heard a police whistle, and a police car with a spotlight moved to the entrance of the mews. Then, just as he was approaching the doorway of one of the flats, a man holding a knife came out of the shadows. Johnson saw the glint of metal and cowered back against the wall. Then he recognised Robin Lane.

"This is where you get a taste of your own knife," said Lane. His voice was little more than a whisper, but its tone struck terror into Victor Johnson. He looked frantically round for some means of escape as Lane walked slowly and inexorably towards him, the knife held rigidly in his hand. As Lane's arm was raised to strike, Johnson screamed. He warded off Lane's first thrust, and his cry brought Christian and two policemen running from the back door of one of the flats.

The spotlight from the police car swung along the mews and picked up the two struggling figures on the cobblestones. It took the combined efforts of two policemen to drag Robin Lane away from the terrified Johnson. Lane was almost sobbing with rage and frustration, as he struggled with the policemen.

"Take it easy, old man," said Christian gently. "This is *my* bird."

*****

The following morning Christian looked up from his desk as Detective Sergeant Hale, his assistant, came in with a sheaf of papers. "How's Johnson's statement coming along, Tom?" he asked.

"Practically ready," replied the sergeant. "But he's getting his nerve back now and asking for a lawyer already."

Christian smiled grimly. "He'll need a good one."

"All the same," went on Hale, "I can't understand why Johnson should run a racket like that from a roadhouse miles out of town."

"It suited his purpose," said Christian. "His idea was that Eddie Porter should attract all the attention and run all the risks. Then, when it suited him, Johnson could take over. A bright boy, our Victor."

"Very cosy," remarked Hale. "And they might easily have got away with it if you hadn't had such a bee in your bonnet about that girl's face."

"Yes," said Christian thoughtfully. "I really believed my memory for faces was slipping."

An hour later, the superintendent sat facing Assistant Commissioner Blackburn, who was turning over Johnson's statement. "Seems open and shut now," said Blackburn. "You've done a first-rate job, Christian."

"Thank you, sir," replied Christian. He yawned widely and stretched. "If there's nothing urgent at the moment, I'd like to go home and catch up on some sleep. I've been going a bit short lately."

"You'll do more than that," said the Assistant Commissioner. "You're going away for three weeks. I've just checked your record, and it seems you haven't had a proper holiday for four years. Go away and lie in the sun, somewhere where they haven't heard of Scotland Yard."

"That sounds good to me," said Christian. "I'll go down to Devon. I've got some friends at a place called Torcross." He laughed. "Believe me, sir, nothing exciting ever happens at Torcross."

But Max Christian was wrong – very wrong. Three weeks later, the Torcross poison case hit the headlines. But that's another story.

PAUL TEMPLE SHORT STORIES

Published in the London *Evening Standard* on twelve Fridays, 10 January – 28 March 1947

Most of these neat short stories show Temple solving a mystery by exposing the criminal's one small slip. Although some other Paul Temple newspaper/magazine stories have been reprinted in recent years as bonuses in the HarperCollins reprints of Durbridge novels, this set of twelve has never re-appeared in print in the UK – except that *Paul Temple and the Elstree Affair* was recycled by Durbridge several decades later for a London theatre programme in 1971 as *Coffee Break*, replacing Temple with Detective Superintendent Hamer. All of these twelve stories in German translation were included in the collection *Paul Temple: Die verschollenen Fälle* (Pidax, 2018).

PAUL TEMPLE AND THE ELUSIVE MR. WADE

The BBC announcer glanced at his wristlet watch, walked past the studio attendant, pushed open the swing doors, and entered the studio.

He stood for a moment staring up at the electric clock, then with a friendly nod to the programme engineer in the glass cubicle he faced the microphone. The red light flickered. The announcer looked very serious. He said: "We are asked by the Commissioner of Police to broadcast the following. Listeners are requested to be on the look-out for Richard Edward Wade, who escaped from Ridgeworth Prison in the early hours of Tuesday morning. Wade was last reported to have been seen in the Bramley district of Evesham. It is believed that he is wearing ..."

When the programme was over, the studio attendant said: "If you ask me, they'll never catch that bloke Wade. He's a blinkin' Houdini, that's what he is!"

The announcer said: "He may be Houdini to you, Sam, but to me he's a pain in the neck! That confounded announcement made me miss the early train."

* * * * *

Inspector Merritt was out when Paul Temple called at the local police station, but the novelist was welcomed by Detective Sergeant Ross. As the sergeant sprang to his feet, Temple placed a bottle of whisky on the corner of the desk. "A New Year present for Inspector Merritt," he explained. "It's a little late I'm afraid, but Steve and I only arrived back from Switzerland this morning."

He picked up the newspaper that the sergeant had been reading. There was the usual photograph of Wade on the front page. "I gather this Wade affair is keeping you pretty busy," he said.

The sergeant sat down again and nodded towards a vacant chair. "One or two of the local people seem to think he's hiding in Foxdown Wood," he said.

Temple extracted his cigarette case, took out a cigarette, scratched a match and said: "Do you think that's very likely?"

Ross shook his head. "I hardly think so, sir," he replied. "But just to be on the safe side we've got most of our men combing the wood."

Temple put the burnt-out match in the ashtray and glanced out of the window at the grey sky. The light was fading, but he could still see the bare trees and could almost feel the cold night air. The thought of spending seven or eight hours in Foxdown Wood struck him as being a particularly unpleasant assignment. "There's something to be said for an office job, eh, sergeant?"

The sergeant grinned. His thoughts had run along very much the same lines during the past forty-eight hours.

Temple turned up the collar of his overcoat and moved towards the door. "Give my regards to Inspector Merritt," he said. "I'll drop in again one day next week."

There was a policeman waiting for a bus on the corner of the road near Foxdown Wood, and Temple pulled his car to a standstill and offered to give him a lift. The young man was cold, tired and thoroughly miserable. As he climbed into the car, he said: "I'm just about browned off! I've been hanging about here all the blasted day. I heard the church clock strike eight this morning an' I heard it strike five this afternoon, an' that's about all I have heard!"

"No sign of the elusive Mr. Wade?"

The constable laughed. "I'm afraid not, sir – an' if you ask me it's a wild goose chase. He's probably in Scotland by now!"

Temple said: "What you need, officer, is a good stiff drink. You'd better come along to my place."

*****

"What would you like to drink?" asked Paul Temple. It was a quarter of an hour later, and they were standing by the cocktail cabinet in the lounge at Bramley Lodge.

The constable said: "I'm not one for whisky, Mr. Temple. A nice glass of beer is more in my line."

Temple smiled, put down the whisky decanter, and walked across the lounge, through the hall, and out into the kitchen. When he returned a few moments later, the young man was examining a statuette on the mantelpiece. Temple stood watching him for a little while, then he said: "Here's your glass of beer."

The constable put down the statuette and took the glass of beer. He smiled at Temple before lifting the glass to his lips.

Temple said: "You must have had a pretty tough day of it. What time did you go on duty this morning?"

"I was supposed to be on duty by seven o'clock, sir."

Temple splashed a little more soda water into his glass, and said pleasantly: "Do you live near here?"

There was a moment's hesitation before the young man replied: "No, as a matter of fact I'm in digs in Evesham."

"Then you're a new man – new to the district, I mean."

Their eyes met. The young man said softly: "I've lived in these parts all my life, sir. Whichever way you look at it, I'm not exactly a new man."

Temple said: "When I went through to the kitchen just now to get you a drink, I took the liberty of telephoning Sergeant Ross. He tells me that they nearly caught the enterprising Mr. Wade, only at the last moment he knocked one of the local boys stone-cold, borrowed his uniform and made a dash for it."

The young man smiled. He knew that the game was up. He hesitated for a moment, then took a revolver from the pocket of his tunic. His manner was grim and determined, but he was quite unperturbed. He said: "There's no need for any unpleasantness, Mr. Temple. The position is really quite simple. I want a new suit of clothes and all the cash you've got in the house."

Temple ignored the demand and said: "Do you know what made me suspect you, Mr. Wade?"

Wade shook his head. "I was under the impression I'd played my cards rather carefully."

"Your reference to the church clock gave you away," said Temple. "You couldn't possibly have heard the clock strike – it hasn't struck since it was damaged by a piece of shrapnel in 1941."

Wade said: "I'm going to give you precisely two minutes, Mr. Temple. I want a new suit of clothes, and all the cash you can lay your hands on." He prodded Temple with the revolver. "Now lead the way," he said.

"If it's a change of clothing you want," said Temple, "then I'm afraid you'll have to follow me upstairs." He half turned towards the door, and Wade started to move with him. Temple swung round again and caught the butt of the revolver with the palm of his hand. He heard the explosion and felt a burning sensation across the tips of his fingers. He brought his left fist forward with a tremendous heave and slammed the young man's chin for all he was worth. The punch was a beauty. The elusive Mr. Wade fell like a log.

*****

Steve had finished bandaging his hand, and Temple was ready to climb into bed. Steve said: "I don't know why it is, but whenever I'm out shopping you always seem to get yourself into mischief."

Temple said: "It's cheaper than going with you, Steve, and much more exciting."

Steve smiled, patted her hair, and asked: "What made you suspect the constable?"

In spite of his hand, Temple was feeling very pleased with himself. He said rather airily: "I had a feeling that he was a stranger to the district, and that slip about the clock convinced me."

Steve said: "It was clever of you to notice the slip, my sweet – but there's something you ought to know."

Temple looked puzzled. "What do you mean?"

Steve was smiling, and there was a twinkle in her eyes. She said: "Things have been happening around here while we were in Switzerland."

"What sort of things?"

Steve laughed. "Well, for one thing," she said, "they repaired the church clock!"

PAUL TEMPLE AND THE ELSTREE AFFAIR

Carl Sherman, chief executive producer for the Harrison Film Corporation, was surprised when Paul Temple paid a visit to the Harrison Studios at Elstree. It was twenty-four hours after Sylvia Lincoln had swallowed the fatal dose of arsenic.

Temple said: "You know why I'm here, Mr. Sherman. I used to know Sylvia Lincoln pretty well in the old days, and Sir Graham Forbes suggested that I should make a few discreet inquiries."

Sherman took the cigar from his mouth and snapped into the telephone: "Don't disturb me for the next fifteen minutes. I'm all tied up." He looked at Temple. "I only got this job by poking my nose into matters which didn't concern me," he said. "You ask the questions, Mr. Temple, and I'll answer 'em."

Temple smiled and said quietly: "I'm given to understand that you had Miss Lincoln under contract for two more pictures." Sherman nodded. "What was her position so far as the studio was concerned?"

There was a momentary hesitation before Carl Sherman replied: "We wanted to renew her contract. We had every intention of doing so, but ..."

Temple said: "It's the 'but' that interests me, Mr. Sherman."

"Sylvia was in pretty bad shape. Her figure seemed to be going to pieces, and –"

Paul Temple interrupted him. He leaned across the desk. "Don't let's beat about the bush," he said. "We all know that Sylvia was a personal friend of yours."

Sherman replied, somewhat acidly: "Miss Lincoln was under contract to the Harrison Film Corporation, but that doesn't mean to say that I had either the right or the inclination to interfere in her private life."

The novelist asked: "Is it your opinion that Miss Lincoln committed suicide?" Carl Sherman hesitated, stared at his cigar for a moment, then nodded his head. Temple said: "Had anyone in the studio a particular reason for wanting to get rid of Sylvia Lincoln?"

"So we're looking for the good old motive!" exclaimed Sherman with a pained expression. "This is just like a corny situation out of a Hollywood who-dun-it!"

Paul Temple said: "Don't let your sense of humour get the better of you, Mr. Sherman. I've got a hunch that someone in this studio played a pretty unfunny trick on Miss Lincoln."

Carl Sherman looked the novelist straight in the eye. He said quietly: "Any ideas, Mr. Temple?"

Temple replied: "Suppose we accept the suicide theory for the present. Have you any idea why she should have committed suicide in the canteen?"

"I haven't the remotest idea," said Sherman, and added with a smile, "Your guess is as good as mine, Mr. Temple."

Paul Temple said quietly: "My guess is that Miss Lincoln didn't commit suicide."

"But she must have committed suicide!" Sherman laughed. "We all know the coffee's pretty bad in the canteen, but it's not that bad!"

Temple paused and said: "I'm going to ask you a very personal question, Mr. Sherman."

Sherman stubbed out his cigar in the ashtray. He looked uncomfortable, but his voice was quite steady. "You're the most persistent guy I've met since I've been over here," he said. "However …"

Paul Temple said: "Was Sylvia making a nuisance of herself?"

"You mean here, at the studio?"

"No."

Carl Sherman shook his head. His hand was trembling slightly. "I'm afraid I don't get you."

"It's really quite simple," said Temple. "I'm asking you whether Sylvia Lincoln was making a nuisance of herself."

"What you're really asking me," said Sherman, "is whether my private affairs caught up with me and started to interfere with my duties as chief producer for the Harrison Film Corporation."

"You can put it that way if you like," said Temple.

Carl Sherman said: "Whichever way you put it, I guess it whittles down to the same thing. Did I murder Sylvia Lincoln?"

Paul Temple said quite simply: "Did you, Mr. Sherman?"

"No, I didn't," said Sherman emphatically. "Though God knows there were times when I was tempted."

Paul Temple smiled, and crossed to the door. "I'll see you later," he said. "I'm going down to the canteen."

As he strolled down the corridor, he could hear Sherman on the telephone. "I can't make it this afternoon," he was saying. "I'm all tied up." He sounded very worried.

*****

Mrs. Muriel Cross had been in charge of the canteen at the Harrison Studios for seventeen years. She was a stoutish little woman with a jovial manner and a tongue that never stopped wagging.

After he had signed her autograph book and accepted a cup of tea, Temple said: "Now tell me exactly what happened yesterday afternoon, Mrs. Cross."

Mrs. Cross said: "Miss Lincoln came into the canteen about half past four. She was with Charlie West, our dress designer, Beryl Drake the actress, Tim Lowe the assistant director, and Mr. Sherman. They ordered coffee and sat over there at the corner table." She pointed to a table at the end of the canteen.

Temple asked: "Who served the coffee?"

Mrs. Cross said: "I poured it out myself, but Mr. Sherman was at the counter buying some cigarettes and he insisted on carrying two of the cups across to the table."

"Did Miss Lincoln strike you as being downhearted about anything?"

"I don't think so, sir. If you ask me, they appeared to be quite a jolly party."

"And what about Mr. Sherman?" asked Temple. "Did he strike you as being particularly jolly?"

"He was pretty much the same as he always is," said Mrs. Cross. "Until his stomach started to bother him."

"And then what happened?"

Mrs. Cross said: "Well, it was most unusual. He was perfectly all right one minute, and the next minute he was howling his blinkin' head off for some magnesia."

Paul Temple said quietly, "Thank you, Mrs. Cross, you've been a great help." He finished his cup of tea and strolled out of the canteen.

*****

Carl Sherman was on the telephone when Temple returned to the office. As soon as he saw Temple, he barked into the mouthpiece: "I can't discuss the schedule any further at the moment. I'm all tied up." He put down the receiver and smiled.

Temple said: "I'm afraid Superintendent Bradley will want to ask you one or two rather awkward questions, Mr. Sherman."

"What do you mean?"

"I've just had an interesting chat with Tim Lowe," continued Temple. "He tells me that shortly before you had your spot of stomach trouble you laboured under the impression that you'd taken a drink from the wrong cup — from Miss Lincoln's cup, in fact."

Sherman looked angry. He said: "What precisely are you getting at?"

"I'm getting at the fact that you knew perfectly well that one of the cups contained arsenic. You thought you'd taken a drink from that cup — that's why you suddenly got frightened and demanded some magnesia." Temple paused. "You know as well as I do," he said, "that magnesia is a rough antidote for arsenic poisoning."

Sherman opened his mouth, then closed it again. He looked very frightened. The telephone rang, and Temple picked up the receiver. A curt, crisp voice said: "Listen, Carl. We want you for an executive meeting on the fourteenth, a personnel meeting on the seventeenth, and a script conference on the twenty-first."

Paul Temple said: "I'm sorry, but Mr. Sherman won't be able to make it." He added, as an afterthought: "He's all tied up."

370

PAUL TEMPLE AND "THE COLONEL"

It was in the autumn of 1946 that Paul Temple first heard of Joseph Dalbriax, alias "The Colonel".

Temple and Steve were giving a cocktail party at their flat in Half Moon Street, and among the guests was Major Hazlitt of the Special Branch. As he handed the major a dry martini, Temple said: "I was interested to hear that you think you know who stole the Baxter emeralds."

Hazlitt helped himself to a biscuit and said casually, "We've reason to believe that the emeralds were stolen by a man called Joseph Dalbriax, alias 'The Colonel'". "Dalbriax," he went on, "is a first class con man, a cat burglar without equal, and a past master at the art of disguise."

"He doesn't sound a very easy bird to catch up with," commented Temple.

The next time Paul Temple heard of Dalbriax was at a stag party given by the European director of a prominent American publishing firm. Temple had said goodbye to his host and was on the point of leaving the hotel when a dark, thick-set little man caught him by the arm and pulled him over to an alcove in the lounge.

The stranger introduced himself as Charles Hemingway, vice-chairman of the Hemingway Trust Combine. He said: "I've been wanting to have a chat with you for some little time, Mr. Temple, but I didn't quite know how to go about it." Delving into the pocket of his jacket, he produced a small box. He opened the box and displayed a single diamond ear-ring. "Six months ago, I bought my wife a pair of ear-rings, but two months later my house at Epsom was robbed and one of the ear-rings was stolen."

Temple looked at the ear-ring for a moment, and then lifted it out of the box. "How much did you pay for the pair?" he asked.

Hemingway said: "They wanted eight hundred and fifty pounds, but I persuaded them to accept eight hundred. I don't care what it costs me, Mr. Temple, but I've got to find that ear-ring! Ever since it was stolen, my life's been absolute hell. I've offered to buy my wife a completely new pair of ear-rings, but she won't hear of it. Nothing will satisfy her except the return of the stolen ear-ring.

"I'll be frank, Mr. Temple. You're on pretty friendly terms with a lot of people in this town that the police wouldn't dream of contacting, so I thought –"

Temple interrupted. "To be brief," he said, "you want me to find the ear-ring."

Hemingway nodded. "Find the stolen ear-ring," he said, "or one identical to it, and I'll pay you two hundred pounds – quite apart, of course, from what you've got to pay for the ear-ring itself."

Paul Temple smiled. "I'll see what I can do," he said.

*****

It was exactly a fortnight later that Temple received a telephone call from a man called Clancy Edwards.

Clancy was a fence, and the proprietor of a small antique shop in the Edgware Road. He said: "I don't know whether you remember me, Mr. Temple, but I was mixed up in that spot of bother over at Ealing about –"

Temple said: "Yes, I remember you, Clancy. What can I do for you?"

"The boys tell me that you've been making one or two inquiries about an ear-ring," said Clancy. "An' I've a hunch I've got just the ticket you're looking for."

Temple said quietly: "What sort of an ear-ring have you got, Clancy?"

"A diamond one in a platinum setting," said Clancy, "and there's a fancy bit o' scrawl where it clips on the ear."

Temple smiled to himself. "How much are you asking for it?"

Clancy said: "I'm practically giving it away, Mr. T. I'm only asking seven hundred and fifty pounds."

"I'll be with you in half an hour," said Temple. "If it's the ear-ring I'm looking for, the money's yours."

Clancy said: "It's the one you're looking for, Mr. Temple - I'm sure of that." He added, as an afterthought: "If it's all the same to you, guv'nor, bring cash."

*****

Temple recognised the ear-ring as soon as Clancy Edwards pushed it across the counter. He counted out the bank notes, picked up the ear-ring, and within fifteen minutes was back at the flat.

Steve said: "I telephoned Mr. Hemingway as soon as you left, darling. He's promised to be here by ten o'clock, to give you a cheque and pick up the ear-ring."

Paul Temple laughed. He laughed for quite some little time. When he had finished laughing, Steve said: "What's this all about, Paul? Something seems to tell me that you've got something up your sleeve!"

Said Temple: "Well, if you'll pardon the vulgarity, my sweet, I'll tell you. Our esteemed friend Mr. Joseph Dalbriax, alias 'The Colonel', tried to make a sucker out of me. He impersonated a man called Hemingway and showed me a diamond ear-ring worth approximately four hundred pounds. He told me that if I could find an ear-ring to match the one he already had, he'd pay me two hundred pounds. He assured me that he was quite prepared to pay almost anything for the ear-ring, providing it completed the pair."

"But it does!" exclaimed Steve, picking up the ear-ring from off the small table.

Temple said: "It's the very same ear-ring, my dear – but that's the catch." Steve stared in amazement. "It's the oldest trick in the world," continued Temple. "'The Colonel' tipped off Clancy Edwards, and provided him with the ear-ring – the one he originally showed me at the party."

Steve said: "So you paid seven hundred and fifty pounds in cash for an ear-ring that is worth only four hundred pounds?"

"Precisely," said Temple, but he looked very pleased with himself.

Steve was annoyed. "I fail to see why you should be so pleased with yourself," she said. "It's quite obvious that you'll never see Mr. Hemingway again."

Temple laughed. "But the fun hasn't started yet," he said. "Just you wait …"

Paul Temple was right. The fun hadn't started. But it started forty-eight hours later when Joseph Dalbriax, alias "The Colonel", was arrested for passing forged banknotes.

PAUL TEMPLE AND THE GRANVILLE SISTERS

Paul Temple climbed over the barbed wire fence and followed P.C. Rodgers down the deserted lane to the edge of the field. He saw the body of the girl as soon as he turned the corner. She was lying exactly as the constable had described her, the legs sprawled across the grass.

Temple made a quick examination of the body, then turned towards the constable. "She has been strangled," he said, pointing to the marks on the side of the girl's neck.

Rodgers said: "Who is she, sir – do you know?"

"Yes," said Temple. "Her name's Granville. She lives with her sister in the big house on the top of Minsdale Hill."

"How long do you think she's been dead, sir?"

Temple said: "About thirty minutes. I should imagine it happened about nine o'clock."

The constable looked perplexed. "It's lucky for me you decided to take a stroll this evening," he said. "To tell you the truth, sir, I wasn't sure what I ought to do next."

Paul Temple asked: "Did you touch anything?" Rodgers shook his head.

*****

Temple was in the bath when Inspector Merritt telephoned. He wrapped the bath towel round him and crossed into the bedroom.

Merritt said: "I'd like you to have a chat with Miss Ursula Granville, Temple. I've got a hunch that she knows a great deal more about this business than she cares to admit."

Paul Temple said: "Had she a motive?"

He could hear the inspector chuckling at the other end of the wire. "She'd a first class motive," he said. "That is, if you consider forty-five thousand pounds a first class motive!"

"It's certainly an incentive," said Paul Temple.

The inspector said: "Have a talk with her, Temple – you might get more out of the old girl than we did."

*****

Miss Ursula Granville was on the telephone when Paul Temple entered the lounge. Miss Granville, a tall, well-dressed woman of about fifty, was saying: "… It's no good arguing the point, Mr. Wallace – the set is completely hopeless. I can't get the Home Service at all, and the reception on the Light leaves a great deal to be desired." She banged down the receiver with a gesture of impatience, and turned towards Temple.

Paul Temple said pleasantly: "I do hope I'm not making a nuisance of myself, Miss Granville."

Ursula Granville said: "You want to know all about my sister, I suppose? You want to know where I was and what I was doing when she was murdered."

Temple's eyes rested on the travelling trunk and two suitcases in the corner of the room. "Tell me about your sister, Miss Granville," he said quietly.

Miss Granville hesitated, then crossed over to the sideboard. "She was a strange, moody type of girl," she said. "At times I do believe she suffered from a persecution complex."

Temple asked: "Did you get along well together?"

Ursula Granville handed Temple the drink she had mixed for him and picked up her own glass from the sideboard. "We didn't get along at all well together," she said frankly. "To be perfectly honest, Mr. Temple, we mistrusted and disliked each other."

Temple said: "Well, that's frank enough, Miss Granville." He raised the glass to his lips, then hesitated and crossed to the doorway. Quickly he opened the door and went out into the corridor.

"Was there someone in the corridor?" asked Ursula Granville when Temple returned a few moments later.

Temple said: "How long have you had your housekeeper, Miss Granville?"

Miss Granville looked annoyed. "She's been with me for fifteen years," she said, "and I trust her implicitly."

Temple nodded towards the door. "I'm glad to hear it," he said, "because I'm quite sure she hears a great deal of what goes on in this house."

Miss Granville frowned. "I don't wish to appear rude, Mr. Temple," she said, "but I've got rather a busy afternoon ahead of me."

Temple held the glass in the palm of his hand, and slowly raised it to his lips. He peered at Miss Granville over the top of the glass. "Inspector Merritt tells me you were in bed when he phoned you the news about your sister."

Ursula Granville said: "That's quite true, Mr. Temple. My sister and I had dinner together, and then at about half past seven she decided to go for a stroll. I did one or two odd jobs, read a library book for a little while, listened to the nine o'clock news, and then went upstairs to bed."

Temple said: "And your housekeeper?"

"My housekeeper was out for the evening."

Paul Temple said: "I wonder if you'd take the trouble to explain something to me, Miss Granville?"

"Well?"

"I'm rather curious to know how you can listen to the nine o'clock news on a radio set which can't get the Home Service."

There was a moment's pause, then Ursula Granville smiled. "You think you're smart, don't you, Mr. Temple?" she said. "But unfortunately, my friend, you're not quite smart enough." She pointed to the drink he was holding. "I took the liberty of dropping a phial of heroin into that drink."

Temple grinned. "You obviously don't believe in taking any chances," he said.

"Not if I can help it," said Ursula Granville.

"I don't blame you, Miss Granville. I don't believe in taking chances either." Temple continued to grin. "Why do you think I went out into the corridor?" he said.

There was a cold light in Ursula Granville's eyes. She suddenly seemed very uncertain of herself. "Why did you go outside?"

Paul Temple said: "I'm rather afraid I took advantage of your aspidistra." He opened his hand and revealed the glass empty.

PAUL TEMPLE AND THE CRAWFORD CASE

Detective Sergeant Ross looked tired when he arrived at Bramley Lodge.

"What's the trouble?" asked Paul Temple.

"We're in rather a quandary, Mr. Temple," said Ross. "Yesterday afternoon a farm worker called Ted Morgan met with a fatal accident. He was ploughing a field, and the tractor went too near the ditch and toppled into it. Morgan apparently fell from the tractor and caught his head on the front wheel."

Temple made a note of the word "apparently". He said: "Did anyone see the accident?"

The sergeant said: "Yes, Morgan's boss saw it – a farmer by the name of Fred Crawford. Crawford was repairing a fence about fifty or sixty yards away."

Temple looked at the sergeant. "You don't think it was an accident, do you, Ross?" he said.

"To be frank, Mr. Temple," said Ross, "I don't and neither does the inspector. We know there was no love lost between Morgan and Fred Crawford."

"Have you moved the tractor?"

"Nothing's been moved except the body," said the sergeant. "I've even had the ditch roped off in case you'd like to see it."

Temple said: "How long will it take us to reach this place?"

"About forty-five minutes, sir."

Temple nodded. "Wait for me in the hall," he said. "I'll get my hat and coat."

*****

Paul Temple was beginning to share the sergeant's dislike for Fred Crawford.

He asked: "How long had Morgan been driving the tractor before the accident happened?"

Crawford said: "He started at about ten in the morning, knocked off for a bite to eat round about one o'clock, and started again just after two. The accident happened at about a quarter to four."

"Did Morgan have a break during the afternoon?" Crawford shook his head, and Temple said quietly: "Then correct me if I'm mistaken. The tractor was at work all the time, without a break, from just after two o'clock in the afternoon until the time of the accident at approximately a quarter to four?"

Crawford said: "That's right, Mr. Temple."

Sergeant Ross said: "You're quite sure, sir?"

Crawford glared. "Of course I'm sure!" he exclaimed. "From where I was working, I could see and hear the tractor."

Temple walked over to the far side of the tractor and examined the tyres. He stared at the ground, appearing to be deep in thought.

Crawford said to the sergeant: "I'd like to get the tractor started and take it back to the farm."

Temple nodded and moved the gear into neutral. "Let's see if we can pull it out of the ditch," he said.

When the tractor was on level ground again, the sergeant said: "She's stone cold. Take a bit of starting, if I know anything about tractors."

The farmer looked at him. There was a contemptuous grin on his face as he moved to the front of the tractor, took the handle, and swung it for all he was worth. The tractor coughed, spluttered and then finally started.

Crawford jumped into the seat and turned the tractor round so that it faced the gate. "You'll find me up at the house," he shouted.

As Temple and Ross strolled across the meadow towards the main road, the sergeant said: "I'll tell you what struck me as being rather odd, Mr. Temple. Crawford didn't switch the engine on just now before he started it up."

"The tractor was already switched on," said Temple. "Don't forget it hadn't been touched since the accident, and at the time of the accident it didn't switch itself off."

Ross nodded. "I see what you mean," he said. "The engine conked out when the tractor hit the ditch."

When they reached the car, Temple said: "I should keep an eye on Crawford if I were you."

The sergeant said: "He's a shrewd bird, Mr. Temple. Men like Fred Crawford don't make many mistakes."

"I think there's something you've rather overlooked, sergeant," Temple said quietly. "When you first start a tractor, you run it on petrol for probably five or six minutes to get the engine warmed up, and then you switch it over to paraffin. Now according to Crawford, the tractor was in use from just after two o'clock until the accident at a quarter to four."

The sergeant said: "I don't see what you're getting at."

Temple said: "I'm simply getting at the fact that by the time the accident happened the tractor would be running on paraffin. When the tractor hit the ditch it would in fact have been switched over to paraffin."

The sergeant said: "I may be pretty dense, Mr. Temple, but where does that get us?"

Temple laughed. "But you saw Crawford start the tractor," he said. "It hadn't been touched since the accident, and yet it started like a bird."

381

The sergeant looked serious. "Gracious!" he exclaimed. "It must have been switched over to petrol at the time of the accident."

The novelist said: "Well, you certainly can't start a stone cold tractor on paraffin, sergeant."

"So what do you think happened, sir?"

"I'll tell you what happened," Temple said. "Morgan started ploughing and was interrupted by Crawford. Morgan stopped the tractor. There was a row during the course of which Morgan was murdered and taken down to the ditch. But suddenly Crawford hit upon the idea of making the whole thing look like an accident.

"He went back to the tractor, but by this time of course the tractor was pretty nearly cold. So Crawford had to switch over to petrol in order to start it again. He then drove the tractor down to where he had placed the body, and toppled it over into the ditch."

The sergeant said: "Well, he certainly made a good job of it. It looked exactly like an accident!"

Paul Temple said quietly: "Yes, but even men like Fred Crawford make mistakes. He forgot to switch back to paraffin."

PAUL TEMPLE MEETS AN OLD FRIEND

It was exactly the sort of bracelet that Steve wanted, and Temple decided to buy it for her. The jeweller's assistant, a rather nervous young man, smiled at Temple as he entered the shop and nodded his head towards the chair. Temple leaned against the counter, and amused himself by studying the tall, grey-haired man who was examining a diamond ring.

The man looked up, then carefully placing the ring on the velvet pad he said crisply: "I'd like to see that ring in the window. The square cut diamond. It's marked six hundred and fifty pounds."

The young man nodded and produced a tray. "I think this is the one you mean, sir," he said, pointing to a ring in the centre. The man picked up the jeweller's eye-glass, and lifted the ring from the tray. Temple watched him with interest. He felt sure that there was something familiar about this distinguished-looking man.

The assistant turned towards Temple. "Is there anything I can show you, sir?"

Temple said quietly, his eyes still on the stranger: "You've got rather an attractive little bracelet in the window." The assistant nodded and brought out the bracelet.

As he passed it to Temple, the grey-haired man looked up and caught Temple staring at him. He smiled and nodded towards the ring. "It's not worth a penny more than four hundred pounds," he said. He put the glass down on the counter and replaced the ring.

The assistant said to Temple: "That's just the same as the bracelet in the window, Mr. Temple, but we have an exceptionally nice one at ninety-five pounds." He turned towards the stranger again and picked up the glass.

The man said: "The ring isn't worth six hundred and fifty pounds, and if you want my frank opinion —" He stopped short and stared at the tray. Temple and the assistant followed his gaze. The ring was missing. The stranger said: "That's extraordinary! I put the ring down there." He pointed to the centre of the tray.

The assistant moved the velvet pad, lifted up the tray, and ran his fingers across the top of the counter. There was no sign of the ring. Temple continued to stare at the grey-haired man. Suddenly he smiled, a smile of recognition. "I've been trying to place you," he said. "Your name's Gray Freedman. Chief Inspector Davis nicknamed you Light-Fingers."

The grey-haired man looked indignant. "My name is Rolson," he announced coldly. "Colonel John Wynford Rolson."

Temple smiled. "I never forget faces," he said pleasantly.

The assistant said nervously, "We don't want any trouble, sir, so if by any chance you have the ring —"

The man exploded. "I most certainly have not got the ring!"

Temple said: "I take it you've no objection to being searched?"

The man brought his fist down on the counter. "I have every objection to being searched, sir!" he said, then added as an afterthought, "except by the proper authorities."

The assistant said: "Could I trouble you for your identity card, sir?"

"It's quite obvious that you choose to accept this gentleman's word instead of mine," said the stranger. "You leave me with but one alternative." He went to the telephone and dialled a number. After a moment's delay, he said: "Is that the police? Will you please send one of your men to Frinton's, the jewellers in the High Street? It's very urgent." He added, just before replacing the receiver: "My name is Colonel Rolson." Then he sat down on the chair to wait for the detective.

*****

The detective was businesslike. He examined the man's identity card and made a thorough search of his person. When he had finished, he said to the jeweller: "There's no sign of the ring, sir, and it seems that this gentleman is the person he says he is."

The stranger straightened himself, buttoned up the jacket of his suit, and pulled on his gloves. He said to the assistant: "Don't imagine that you've heard the last of this, young man." He ignored Temple and strolled out of the shop.

When the detective had gone too, the assistant said dejectedly: "It's not like you to make a mistake, Mr. Temple."

Temple smiled, opened his left hand, and revealed the ring. The assistant gasped: "But where on earth did you get it?"

"I took it out of his pocket, while I was shaking hands with him," said Temple.

"But you didn't shake hands with him!"

Temple grinned. "I'm referring to the bogus detective, my friend. Gray stole the ring, pretended to dial the police, and then waited for his accomplice. The bogus detective turned up, and Gray simply passed him the ring."

The assistant heaved a sigh of relief. "It's a good job you spotted him, sir!"

Temple said: "I've got a memory like an elephant."

PAUL TEMPLE AND THE ECCENTRIC MILLIONAIRESS

Paul Temple was interested in the strange death of Mrs. Clarence Wharton, the eccentric millionairess. It seemed that even her exit from the world had been unconventional, for she had been stabbed to death on her own hearthrug, her head resting on a book by Edgar Allan Poe.

When Temple arrived at the house, Inspector Thompson had placed three items on a side table. Temple said quietly: "Exhibit A, a clasp knife. Exhibit B, a wristlet watch. Exhibit C, a book."

Thompson said: "That's the Edgar Allan Poe, sir."

"I see," commented Temple. "Now tell me what you know."

Thompson said: "Soon after nine last night Mrs. Wharton's niece, a Miss Lucy Davenport, telephoned the Yard and said that she'd just got back from a lecture at the public library and had found Mrs. Wharton lying on the floor. The room was a shambles. Miss Davenport found this clasp knife in a corner of the room – you can see it's covered in blood."

"No fingerprints, I suppose?"

"Not a sign. I showed Miss Davenport the knife and asked her if she recognised it, but she said she didn't – though I'm not altogether sure that she was telling the truth."

"Is there any reason why she shouldn't speak the truth?"

Thompson shrugged. "She might be shielding her brother."

"And is there any reason why the brother should have killed Mrs.Wharton?"

"That's the peculiar part," muttered Thompson. "According to the will I saw this morning, Miss Davenport inherits the entire fortune. Yet she couldn't have killed Mrs. Wharton, because it appears the murder was committed at a quarter past eight and Miss Davenport was most certainly at the public library then."

Temple stared at the wristlet watch, with the hands pointing to eight-fifteen. He picked up the book and began to turn the leaves. He noticed that only the first four pages were cut. He said: "How long was young Davenport in South Africa?"

Thompson raised his eyebrows. "What makes you ask that, sir?"

As Temple indicated the clasp knife there was a knock at the door, and Miss Davenport entered followed by her brother. At Temple's request, Lucy Davenport recounted how she had accompanied Mrs. Wharton to the lounge immediately after tea, and the older woman had read aloud from the book by Edgar Allan Poe.

"Never met a woman with such a morbid taste in books," said Tom Davenport. "And how she loved the sound of her own voice!"

"What time did Mrs. Wharton start reading the book?" asked Temple.

Lucy Davenport said: "Mrs. Wharton started to read at about five o'clock and finished at about seven-thirty. I then went upstairs and prepared myself for the lecture."

Temple nodded and turned towards Tom Davenport. "And now, Mr. Davenport," he said, "what about your alibi?"

"I'm afraid it doesn't amount to much. You see, I was in my room on the other side of the house the whole time. I happen to be writing a novel."

Temple smiled. "You have my deepest sympathy," he said. He added as an afterthought: "I daresay your experiences in South Africa will come in useful."

Davenport said in surprise: "How did you know I was in South Africa?"

"Because I have an idea that this is your clasp knife."

Davenport picked up the knife and examined it. He seemed surprised. "Good Lord, yes! I haven't seen it for ages," he said. "I thought it was lost."

Lucy Davenport made a movement. "Tom!" she gasped. "That's the knife – the knife that stabbed Mrs. Wharton."

Paul Temple slowly shook his head. "The weapon that stabbed Mrs. Wharton," he said quietly, "penetrated at least three inches. This blade is not more than two and a half. The murderer clearly hid the knife or dagger he used and smeared this knife with blood to divert suspicion."

"Now I come to think of it," said Tom Davenport, "what's become of the old girl's paperknife? She used one of those Oriental daggers."

"I suspected as much," nodded Temple. He smiled at Tom Davenport. "It's my bet that the murder did not take place at eight-fifteen, but sometime around six o'clock. After Mrs. Wharton was dead, the murderer turned her wristlet watch to eight-fifteen and smashed the glass. You see, Mrs. Wharton could not have read solidly for over two hours without cutting more than four pages of the book."

Tom Davenport looked serious as he said: "But who would be particularly anxious to establish an alibi for eight-fifteen, Mr. Temple?"

Paul Temple swung round quickly and said: "Miss Davenport, I think I shall have to ask you a few more questions." But, for the first time in her life, Lucy Davenport had fainted.

PAUL TEMPLE AND THE GIRL IN GREY

Paul Temple had just left Sir Graham Forbes's office at Scotland Yard, when he bumped into Inspector Vosper.

Vosper looked serous. "I heard that you were in the building, Mr. Temple," he said, "so I thought I'd better give you a word of warning. Have you ever heard of a girl called Sue Dearman?"

"Can't say I have," said Temple.

"She was Ted Waring's girlfriend," said Vosper quietly.

Temple whistled softly. He had just solved a forgery case which had resulted in Ted Waring getting five years.

"I had the word passed to me this morning that Sue is out to get even with you," said Vosper. "And she's liable to be dangerous. She got two years for throwing acid during the war, and she's been mixed up in several other unpleasant jobs."

"Well, I'm afraid I can't help Ted Waring's deplorable taste in girlfriends," murmured Temple.

Vosper said: "I've always maintained that prevention is better than cure, Mr. Temple, so I think I'll detail someone to keep an eye on you during the next few days."

Temple shrugged. "If you can spare a man in these hard times, Vosper, I promise you I won't lead him much of a chase. I'm pretty busy on a new novel just now."

On his way home, Temple found himself looking over his shoulder for the notorious Miss Dearman. He paused at the entrance to his flat and glanced quickly in either direction, but there was no sign of her.

It was not until he was leaving his tailor's in New Bond Street that he noticed a woman standing on the opposite side of the road. She was watching him out of the corner of her eye. He glanced at her quickly and moved on, giving no sign that he was aware of her.

During the next few minutes, he caught further glimpses of her. She was dressed in a smart grey suit. Temple smiled to himself, crossed the road, and jumped on a bus for Victoria.

He left the bus at Hyde Park Corner and caught another bound for Piccadilly Circus. Turning up Air Street, he doubled into Regent Street, walked a hundred yards, and then took a taxi to the Strand. He was rather pleased with himself as he strolled into a hotel. When he came out half an hour later, the girl in grey was waiting for him – she was apparently studying the photographs outside a theatre.

Temple felt annoyed and irritated. Apparently, Miss Sue Dearman had a plan of campaign. On his way back to the flat, he made no effort to elude the girl in grey. He was almost hoping that she would make some move.

*****

The next morning, when Temple peered through the curtains, the girl was walking slowly along on the opposite pavement. Temple hesitated, then made up his mind. He went into the study, unlocked a drawer in his desk, and took out a small automatic pistol which he slipped into his coat pocket. "We'll give Miss Dearman a run for her money," he said to himself.

After calling on his agent in the Haymarket, he caught a tube to the East End, lunched in a carmen's dining room, roamed around the dock areas for a couple of hours, crossed the river through the Blackwall Tunnel, and then travelled by bus and tram as far as the Crystal Palace. He returned through Camberwell and the South London slums.

It was after eight o'clock when he arrived back at the flat. He felt tired, dishevelled, and in a bad temper. He had good reason to be – the girl had trailed him all day.

Late that night Steve fetched her husband out of his bath, to take a telephone call from Scotland Yard. Temple recognised the voice of Inspector Vosper. "I thought I'd let you know that you don't have to worry about Sue Dearman, just in case you were concerned," said the inspector.

"I'm not exactly worrying," replied Temple, "but I'm more than a little interested. What happened?"

"We picked her up on the Cornish express. The silly girl had a neat little plan to help Waring to escape – they were taking him down on the train this morning."

Temple said: "I don't quite understand. There's a woman in grey been trailing me for the past couple of days. I'll bet a fiver she's outside the flat at this very moment."

He heard Vosper laughing at the other end of the wire. "I'm afraid that was Gail Marvin," said the inspector.

"Gail Marvin?"

Vosper said: "She's one of our brightest girls, Mr. Temple. You wouldn't lose Gail Marvin in a hurry."

"By Timothy, you're telling me!" said Paul Temple.

PAUL TEMPLE AND THE GARAGE MYSTERY

Paul Temple had an appointment at eleven o'clock, and shortly after a quarter past ten he strolled down to his private garage in Exeter Mews.

He was lifting the bonnet of his car, when a somewhat agitated middle-aged man pushed open the garage door. "Forgive me for intruding, sir," said the man, "but aren't you something to do with the police?" Temple recognised a doctor who garaged his car a little farther along the mews. "My name is Arlington-Smythe," continued the doctor. "I'm sorry to trouble you, but I'm rather afraid my wife has met with an accident."

He hesitated a moment, and then said: "I'm afraid it's suicide, sir." The doctor indicated a half-open garage door. "I'd just come down for my car," he explained, "and I found the place full of exhaust fumes. My wife was in the back of the car, with a tube connected to the exhaust pipe."

The two men went to the garage, which was just large enough to accommodate a sixteen-horsepower saloon. It was a gloomy garage, and Temple tried rather unsuccessfully to peer through the back of the car. "Can't we have some light?" he asked.

"I'm afraid the roof light in the car is out of order, and the electricity is switched off at this time," explained the doctor.

"Have you touched the car?" Temple asked.

"No."

"In that case, we'd better get the car outside. I should think most of the fumes will have gone by now."

Arlington-Smythe nodded. "I've had the door open for some minutes," he said. As he spoke, he climbed into the front of the car, switched the engine on and backed out into the yard. Before the doctor had stopped his engine, Temple had opened the back door and was looking at the attractive but rather weak features of Doris Arlington-Smythe.

"I suppose it's no use trying artificial respiration?" Temple asked.

"Not a chance, I'm afraid. She's been dead several hours."

Temple frowned. "Then she must have been missing for some little time," he commented. "Didn't you wonder what had happened to her?"

The doctor looked worried. "As a matter of fact, we haven't been getting on too well lately," he said. "To be frank, Mr. Temple, she'd fallen victim to the drug habit, and she tried to persuade me to let her have some cocaine."

"When did she ask you to get her the cocaine?"

"Shortly after midnight. We had rather a row, I'm afraid, and Doris dashed out of the flat in a temper."

Temple picked up the hands of the dead woman, then let them fall to her side again. He said quietly, "She doesn't appear to show the symptoms of a drug addict." He looked at Arlington-Smythe for a few moments. "You know, doctor," he said, "it's my guess that your wife didn't commit suicide."

"What are you suggesting, sir?"

"I'm suggesting that she was carried out to the garage, probably under the influence of an injection, and that a very effective suicide set-up was arranged. I'm suggesting that she was murdered."

Arlington-Smythe looked angry. "What makes you think that?" he asked.

"I watched you very closely just now," said Temple. "I watched you switch the engine on, start the car up, and back it into the yard."

"Well?"

Temple smiled. "If it had been suicide," he said, "there wouldn't have been any necessity for you to switch on."

"You mean –"

"I mean," said Paul Temple, "that your wife couldn't very well have committed suicide, my friend, and then switched off the engine."

PAUL TEMPLE AND THE BLONDE CASHIER

Paul Temple was still thinking of Hedy Lamarr, as he emerged from the Splendide Cinema in Leicester Square and bumped into the stalwart figure of Inspector Vosper.

"I didn't know you were a film fan," said Temple.

Vosper shook his head with a rueful grin. "I'm here on business, Mr. Temple. While you and Mrs. Temple were feasting your eyes on Miss Lamarr a couple of men made a neat little raid and got away with the best part of seven hundred pounds."

"Any sign of a clue?"

"Not so far. The men wore masks, and they were in and out again in less than five minutes. They chose exactly the right moment. The manager was checking the day's takings."

"Rather looks to me as if they got an inside tip-off," said Temple.

Steve asked: "Was anyone hurt, inspector?"

"Nothing serious, Mrs. Temple. Although the girl in the cash desk got a scratch from a stray bullet which one of the men fired."

Vosper led the way into the manager's office, which was still in a state of disorder. In the far corner sat a tall, good-looking blonde. There was a bandage round her left hand, near the wrist. "This is Miss Daphne Stirling," Vosper said.

Temple nodded to the girl, inquired after her injury, and asked her if she would mind repeating her account of what had happened.

In a slightly affected drawl, the girl said: "I was in the cash desk, taking a telephone booking for the big charity show tomorrow night. I had just started to write down the name of the person booking the seats, when I saw two men rushing out

396

of the office. There was a commotion, and two shots were fired."

"What did you do when you heard the shot?"

"Well, almost immediately on top of the shot I felt something red hot stinging the back of my hand – the one holding the telephone. I dropped the receiver, and – well – after that I'm rather afraid I fainted."

Temple glanced at the statement Vosper had taken, then went over to the manager's desk, selected a pen and passed it to her. "Perhaps you would sign this statement you gave the inspector," he suggested. "Then we shall know it's authentic."

The blonde shot him a suspicious glance but took the proffered pen and scrawled her name in the book. Vosper was watching them closely, as Temple took the pen back and said: "I'm glad to see your injury doesn't prevent you from writing, Miss Stirling. I'd no idea you were left-handed, or I wouldn't have suggested your using the injured hand."

"That's o.k.," she replied jauntily. "It's only a bit of a scratch."

Paul Temple looked serious, as he said: "And I very much doubt if the scratch was caused by a bullet, Miss Stirling."

"Here, what are you suggesting?" she demanded.

"I'll tell you what I'm suggesting," said Temple. "I'm suggesting that you tipped off those men when the cash would be checked in the manager's office. In order to divert suspicion, they fired a couple of shots in the air and you gashed your hand with a penknife. But unfortunately, young lady, you gashed the wrong hand."

"What do you mean?"

Paul Temple said: "If your hand had been hit by a bullet while you were holding the telephone, it would have been your right hand – because you would, in fact, have been taking down the caller's name with your left."

PAUL TEMPLE AND THE CAR ROBBERIES

Steve came into the study at Bramley Lodge as Paul Temple was about to start the last chapter of his latest novel. "Your old friend Inspector Vosper is in the lounge."

"What on earth brings Vosper into this part of the world?" asked Temple, throwing down his pen.

Vosper, who was absorbing a whisky and soda, enlightened his host. "I made a little detour," he explained, "to see if you would care for a run into Herefordshire. There's a very peculiar business going on there."

"Don't tell me there's a sinister criminal organisation among the cider orchards," smiled Temple.

Vosper shrugged. "Maybe not as sinister as all that. But there's something very fishy going on. It has to do with these car robberies. Twice during the past month, we've had clues that led us to the village of Morpham, about ten miles from Hereford."

"You mean you've traced the stolen cars to Morpham?"

"Yes, but unfortunately we haven't got beyond that point. We suspect the number plates are changed for the second time at Morpham, and after that the cars are taken to one of the South Wales towns and generally made unrecognisable. We sent out one of our special men – a young fellow named Ronson – to try to find out what's going on, but we haven't heard from him for over a fortnight."

"What sort of a man is Ronson?" asked Temple.

"I've never met him," said Vosper, "but he's considered to be pretty smart at his job. He distinguished himself over that Park Lane murder case."

"I'll get the car out," said Temple, "and we'll run over to Morpham."

*****

Morpham proved to be a typical Herefordshire village, with a tiny railway station, two public houses and a handful of shops. After they had parked the car, Temple and the inspector explored the place on foot, finally calling at the railway station where Temple chatted to Fred Hodgson, the stationmaster-cum-porter-cum-booking clerk.

When Temple returned to the inspector, he found Vosper still speculating upon the activities of the car gang. "I can't think what's happened to young Ronson," he murmured with a worried frown. "Judging by the reports, whoever's running this gang is in pretty close touch with what's going on at the Yard, and I can't help thinking he was on to Ronson as soon as the poor devil got here."

They strolled into the saloon bar of the Salop Arms, and a few seconds later a smart young man wearing a dark double-breasted overcoat and a bowler hat came through the swing doors. He noticed Vosper almost immediately and crossed to the inspector. "Inspector Vosper?" he said quietly.

When Vosper acknowledged his identity, the young man grasped his hand. "I'm glad to see you, sir," he said. "I was afraid I'd missed you. When I telephoned the Yard, I understood them to say you were coming down by train and I met both the afternoon trains. I've been cooling my heels in that confounded waiting room for hours!"

"You telephoned the Yard?" repeated Vosper. "I'm afraid I don't quite –"

The young man laughed. "I should have introduced myself, sir. My name is Ronson."

"So you're the gentleman who vanished into nowhere," said Temple, after Vosper had introduced him.

400

The young man ignored Temple and addressed himself to Vosper again. "I've had a devil of a time, but I think I'm at last on the right track." Then he lowered his voice to a whisper.

To avoid embarrassing the inspector, Temple excused himself and said he wished to telephone his wife. There was a telephone in a small room at the back of the public bar, and when Temple returned ten minutes later he found Vosper and the young man still in conversation.

Vosper looked up as Temple approached. "Ronson's going to take us to a farm that the gang is using," he began, but Temple slowly shook his head.

"On the contrary," said Temple, "we are taking Mr. Ronson back to Hereford, where I understand the cells are particularly comfortable."

The young man seemed to lose his air of self-confidence, as Temple said to the inspector: "I've just been on the phone to Scotland Yard. They have received no telephone call from Mr. Ronson, for the very clear reason that the real Ronson was discovered in the River Severn early this afternoon!"

Temple turned to the young man. "It was an ingenious plan, but you should pay a little more attention to details. When you tell an elaborate story about cooling your heels in a station waiting room, you should make quite certain that Morpham station can claim such an amenity."

PAUL TEMPLE AND THE DARK STRANGER

It was growing dark when Paul Temple and Steve, on their way to London, turned an S-bend beside a pair of white lodge gates between Oxford and Reading.

The headlights of the car suddenly picked up the hurrying figure of a swarthy, middle-aged man. Temple stepped on the footbrake. "Can I give you a lift?" he asked.

"I'm going for a doctor," the man said in a hoarse voice. "My man, Burford, has met with an accident or had a seizure of some sort. I tried to telephone, but the gale has evidently blown down the wires and I couldn't get through."

On the way to the nearest village, the man introduced himself as Professor Ersdale, formerly of Columbia University in America. "I'm writing a survey of English literature, so you can imagine my time is pretty well occupied," he explained.

The professor found the doctor at home, but as his car had broken down Temple offered to drive them back to the house. It was a Victorian mansion at the end of a winding drive. Ersdale led the way into a small sitting room, where a man lay slumped in an armchair.

The doctor made an examination, then straightened himself. "There's something strange about this," he said. "It looks to me as if this man has had an injection of some poison." He turned to Ersdale. "When did you last see this man alive?"

"It would be about eight o'clock," said the professor. "He brought me a cup of coffee and a book I'd mislaid."

"This wouldn't be the book, by any chance?" asked Temple, indicating a volume that was open on the table.

"That's right. It was a favourite of mine, *In Defence of Women* by my old friend George Jean Nathan."

"But if he brought you the book, what's it doing here?" demanded Temple.

"He asked if he could borrow it. You see, Nathan visited us several times in America and Burford was curious about the sort of thing he'd write."

"I take it there's only the two of you living here?" said Temple.

"That's right. Burford has been with me a number of years – I found him in America, and he's been very loyal. I'll never be able to replace him."

"I don't think it will be necessary to replace him," Temple said quietly.

The doctor swung round. "What do you mean, sir?" he said.

"I mean that the inestimable Burford was not murdered," replied Temple.

The doctor looked bewildered. "You mean it was suicide, or possibly an accident?"

Paul Temple said softly: "It wasn't suicide and it wasn't an accident, doctor. In fact, our friend Burford is still alive, and he's standing immediately behind you!"

The pseudo-professor made a sudden dash for the door and had almost reached it when Temple picked up a vase and hurled it with all his force. It caught the man on the back of the head. "We'd better carry him to the car while he's out!" said Temple.

When Burford had been handed over to the police, Steve said: "I can't imagine what made you suspect that man, darling. He seemed quite well-spoken and might easily have been mistaken for the professor."

"Yes, it wasn't a bad impersonation," said Temple, "if only he hadn't gone into quite so much detail about his friend George Jean Nathan."

Steve said: "But surely a Professor of English at Columbia University might well have been a friend of George Jean Nathan?"

"In which case," smiled Temple, "the professor would most certainly have known that *In Defence of Women* was written by Mr. Nathan's friend H.L. Mencken."